MILLENNIUM

*Afterlife is here with us now,
for those who have gone before*

MILLENNIUM

JULIAN BEALE

With best wishes,

Julian

Jul '18

UMBRIA PRESS

Cover image: Shutterstock

Umbria Press
London SW15 5DP
www.umbriapress.co.uk

julianbealebooks.com

Printed and bound in Poland by Totem
www.totem.com.pl

ISBN 978 1 910074 15 2
E-book ISBN 978 1 910074 16 9

MAJOR CHARACTERS

THE TWINS
Tomas
&
Tetrarch

THE PRIEST
Pente Broke Smith

THE SPOOK
Kingston Offenbach

Vanda Deveridge

Hannah   William   Charlotte
=
Simon Goring

Part One

GENESIS

In the beginning

PROLOGUE — MAY 2015

'That's correct', said the distinguished Professor from Harvard. He ran a hand through his overlong, greying hair and tweaked at his yellow spotted bow tie.

'Yes, I do believe the Mountain Men are alive today. Not the original version, of course,' he allowed himself a wintery smile, 'and not as individuals either. We must regard the name for what it always was – a catchy title for a clandestine organisation.'

It was a warm, fine day in May, the start of the summer of 2015. The setting was the White House, Washington DC and the location was one of the smaller conference rooms in the West Wing. Seated in auditorium style were about twenty people, most of middle age, all formally dressed, the majority male but including four women. The Professor sat facing them at a large, heavy table and alongside him was their host for the occasion. She was an important lady, the assistant to the President of the United States of America for National Security Affairs – a title generally abbreviated to the NSC Advisor.

The gathering was made up of government security professionals from around the world. Six were from US Agencies, ten from European Community countries including Great Britain, France and Germany, plus there was representation from Canada, Australia and Scandinavia.

The Professor was not intimidated by the company. He spoke in the dry, measured tones which he used to address his students.

'I can give you any amount of detail on the origins and development of the Mountain Men. Much of it is proven fact but there's a good deal of speculation too. That's bound to be when you're dealing with events of almost a thousand years ago. But I expect you would prefer me to start with more recent times and what made me come forward.

'I'm a historian. My specialisation is in the cultures which originated and flourished throughout the region which we now refer to as the Middle East. Like most in my profession, I can't help myself from being side tracked into criminology. When you study the past, the influential figures include those of doubtful intent and amongst these, you will come across mysteries which are tempting to research. In my case, a career long interest in a sect called the Assassins, which was formed in Persia around the start of the thirteenth century, led to my knowledge of the Mountain Men. I have known for a long time what they did, why they came into existence and why they were so called. But it was only two months ago that I came upon the same title in a modern context.

'I would have liked to introduce you to the lady who supplied me with the crucial information but that, sadly, will not be possible. She died in April this year, succumbing to a cancer which destroyed her body but not her mind. It was entirely fortuitous that I had the chance to meet her and to be honest with you all, I didn't expect much from our conversation. One learns to anticipate disappointment in this sort of work. Nevertheless, she had apparently made frequent mention of the Mountain Men so it seemed worth making the effort of travelling to Europe to see her and since I was anyway going over to a conference in Barcelona at the beginning of March, it was simple enough to add on a couple of days and visit her in her home city of Poitiers, France.'

'Just a minute, Professor,' the interruption came from the leader of one of the US Agencies, seated in the front row, 'your interest at this point sounds to have been pretty casual. Why weren't you more excited to hear the Mountain Men being mentioned?'

'Because it's happened before – quite often actually. I guess it's a useful, alliterative title and most often it turns out referring to wrestlers or runners or cyclists.'

'So why bother going over to find out? Why not pick up the phone?'

'It was the manner of introduction, Sir.' The professor was unperturbed by the sharp questioning and he added, 'that and the nature of my informant's profession.'

'Was she another historian?' this from the representative of the Canadian Security Service, a smartly presented, savvy looking woman.

'She was a courtesan, Madam, and she owned a most select establishment. She catered for wealthy men with particular tastes, especially sadism and masochism. She opened her salon in the mid nineteen-sixties when she was only about twenty-five herself. The business was discreetly managed, operating from a large house in a quiet suburb of her own home city. She must have been very well connected with the authorities in Poitiers as she stayed in business for over forty years, finally closing the door as we turned into this new century. Her name was Collette. I don't know if that was her birth name or if it was a working title. I don't know her surname.

'She told me that the clients who came to call themselves the Mountain Men appeared in December 1995. On the first occasion, there was only one of them and she recognised him immediately as both trouble and opportunity. He was very powerfully built and had a brooding, hulking look to him. He talked very little. French was his birth tongue and he spoke it with a North African accent. He was willing to pay and did not argue over the top price which she quoted. He wanted two women and they must be capable of extreme and violent sexual behaviour.

'He kept returning, this strong and silent type who demanded much physical activity but otherwise made no trouble. He paid the fees and the medical bills which resulted from his excesses. He made regular visits and a year later, he arrived with a companion, an Ethiopian of quite different size and temperament. This man was garrulous and jokey, almost as keen to talk to Collette's girls as to get into the action. As a pair, they visited more and it was the Ethiopian who announced one evening that they should be known as the Mountain Men.'

A visitor from Germany posed the next question, asking how the Professor had come to hear of Collette and to meet her.

The Professor fiddled with his flamboyant tie as he replied.

'I have been for all my adult life a practising homosexual and of course I can speak freely about that in today's world. But it was a different matter thirty years ago and in that era, my partner of many years was trying to rid himself of his natural sexuality. He's Austrian by birth, scion of a rich and prestigious family and he went knocking at Madame Collette's door looking for a solution. Collette took to him, told him to stop fighting it and to enjoy himself, sorted him out with a few young fellows. They became friends and Jim, as he now calls himself, would drop by from time to time for dinner with her and a talk. Part of Collette's therapy was to show him that many of her "normal" clients were much less so than he, himself and one man whom they discussed was the big guy with the tendency to damage.

'Now, fast forward to 2014. Jim, who is a fine art auctioneer, had been living with me at Harvard for over a decade but still travelling a good deal in Europe. Still calling on Collette and she is still doing a little introductory business in her retirement. Demand for some things just never diminishes,' he said wryly.

'In the fall of last year, Collette was diagnosed with cancer. She's a brave lady, knows she's on her way but reckons she has time to sort out her legacy before she goes. She talks quite candidly to Jim after she received her sentence of death and she shares some particular memories which are mostly about her former clients and prominent amongst these are the Mountain Men. Jim, of course, knows all about my work and special interest and so the next and last time he visited Collette, I went with him. We stayed a week in Poitiers and I spent as much time as I could with her. She was as sharp, composed and knowing as Jim had always described her to me. She supplied me with a lot of detail about visits from the Mountain Men but it wasn't until I was leaving that she said the tough guy hadn't called himself that to start. He'd given his name as Tetrarch.'

There was a collective sigh of understanding from his audience. Now this was starting to make real sense to them.

The NSC turned immediately to him and said, 'That name is very significant to us, Professor, and I know that you've got more to tell us with the further research you've been doing. Can you take us through all that now please?'

There were murmurs of assent around the room and the Professor inclined his head in acknowledgment.

'Of course, but there are some further revelations which you will want to debate, so I'm afraid it will all take a little time.'

That was a considerable understatement: the meeting finally broke up at 1.30 the following morning.

1. VANDA MADDOX — 1960

The path became steeper and the young couple braced themselves for the final push to the summit of the well-known track and burst together onto the flat rock which commanded an extensive view over the heavily wooded valley. As children, this lookout point had seemed to them to provide a window to the whole world and it had required daring to negotiate the gloomy woods as well as effort to climb the mountain in order to reach this vantage point. Now, armed with the sophistication of their mid teen years, it was just a stroll through the trees with a little more energy needed to climb to the rock which smiled down on a benign patch of English countryside, outside a small village called Foy with the County town of Hereford to the north west.

Even for the English climate, the year of 1960 had offered a pretty miserable summer but this Friday, the first in the month of August, produced an interlude of tepid sunshine which encouraged them to escape for a few hours in which to enjoy each other's company and the familiarity of this favourite walk.

He was seventeen, already tall, wide and well developed. She was a year younger and another of nature's early starters, a girl with a pretty face and a Rubens figure. She had vivacity and sex appeal. You would guess that the years to come might not be kind to these looks but that was for tomorrow and another world. Today was for living.

They sat companionably together on their rock, saying little to start with while each concentrated on the call of familiar birds and the hope of seeing some wildlife. Rabbits were numerous and not worthy of remark, but sometimes they would see a hare and very occasionally, a group of deer would pick a cautious path through the wood which lay beneath them. Not today,

8

however, and presently the girl broke the spell by rummaging noisily through the small haversack which she had brought with her to find a battered flask and a wedge of coffee cake, casually wrapped in an old newspaper. They started to gossip, sharing news of school contemporaries, views on latest music, thoughts of how to make the most of the harvest barn dance, always held over the August bank holiday weekend at the end of the month.

'I don't reckon Polly'll be going anyway.'

'Who's Polly?' asked the boy.

'Oh you know, Roo, she's that horse faced girl with the big bust. She's in the class below mine – not that she's younger than me, just a bit thick. She must be stupid to have allowed her Dad to catch her spooning with that drippy Luke Deveridge. Now she won't sit down for a week and her Mum'll keep her back from the dance.'

She could see him searching his memory and knew which of Polly's features would come to him first, so she lay back on the rock and allowed her own impressive breasts to distract him.

The boy swallowed the last of his share of cake and leaned back on one elbow whilst his free hand lighted on one of her ankles and commenced a tentative, northbound journey of discovery. It was above her knee before she slapped him away with a giggle.

'Don't you try that on me, Roo pert', she said, drawing out his name to tease him, 'I'm not getting into trouble with the posh family of the village'.

The boy smiled down at her. 'I may be posh, Vanda, but I'm also poor. Plus I've got a daft name which I didn't ask for. You should have pity and give me a bit of comfort. You could blame it on that snake the vicar was telling us about.'

Vanda goggled at him. 'Honestly, Roo, what you do go on about. What's this snake?'

'Well you were in church same as I was last Sunday. You must have heard Reverend Albeith preaching on the Garden of Eden and Eve's excuse that the serpent beguiled her.'

'Oh yes, I remember alright,' she replied sitting up abruptly and giving him a kiss which was not as innocent as she had intended. Then she pushed a strong knee into his groin and wiggled it knowingly as she said, 'and I'm telling you, Roo, I may fancy you but I'm not being beguiled by this serpent, not this afternoon anyway!'

They laughed together. They were always laughing and that was the strength of the friendship. Rupert Broke Smith, only offspring of an ageing couple, lived on the edge of the village in a smart but small house, no more than a cottage. Roo was always on his own and had been since he was quite a little boy, not that his parents weren't there at home, but they were distracted by their passion and precarious living in antiquarian books so had not much time for their son and none at all for children's parties and the like. In sharp contrast, Vanda Maddox was one of six children who rattled around a large and draughty old farmhouse which generations of the family had occupied while milking their herd and cultivating a hundred acres of arable flats down by the river. Vanda was the youngest and the only daughter, so she understood from an early age that she would be the first to leave Foy Farm. She was bright too, the only child of her family to follow Roo from the village primary to the grammar school and she was doing well there, but she was the first to acknowledge that she was not as clever as her very best friend, Rupert. Except, that is, in matters of intuition. She was female, of course, and that alone made her the more perceptive, but there was more besides. It was Vanda's mother Trisha, whose own family background lay in Snowdonia, who recognised in her daughter a gift inherited from her maternal grandmother, now long dead and gone. Vanda had the 'vision': a sense of knowing what to expect. It didn't make her a witch but it did give her foresight.

All that apart, Vanda was hugely dependent on her friendship with Rupert. In her own household, her father and five brothers were completely absorbed by their land and the large herd of milkers, while her mother was both preoccupied and exhausted by the tasks of tending to her menfolk. Only by turning to

Rupert, and sometimes to his parents, could Vanda nourish her yearning for wider education and knowledge for its own sake. In addition, she was very much attracted to Roo and she had no doubt that in due time, each would claim the virginity of the other. But her vision told her that she must make the most of the relationship. Deep within herself, she knew that they would always be close, but not together for much longer.

Vanda stuffed things back in her haversack and stood up, brushing a few pebbles from her skirt. She took Roo's hand in hers and they started their descent together. It would take them almost an hour to regain the village, plenty of time for more gossip and banter. If there were deer in these woods, they would hear the ever present laughter.

2. MONIQUE DORCAS — 1965

The sun was coming up, on pattern, on power and on time. There was no reason why it should not. In this harsh environment, the sun was one of the few constants and it came blazing forth every day of the long year.

A light vapour trail revealed the path of a passenger jet on the short overnight flight from Europe, most probably out of France and perhaps making for Nouadhibou, just over the border into Mauritania, where the passengers would be greeted by searing heat and whirling dust across the barren landscape. Even less hospitable was the country which they were overflying now: they called it 'the Land of the Unforgiven'.

Western Sahara, formerly a colony of Spain, was then the subject of squabbles between Morocco, Algeria and Mauritania. It would soon be plagued by guerrilla warfare as a nationalist group became established and introduced itself as the Polisario. God knows, however, why anyone should want this country which has no minerals, little vegetation and hardly any water. It offers instead an unchanging diet of sun, sand and solitude.

From the flight deck of the aircraft, the captain had a fine view of the region which lies between Ad Dakhla and Awsard. He could make out the collection of tents and ramshackle buildings which made for a semi nomadic settlement and as he tucked into coffee and a croissant thirty thousand feet above, he was happy not to be facing a day in the furnace of that landscape. If his aircraft had been equipped with the latest American camera technology, he might have wondered at the knot of figures starting to converge upon what seemed to be a football lying in an open area of sand and scrub a hundred metres from the camp.

But it wasn't a football: it was a head and it belonged to

a human body which was still living, although not for much longer.

On the last morning of her life, Monique al-Jabri, nee Dorcas, was long past reflection and was scarcely holding onto consciousness but she might have felt with reason that the cards of fate had been stacked against her since the day of her birth. She was thirty-one years old and looked closer to forty-five. She was the youngest of five children, the family of a French couple who had spent all their lives in the bled, the countryside of Algeria which had suffered the worst violence in the bloody campaign to escape the colonial rule of France. Like many contemporaries, the family Dorcas had lost their livelihood and their lives. Monique's father and two of her brothers had died in the bitter fighting, her mother lost her mind and killed herself, her sister had simply disappeared. Monique and her surviving brother managed to stay alive long enough to abandon the family farm outside Djelfa and make their way to Morocco. They had tried to settle in Rabat, scraping some sort of a living together until her brother Gilbert became involved with a girl from Casablanca and packed up almost overnight to move there, making it clear that Monique was not welcome to accompany him.

Left entirely on her own, Monique did not hesitate when she received a marriage proposal from Manaff al-Jabri. She knew, of course, that he was a Muslim, believed he was a citizen of Morocco, thought he would look after her even if along with other wives and women. He was pleasant enough company, rather diffident in manner and appeared to treat her with respect and some old fashioned gentility. He made infrequent and perfunctory love to her and these liaisons resulted in her pregnancy with the twins which she produced in late 1960.

It came as no surprise to Monique to find that she was expected to be a single parent to the infants. Manaff was always too busy with weighty business matters to concern himself with any aspect of raising his children. There were forever meetings to be arranged, discussions to be held, social events for men only. Monique was content to be treated as an object of ownership, deemed of little worth and deserving of scant attention. None of this troubled her. She had received little attention as a child before the trauma overtook her family and now she was happy to be left alone with the offspring which consumed her life.

Monique called them Tomas and Tetrarch, the former and by minutes the elder named for one of her own long gone siblings and Tetrarch, because although bigger and stronger, always took a lead from Tomas. Monique had delved into her Bible and was inspired by King Herod the Tetrarch – a dominant character but a subordinate ruler.

She delighted in the growing children who kept her busy and provided a channel of introduction to other women and offspring in the neighbourhood. She ceased to remember her dead parents, her brothers and sister: she no longer worried over the abrupt departure from her life of her surviving brother Gilbert. Best of all, her husband Manaff made few demands on her as she had come to dread his flaccid embrace, garnished with increasingly bad breath.

Monique was a simple woman from a simple background, content enough with her lot. But then came the day which changed everything. She had never enquired after her husband's business affairs, would never have presumed to do so and would hardly have understood. In truth, Manaff was disastrously incompetent and worse, he was dishonest. He talked big and delivered small. He made unwise commitments from which he was too often obliged to withdraw in ignominy. In personality and behaviour, he was unsuited to a culture which expects a man to be good to his word.

Manaff had a crisis which was waiting to happen and on that day in October 1964 when an enraged business partner threatened him with exposure followed by death, he went home in a rage fuelled by panic. In a flurry of words, he announced to his wife that she must pack minimum belongings and be prepared to leave Rabat the following day at dawn. He revealed to her that he was not Moroccan, rather that his family was Tuareg, originating from northern Niger and Mauritania, now living at Awsard in Western Sahara. They would go there immediately and the journey would take three days.

Monique was simply bemused. She wondered where these ravings were coming from and refused to believe that this was reality. Her natural sense demanded protection of her children, in whose defence she started to argue. Manaff fulminated and became violent, insisting on her obedience to him without further question. She refused. He hit her and she struggled. Their modest furniture was scattered about the room and ornaments were broken. The twins started to scream in fear and astonishment. Their father reacted by turning on them. Plucky little Tetrarch tried to shield his sibling and was kicked for his pains. For Monique, this brought back the horrors of her own mother losing her reason and she sought to protect her children by striking out at her husband. All too typically, Manaff broke off to swear viciously at her and then ran from the house.

Galvanised by this crisis, Monique followed her immediate instincts without thought for the consequences. In Algeria, as the child of a pied noir family, she had been raised as a devout Catholic. During her years of living with Manaff in Rabat, she had maintained her religion and he had not questioned it. Monique had worshipped regularly in the cathedral and the twins had been baptised there. She had come to know the bishop and his clergy. In particular, she had become close to Father Christophe, the son of a French émigré family and like herself, brought up in colonial Algeria. In desperation, Monique now swept up her twins and ran to him for protection and advice.

Father Christophe received her kindly, listened to her woes and promised to help. He installed her with her children in a room in the cloisters of the cathedral and left her in peace to reflect. She was devoutly grateful.

A day later, the relief turned sour. Christophe reappeared and with him was Manaff. It became clear that they were friends and shared the same interests, including similar predilections and practices. Monique listened with steadily mounting horror as the two men agreed their deal. Christophe would maintain a discreet and ecclesiastical silence. He would disclaim knowledge of Manaff and his activities. Neither man expected there to be any enquiry after Monique or the twins which was helpful as the bargain included the gift of Tetrarch to Father Christophe. The lively, good looking five year old was to be left in the Father's care – forever.

Afterwards, Monique was to berate herself that she did nothing to save her son. She should have shouted, screamed, fought and run and yet she knew instinctively that escape was never an option. In the gloom of the cloisters, there was no one to hear, still less to help. She was encumbered by two children, always a handful in themselves and quite persuaded that life was a constant game. How quickly and savagely were they to learn otherwise. Christophe caught up Tomas while Manaff twisted his wife's arm behind her back and pushed her bodily through the massive oak door which had been guardian of their security and now became a prison for Tetrarch as the Father turned the key in the door and the mounting cries of the little boy left behind it were blocked from his mother's ears but never from her heart.

The men hustled their human loads up the stone flagged corridor and into a courtyard where waited an old grey van marked with the insignia of the Order of monks which ruled the daily life of the cathedral. The scruffy old man at the wheel showed neither surprise nor interest at his cargo.

The vehicle wheezed into life, moving from the courtyard into another, larger version and thence through the main gates and into the busy streets of Rabat. Crushed in the windowless rear, Monique could see nothing of their progress. She had seen no sign of a farewell between the two men and Father Christophe had said nothing to her as he thrust the bundle which was Tomas into her arms and slammed the door of the van in her face. Manaff had climbed into the front by the driver and although there was a solid steel wall between her and the front seats, a grille was let into it and she started to implore him for some explanation and comfort. He offered no word of reply. He was never to speak directly to her again.

It took them a full three days to reach the camp outside Awsard, endless hours of discomfort, delays and distraction in trying to keep Tomas quiet and biddable. They travelled in a succession of mini-buses, each more crammed and decrepit than the last as the roads grew worse and became rock strewn tracks.

There was nothing to tell Monique that they had finally arrived: no word from her husband, no sign on the track, no evidence of life. They were simply dumped in the bush in the middle of a barren, windswept landscape which baked under the searing sun. They watched the rusty old van which had transported them over the final leg of a hardship journey as it ground away. Man, wife and child stood amidst their pathetic bundle of belongings until Manaff swept up his share, leaving Monique to struggle with the remainder with a hand held out for Tomas to walk beside her. The group made slow and painful progress in walking a further two kilometres over a winding path until they came into the camp which was to be a final home for Monique.

By her rough reckoning, they had survived there for about a year before the crisis. A year during which she lost all hope of regaining any normality of life, twelve months of a constant battle to get through each day whilst protecting her child. She was conscious that Tomas was better able to tolerate the circumstances as there were other children of similar age amongst the hundred odd humans who populated the settlement which existed in this location simply because of the supply of well water sufficient to keep them all alive. The effort to survive consumed so much energy and concentration that most of the inhabitants were withdrawn and surly.

Monique rarely saw Manaff but from the moment of their arrival, she was taken in hand by his mother, a tall and surprisingly graceful woman who lived with her husband and his brother at the centre of the encampment in a rusted old shipping container which had a tent attached. Little by little, the background story became clear to Monique. Manaff was an only child, his father was a wastrel and his uncle was mentally deficient. Manaff had disappointed his parents, first by running off to the fleshpots of Morocco and then worse, by returning in failure, penniless and trailing his own baggage. His mother ruled the roost and she was all the more frightening for her calm. It was a redeeming feature that she took strongly to Tomas. Monique guessed that she had been unable to conceive a second child and was thus all the happier to welcome a grandchild. But as the weeks passed in their grinding discomfort, she came to see her mother-in-law as an ever more sinister threat. The woman was for ever finding further tasks for Monique whilst she monopolised Tomas, and worse, very much worse, she appeared to encourage her husband in the unwanted attention which he paid to Monique. This awkward, extended family was living with little privacy in confined quarters but this did not deter the grizzled older man from taking every opportunity to leer and to touch. Monique was horrified. There was real danger here, irrespective of Manaff's indifference to his father's behaviour and in addition, the old man repulsed her: he smelt like a dead goat. She kept pushing him off, hit out at him a couple of times, appealed to his wife who simply smiled vaguely and concentrated on attending to Tomas.

Then, two nights previously, Monique had woken abruptly. As normal for her, she had been sleeping face down, her head to one side so that she could look over to the little alcove in which Tomas lay. She suddenly felt a weight on her back, hands at her neck and she smelt the dreadful breath as he tried to push himself between her legs. A filthy rag was stuffed into her mouth as she started to scream and while one hand stayed at her throat, the other pushed its way over her breasts and down, over and round her buttocks, seeking to ease his passage into her. Monique fought, bucked and won. She was a young woman made strong by the privations of her life while her father-in-law was of slight build and under exercised.

Much later that day, she was trying to recover from the attack by spending much longer than normal in fetching water and so giving herself some precious time of solitude. When she did return to the container home, she found waiting for her a senior member of the Elders Committee, a self-styled group of five men who adjudicated on any matter of dispute within the camp community. With him stood her mother-in-law, now ranting in a manner which Monique had never seen before. The Elder told Monique that she would now be tried on a charge of adultery, the claim being that she had wilfully seduced her father-in-law and that evidence of this would be advanced by his wife. At this, Manaff's mother recommenced her verbal assault, backed up by a physical attack and Monique had to fight her off before more members of the Committee intervened to separate the women.

Monique was then led away to be held securely overnight. Her trial before dawn the following morning was a charade, carefully orchestrated from behind the scenes by her ruthless mother-in-law. Monique was duly convicted and sentenced to die by stoning before the sun rose. The wretched woman was by then in a state of trance, unable to comprehend and incapable of fighting back. She was ready to give up on this world still caring enough for her surviving child to recognise that the whole episode had been contrived by Manaff's mother so she could take full charge of Tomas as her own.

It was still dark when they buried her up to the neck but soon there was light enough to start the gruesome business of execution. As the cuckolded husband, Manaff was entitled and required to cast the first stone. Being an established incompetent, he could be expected to miss by a mile and thus make the victim yet more desperate. But Manaff disappointed his parents again and his stone struck his wife not very hard, but with great accuracy on the forehead right between the eyes. Monique immediately lost the consciousness that she was never to regain. Her last thought was for her twins and her love for them.

Tomas, at five years old, sat away from the crowd of onlookers, hands over ears to block out the sounds of a precious head being turned to pulp. But the child's eyes remained open, staring with vivid determination into the middle distance of that harsh landscape, willing forward the time and opportunity for revenge.

3. KINGSTON OFFENBACH — 1967

As soon as he got out of the beaten up old cab, he knew it was a mistake, a put up job. He knew he should turn on his heel and leave – right there and then.

King Offenbach had the required personal qualities and the training for his profession. He was a highly intelligent young man, perceptive, patient and painstaking by nature. He had been schooled at the expense of the US Government and enrolled into the CIA for further education and development. His success as a diligent student had led to a post-graduate course at Oxford University in England, so for almost a year he had been unable to pay his routine monthly visit to his single mother Maisie, quite content to be getting on with her small town life in the depths of South Carolina.

It was just as well that Maisie cherished her independence as her son, in whom she took such quiet pride, then went on to land a plum job which was based at the American Embassy in London. During the 1960's, the US Administration was increasingly concerned at the proliferation of the drugs trade throughout the States. Cocaine was becoming the stimulant of choice and perceived sophistication and whilst the majority of the white powder found its way via the Caribbean from South America, a rapidly developing volume was being trafficked via countries in West Africa and the CIA's interest in that entire continent was managed from the UK. King had joined the small team in Grosvenor Square shortly after his stint at Oxford and he had been making good progress. His boss and his colleagues recognised his natural ability, warmed to the character of this relaxed, unhurried young guy with his diffident charm and languid good looks. And there was more: operating as they were in Africa, it helped that Kingston Offenbach was black.

King stood for a moment in the dust outside the scruffy looking bar, ill named as the Etoile. It was located pretty much in the centre of Pointe Noire, second city of the Republic of Congo in southern Africa. King had been spending time in neighbouring Zaire, finding his feet and some facts from a secure base at the US Embassy in Kinshasa into which America was busy pouring support and finance in return for which Zaire was supposed to become a bulwark against communist influence. His colleagues at the Embassy were welcoming enough but distracted. They had enough to do in progressing this initiative for the US of A to assume centre stage in Africa without troubling themselves too much over the programme for a small fry CIA operative intent on penetrating the local drugs gangs. Plus there was discrimination ingrained in these Ivy League diplomats. Polite and charming on the surface but he had overheard an aside whilst being introduced around at a social occasion: 'can you believe the lengths they're going to at Langley to ensure mission disguise!'

King had experienced way too much of such smart talk to be offended, so he kept his head down and ploughed his own furrow. He suffered nearly ten days of interminable briefings on the American diplomatic objectives, the complex background of this huge and testing country, the vital wooing of Mobutu Sese Seko, all powerful President of Zaire through ruthless intrigue, bloody assassination and breath-taking corruption. By then, King had had enough of being lectured. He reported at length by Telex to Jeb Ambrose, his Chief in London and finished by saying that he would now move on to make contact with 'Marco', at that point just a name to all of them but a character reputed to be well informed as to the methods and men being used to shift high volumes of cocaine through Africa and on to the society sophisticates in Europe. It was unfortunate for both of them that Jeb had been summoned to Washington and was delayed in reading the message. By the time he had sent his reply to counsel caution, King had already made his first move.

21

Marco had been suave, courteous and very persuasive as to the value of his local knowledge and experience. When King had called, Marco had been delighted to hear from him and insisted on buying him an excellent lunch at one of Kinshasa's better restaurants – and in those days, there had been a wide choice. They sat outside in comfortably cushioned cane chairs under a wide parasol and watched the chic pedestrian traffic moving down their boulevard. They might have been in Rouen or Orleans on a warm summer afternoon.

Marco was expansive and relaxed as he lounged in his smart tropical suit, his hat thrown casually on the table in front of them. He recounted that he was Panamanian by birth, had lived in Rio, Buenos Aires and Bogota before moving across the Atlantic ten years previously to start a new life in Luanda, Angola. This sounded to King to be a strange choice and he said so.

'Ah well, you must understand Keeng', Marco explained in his flawless English garnished with Spanish accent, 'I became an unpopular man in Columbia and that is a dangerous condition in Bogota. I was a soldier in Brazil and a policeman in Argentina. I progressed to ingratiate myself with some of the emerging drug barons, to be an informant, thus to help limit this pernicious trade. But to do that in Bogota, you must settle for a short career or a short life – and for some, it means both things. As for me, well, I was lucky but also, I had cultivated my contacts around the globe and had the offer of a career with an American oil giant, helping to protect their interests in off shore rigs operating in the waters of Angola. I have been based in Cabinda these last few years and there I have made good money whilst being well away from the orbit of my former life in Columbia. I am protected by living far away and in anonymity.'

Marco paused to light himself a cigarette before concluding. 'But, of course, I still keep myself informed and I'm happy to enhance my lifestyle by passing on observations of value. How is our mutual friend Jeb, incidentally? We've only met once, but as you will know, I am in regular communication.'

King took his time before making his reply and even then,

it was not to respond directly. He stretched out his long legs and steepled his hands in front of him as he played over in his mind the little summary which Marco had just delivered. Too short, too sparse and also too pat, he thought to himself and yet it did fit well enough with the brief Jeb had given him back in London. Finally, he responded with a question.

'I guess you know that I'm here on a fact finder. You've seen my credentials and you know I'm legit. Can you give me any more on the latest shipments coming in here to Zaire and how they are leaving for Europe?' King was deliberately using the sort of language that would be expected of a keen, young CIA Agent.

'I can tell you you're in the wrong place.' Marco smiled disarmingly as he dragged on his cigarette and sat back in his chair. 'Look, things been moving on gradually during the last few years. This part of Africa is still a major staging post but now more and more of the product is being transhipped through next door rather than our Port of Matadi and then Kinshasa.'

Marco saw the question mark in King's eyes and he went on,

'I'm talking about the Congo and their Atlantic outlet at Pointe Noire. There are two advantages for the traffickers. First, there's less interference, not much of a police or customs presence so fewer hands to bribe. And second, the airport there is pretty large as it was reconstructed by the French during World War Two. It's not much used today and security is light so they can fly the stuff straight out – even directly into Europe. Whereas here in Zaire, they have to use trucks from the coast into Kinshasa and then the airport is a bugger to get through. So it makes sense for them to have moved next door.'

He gave a shrug and waited for the next question which came immediately.

King asked, 'Why didn't you tell us this before?'

'I've given some clues to Jeb but I don't like to commit this sort of news to paper or phone or telex come to that. I was waiting for Jeb to come down here or for him to send someone in his place and now, here you are!' The charming smile lit up again under the heavily tinted sunglasses.

King was mulling over this and thinking that it didn't fit too well with the last briefing he'd received from his boss for all that it was sure as hell interesting, when Marco resumed.

'The big man in these parts is Belgian but also he's black – or just possibly mixed race. Very bright, hard as nails and ruthless with it. I don't know his real name but he's known to all as le Mot – the Word. These days he's mostly in the Congo but they say he travels a fair bit. Wherever he is, you can be sure he's your No 1 target.' Marco paused to light up again and then he leant forward to speak more softly.

'There's another contact I can give you, King. A guy called Guillaume who lives in Pointe Noire. He's a Frenchman who's been there for years. He's pretty low life, always involved in petty theft and various scams but he's well connected and knows his way around. The drug trade is now so profitable that Guillaume has involved himself in the fringes and is probably a user himself. He'd be worth talking to now you're down here and it won't take much time or effort. You can be in and out in a day.'

King thought about this but not for long. In his profession it was generally worth following every lead even if the majority ended in a cul de sac. So he thanked Marco for both lunch and his advice, taking guidance as to how to find Guillaume. Then he stood to leave with the promise that he would report back on his return and they could have another meal together before he flew back to London. King left Marco to enjoy a final coffee and a digestif in the afternoon sunshine while he set out on foot. His long strides had carried him a couple of blocks towards the Embassy compound when two police motor cycles followed by an ambulance blared their way past in the opposite direction, shattering the relative peace and causing unwary walkers to leap for their lives. It was a familiar occurrence to King although he had spent only a few days in this vibrant city and he thought nothing of it as he made his way, recalling and analysing every facet of his conversation with Marco.

Two days later, King took what is said to be the shortest international flight on the planet – from Kinshasa, Zaire across the Congo River and into Maya Maya Airport which serves the Congolese capital of Brazzaville. There he had a couple of hours wait before he could fold his long frame into an ancient Constellation which trundled its way due west to land in Pointe Noire. He took a Peugeot cab into the centre and found the Bar de l'Etoile to which he had been directed by Marco. Despite the doubts which assailed him as he stood in the dust outside, he straightened himself up and turned to walk in. He was still young enough for age and pride to trump experience.

The interior of the Etoile was an encouraging improvement. The place was much bigger than it appeared from outside, extending a full block back and it had a fine mahogany bar running the full depth of the establishment and thus at right angles to the entrance. Round tables of equally solid construction were dotted about the remaining floor space and the bar itself was curved through ninety degrees at the extreme end of the building so that customers could drink or eat with their backs to the end wall whilst looking down and out of the front entrance.

It was mid-afternoon when King walked in and the place was not humming. A few of the tables were occupied and a handful of drinkers stood at the bar, some flirting with the garishly presented girls who perched on stools wearing skirts so short as to barely cover their most valuable commodity.

King strode purposefully towards the bar, intent on asking for Guillaume in his just adequate French. Before he could open his mouth, a slightly built man with matted ginger hair, wearing a filthy pair of jeans and a T shirt rose from a table in the centre and leaving the group which remained seated there, made his way up to King. He had a pronounced limp.

'M. Offenbach? Moi, je suis Guillaume et on m'a dit que vous me cherchez. Oui?'

King smiled down at him from his much greater height and opened his mouth to make a laboured reply. Guillaume interrupted him almost immediately and invited him to join his table and to meet his colleagues. This was the last thing that King was expecting but he dutifully followed the small man over and found himself looking at a hard face set in a bullet head which surmounted a wide body. The unsmiling mouth opened and a gravel voice spoke in very adequate English.

'I am le Mot,' it said,'why are you looking for me?'

King managed to look calm and relaxed while his heart was pounding and his thoughts were furious. He had been right by instinct and should have left before he started. He smiled at the malevolent face and very slowly reached into the pocket of his lightweight jacket as he spoke in reply.

'I'm glad you speak English. My French is very poor but my intentions are good.' He exaggerated his American drawl as he went on.'I'm a writer doing an article for the *National Geographic* magazine. Here are my credentials.' King laid a slim wallet emblazoned with the correct emblem on the table and gave it a push towards le Mot. The man held his gaze and nodded sharply. One of the four cohorts who sat beside him, two on either side, moved the wallet further on until it lay immediately in front of le Mot, who picked it up and flicked idly through it.

The documents were quite false but expertly prepared and should pass muster, King had time to think to himself as he took his chance to inspect le Mot's companions more closely. All regarded him unswervingly. They all looked fit, tough, hard and unfriendly. Too much competition and too good. He was in real trouble here and there was worse as back up. Behind this table was the bar extension and behind that stood yet another big guy, much blonder, heavily muscled, chewing at a baguette with a tall, long glass of beer halfway towards his mouth. He had just a few seconds to take all this in before le Mot was speaking to him again.

'This is bullshit. I don't know who you are but I don't like people digging around in my business affairs.'

King leant forward and placed his finger tips on the edge of the table. He looked into le Mot's jet black, piggy eyes and made his reply.

'I believe I can surely explain, Sir, if you let me sit down here and just talk awhile.' King gave le Mot his best, disarming smile and raised one eyebrow in polite enquiry. There was a pause before the head nodded briefly. King stretched out a long leg to hook round the leg of an empty chair at an adjoining table. Smoothly, he pulled it closer and keeping his eyes on le Mot, he swivelled the chair and sat facing him.

'Now then, Monsieur le Mot, you can check me out however you wish but the truth is that I'm a freelance American journalist. I specialise in hot stories from anywhere around the world. I've covered the Mafia, kidnap and ransoms, a few bush wars. I've done a fair bit of work for the National Geo and this now is a big project. They want a number of articles on the drugs business, but particularly coke. Their angle is to show how and where it's mostly grown, how transported across the globe, how sold and used. We'll cover technicalities of production, they'll be maps aplenty, photos as they do and there'll be comment but no quotes. If you can help me with my research, well swell, but if you don't want, that's OK too and I'll be on my way.'

There was no direct response from le Mot. Instead, he shrugged and turned the bullet head to nod an instruction to the burly young man sitting on his immediate right. The guy reached down to the floor and came up with a thin, foolscap sized manila envelope which he placed on the table in front of his boss. Then le Mot spoke to King.

'I know how you found me and that was easy enough. Leaving will be harder. But first, have a look in there.' He flicked the envelope across the table and King opened it to draw out a single sheet which was a colour photograph, made a little fuzzy by the degree of magnification but quite clear enough with its damning message.

Marco was still sitting where King had left him in the restaurant. He looked comfortable in the cane chair under the parasol, his hat thrown carelessly on the table in front of him, alongside the coffee and glass of Armagnac. But there was no life left in the smiling eyes and the smart shirt had been ruined by blood spilt from the wound in his chest. A knife – a throwing knife to King's tutored eye – was still lodged deep in his body. Marco was very dead and the noise and drama of those emergency vehicles came back to King.

Le Mot was speaking now. 'Marco was a greedy man. Also foolish. He took risks and now he has crossed my path once too often. I warned him before, even a few times. He was not like le petit Guillaume here who needed only one lesson.' He gestured at the ragged and pathetic figure who was cowering away from the table. 'Non. As soon as his leg was broken, I knew he was mine for life and if there is a next time, he knows I will have his balls and then much later, his brains. But Marco was different and too clever for himself. He is lucky to have died quickly.'

He stood then and King saw that although le Mot had a broad and powerful torso, he was very short and his bodyguards towered above him as they also rose. The boss was leaving but first, he had a final message for King.

'Monsieur Offenbach,' he began, his gravelly voice all the more threatening for its calm and measured tone, 'I know you work for an American Intelligence service, probably the CIA although I don't know and don't care, because you were followed from that bistro where you talked with Marco. We followed you back to the Embassy. You did not conduct yourself professionally then and now you come to me with lies. I have no wish to bring the Marines down on me in revenge, therefore you will live but you will be returned to Kinshasa in a considerably damaged state. My men here will see to that but for myself, I have better things to do and am now finished with you. Adieu.'

Le Mot turned to go and King was trying to prepare himself for a painful onslaught when he heard – they all heard – the smash of breaking glass, followed by a very American voice swearing: 'goddamn it'.

The accident was obvious. The blond guy with the beer and baguette must have been bending to catch more of their conversation and in doing so, had knocked his glass onto the floor where it burst in spectacular style. King felt a momentary lift. At least this man was apparently not another member of the muscle party and to confirm this, le Mot said immediately,

'Clear up your mess and then leave. I don't need another Yankee mec involved in this.'

'Well Jesus and goddamn again. I was just interested but now I'm pissed. How many times do I have to say that I'm not a fuckin' American. I'm Canadian. Right?'

As he completed this announcement, the blond left his position at the bar and it became instantly obvious that the guy had not been standing there, but sitting on a stool. He was immense, well over two metres tall and built like a barn. He had huge hands and was cracking his knuckles with relish as he advanced towards the group. He moved swiftly and smoothly, picking up one of the large tables and was holding it comfortably in front of him, its legs sticking out in challenge as he came to a halt in front of them.

'OK then you bastards,' he invited, 'all together or one at a time?'

King had no time then to wonder why this salvation had appeared and events started to move very quickly. His peripheral vision told him that Le Mot was making swift progress towards the double doors onto the street while little Guillaume was heading at his limping run for some exit at the rear. That left four opposition against the Canadian, but King's instinct told him there must be more. He was sure there would be no guns or knives. Le Mot had been clear that there was to be damage but not death, but he was equally certain that there would be more back-up scattered around the Etoile and as he swung around, he saw the first of it immediately. Two fellows of similar stamp and build to those sitting at le Mot's table were breaking away from the group of working girls standing at the bar and were heading to join the fracas.

It was then that the advice King had received from one of his trainers at Quantico flashed across his memory. 'You're tall but not big and you never will be. You've got speed but no bulk. So use the speed and look for the unexpected. If you ain't got size, rely on surprise'.

Now King's reaction was to move fast towards the new

entrants. With quicksilver movement he dodged around one of them and grabbed the first of the girls who came within reach. She was no slimline but light enough for him to swing up to become a battering ram in front of his face with his nose sticking into the clip of her bra, straining to hold it together across her back. She was screaming, struggling with flailing hands and kicking feet as King held her under the arms. He ran her like that into his first assailant and the guy staggered back under the assault to his face from a pair of heaving, sweating breasts whilst further south, her panic driven feet were threatening him with serious harm. King pushed harder and then dropped the girl, leaving that little melee to sort itself out as he turned to meet the second thug who was short and squat, making the mistake of rushing in with arms held wide, intent on taking a hold which King would struggle to break. But he didn't need to. He pirouetted like a bullfighter and as his man went past, he grabbed one leg around the muscle bound calf and swung the guy off the ground and into a whirling circle once, twice and on the third circuit he released him to fly head first into the base of the bar with a satisfying thud.

In the brief respite which followed, King turned to check on the Canadian who by now had three down, two of them out and was in the act of landing two massive blows to the fourth, the first with a leg ripped from the table which caught the man in his stomach while a mighty fist smashed into his face. Not pretty but effective.

King heard noise at the rear of the bar and was not surprised to see more figures appearing. There would be no shortage of le Mot's men in this joint and eventually, he and his saviour would be worn down by numbers with a fierce final reckoning to be paid. The Canadian followed his glance and they reached unspoken agreement in unison: time to leave.

Shoulder to shoulder they dashed for the front doors and burst through together to find the centre of Pointe Noire neither busy nor empty, simply idling along under a hot sun. King was the quicker on his feet and he sprang straight off the pavement and into the main road to land in front of a rusty old Citroen driven by an elderly man who stamped on his brakes in alarm. The Canadian wrenched open the door and pulled the driver out, pushing himself behind the wheel as King hared around the vehicle to climb in beside him and they took off before the doors were closed. King could only hope that his companion knew the city and where he was going but he gesticulated as they passed a sign with the plane symbol which means airport in any language.

'Not that way?' he blurted as the worn tyres squealed on cobbles.

'Got a better idea,' came the reply, 'you just hold on'.

King did as he was told and kept silent until the alternative was revealed as the railway station at which they arrived in a shower of loose gravel. They swept past the foot passenger entrance, which looked grim enough, and continued to bump over an unkempt track to some sort of goods marshalling area in which the old car was abandoned with, King noted, the keys left in the ignition.

'The old guy will find it soon enough,' said his companion, 'you just follow me'.

He led the way at a brisk jog and King was sweating profusely through his lightweight jacket before they finally pulled up outside a shack which bordered the railway track. The Canadian did not hesitate to dive straight in and within seconds he was embracing a middle aged black man with a grizzled face, a greying beard and an enormous paunch.

'This is Chomu', he said by way of introduction. 'He's my best buddy in Pointe Noire and he'll get us on the right transport outta here. But we'll have to wait awhile so grab a corner and make yourself comfortable. I'll try and get us a beer.'

King looked around the confines of the scabby cabin, noting the sparse furniture overflowing with ancient files which were also stacked all over the floor, interspersed with what looked like rat droppings and he sniffed at the smell which overpowered the whole place. It was still a whole heap better than the place he had just left, he decided to himself, and so removed his jacket with relief and subsided on the floor in one corner.

From there, he cocked an ear to the conversation between the Canadian and Chomu, noting the quick fire French and understanding some of it. It was clear that Chomu marshalled freight and that the plan was for them to hop a goods train to Brazzaville but on a service which would not leave before 0100 the following morning and right then, it was scarcely five in the afternoon. But King was a patient man so he settled down to wait.

It was nearer three in the morning before they left, guided aboard a freight car by the tireless Chomu and a further twenty-four hours before Brazzaville raised its head above the horizon, yet all that time they had been unmolested by the men of le Mot seeking vengeance so King felt both contented and relieved. What puzzled him was the reluctance of his big companion to get into any sort of conversation. He remained companionably quiet until they had checked into a prime hotel in Brazzaville and over a couple of beers, the Canadian underwent a sea change and started to talk.

'The name's Hank Devine', he said stretching out a great paw to grip King's hand. 'Canadian citizen, oil man by profession, old Africa hand by experience and inclination. I'm pleased to meet you.'

'Kingston Offenbach but call me King. CIA since schooldays and now based in London. On the Africa drugs team.'

'OK. Well, I guess that means that our friend le Mot had something right.'

'Yup, he surely did. And before you say it, I made the near disaster for myself by rushing in there without checking out my informants first. I was so damn lucky you were there, Hank, and first thing for me is to say a big thank you.'

The big man waved this aside. 'Glad I was able to help and truth be told, I don't mind a bit of a scrap. Those fellas are bastards anyway, sucking the life out of anyone around them. I've had to deal with le Mot before and he saw me before he took off. Knew what he'd be in for.'

King nodded his understanding and appreciation. 'I guess you have the right to know a bit more about me,' he said and he went on to give Hank a brief summary of his background and what had brought him into Pointe Noire.

'It sounds like you're developing quite a career,' said the Canadian in response, 'and if you were a might hasty yesterday, I guess you'll benefit from the experience. Mind you though, this country of the Congo and Noire in particular is generally pretty relaxed and not too bad a place to be visiting. Just that you got yourself in a tangle with some real mean hombres and I expect that Marco was another of the same.'

'I guess you're right but still, I should've known better and hell, I've seen enough of that sort in this line of work. But do tell, Hank, what brings you to this neck of the woods?'

Devine sprawled in his chair and lit himself a cigar as he composed his reply.

'In just one word I can tell you all, King, and that word is Oil with a capital O. I've been in the oil business most all of my working life and I reckon I'll never leave it. There's kind of a compulsion that gets to you and then there's this continent of Africa. I've been knocking around these parts for years, places which get into my blood and under my skin. It's rough and ready, sometimes dangerous and pretty much always uncomfortable but I guess to me it's home and always will be.'

'And it's that which keeps you in Africa? The people and the places?'

Hank shook his great head. 'Nope, it's still the oil. I'm at the cutting edge here and I want to see up close how it all plays out. I'm no geologist but I've the sense for it. I can smell oil, King, and I'm telling you that in the waters around this coast there are fortunes to be made out of reserves you wouldn't dream about. There's a hundred billion barrels off the west coast of Africa and it's all waiting to be harvested.'.

4. VANDA DEVERIDGE — 1969

The cold wind blowing in from the east kept the rain off the small knot of mourners but there was little else to comfort Vanda as she stood shivering beneath her thickest coat and watched Rupert Broke Smith lower his bulk to kneel by the graveside.

His mother Constance had been both a friend and an inspiration to Vanda over many years of living close to each other in this rural community, isolated in the backwoods of Herefordshire. Constance and Geoffrey, Rupert's parents, had settled into Forty Green Cottage in the heart of the village when Vanda had been only about five years old. They had moved there from London and Vanda had felt a child's wonder that a couple from the capital should come to live amongst such country folk.

Constance was never a woman for babies and young children. Indeed, during the years that followed, Vanda had come to believe that Rupert had been conceived in a passing moment of absent mindedness or perhaps when she and Geoffrey had been distracted by a doodle bug bomb interrupting their placid life in a south London suburb during the war years. But as Rupert had come to be her best friend during their early school years and they had moved together into adolescence, Vanda had been a regular visitor to the cottage and had developed a close relationship with his mother. Her outstanding merit to Vanda was that from the earliest days she treated her as already grown up and spoke to her as an adult.

Vanda had enjoyed her senior school years, distinguishing herself in her studies and scoring particularly high marks in history. She had nevertheless been astonished when the headmaster had taken her to one side and asked her if she would consider trying for a place at Cambridge University. He was confident of her success in gaining a place. She immediately shared this news with Rupert who was full of encouragement and then she discussed it with Constance over a cup of tea in Forty Green Cottage. The reaction surprised Vanda. Constance needed no persuasion that she had the brain and application to make a successful undergraduate career and she spoke wistfully of the opportunities which a decent degree would open up for Vanda but she shook her wise old grey head as she pondered aloud on the effect all this would have on Vanda's family.

'You'll have to face it, girl,' she said gently, 'you'll be leaving home and it may be hard to go back.'

Vanda couldn't credit this. There were already five Maddox brothers working on the farm and committed to taking over from their father, Frank. There had never been any suggestion that their only sister would be welcome to join them and surely her whole family would be proud to see her take off in search of some academic fortune.

But Constance was right in her foreboding. Vanda's mother Trisha was pleased enough by the news but as always, she was preoccupied by the toil of looking after her family. Her father, however, big bluff Frank expressed his view in as he sucked on his pipe after supper and it was plain that wild horses would not change his decision.

'No, Vanda lass, that's not for you. You've done well at school, mind, there's no denying that but education's one thing and life is another. What would you want with more qualifications? I can't see the benefit and then the cost of it would be another thing. Three years of travel and accommodation and such like? Honestly, love, it's better to settle down here where you belong – amongst your own.'

While he was delivering this little speech, abnormally long for the taciturn Frank, Trisha continued to swab down the Aga, keeping her back firmly turned so that Vanda knew she should expect no support from her mother. She resolved instead to go round the following day to take some advice from Constance but as soon as she reached Forty Green Cottage, she was hit by a second blow.

The news had come in by the Post that very morning. Her best friend Rupert had triumphed in his own exams and was now offered a place to study physics at Oxford and would be going off to start there in the autumn. Vanda felt instantly crushed. She did her best to rejoice with him and his parents but she was weeping inside. She was losing her own chance and would be losing his nourishing companionship. She would be left marooned in this all too familiar backwater.

Over the next year or so, Vanda managed a sometimes cheerful existence by living some of her young life vicariously through Rupert. She yearned for the vacations when he came home from Oxford and they spent all the time they could manage together, although she was working full time at the pharmacy in Hereford. He told her all about his new life in the University City, reported on the progress of his studies, used his descriptive language to walk her around the sights of Oxford, told her about his games of rugby, spoke about his friends.

During these brief interludes, they were as happy together as they had ever been in childhood or whilst growing up. Over the period of New Year 1964, Rupert had taken her out from work to lunch one day and started to speak seriously about the prospects of marriage after his graduation the following summer. He had been so fidgety in manner and circumspect in speech that Vanda had immediately recognised his proposal for what it was, an invitation to have a bit of carnal before Communion – in old fashioned country speak. She had been happy to agree and had contrived an elaborate excuse to be away from home for a couple of days. And so they had become lovers, going off to a quiet hotel in North Devon where they spent the hours of these brief, stolen days and nights in exploration of both hearts and bodies. Vanda had returned to her humdrum life and farmhouse home fulfilled in every sense and believing that she had at last a secure and exciting future.

But 1964 went on badly and became worse. First, Vanda's oldest brother Matthew died in a wholly avoidable farm accident, leaving a widow and one small child. After the shock of this tragedy, their father Frank became morose and withdrawn while a deep gloom settled over the surviving members of the family. The mood was beginning to lift with the coming of spring when Vanda received a long letter from Rupert, saying that he felt moved to go to India on a form of spiritual retreat during his summer vacation and would therefore be coming home to his parents' cottage for only a short time in September. Vanda was very unsettled by this pronouncement and went to discuss it with Constance but found her to be equally puzzled. Whilst years apart in age, they were both wise women and could understand that Rupert might be seduced away by some siren song in Oxford, but not that it should be sung by the Almighty from continents away.

That proved, however, to be the case. When Rupert came home for a week in late September, he was on one level the same character as he had always been. There was plenty of conversation, much humour and solicitous attention. He seemed very calm also, very determined and sure of his path. He told her carefully and without inhibition of the 'calling' he had received and of its confirmation whilst he had been in the Hindu Kush. He told her that he was determined to join the priesthood. He would become a monk and whilst he would love her forever, it would be a love of care and not of passion.

Rupert left her then to return to Oxford and in the void of his absence, Vanda felt confused and frustrated but above all, she felt lost. For want of alternative, she fell back into a routine of life, taking the bus to and fro to Hereford every day to her undemanding job, performing her share of chores at home on the farm, entirely puzzled as to how she was going to find some meaning for her life.

The months passed with agonising slowness. She managed to get through Christmas and the New Year without seeing Rupert. She had some letters from him, just news and views which she read avidly, hoping against hope that he might have a change of heart. But there was none of that, simply a change of name. He wrote her a long account of the training course at a seminary which he had attended over most of the Christmas break. He and his fellow students had been hard worked and for relaxation they would gather in the bar of an evening where Rupert would down his pints of bitter and chew on the pickled onions which he loved to the violent detriment of his digestion. The noisy results had led to another christening and now all his friends called him 'Pentecost' after the biblical rushing, mighty wind and this had been shortened to 'Pente'.

Vanda had managed a genuine laugh at this and had replied to say that she sympathised with his new colleagues but that to her, he would always be Roo. Then she went on to give him some local news, feeling ever more lonely and miserable as she wrote although she strived for a bright tone. There was nothing now to be done except to preserve the close friendship of many years which could have been so much more.

Barely two months later, whilst still feeling raw and vulnerable, Vanda drove one Saturday morning with her father Frank to look at some milking parlour equipment which was offered for sale at an unexpectedly low price. She suspected something from the moment Frank had proposed the outing. Vanda herself knew little of cows and milking but she did know the vendor who was Mr Deveridge, wealthiest farmer in the district and the father of 'Drippy Luke' of whom she had spoken in such demeaning terms to Rupert years ago.

The Deveridge land holding was considerable and the farmyard immaculate, arranged to impress with its spacious buildings and modern machinery. The owner was pleasant enough in his own way but Frank had reminded her while they were driving over that Tom Deveridge had inherited an enterprise which had been established and built up by his grandfather. Tom was no farmer himself but he was astute with his finances and had invested wisely to increase the value of his sprawling property. His wife Margaret had produced two offspring – their son Luke who was a contemporary of Vanda and who followed and older sister, Sarah.

It was obvious to Vanda that she was being set up with Luke

and she resented her father's attempt at an arranged marriage which would likely bring more benefit to him than to her. As the late winter sun shone warmly on these palatial surroundings, two thoughts arrived to mollify her. The first was that she had nothing more to lose now that Roo had ruled himself out of her life and then secondly, the Luke who came dashing out of the grand house looked nowhere near as bad as she remembered him.

And so matters took their course. Vanda and Luke were married in the July of that same year, almost on the very day that the first love of her life was graduating from Oxford and setting out on his lonely journey of service and penitence. Vanda and Pente had not met again until this cold winter day, four and a half years later when they were laying his mother Constance to rest in the quiet village churchyard.

One thing that had not changed during this time was Vanda's fondness for Constance. The two of them had remained in close and frequent contact, culminating in almost daily visits by Vanda to Forty Green Cottage. As the cancer which claimed her had been draining the strength from her body, Constance had been desperate to stay in her own home until the end and with Geoffrey quite unable to cope, it had been Vanda who came to the rescue with visits to supplement her nurses' attention and to bring the comfort of idle talk and shared memories.

When they had all gathered in the cottage after the funeral, the first words Pente spoke to Vanda after a giant's embrace were of thanks for her loving care. Vanda thought to herself that quite apart from the pressures of the moment, distress at losing his mother and concern for how his father would survive without her, Pente looked older than his twenty-six years. Much of that was to do with sheer bulk, the weight which had crept on as he had shed his rugby fitness but not the beer consumption which had accompanied it and then there was the great, shaggy beard which he had grown. In character he seemed completely unchanged and she loved him anew for that as soon as he started to speak to her. His perception was also undiminished.

When all the other mourners had left and she was standing in the small hall which she knew so well, belting her coat around her and preparing for the drive home, he stopped her with a gesture, saying,

'Hang on just a moment while I settle my dad with a whisky and let's have a quick word before you go.'

'OK, but I really mustn't dally. Luke will be looking out for me.'

'Hah! Well he should have come himself,' Pente shot back as he slipped past her to attend to Geoffrey and Vanda had to smile to herself. Punchy, but also correct, she thought and then with mischief, I wonder if he still fancies me? As well he might. Vanda had remained a very good looking girl and thus far had succeeded in her battle to keep slim. But two pregnancies had done nothing to help and she was conscious that it would become a tougher battle with each passing year. At least there was no chance of a third child. Hannah had been born in March '66 – almost a honeymoon baby and her brother William had followed in the first month of 1968 so that she had her hands full with two under four. She was proud of her children, loved them both and was absorbed by them.

'Just as well I have them,' she was saying to Pente on his return to the hall and they were exchanging intimate news at an unseemly speed, 'because I get no life nor love from Luke. I married him on the rebound from you, Roo, and I should have known better. He seemed fine to start, dashing, fun and all the more attractive for his money. I don't mind admitting to all that and I shouldn't have been in such a rush. But whatever, I don't believe I could have guessed at the drink problem. Probably it was there before but only became crystal clear to me about a year ago and it's been accelerating since then. These days he's hardly sober by day and absolutely never at night. At least he doesn't get violent and he's become so weedy I think I could cope with that anyway. But Luke's no sort of company and scores zero in the romance stakes these days. If he could ever get it up, it wouldn't stay that way for long.'

It was still her Rupert – or Pente if she must – to whom she was talking and she was not prepared to avoid the sort of direct language they had always used together just because he was now dressed in a habit tied together with a superior looking dressing gown cord.

Pente seemed quite unmoved.

'You poor, poor thing. What a rotten situation and how undeserved. I suppose you're quite on your own in this? No help from his father or the rest of the family?'

'Not a chance. They don't want to know, much less to get involved to help. The truth is, I think, that Luke has had this and other problems from way back. They managed to smarten him up enough to catch me and now they're prepared to throw enough money at us to keep the lid on things. We have a beautiful big house, any amount of money, lots of help but we pay the price that they don't want to recognise the state of their son. They just want me to keep him out of their way.'

Pente nodded sorrowfully. 'What about your people?' he asked gently.

'No,'Vanda was shaking her head,'No. Well, you know them well enough. Both my parents and all my brothers are such private and mostly undemonstrative people who never stop working and simply don't understand a man who won't do a hand's turn. Plus they can see all the wealth and know that Luke's indolence isn't keeping the food from my mouth or his children so they just shrug and walk away. And as for the drink, it would be an embarrassment to talk about it, much less to consider a remedy. So, all in all I'm afraid it's the old adage: I've made my bed etc.

Pente had been slumped against the door post but now he drew himself up to full height.

'I'm not so sure about that last bit. You really can't be settling for another thirty years or so of this sort of life and there are things that can be done. There simply must be and I'm going to help you find them. You've got to go now, Vanda but I'll be here for a couple of days and a few more in London before I fly back to Africa on New Year's Eve. I'll ring you tomorrow but I can tell you now that the first thing you've got to do is to get away for a while, just a few days to recharge the batteries and give yourself some thinking space. For now, sort out how you can leave Hannah and William so they will be safe and sound and I'll have a word with my good old chum from Oxford – King Offenbach. King's got contacts everywhere and I'm sure he'll be able to come up with some ideas.'

'You're so kind and understanding,' she said drawing him into a hug, 'and how awful that I haven't asked before but how goes it all with you?'

'A bit rocky also,' he replied as he squeezed her, 'but I guess that's the way the good Lord intended it to be'.

He held her away from him and gave his warmest smile.

'I'll tell you more when we speak on the phone. Just hang on for now.'

5. TOMAS AND TETRARCH —1974

The very faintest breeze stirred the torpid air, signalling the approach of dawn. This was the way that each day of the year announced itself in Awsard, Western Sahara, with this brief refreshment before the landscape and all who survived in it were plunged into the familiar cauldron of sand and searing sun, to be followed eventually by the scarcely cooler hours of the night.

Inside the al-Jabri compound in its pride of place at the centre of the encampment, the family was trying to gain some final minutes of repose before the swelter of another day overtook them. On the truckle bed by the door lay the matriarch, the tall woman with the air of menacing calm who had contrived the execution of Monique nearly ten years previously. At right angles and against one of the shorter sides of the old container which made for their hearth and home, a pile of old sheets and rags covered a filthy mattress on which the snoring form of her husband remained comatose, a slave now to the mixture of desert cactus juice laced with meths which he used as a crude anaesthetic every night. The matriarch wrinkled her nose: she could smell him from where she lay but at least his older brother was out of their lives. He had died about two years back. She didn't know why and cared less.

In the centre of the container floor stood a battered steel table and beyond it, two roughly constructed wooden beds, one for an adult and the other much smaller but enough for a child. The table was covered with cutlery, metal platters, a large jug of purified water, general bits and bobs – and against the other short wall stood their most valued possession, an ancient refrigerator which was powered by gas from bottles outside the container.

It remained, both inside and out, almost as sordid a structure as the day when the luckless Monique had been introduced to it but the comforts of home had improved over the years and they were reflected in the general condition of the whole camp. A roughly made sign now greeted any casual visitor who dared to trek down the kilometres of rough track from the main road and this read simply "Romany. Keep out": hardly a welcome, but at least a warning.

The population of the camp had not changed and was still about a hundred souls but the make-up had altered considerably. Many had left, either to seek somewhere, anywhere that was less dire, and many more had departed the world, their remains inadequately buried somewhere in the rock strewn ground which surrounded the encampment. It was the relative newcomers, however, who were significant.

In 1971, the name of the Polisario Front had been coined and had even managed to gain a little recognition on the world stage. This fledgling organisation was at that point a simple guerrilla outfit with the single objective of ending the Spanish colonial rule of this territory and to pave the way for an independent nation. Eventually, the Polisario would come to succeed but only when the President of neighbouring Mauritania was forced to concede that his miserable military strength could not deliver the control and security which he had promised to Spain. But that was still to come and in 1974, the guerrillas were under ceaseless pressure from coalition forces which harried them viciously. To gain respite from time to time, groups of freedom fighters would melt away into the harsh bush country, finding retreats in which they could regroup and rearm themselves before launching fresh attacks against their prime government targets of main roads, the railway, ports and mines. The camp outside Awsard was a perfect refuge for as many of them as it could accommodate, an opportunity to become gypsies for a while as they licked their wounds.

Such an arrangement suited the genuine inhabitants well enough as these hard men brought with them their own form of security and much more important, they brought money. The matriarch, reclining in the best bed of the wretched container, hugged to herself the thought of the growing stash of currency notes in the box which she kept out of sight behind the fridge. In another month or so, she would have enough to ditch her hopeless husband and make her way towards a new and better life in Nouakchott, capital of Mauritania. After much thought, she had decided that she would also abandon her son Manaff, finally convinced that he was incapable of advancing from being a spineless incompetent, made worse now by going the way of his father and drinking anything which would make him both insensible and incontinent. That would leave only Tomas, Manaff's brat whose mother she had removed from the picture. The matriarch had invested much effort in Tomas but received very little in return. The child was stunted in growth and retarded in development. She smiled to herself mirthlessly: three generations and not a real man amongst them. Tomas was willing enough, always obedient and definitely intelligent. But the large, jet black and unblinking eyes in that young face were spooky and the likeness to Monique was unsettling. Yes, she thought, it would be best to ditch this final piece of baggage along with the rest of her family. She had carried too much of a burden for too long. Very soon, she would make a completely new start, by herself and for herself.

But for now, another day. The matriarch propped herself on one elbow and looked over the steel table. Manaff's bed was empty of course. He had been away for two nights, on a mission to buy more supplies in Awsard. He should return today after a little shopping, a lot of drinking and no doubt some screwing around if he had found himself capable. On the smaller bed next to Manaff's, the huddled pile under a grubby sheet showed where Tomas was sleeping, Tomas who should by now be rising to go out to rekindle the cooking fire and to get some coffee brewing for breakfast.

By the head of the matriarch's bed was cut the single door sized access into the container. This gap was closed during the hours of darkness by a heavy mesh grille which was hinged on one side and padlocked on the other. The key to the padlock hung on a string around the neck of the matriarch so that she was, in effect, gaoler to all the occupants of the container. Behind and above Manaff's bed was their alternative source of ventilation, a rectangular section cut out of the container's side, up at the top where the roof met the wall.

She opened her mouth to call to Tomas, a bark loud enough to be heard above the rumblings of the old fridge but stopped abruptly when she realised that the machine had fallen silent. It wasn't working but this was not unusual. It would be because they had run out of gas and the bottle would need changing. It always seemed to happen at night but now it needed quick attention. She didn't want the risk of dripping water finding its way into her cache of bank notes so she came off her bed in a rush and started to pad her way over to shake little Tomas into useful activity.

The matriarch stopped short with her hand on the metal table. There was something different here, an acrid smell which overpowered even her husband's foul body odour and the pervading stench of methylated spirits. She twisted her head to locate the source and then her eye was caught by a glimpse of the explanation. The fridge might be short of gas but the interior of the container was not. She could see clearly in the gloomy light that the rubber supply pipe from the bottle outside had fractured so that gas was pouring freely into their quarters. She moved quickly to push the pipe back out of its access hole through the container wall and could see the obvious as she did so: that pipe hadn't perished or snagged or chafed. It had been cleanly cut.

The smell of the gas was bad but now it couldn't get worse so she gave herself a few precious seconds to check on her money box in its hiding place. Her questing fingers found it immediately and she snatched it up and whirled around to smack it down on the table, a huge relief flooding through her which was instantly replaced by a panicked fury as she tore open the box and found it completely empty.

She goggled at the sight of nothing in sheer disbelief as she fought down the urge to scream in anguish. She was robbed of all she had and the culprit had to be right here. Her husband? The hopeless sot was incapable. Manaff? He had been gone for two days already and she checked that box each night before sleeping. It had to be that little bastard Tomas and she lunged across the container to tear away the pile of rags under which the child was hiding.

But Tomas wasn't there. The bed space was filled instead with all manner of detritus which comes with camp life: plastic bags, discarded clothes, unwanted children's toys, old newspapers, empty water and fizzy drink bottles, some with liquid still sloshing in them. She sniffed at this pile of garbage and had the sense that her husband's meths had found their way into it. If so, it wouldn't be by his hand as he was still comatose and snoring.

The matriarch simply didn't get it. She couldn't understand what had happened or work out what was still to happen but she was conscious that she wasn't thinking at her best. She wasn't spooked but she was furious. Somebody, and it simply had to be young Tomas, had got her money, so the first priority must be to find where the little sod had got to. There was only one way out of this container and she herself had the key to that door.

Then it came to her that there was another exit, if you were small enough. Her eyes flicked up to the ventilation port at the top of the wall above Manaff's bed and immediately she saw traces of blood on the rough, lower edge where the slot had been crudely cut. That had to be it! The wretched child had squeezed out and suffered a cut or so in the process. That would be nothing compared to the suffering when she took her retribution!

Newly energised, she lunged towards the main door. First, get out and her hand flew to the key hanging from its cord around her neck. She couldn't find it and her anxiety started to mount as she stripped off her loose flowing robe and the grubby

T shirt which she wore at night. Her naked breasts heaved as she passed the full length of cord through both hands before she whipped it over her head and held it before her own eyes. The key had gone, no question of that and in place of it, the ends of the cord had been tightly knotted. During the hours of the night, wily little hands had cut the cord, removed the key and tied the knot. It was a symbol of capture.

The anger in her was moving towards panic as the matriarch scrabbled for the money box which she had left on the table. She kept the spare key to the grille door in there with her precious cash. She knew even before she tore open the lid that the second key had gone also. The empty box mocked her.

Irresolute, she stood in the middle of the container with both hands resting lightly on the table. A potent mixture of fear and the growing heat of the desert day was causing the sweat to rise on her brow and body: a few drips fell on the table and she brushed one hand over them. It was then that a scrabbling noise from outside attracted her attention and she looked up at the ventilation slot. The child's face appeared there and the big black eyes looked down at her dispassionately.

'A la memoire de Maman Monique'.

The small, still treble voice spoke the few words tremulously but the matriarch could sense the deliberate calm overlaid with emotion. She took a step closer and reached up a hand in the vain hope of closing a gap which she herself had opened too wide over too long. She heard the scratching again and recognised the sound of small feet shifting on an upturned crate or maybe a step ladder which the child had used to gain the height to access the window. The face had disappeared but now an arm replaced it and to her horror, she watched the hand release a twist of bank notes. They were of different currencies and amounts but she knew instinctively that they had formed part of her hoarded nest egg. They were also on fire.

The matriarch dived forward and was on her knees as she tried to catch the burning cash and extinguish the flames with her bare hands. The reaction to save her money turned rapidly to desperation to save her own life. The shower of bank notes kept falling from the little window above her head, all of them alight and for each one that she grabbed, a further five or more fell into the bedding and the rubbish which Tomas had prepared to receive them. Frail flames became stronger as they fed hungrily on the methylated spirits which Tomas had stolen over the previous weeks from the store of the old man who was never conscious of its loss. The fire started to spread, despite the frenzied efforts of the matriarch, and it started to eat its way into the bedding on Manaff's empty bunk, in which Tomas had hidden more old tins and jars, part filled with the juice and spirits mix.

The woman felt a fear which was starting to petrify her. She spared a glance for her husband who would be of no help, knocked out by a boozing session. She smelt the gas, still escaping from the severed pipe to the old fridge. She hoped for an explosion which would be a better end than being cooked alive in this human oven.

She got her wish. After just a few minutes which would have seemed to her a lifetime of pain, while she was screaming in fear, her hands burned in her attempts to snuff out the pyres of banknotes and with her bare feet scalding on the steel flooring, the gas which permeated the makeshift habitation was ignited by the developing fire and the entire container exploded in a fireball, spreading burning debris onto surrounding shacks and tents, causing instant chaos throughout the encampment.

By this time, Tomas was halfway up the track towards its junction with the main road and moving as fast as the rocky pathway, now roasting under the habitual Sahara sun, would permit small feet to travel. It was a fair estimate that there would be no one walking the track for at least a further hour. The decrepit old bus came out from Awsard once a day, normally groaning under a load of passengers and belongings crammed inside with as many more on the roof as could manage to hold on. By the time it arrived that morning, Tomas was hidden behind the outcrop of rock which bordered the road, waiting for the tell-tale plume of dust rising from the passage of the vehicle far down the gravel road.

When the old Berliet finally pulled up beside the start of the track, the driver was surprised by the lack of passengers waiting to go with him into town but he was not to know of the explosion and consequent drama at the camp which had caused people there to abandon their plans for the day. No more did Manaff al-Jabri know of his parents' fiery demise so he followed his normal routine and waited for his fellow travellers to start moving off on the track to the camp before he sauntered towards the rock where he hid the useful handcart while he was away on his excursion. He was burdened with provisions and the cart was a porter to help him on the last stage home. It would be better still if his mother had remembered to send young Tomas to meet him and to push it for him. It would do the little bugger good and might at last start building up some muscle. Not for the first time, Manaff wished that he had traded this one and kept the twin who had always looked the more useful, but then again, it had been for Father Christophe to choose and he had his preferences.

As he walked around the rock, Manaff was relieved to see his cart still there but sagged on its axle with one wheel missing. Fine. That was how he left it to discourage thieving hands and now he put down all the bags he was carrying and rummaged in them to find the wheel which he had taken with him. He started the business of putting it back on the axle, thinking as he worked that it had not been a bad trip. He had bargained over his purchases to save some of the cash which his mother had dug out of her storage box. Then he'd gone to his preferred bar and drank a great deal of beer but still keeping enough back for a bottle of cheap Algerian Red which would help him bargain for a woman's favours. The disappointment had been that he couldn't find his favourite whore and had to settle for some monster from Smara with huge, drooping tits and the thighs of an ox.

Manaff was tightening the wheel nut when the rock struck his head. It wasn't a killing blow, more as if he had stood up suddenly in the wrong spot and cracked himself against a door frame. But it was quite enough to drop him in a sprawl on the dusty, pebbled ground and away from the small patch of shade provided by the outcrop. Instinctively, he put a hand up to feel for the damage and immediately took it away again, sticky from the blood seeping from a scalp wound. He recoiled, jerking his head and causing a wave of nausea. Manaff was always squeamish at the sight of blood, especially his own: then came some relief as he heard the familiar, childish voice of Tomas speaking softly.

'Take a drink, Papa, it will help the pain.'

A small plastic bottle was pressed into his hands and Manaff raised it to his lips, uncaring that it was made invisible to him by the sun boring into his face. He drank down three gulps before he recognised the taste of his father's favourite tipple and he gagged, trying to raise himself on one elbow and to clear his throbbing head.

The alcohol took an immediate effect on him and, combined with the effect of the blow to his head, made Manaff squirm in the dirt as he struggled to understand his situation. He sensed Tomas kneeling beside him and he tried to clasp his child to him but the slight body wriggled away from him like an eel and Manaff was grasping at thin air as another blow struck his head at the same point as the first. He screamed with the pain of it and in rage that this unprovoked assault should be coming from his own flesh and blood. He bellowed in outrage, swearing that he would beat the life out of Tomas but as he tried to struggle to his feet, he found that his legs were tied firmly together. God knows how, but the little shit had bound them with one of the webbing straps they used to secure their tent in the camp and those nimble little fingers had made an uncomfortably thorough job of it in record time, the webbing going several times around his legs and then tied with knot after knot. He had no knife and it would take him a long time to free himself but when he did, there would be vengeance and hell to pay.

Suddenly, Manaff was confronted by a greater and worse horror. The sun was still blinding him but he could just make out the image of Tomas' small hand, holding the same plastic bottle and tilting it so that the warm liquid of cactus juice mixed with meths ran out in a steady stream over his crutch, soaking through his jeans and brief underwear to moisten his genitalia and surrounding body hair. Manaff had no time to react, not even to swear, before Tomas had struck a match and dropped it into the very middle of the wetness. There was an immediate whoof as the fire took hold and Manaff started to be burned alive. He screamed in horror and pain, beating at his balls with his bare hands and then attempting to roll over on his face, hoping to bury the fire in the sand and the dust. But he was too late and he was pushed back by the weight of the handcart as Tomas manoeuvred its wheels over his head and shoulders. The last sight to Manaff before an endless descent into an excruciating death was the small, smooth face dominated by the jet black eyes which did not blink as they looked down on him without mercy through the shafts of the cart.

It took Tomas a whole week to travel to Rabat. It was a hard journey for any traveller but for a child with little money, few clothes, a minimum of water and no companion, it was perilous. But Tomas had one break of good fortune. After one day of waiting and another of walking through the consuming heat, dawn was just breaking on the third morning when the driver of a minibus carrying a family home to Rabat saw a bundle lying by the road which sprang to life as the noise and dust sent their signals. The vehicle stopped. The Good Samaritan at the wheel asked some questions and made an assessment. A minute later, the minibus was moving again with Tomas inside and squashed into the small space which was still available amongst the luggage. Even then, their progress was slow with multiple stops for minor breakdowns and tyre changes and they were further hampered by being unable to drive in the cool of the night as only one rear light of the vehicle would work and none at all at the front. Finally, they pulled up close to the Cathedral and Tomas left the family of new found friends, assuring them that the vast building was indeed home.

The Cathedrale Saint Pierre de Rabat stands in the Place du Golan in the heart of the city. The tall white towers announce the presence of the Cathedral from miles away and are an impressive addition to the building which was first consecrated in 1921.

Father Christophe still ministered there. Ten years previously, after the deal had been struck with Manaff, the hurried departure made and the one wailing small boy left behind, Christophe had left him all that day and most of the night while he himself became steadily more conflicted by doubt, terror and remorse at the likely results of what he had permitted himself to do. It was certain that the rest of the family al-Jabri was gone forever. He had no idea of Manaff's intended destination and he didn't expect to see any of them again. The irony of all this was that it quite killed his lust for the child, so that he never did manage to rouse himself to abuse the boy.

Tetrarch was briskly dumped into the care of a home for orphans which was financially supported by the Catholic Church in Rabat, in return for which the orphanage supplied boys for the cathedral choir. Conditions in the home for these waifs were poor and the treatment harsh. The boys were all beaten regularly and abused occasionally. Their food was scarce and inadequate, their bedding threadbare and the sanitary arrangements were slight. They were worked hard by a succession of minor clerics who lodged in the Cathedral precincts with some city dwellers drafted in to help. The staff was all male, all single, all of dubious virtue. The boys in their charge were given the rudiments of basic schooling and otherwise put to tasks such as cleaning the building and its surroundings, helping in the laundry and the blacksmith's shop. Their miserable clothing – rags and tatters and cast offs – was covered three times a week and all day Sundays by the lily white surplices they wore for choir practice and the services in the Cathedral. There were about thirty of them with an ever running changeover as the older ones reached puberty and were chucked out onto the streets from which they had been rescued.

There were some exceptions for whom continuing work and lodging was found, a select few who showed promise of developing into attractive young men. At the age of fourteen, Tetrarch had joined this group of survivors but for different reasons. His voice had broken early so he had been out of the choir for almost a year and should have been dismissed from the premises but he had come to make himself very useful as a competent gardener, always to be found sweeping, tidying and tending. He was not very tall but he was unusually strong and well developed for his age so some of the staff were speculating lasciviously as to the roles he might come to play. It helped also that Tetrarch seemed to be a genuine dullard, very slow to learn yet impervious to any number of vicious thrashings. He would plod about his duties without complaint or resentment, eventually understanding some fresh instruction and all the while filling out and becoming more muscular despite his wretched diet. No thought had ever been given to the effect on his mind of losing his mother in a flash and without explanation.

Tetrarch had benefited from an unexpected protector. Father Christophe had little to do with him from the moment he handed him on to the orphanage staff, but he had continued to keep an eye open for the boy. His motives were partly guilt at his own action but mostly because he feared that Tetrarch might one day blurt out his version of what had happened that day which could have led to awkward questions for the priest to answer. The likelihood of this diminished fast with the passing years so he liked to persuade himself that his concern stemmed from Christian charity, nevertheless it always comforted him to see the boy toiling away in the gardens where he could be in sight but out of mind.

Tetrarch was there again, weeding in one of the large rose beds, when Tomas walked into the grounds of the Cathedral. Tomas stopped dead, looked and stared. It was Tetrarch, without a doubt. All the features of the face were so compellingly familiar but they surmounted a body which was so changed and was now on the verge of manhood. Tomas moved closer and sat down on the grass in front of the flowers, just waiting for the moment of recognition. It took a further five minutes before Tetrarch looked up from his work, dropped his hoe and gave an anguished howl as he threw himself across the newly tended bed and into the arms of his twin.

They didn't speak a word for some minutes, just clutched each other while the tears flowed. Then Tomas broke away and they walked together out of the Cathedral grounds. They made their way through neighbouring streets to a quiet alley known to Tetrarch and there they spent that night recalling and recounting all that had happened to them since they had been torn apart nearly ten years previously. In the dawn of the following morning, Tomas took the lead as they started on a long journey which would take them first to Tangier. They had very little money and just the clothes they were wearing. But they did now have each other with priceless resources to pool. They had brains, brawn and blood.

As the Twins walked out of Rabat on the road north, they did not look back. They were two ragamuffins who would change the world.

6. PENTE BROKE SMITH — 1977

On Thursday, 9th June, Pente was in central London, joining in the celebrations to mark the Queen's Silver Jubilee. He had been there for two days already because his old friend David Heaven had thrown a happy bash two days earlier, inviting a group of close contemporaries from his university days at Oxford to party at his firm's smart new offices in Piccadilly and from there to go on to see the Royal procession. Pente had some leave between ministries in Tanzania where he had been based for his Order for a number of years and he was very happy to be spending this three-month break in England with quite a proportion of it in and around the capital. This week, he was staying at the Basil Street Hotel in Knightsbridge, an extravagant luxury which he adored and justified because the location made it easier to meet up with people. One of these was his long established friend Kingston Offenbach who lived and worked at the US Embassy, then in nearby Grosvenor Square.

King and Pente had hatched a plot. They had schemed to collect some mutual friends together to watch the Royal River progress on the Thames. At Pente's invitation, Vanda Deveridge was coming up to London from her farmyard in Herefordshire, bringing her three children Hannah, William and little Charlotte. For his part, King was bringing along just one guest, his godson Simon Goring who was aged about thirteen and lived with an uncle and aunt at their home in South London.

Pente went to Paddington to meet Vanda and her brood off the train and then delighted in spending some money on a taxi from the station which dropped them all in Birdcage Walk, from where they walked into St James Park and were on time for the rendezvous which he had arranged with King Offenbach.

There were introductions to be made. Vanda knew all about King but she had never met him before and none of the younger generation knew each other so there were a few awkward moments as can be the case when young teenagers meet for the first time.

Then they went off as a group, Pente leading the way in boisterous spirits, walking down Great George street and round Parliament Square to reach the Victoria Embankment and a little later, the Embankment Gardens. Quite a crowd had assembled there to watch the spectacle of the Monarch's passage, complete with all its royal regalia and shepherded by the flotilla of craft both large and small. They managed to squeeze in to give themselves a decent view and young Charlotte won the best spot being perched up on Pente's broad shoulders. A happy atmosphere pervaded amongst the onlookers and the camaraderie was infectious. The older children started to relax in each other's company and King was amused to see his godson Simon making some chivalrous space in front of him to offer Hannah a better view.

When it was all over, they made their way slowly through the crowds up Northumberland Avenue into Trafalgar Square and thence to an Italian restaurant in the Strand where Pente had made a reservation. It was by now a lively, joking party which sat down to eat, making merry until the last of the huge ice creams had been demolished and it was time to find a friendly cab driver who was prepared to cram them all in for the short journey to the American Embassy where King had arranged a final treat of the day. An obliging colleague took Simon, Hannah and William off for a tour of the public parts of the building and then into the gardens which were spacious and impressive. Simon tried to get a bit more out of Hannah. She intrigued him as he worked to tease a few more smiles from her. She was a tall girl, slim and self-assured for her age with a budding femininity. But she seemed also to take life pretty seriously and to hide herself away behind the heavy rimmed glasses which she never removed.

With the three young people gone, Vanda, Pente and King relaxed in his spacious office, with the worn out Charlotte dropping off on a sofa with her mother beside her and the men sprawled in arm chairs.

Vanda opened the conversation.

'It's been a marvellous day, it really has and I'm really grateful to you both for taking so much trouble. It's been quite an outing for us country bumpkins and I should think we'll all be zonked out before our train pulls out of Paddington. Oh God, that reminds me, how much time have we got? I can't miss it.'

'Relax, Vanda,' said King in reply, 'you've got plenty and if I have to, I'll get a cavalcade together with outriders to escort you guys to the station'. He gave a broad wink as he spoke.

Picking up the theme, Vanda retorted, 'Well let's make ourselves late then. William would just adore that, probably Simon too, wouldn't he? And what's the story with him, King? Seems like a nice boy - very polite too!'

'Yeah, you're surely right, Vanda. He's a helluva nice young fellow is Simon and a real pleasure to have around. I like to see something of him while I'm in London. He's my godson, you see, and he was orphaned at a very young age so quite apart from enjoying his company, I feel I need to do all I can for him.'

'That's rough for him,' put in Pente, 'I didn't know about him, King. What happened?'

'Plane crash. That was in '64 when Simon was only four: old enough to know but way too young to understand. His Mom Patsy was an old friend from my College days. We dated some, decided it wasn't going to work but stayed close and well in touch. She came over to do a bit of Europe, met up somehow with Ronnie Goring from a very naval family. He joined up, went through Dartmouth, then switched into your Royal Marines. That was after Patsy and he married. I couldn't make the wedding but I was real happy to be asked to stand godfather to Simon when he arrived only a year or so later. That was around the time when I got over for my year's course at Oxford and met up with you, Pente, and all the others. Well, the first time I met

Ronnie was at the little fellow's Christening. We got on real well after Ronnie's shock: Patsy had never thought to tell him that I'm black! Then they had postings here and there while I was back in the States. We didn't exactly lose touch but you know how it is, there was a while without too much communication.'

Offenbach broke off, shuffled around in his seat and gave a long sigh. The other two didn't interrupt him. They knew he would resume.

'I was working at Langley when I got the news and even then, that was only by reading an account in the Brit Press. It was a big deal at the time with a fair bit of coverage. It was an Irish aircraft, that's to say an Aer Lingus plane, Flight number 712 as I remember too damn well, from Cork to London and it came down in the sea off the coast. No survivors out of the sixty-odd passengers and crew. They never did recover many of the bodies and it took two years and more for an inquiry to decide that the cause was metal failure in the tail plane: so an accident pure and simple. But before that, there were rumours and speculation, a suggestion that the plane was brought down by some experimental rocket that you Brits were developing at the time. There was another wild theory too, that it was sabotage and the true start of the Irish Troubles although the Londonderry March drama wasn't till a lot later that year. But some reporter found out that Ronnie wasn't just a Marine but was also in the SBS – the Special Boat Service – so tried to make out that he'd been on some sort of special mission. All total bullshit. He and Patsy had been to Ireland for a week's leave and they left Simon with Ronnie's sister in London just to have a little romance time together. They were trying to get number two going and whether successful or not, it all ended in tragedy. Yup, that's for sure. And now her sister Caroline and Benny, along with their own four kids and a couple of cats, they're all giving Simon a home and I see him when I can to give them a break and him a change. So, that's the whole story.'

There was some silence between them before Vanda broke the spell.

'That's a sad story, King, a dreadful way in which to lose your parents, your whole family in Simon's case. But then again, he's been lucky to have his aunt and hers to take him in and to have you looking out for him as well. All that is, well it's heart-warming actually.'

This started Pente nodding his head in agreement but King went straight in with a question for Vanda.

'You've got a fine brood yourself, right there. How do you make the time for each of them?'

Vanda knew immediately that King was prodding for more candid information and she gave a characteristically direct response.

'Well, I am very much on my own. My husband Luke is a pretty hopeless case as Pente knows well. He's an absolute slave to the bottle and with the effect that his drinking is having, I honestly don't know how long he can last. It won't be a very glorious death, that's for sure, and it won't leave a memorable figure for Hannah and William. It's not that he's violent or abusive. Not to me or the kids. He's just not there.'

'So how do they cope with it?'

'Good question, King. Luke and I got married twelve years ago', Vanda glanced at Pente as she said this; she couldn't help herself but was grateful that the big man held her gaze. 'Hannah was born about a year later and at first Luke was very good with her. Unusual for a man, I suppose, but he really was besotted with her as a baby, spent a lot of time with her. I was encouraged, of course, and thought it was a turning point in our marriage, that he would settle down and make more of his life and his family. Luke's never been short of money, you see: too much of it in fact. He was spoiled as a child himself and became a bit of a wastrel as he grew up. I thought for just a short while that I was going to change that, with Hannah's help, so I was even happier when I got pregnant with William. I honestly reckoned that with two babies around, their father was going to improve. To grow up a bit with his own children if you see what I mean.'

There was almost an imploring look in her eyes as she broke

off. King gave her his charming smile and said, 'I surely do understand. But I guess it didn't work out as you hoped,' and he made it more of a statement than a question.

'Oh, God no. No, it really didn't. As the babies became children, Luke got worse and worse, slipping away from us into his own gin and whisky filled world. I had plenty of help at home but even so, it's a full time occupation with two under four and then to be honest, my concern was turning to disgust. There was a time when I'd have done anything to support him, found the professionals, got him into groups, researched where he could dry out. Luke was always making promises, but the truth is that he didn't want to try, he didn't want help and therefore there could be no help. He's taken himself into his own hell and now I've got no sympathy left, really no time for him anymore. And so, of course, Hannah and William have learnt a bit from my example. They see him around, but he's not there for them so they're making their lives without a father. It's just as if he were dead or gone except it's worse because he's not.'

There were tears in her eyes as she finished speaking. There must be a lot of crying in the loneliness of that big house, King thought to himself, and then he put the question to her that had been growing in his mind.

'So how did young Charlotte come to be,' he said as he smiled towards the little girl who lay fast asleep beside her mother.

'Ah, well,' replied Vanda, brightening with a smile of her own as she responded simply, 'You know, King, I believe you have some responsibility for Charley!'

Pente came bolt upright in his chair at this remark while King simply goggled at Vanda. Just for once he was completely taken aback and bereft of any response, so it was Pente who spoke out.

'It looks like you've lost us both with that one, Vanda my love,' he said mildly, 'but we're all ears. You'd better tell us more.'

'Well look, first off it's true that Charley is a half-sister to the other two. I'm her mother of course, but she has a different father. And how did that come about? Well, Pente - gosh it sounds strange to be calling you that but I'd better get on and join the rest of the world! Anyway, let me answer my own question. You'll remember well enough that at the time of your mother's funeral, you found me in a pretty bad way and before we parted, you were insisting that I should give myself a break and get away for a few days. Remember?'

Pente nodded at her. 'Of course I do, yes.'

'You told me that you would have a word with King and thought that he could probably help with ideas and contacts.'

'Victor.' The single word came from King as he struggled back into the conversation.

'That's right. Victor: your French friend, Victor Sollange. He came to my rescue and in more ways than one. It still seems like a complete fairy tale.'

Vanda leaned back into the comfort of the sofa. She tucked her legs up under her and adjusted Charlotte's head on her lap before looking dreamily at the two men. Pente climbed to his feet with a sigh, fishing in the pocket of his hassock as he did so and coming up with a tin of the short, black and noxious cheroots which he delighted to smoke. He glanced at King for permission and then moved to stand by the open window as he lit up.

'Tell us all about it, Vanda,' he invited and her response was immediate.

'It was a truly miserable Christmas that year after your mother died and I felt especially cheated because it was the last of the sixties. There was no logic in that of course, but I felt it anyway. Luke was particularly bad and only got out of his dressing room to return to his study and his bottles various. Your father was in mourning and wouldn't open the door of Forty Green Cottage and frankly, without your Mum there I didn't want to go calling anyway. Worst of all, Pente, you didn't ring me for days and I was just desperate to carry on the conversation we had started after the funeral.

'But finally you did phone and suddenly the sun started to come out for me. That was on New Year's Eve and bless you, you had got it all arranged - just as you promised. So I went off to Paris and just for once, my Mum really came through and helped me out by having Hannah and William to stay and it was all quite a success. My Dad seemed to enjoy having his grandchildren around and my youngest brother, Ted, the only one still living at home, he spoilt them rotten.'

As she spoke, the men were lost in their own memories. King Offenbach was recalling how he had flown into London from the States early in the morning of a new decade, January 1st 1970, going straight to his desk in the US Embassy to prepare for a big meeting the following day and finding messages from Pente who had been trying to reach him for days. King had phoned immediately and taken the brief. Could he suggest a reliable contact who might arrange a refuge for a very special friend who was finding herself in great difficulty and needed some space and time in a safe haven, preferably outside England but not too far away. King thought he knew someone to ask and better still, he was going to see him the following day. They had discussed it and Pente had been hugely relieved, so much so that he had wanted to give all the details and the background of his involvement with this girl from the backwoods of Hereford. But King had cut him short. He was up to his eyes in it and the full story would have to wait until they could get together at some future date.

Now, seven years and some later, Pente Broke Smith stood by the open window puffing at his cigar as he remembered the state he himself had been in on that New Year's Day, preparing to return to his monk's ministry in Madagascar, gloomy at the prospect and much troubled at the fragility of his faith. It wasn't until many months later that he had been able to share his troubles and the memory struck him hard now that his closest confidant was beside him again.

But King, lounging in the chair behind his desk, outwardly calm and quiet as always, was himself in a turmoil of reminiscence. That New Year's Day in 1970, he had finished the call to Pente with an assurance that he would contact Vanda and somehow find a solution for her. Just a few hours later, the phone rang again and there was the answer on the line: Victor Sollange!

King had met Victor about a year previously. Sollange was maybe ten years his senior in age and the gap between them wider if measured in experience. The Frenchman had been born in Sicily, a fact of which he was very proud, but his family had moved to Paris during his early schooldays and he had spent all his adult life in the capital. Victor entered the Gendarmerie from university and made such rapid progress that he had been recruited into an elite cadre of the French Security Service before he turned thirty. He was hard as nails on the outside and guarded his privacy closely as in his personal life he was something of an aesthete, with a passion for the arts, a profound knowledge of Greek sculpture and a love of opera. He was also a committed Catholic who took his religion seriously. It had taken time and effort by King Offenbach to garner this background information as Sollange had been initially suspicious of an American, a CIA Officer and a black man to boot. Communication had not been straightforward either as each was less than fluent in the language of the other but gradually they had formed a mutual regard and respect as they worked up a strategy together to combat the rising threat of South American sourced drugs being trafficked into Europe via various staging posts on the continent of Africa.

As the dusk was gathering, Victor was calling to say that he was already in London for the conference the following day and could he and King get together to compare notes in advance. King was delighted and readily agreed, thinking to himself that here was an ideal character to help out also in the matter of Vanda Deveridge. And so it proved: Sollange listened to King's request for help and announced that he, personally, would be happy to receive Vanda in Paris, would show her around and look after her.

It seemed now that he had done just that, King was thinking as he pulled himself together and asked his question directly.

'So, Vanda, are you telling us that Victor Sollange is Charlotte's natural father?'

'Yes, he is.'

'And how many people know this?'

'Well, as of now, just the three of us in this room.'

'So not Victor himself?'

'Absolutely not. I haven't seen him nor even spoken to him in the last seven years.'

There was a stunned silence, softened by a slight snuffle from Charlotte as she slept deeply with her head in her mother's lap. Then Vanda went on:

'You two must both understand that I have no regrets and nothing to say against Victor. Quite the reverse in fact and I adored the short time I spent with him. Neither of us could have expected in advance the intense attraction we felt for each other from the moment he met me at the airport. It was just a magical interlude and I am very happy to have Charley as a constant reminder of the love affair that gave me back some sanity and belief in myself. It wasn't all about sex, you see, although there was plenty of that. Neither was this just a special holiday romance even though he introduced me to some of the sights and sounds of Paris which would normally be hidden from a tourist visitor. No, there was much more to it and especially the all night conversations during which I was able to share with a like mind a lot of troubled history and considerations of how I could change myself to enjoy my life again and to make the best of my opportunities. It wasn't all one way either. I learned a great deal about that man and his background, his demons and aspirations. To be honest, Pente, Victor was the first person I've been able to talk to since I lost you and your mother.'

Pente was stubbing out his cigar on the window ledge as he turned to look at her and there were tears in his eyes. He nodded his great head but he wasn't capable of speech. Vanda resumed,

'Being men, you two won't understand but I knew I was pregnant even before I left Victor in Paris and I knew I wouldn't tell him or anyone else until I felt the time was right. Mind you, my circumstances at home have made that a whole heap easier. I'm not sure that Luke ever even noticed that I was getting bigger, never said anything, never asked a question and he was happy enough to greet a new baby in the house with the unspoken assumption that it was his. And his parents were quite delighted of course, believing that we must have got things together and that they would have a bit less to worry over. As for Victor, I would have told him if he had asked but he's never been in touch and I don't hold that against him. He's a very reserved and private person and that was our deal at the time. We were ships passing in the night and I'll be happy if he holds the same sort of memories as I do myself. Quality can't always be quantity as well.'

Pente gave a long sigh as he spoke at last.

'Well I am glad you've told me now, anyway. Glad you've told both of us. And I don't think I need ask if there is anything I or King can do for you now. You really are sorted, aren't you? You're as happy as you can be with your lot and determined to make the most of it.'

They heard excited voices coming back down the passage towards King's office. Simon, Hannah and William were back on cue to terminate this revealing conversation.

'Yes I am', Vanda replied, 'but I'm also very happy to have told you, Pente, or rather still Roo to me. In your own way, you will always be the most important man in my life.'

She smiled at him as she roused Charlotte and sat up herself, looking up at him and crossing her legs. There was a symbolism of which Pente was deeply aware. You've had your chance but preferred to seek your reward in Heaven. He hoped he'd got it right.

7. VANDA DEVERIDGE — 1979

Her husband Luke died on or about the second Monday of the New Year. They couldn't be sure of the when, but the where and the why were plain enough. At the Inquest, the coroner sifted through the sparse details and recited the Police account of events. They had been alerted by Mrs Deveridge's report that her husband was missing, that neither she nor any member of the household staff had seen him for a full day and a night. It was understood that this pattern of behaviour was not unusual and it was recorded that the deceased was in an established habit of wandering off by himself to any part of the substantial estate which was the family home. Questions might have been asked as to why the alarm had not been sounded rather earlier, but then this was a part of very rural England. Amongst the local community, it was accepted and understood that Mr Deveridge was given to eccentric practice. The villagers and the occupants of surrounding farms acknowledged without drama that this was a minor tragedy which has been waiting to happen for a number of years. The young man had been a hopeless case with his drinking spiced with drugs and with his indolence which had been allowed to persist since his childhood. A sad story, then, but not one over which to shed too many tears and most of those would be for his wife and children.

They had found the body in the crumbling old shed which Luke's father had built as a summer house, perched on a bit of flat ground over a mile from the house. Luke would often retreat there, sometimes for a day and more at a time and Vanda worried that the children might find him there in a state of collapse, so that January morning when a heavy frost lay on the ground, she sent old Jethro, the cowman, to look for his nominal boss. Death was part of life to Jethro with his profession and experience so it didn't trouble him to find the body, but its condition was distressing. Luke was slumped in a decrepit wicker armchair, placed just inside the door which sagged open on its hinges and beside the chair was an equally ancient table, propped awkwardly against the door frame as one leg was missing. On the table were two bottles of vodka, one empty and a saucer covered with a white powder which Jethro assumed to be some form of drug. He had no need to check for signs of life. It was bitterly cold there and one arm dangled at an awkward angle, already stiffened by rigor. Worse to see was the evidence that a fox or two had come calling during the night.

Jethro covered up the remains of Luke Deveridge with a bit of old carpet which he found in the back of the cabin and went off to get help from another of the farm workers. It would take two of them and the Land Rover to recover this sorry burden back to the house.

Vanda was pleased that she had been able to weep for her husband and the broken, wasted life which had given up on him. But the tears had dried quickly as she coped with the aftermath. There were so many necessities to claim her attention. The police enquiry, the Inquest, the lawyers, the announcements in newspapers and the Parish Magazine. Much more demanding was all the personal communication. There were neighbours, villagers, people from all across the county who telephoned or dropped in to express sympathy at her loss and almost all uttered bland words which did not disguise the true opinion which lay behind them: 'this was bound to happen. Pathetic Luke was a loser from birth and a right pisshead with it'.

In its own way more distressing but completely not a surprise was the reaction of her children because they were so totally unaffected. They had scarcely known their father in life, therefore there was nothing to miss in his death.

Her parents-in-law presented their own brand of challenge. Tom and Majorie Deveridge were a perfectly straightforward, upstanding couple, solid bastions of the rural community who perceived their status as landed gentry and had basked all their lives in understated respect from local people on account of their considerable wealth and the support they offered to those in need. In short, they were considered worthy but rather dull and they had always been content to accept this judgement of which they were fully aware because it deflected a little of the opprobrium that came from having a son like Luke. So it had suited them to pretend that Luke had somehow simply not happened. They had been quite unable to understand him since his early teens: they had no concept and no wish to learn of the demons which drove their only son right to the point of his sordid death. Faced now with the inevitability of marking his passing, they opted to leave it all to his wife. She must get on with all the arrangements while they would hover behind the scenes, two grey figures looking more bemused and unhappy than was perhaps the case.

Vanda didn't expect any support from Luke's only sibling either. Sarah had been the first born to Marjorie and Tom and she was a disappointment to them from her first bawl. Tom had wanted a son and Majorie had simply wanted to produce his preference. So when Luke appeared three years later, Sarah had been largely side lined in favour of her brother. As soon as she was of an age, Sarah had escaped the confines of Herefordshire to live and work in London. There she met and married Rufus Slessor, the third son of a prestigious Scottish family from the border country. They made a formidable pair and soon built their independence from their respective upbringings. Rufus worked in the City of London and made his name as a thrusting merchant banker while his wife worked equally hard to establish their position in smart society. They became energetic members of a Chelsea set, elegantly flaunting their wealth and lifestyle. Both were content to have little contact with the families which had spawned them.

Sarah loved her London and made rare forays into the countryside for sporting events or high society weekends. Her Herefordshire homeland was too distant and rustic but she graced them with a couple of visits a year. Tom and Marjorie Deveridge had fallen into some awe of their daughter and were uncomfortably aware that in showing little interest in their daughter whilst favouring her brother, they had backed the wrong horse.

Not that Sarah was any sort of a horse. By this time in her late thirties, she was a good looking woman enhanced by expensive packaging and immaculate presentation. Hard work and dedication to the gym had preserved her excellent figure following the birth of her twin sons and their turnout and manners spoke volumes about this smart London family.

Sarah had long abandoned any relationship with her brother Luke and she could hardly be blamed for that. More questionable was her attitude towards her parents. She had scant contact with them which meant that they saw little of their grandsons and Sarah herself set the pattern by being aloof, speaking to her mother and father in a manner of coolness which stopped just short of disdain. It was not surprising that she made no effort with her sister-in-law but there was some comfort for Vanda in recognising that Sarah saw the steel in her which was absent in Tom, Marjorie and Luke.

Vanda had telephoned the Slessor household in London during the evening of the day on which they had discovered Luke's corpse. To her relief, Sarah had answered herself but in pretty curt terms which made clear that the timing was inconvenient as she was getting ready to go out to a charity dinner.

Vanda gave her the news of her brother's death and was not surprised that Sarah received it with equanimity. 'I suppose we've all been waiting for this, haven't we?' was almost her only comment.

The sisters-in-law did not speak during the following three weeks while Vanda struggled with the formalities but then Sarah appeared alone the day before the cremation. Vanda had been hoping for a quiet evening to herself, trying to find some happy memories of Luke with which to prepare herself for what was sure to be a testing day, but she walked over to Tom and Marjorie's converted stables house to welcome Sarah who was staying the night with her parents. The four of them had a drink together, accompanied by some stilted conversation about the practicalities of the following day.

As soon as was reasonable, Vanda got up to leave. 'I've left the children alone,' she said by way of explanation, 'and I know they'd like to talk things through, plus we should all try and get a night's sleep before tomorrow.'

Tom grunted and Majorie smiled her understanding but Sarah rose to accompany her to the door and to grab a few discreet words as they stood together in the hall.

'Vanda, we should have a talk - just us girls together and sorry, but it needs to be now because I'll go straight back to London from the Cremo tomorrow.'

'Yes, I thought you probably would', Vanda refused to be intimidated, 'but I'd prefer a conversation at some other time because right now I just want a bit of peace and quiet before tomorrow. I'm sure you understand?'

'I do, yes, and that's fine. It's just that Rufus and I both feel strongly that we, you and Guy Sinclair should have a talk about what happens next, about the future of this property, planning for inheritance and all the legal aspects.'

Vanda froze with her hand on the knob of the front door. She turned to fix unblinking eyes on her sister-in-law before she spoke in reply.

'Za,' she said, choosing the childhood diminutive which she knew Sarah disliked, 'Za, Guy is the family lawyer. Like the rest of us, he's been preparing for this situation and I'd be happy for him to explain directly to you and Rufus how Luke's Estate is to be handled. It's relatively straightforward.'

'Maybe so. But what about the future? What happens if you remarry or have more children who are not fathered by Luke?'

There was a long pause while the two women exchanged hostile looks. Finally, Vanda spoke again.

'You should not be amazed to hear that right now, on the eve of my husband's funeral, the very last things on my mind are remarriage and the prospect of more childbearing. If we ever have to speak of this again, it will be on my terms of timing and location. Goodnight Sarah'. She pulled open the door and shut it hard behind her.

The following morning dawned grey and miserable. It was bitterly cold also, the north wind blowing in gusts which drove flurries of snow before it. The weather perfectly matched her mood and she felt bone weary after a long night with fitful sleep from which she had woken often with a persistent anxiety.

What had that cow Sarah meant about children not fathered by Luke? Was she really talking about the future or did she know about Charlotte, that the child's provenance had nothing to do with Luke. Was she just taking a flying, malicious guess? Was there some genuine intrigue and if so, what would she do next? Variations on these thoughts had chased each other round in her head as she tried to sleep until finally, she had given up the attempt and spent a couple of hours downstairs by the fire, dozing a little and trying to get her strength up for the day to come.

As daylight broke, she returned to her bedroom for a long and comforting bath, after which she dressed for warmth, knowing that there would be enough shivers this day without the weather making it worse and conscious that she wanted to look strong and controlled on this of all occasions.

As she completed her preparations, she continued to smart at the implications of the brief exchange with Sarah. What a true bitch to produce that message at that time: and for what purpose? Vanda, by now recovering her courage and determination, suspected that at heart, it was all about demonstrating superiority. It wasn't really about money, it was the lust for power and control. But she hadn't been through all those years with Luke, trying her best for him with neither help nor recognition from his family, for them to now start dictating how she should live the rest of her life.

The service at the crematorium was set for midday and Vanda

got there sharp at eleven, driving herself in the company of Hannah, William and Charlotte. She was proud of her three and the way in which they had already distinguished themselves in their support for her, calmly getting themselves ready that morning, Hannah at thirteen organising their breakfast, eleven year old William suppressing his naturally rowdy behaviour and then Charley, only just nine yet already with a wise look about her which said she understood what her mother had to get through.

Vanda had not been to many cremation services before and the whole process was an entirely new experience for her children. She had deliberately chosen Hereford crematorium as it was a bit farther from home and she hoped that it would be even more impersonal than the norm. The Chapel looked to be exactly that and from the outside it was stark and white, surrounded by its acres of tarmac approach roads and car parks whilst by the entrance door, groups of black clad mourners were waiting to go in or loitering with respect by the exit. This was the production line of death and all must wait their turn.

Beyond the Chapel, the immaculately manicured grounds spread out and Vanda took her three for a walk over the extensive lawns. It remained cold but it was mercifully dry and all four of them were happy to have a little exercise and the chance of time to themselves. Behind the gentle conversation with her children, Vanda had a single thought which pressed upon her and that was how much she wished that Pente Broke Smith could be with them, not just for his religious conviction and familiarity with death but more for his comforting bulk and the feeling of security which it imparted. But that could not be: on this day as for so many on which she would have wished him to be with her, Pente was absent and far away, this time somewhere in the wild wastes of Tanzania, lost in a landscape which she could not start to imagine.

To give him his due, however, Pente had tried his very best. She had sent him a message via his Order as soon as Luke's body had been found and he had somehow found the means of telephoning her a couple of days later. It had been a frustrating conversation with breaks on the line and noises off which had distracted both of them but even so, just to hear his voice had been a comfort. Before they rang off, Pente told her that she would feel him with her this day and that other friends would be present to stand up beside her but she had given little further thought to that.

It came back to her, however, as just before noon they filed into the Chapel and Vanda ushered her children up to the front pew, happy to receive a kindly word of greeting from the vicar of Foy who was to conduct the service.

She was surprised to see how many people had made the effort to attend. Tom and Marjorie Deveridge were there, of course, sitting immediately behind her and with them was Sarah Slessor who looked smart and sharp as she avoided eye contact. Further back was a contingent from the farm, quite a number of Foy villagers and scattered throughout the Chapel were friends and contacts from across the region. Vanda was taken aback and very touched by their presence. She knew they were there for her and hers.

It wasn't until she looked across the aisle and one pew back that Pente's promise came back to her and she felt herself stiffen in surprise. Sitting there was Kingston Offenbach, immaculate in a black suit and a white shirt, turning his good looking face with a slight smile to acknowledge her glance in his direction.

But the real shock sat beside King, another man, equally smartly dressed and quite motionless as he sat with his eyes fixed on the altar and the coffin which lay before it. Vanda swallowed hard as she took in the well-remembered profile, the sharp and hawkish features, softened by the laughter lines which wrinkled around the eyes. Victor Sollange had returned to her life.

8. TOMAS AND TETRARCH — 1981

The nights of mid-August in the Vieux Port of Marseilles can be warm, even at one o'clock in the morning and especially if it's a Saturday. Tomas was sweating freely whilst recording in the ledger the number of men and women entering the bar. They made for an endless procession while the crowd, the blaring music and the candlelight added to the oppressive atmosphere. It was enough to make Tomas jealous of Tetrarch who was stationed in the narrow street outside, teamed with another three bouncers to keep order on the busiest night of the week in peak holiday season. Even so, no cause for complaint: they were alive, well and making good money.

In the six years since leaving Rabat, the twins had negotiated various staging posts. They had walked to Fez, the provincial but historically important city of Morocco where blind good fortune had led them into the path of a significant merchant with something of a conscience who had provided poor food and basic lodging in return for a form of child slave labour. It had been a rough time, but for all that, better than either had known during their brief childhood and it gave them a safe haven in which they could trawl together through the hazy memories of their infancy, recalling the influence and loving attention of their mother, Monique.

They left Fez on an impulse, travelling mostly by foot over many a weary month until they slipped across the border into Algeria and found their way eventually into the region, then the town and finally the village in which their grandparents, Monique's father and mother, had lived with all their offspring. But that had been in French colonial days, an eternity before and there remained nothing and no one to provide Tomas and

Tetrarch with a link to their ancestry.

And so it was time to move again, now yet further east and across another border, this time into Tunisia and its capital city. They struck lucky in Tunis. In a scenario worthy of Dickens and Oliver Twist, the Twins had been begging in the central city market and trying some pick pocketing when they were spotted by a wealthy merchant, Maitre Dhaou, who was well connected amongst the city's governing body and would have had them arrested as vagrants had he not been moved by Tomas' carefully contrived history of all the evil which had befallen them. Dhaou made an instant decision that he should earn some respect from his peer group and hopefully some reward in the afterlife by taking these two in hand and seeing what could be made of them. It didn't take him long to discover that Tomas was bright and quick to learn whereas Tetrarch was abnormally strong for his seventeen years but a dullard. Neither had received any formal education and Dhaou instituted an immediate regime under which they worked for their living and adequate accommodation in the stable block of his large house while for two days a week they were tutored by a retired teacher who owed Dhaou the return of a favour. He reported that Tetrarch made limping progress but could manage a bit of reading and writing after a year of tuition whereas his sibling had a quicksilver mind and was voracious in wanting to learn. After twelve months, Tomas was fluent in French, competent in pure Arabic without losing the rough patois with which they had arrived in Tunis and was outstandingly good with figures. So good, indeed, that Dhaou moved Tomas on to work with his accountants who kept a careful tally on his varied business interests while Tetrarch assumed a wider role in the care of the vast property and developed as quite a promising stonemason.

Life was good in Tunis, with every prospect for further improvement. After more than two and a half years, they were content, developing their talents, comfortable in their surroundings, at ease with their mentor and saviour, enjoying an increasing circle of acquaintances. In addition, they had discovered women whom Tetrarch, especially, was coming to consume in increasing and varied quantities. He was happy to learn that while the girls might not be too impressed with his brainpower or style of conversation, enough of them were attracted to his muscular good looks.

It was then that their world fell apart. Maitre Dhaou had over-extended himself in business, causing a severe lack of liquidity and the worry over his affairs brought on a heart attack which dropped him stone dead in the middle of his extensive garden late one evening. After this tragedy, matters developed swiftly. Dhaou's wife and daughters - there was no son - wanted to move as quickly as possible to one of the smaller properties in the city already owned by the family. That gave free rein to the creditors of his business, including some past business partners who had developed into rivals, to start descending like a swarm of locusts onto the failed empire. For all of the late Dhaou's staff and servants, there was no guarantee of employment but most decided to wait and see.

Tomas did not subscribe to this approach, believing that it was time to take what they could and go. Thanks to Maitre Dhaou, the twins had gained valuable respite and had made the most of it. But that time had been and gone. They must set out again, dependent on each other and as usual, Tetrarch did not demur. He left it to Tomas to make the key decisions while he would be on hand to provide back up with brawn whenever it might be needed.

They slipped away quietly with no word of farewell. One morning, they were simply no longer there and Dhaou's widow and family breathed a sigh of relief that their absence meant one less worry. For a month or so, the Twins wandered in Tunisia, doing a few odd jobs to pay for their cost of living and to keep intact their cash saving. Then came the day in Bizerte on the Mediterranean that Tomas reckoned they should visit the country of their mother's nationality if not her birth and so they had started a sea journey, working their passage on a series of coastal tramp vessels, the last of which landed them in the port of Marseilles.

Instantly, they both liked the buzz of the city and its polyglot population, assembled over generations by arrivals from around the world. It seemed to make them welcome in a way they had never previously experienced. They had no difficulty in finding work and somewhere to live with Tomas going further and enrolling in some night school courses. Sometime during the early months of 1981, by which time they had been in Marseilles for about a year, they moved from adequate lodgings into an apartment, the first abode which they could truly call their own. It was at the top of a tall building just off the Rue du Refuge in the heart of the le Panier quarter and a short walk from le Pelerinage - the Pilgrimage, an odd name for a popular bar and restaurant which occupied a prime site on the quayside of le Vieux Port, with its upper two floors supplementing the owner's income by operating as a classy whorehouse.

The proprietor was called Madame Salazar, although it was never clear whether this was a real or an assumed name. La Salazar lived elsewhere in the city, visiting her business once a week and never on the same day or at the same hour which could be night or day. This lack of routine helped her to keep check on her investment and particularly on her manager who was a great bull of a man known only as Poilu. He was not a pleasant character, with a wily sneer as a permanent feature below his hairless head which shone like a beacon beneath the subdued lighting throughout the club and was in sharp contrast to the remainder of his squat, burly body which was almost completely covered in a mat of hair. Poilu rejoiced to have the reputation of a hard man and took every opportunity to prove it, using his power and his fists to settle the most trifling dispute. He had started as a bouncer and managed to graduate to being the day-to-day boss. Some said he had risen to this station because Madame Salazar was frightened of him, others that she enjoyed a little rough from time to time. Tomas came quickly to the latter view. Poilu might be energetic, but he was hopelessly inadequate in administrative skills and could be relied upon to boost his earnings through any number of little manoeuvres on the side – skimming cash from the bar takings, taking bribes from the food and drink suppliers, pocketing some of the hourly room rents paid by the working girls. All these became apparent because Tomas worked in the airless back office which was located in the basement, without a window and so lacking both ventilation and natural light. It was nonetheless a large room, dominated by Poilu's huge desk which was the centre point of his kingdom.

The Twins chose a good time to make their first visit to the Pilgrimage. They were looking for better jobs to finance the rent of their apartment and wandered into the bar one evening. Tomas asked a busy waiter where the *patron* was to be found. He jerked his head towards the steep stone staircase and the Twins descended, finding themselves in the large office which Tomas was to come to know so well. The three members of day time staff were gone so they were confronted by Madame Salazar and Poilu. He was sitting back in his huge swivel chair, heavy hands with their split finger nails clenching the arms and his shirt open to the waist to reveal the powerful body with its pelt of black hair, flecked with grey. Madame was standing at his side, one long forefinger tracing a column of figures in a large, leather bound journal. She was an elegant woman, somewhere in her fifties with a hard face and a predatory look but stylishly dressed and well presented.

Tomas stated their case, using some economy with the facts. They were recently arrived in Marseilles from Morocco, intending to stay, had just rented an apartment, needed work, had plenty of ability to offer.

It was immediately clear that Madame Salazar had an interest in Tetrarch. She eyed him up and down and asked a few questions about his work experience, her eagle eye taking in his height, muscle and age. At twenty-one, Tetrarch was quite a prime proposition and she remarked to Poilu that they were short of a security guard for front of house now that the idiot Marc had got himself into trouble and been hauled off by the law. They wouldn't be seeing him again any time soon. Poilu agreed they could do worse than see how this guy shaped up. A bit young but he could learn and if he fouled up, there were plenty more like him in Marseilles.

Then Madame turned her attention to Tomas and with some adroit questioning, she established that there could be possibilities here too. Efficient bookkeeping at the Pilgrimage was a permanent challenge for her. She expected to be ripped off a little and could allow for that within the healthy profits of the business, but there were limits and people had to show her respect. Poilu was writhing in his chair, knowing that he had nowhere to go in a debate with la Salazar on this subject. He could do with some help over the drudgery of the figures and from a brief look, there might be a bonus here. Poilu was driven by an overwhelming sexual appetite and used his position of authority to help himself to any number of the prostitutes who used the club as their base. And they were not only girls. There were a number of winsome young poufs who catered for other tastes and sometimes Poilu used them also on the basis of enjoying a varied diet. The slim figure in front of him now just might prove entertaining.

So Tomas and Tetrarch had been hired. Overall, it had gone well for them. They both worked a shift from 6pm to 2am six nights a week. The money was very good and they had the means to live comfortably and to save. They could indulge in some fun too. Tomas went gambling from time to time and normally with success, especially on the roulette wheel. Both enjoyed sex and there was a limitless supply of women available but they treated their apartment as out of bounds for this activity. One reason for that was that Tetrarch sometimes became violent when aroused and could damage his surroundings and his partner of the moment. There were occasions when Tomas had to pay off a girl who was excessively knocked around in the process of satisfying Tetrarch. Tomas could see the connections to the treatment he had suffered as a child and saw it as both wiser and fairer to pay up and hope for better days. But one episode was going to make things worse before they could improve, so that the drama that evening was probably just waiting to happen.

Tomas had returned to the basement office with the working ledger ready to be written up in the master record before the evening shift finished. It was a wearisome process but it had produced satisfactory results for Madame Salazar over the years and no one was going to persuade her that a more advanced system would be preferable. Least of all Poilu who neither cared nor understood provided that the work was done and all the better if in a style which allowed him to appropriate for himself some extra benefits along the way.

So Tomas had done his counting, checked with Tetrarch on guard at the front entrance and gone upstairs to check on the number of clients being entertained in the ten bedrooms spread over two floors. There had been a great deal of noise coming from one room, located at the end of the top corridor. The door should have been closed to indicate activity inside but it stood wide open and even Tomas, well used by now to unusual proclivities of visitors to these brothel rooms, had stood and goggled for thirty seconds before beating a silent retreat towards the staircase. The sight to behold had been that of a late middle aged Caucasian man, face down naked on the wide double bed and secured by wrists and ankles in a starfish position. Tomas recognised him by his overlong, grey hair which straggled past his neck and down his back. He was a local politician who was forever holding forth about the evils of perverted morals, so prevalent in this area of Marseilles. It now seemed that both his principles and his person were open to abuse. His long hair was flopping around in rhythm with the blows he was receiving on his back and buttocks from two girls, one a white Dane whose working name was Cassandra while the other, who called herself simply Mlle X, was thought to originate from the Ivory Coast. She was a big, powerfully built girl with enormous breasts which swung freely as she wielded her leather belt from a kneeling position over her victim, extracting loud yelps from him for all that she was hampered by another man who was standing by the bed and was buried to the hilt inside her. Tomas took one look at the bald head and the apelike, hairy form to realise that Poilu was engaged on one of his many side interludes. It was high time to leave and a scene best forgotten.

For once careless and eager to get the work of the night concluded, Tomas didn't hear the surprisingly soft foot fall of Poilu as he came down the stone staircase and entered the basement office. Moving quickly but quietly, Poilu positioned himself behind the slight figure stooped in concentration over the ledger which was lying on top of a filing cabinet where the best reading lamp was casting its pool of light. The first Tomas knew of attack and danger was the rancid smell of his employer and the encircling grasp of his powerful arms. Poilu lifted Tomas with little effort and carried the struggling figure over to his own large desk where it stood in the centre of the basement room. Tomas kicked out and tried to break the hold but lacked the strength. Poilu bent his victim over the desk, face crushed into a litter of papers and discarded packets of Gauloises cigarettes.

'You're a little shit,' shouted Poilu, 'slinking around spying on me and the girls. You must need a bit of a lesson in violent sex and by Christ, I'm the man to give it to you!'

Tomas squirmed under the weight of the hairy body and tried a reply.

'It was your own fault, you great ape. You left the bloody door wide open and you haven't shown me anything I didn't know. I won't be telling any tales.' But this last came out as a muffled gasp as Poilu's fists came pummelling in.

'No. You fucking well won't. You'll be too busy repairing yourself. D'you know that after that great black bitch I fancy a bit of tight arse and yours might do me pretty well. Just hold still you little sod while I unzip.'

Tomas did just the opposite and kicked out again, desperate to escape the crippling hold. The mighty fists crashed in again and Tomas felt consciousness slipping away, but that changed again as the weight and the smell disappeared, overtaken by the sound of Poilu groaning in pain.

Tomas was able to stand up and turned around to see

Tetrarch standing over the recumbent body. It seemed that the intervention had come about through sheer luck. There had been a lull of custom through the front door and Tetrarch had come looking for his sibling to say that he was free to go. The tableau which had greeted him was clear and his fury had built in an instant.

Tetrarch had jumped in, hauled Poilu off Tomas and set about him with a vengeance. The much younger man had the advantages of both surprise and strength. But there was something more. In his mind made slightly simple by his childhood treatment, Tetrarch knew he was forever in thrall to his sibling and here was a rare chance for some payback. So he couldn't leave it there. Before Tomas could stop him with calming words, he bent down and with a grunt of effort picked up the hairy, groaning body of Poilu, tucked the bald head under one arm and ran him clean across the basement room to slam into the concrete wall and slide to the floor. They both heard the alarming crack as Poilu hit the wall and could see the neck was at an awkward angle as the body slumped in ultimate surrender.

After a full minute's silence, it was Tomas who took charge again, going to kneel by Poilu to check for a pulse. There was none. Tetrarch stood motionless, breathing slightly, hands outstretched in a gesture which said 'Sorry I've gone too far. What do we do now? Help!'

There was only one way forward. Most problems could be resolved in the environment of le Vieux Port of that era, but not murder. That left only one answer, which was flight. They were on a night train out of Marseilles before the dawn broke.

9. SIMON GORING — 1984

It amazed him that he had been here a year already. Simon felt a frisson of expectation as he spotted a parking place for his well-worn Renault 4 from which to hump the contents of his overloaded car up five flights of stairs to the apartment which would be home for this, his second year at Bristol University.

Most of his contemporaries had teamed into groups of four or five to rent houses from the established bank of student accommodation but Simon had got together with a guy of his own age and stage called Harry Bonsor, who had started with him. They had gelled into a contented friendship and before the long summer vacation, they had settled on this bright and airy flat at the top of a house in Clifton, conveniently placed for all their commitments to University life. There was another advantage for him. Harry was the youngest of four siblings. His parents owned an art and furniture dealing establishment in the nearby country town of Melksham. They worked all hours but kept an open house in their rambling old rectory in one of the surrounding villages. Simon got on well with the parents and Harry's siblings so now he was looking forward to developing these relationships. There was more. He was stimulated by the course he was taking in Languages and Politics and fired by the fervour of his tutor who was an engaging and provocative character, determined to get the best out of all his students.

Simon was no less determined. He had been able to further his education at this prime University thanks to three benefactors. First his adoptive parents, his aunt Caroline and her husband Benny who had taken him into their South London home after his mother and father had gone down in the plane crash off the Irish coast. Secondly, there was his godfather King

Offenbach, the genial black CIA man who was always there for him in the background, providing welcome guidance and financial support. And finally, the Royal Marines who were sponsoring his degree course in return for the commitment that, on graduation, he would enter their illustrious ranks for training and service for a minimum of five years. His pal Harry Bonsor, who was personally dedicated to as much work only as was strictly necessary and to an otherwise unchanging diet of parties, womanising and the vague notion of some career in journalism. Harry thought he was quite mad and said so.

'Why would you want to get through education and then volunteer for cold showers, haircuts and ceaseless bollockings? It beats me, Si, but if that's what turns you on then you go for it and I'll enjoy watching! But first, anyway, let's have some fun!'

They did so, and with a vengeance but the nonstop lifestyle didn't prevent Simon from taking his studies seriously and to the delight of his Tutor, Roly Patrick, he was really beginning to shine as the days grew shorter and the nights colder in that first term of their second year.

As the break for Christmas approached, Simon called on Roly one evening to take him a bottle by way of thanks and celebration. That's how he came to see again Hannah Deveridge whom he had first encountered when they were both gawky teenagers being shepherded around central London at the time of the Queen's Silver Jubilee seven years previously.

Not that he recognised her at first but that would hardly have been possible. It was early evening on the last Monday of Term, about 5pm so well after the December darkness had fallen. Simon clumped up the steps of Roly's town house which was within comfortable walking distance of his flat and the favoured pub in which another rousing drinking session was planned. Simon was encouraged to see a light burning above the entrance and not surprised to find the door on the latch as there were forever people coming and going.

Roly looked to be older than a man in his late thirties, with wise eyes twinkling beneath heavy brows and surmounted by a shaggy mane of brown hair which fell over the collar of the corduroy jacket from which he was seldom parted. He had established a considerable reputation for himself at Bristol: a natural linguist with a first class brain, he had retreated from a promising future in the diplomatic service when it came to him that he was at heart an academic and now he conducted his tutorials in the spirit of a shared journey of adventure. He was inspiring and Simon felt privileged to be learning from him.

Roly Patrick was an energetic bachelor and his house was arranged to suit a disorganised lifestyle. The building was tall and thin: the door from the street opened into a large room which served as the kitchen and was dominated by a pine table piled high with books and papers. Along one wall a staircase mounted to the second floor and another large room which was his study. The stairs went on rising to a third and perhaps a fourth floor, but it was the study which was the centre of Roly's existence and it was here that he conducted tutorial sessions for both groups and singles.

Simon pushed open the street door with a cursory knock and stepped into the kitchen room. He called out but there was no response which was not a surprise. Probably, he couldn't be heard above the music being played upstairs and mingled with it, Simon could hear voices. It seemed that Roly was still at work and as if to confirm, the music changed from the Boomtown Rats to a Schubert symphony which meant a teaching session. Encouraged, Simon set off across the kitchen and up the stairs. He would just pop his head around the door to hand over his bottle and card for a Christmas greeting. As he climbed, he could hear the familiar sound of Roly's gargantuan armchair, the throne from which he liked to hold court, being pushed around and into position centre stage. Presumably, Simon had time to think to himself, there must be several of them there. As he reached the little landing from which the staircase turned in its tracks to vanish further upwards, he heard Roly's voice clearly.

'Now are you quite sure about this, Hannah?'

'Absolutely', came the girl's voice in a husky reply, 'it's been bugging me and I've just got to get this done by the end of term. You're my best shot and I'm sure you know what you're doing.'

'Well fine, but try turning your back to me. You'll find it easier.'

Last minute practise for presentation, Simon thought to himself, feeling uncomfortable to be eavesdropping although he really couldn't avoid it. He knuckled his hand and pushed it towards the quarter open door, seeking to announce himself with a polite knock. Then came Roly Patrick's voice again, stopping his hand in mid-air.

'That's me OK. Teaching all term, open all hours. Take in washing on Fridays, deflowering every other Monday'. All this in his familiar, jocular style.

Simon simply froze and then it was just blind fortune, good or bad, which revealed the scene to him as the door swung involuntarily a little further open. His Tutor lay full length on the floor of the study, his feet towards the door in which Simon was standing and his head towards the large window which overlooked the street. The imposing armchair had been pushed well back against the floor to ceiling bookcase. Roly's legs were slightly parted and he appeared to be completely unclothed. Certainly all of his equipment was open to inspection and his penis stood up from the forest of black hair which covered his legs and blossomed out over his belly. The remainder of him was obscured by the body of his partner, a lissom looking girl of slim build with great long legs, one of which was just arching over Roly's recumbent form as she knelt astride him with her back to his face and his hands giving balance to her hips. The top half of her was entirely clothed, a black roll neck sweater with a long, gold necklace swinging between her breasts, hair down to her shoulders and covering most of her face. She was even wearing some sort of trench coat, undone and with the tails presumably flapping in Roly's face. Below this she was naked. She had one hand on his thigh while the other grasped the base of his member as she took aim to encase it. The sheer eroticism of the scene was enhanced by the enormous pair of spectacles which she was wearing and by the sound of her husky voice speaking to herself.

'Well if a baby can come out, this will surely go in ok.'

Instantly aroused and embarrassed in equal measure, Simon backed down two stairs, turned and skipped down the rest. He flew across the kitchen room and through the front door which he left as he had found it. The bottle was still in his hand but he dropped the Christmas card as he vanished into the December evening.

Simon got himself properly drunk in the pub that night but that didn't cause him to talk about what he had witnessed at Roly Patrick's house. He told himself to say nothing and stay well clear but he couldn't help wondering at the identity of that girl with her endless long legs and glasses the size of goggles.

But as he hauled himself out of bed next morning, other matters intervened to claim his attention. First, he realised that he had only two days left in Bristol before he was due to pile into the Renault and hope it would carry him up to Caro and Benny for Christmas in Dulwich. For this, he was completely unprepared so there were presents to buy. Then there was a piece of work to hand in and he had to finish an article which he had promised for the Student Mag, not that it would appear before the New Year. These were all day jobs of course, but the couple of evenings were already taken up with carefully planned roistering and Simon was just juggling priorities in his head when the phone started ringing. He picked it up and listened to the laconic drawl of his godfather King Offenbach who wanted to call by to see him sometime late that afternoon.

Simon put down the phone and sighed. He should be Christmas shopping then but somehow he would fit it all in. He liked the American and If King could make the time, he could manage also, so he set about the rest of his day with renewed energy.

They met at a coffee shop in Clifton which King knew from previous visits. It turned out that he had been to a meeting at the British Security Centre, GCHQ in Cheltenham and Simon was flattered that he was making a big detour to take in Bristol on his return trip to London. Simon started to thank him for the effort but King brushed aside his comments with an airy wave.

'Don't even mention it,' he said, 'it's a pleasure to see you, better yet after a day of a spooks gathering. Actually, that went OK but I'll still be glad to get home to London and start packing my bags.'

'You're going to the States for Christmas?'

'Nope. Not this year although I'll get to spend the New Year with my old Ma in Colorado. But first, I'm going south, into Africa to see my good ole friend Pente Broke Smith and pass Christmas with him in Singida, Tanzania. I guess I won't go short of church but we'll find time together to chew the fat some.'

Simon was scouring his memory whilst attempting to look informed but King spotted it at once.

'You don't remember Pente? The big guy with the booming laugh who smokes the foul smelling cigars?'

'Is he the missionary?'

'Yup. Well sort of. But you've done well to remember that much. He and I became good buddies while at Oxford together. That's what, nearly twenty years back now but we've always got on and kept in pretty close touch even though there's not so many chances to get together.'

'I've heard you speak of him before,' said Simon in reply as he put down an empty cup and signalled to the waitress for a refill, 'and he sounds a larger than life character but I can't picture him. I'm not so sure I've actually ever met Pente.'

'Oh sure you have Si, but not for a few years, that's true. But going back aways, d'you recall we were all together at the Jubilee whenever that was. '77 wasn't it and I picked you up from home to go and see the celebrations? Remember we met up with Pente then and he had that special old girlfriend of his with him, her and her three kids? Yeah?'

The memory sprang sharply into focus for Simon and he could picture the crowds, the excitement, the wandering through the Royal Parks and the press of people as they watched the river pageant.

'Of course', he said clicking his fingers, 'I've got it now. He's a huge man, covered in his black robe and with a beard which makes him look like an Old Testament prophet.'

'You've got him. That's Pente alright.'

'And the family with him: who were they?'

'A lady called Vanda. Vanda Deveridge as she became but I reckon she would have married Pente himself if he hadn't decided to give all that up and go with the priesthood. As things stood, though, she went with a lush who drank himself to death a couple of years back. He wasn't there that day, of course, and I never met him. But I remember the three kids: the girl Hannah, a boy and then a much younger girl who was called Cordelia or Camilla or some such.'

Simon knew King well enough to suspect he was holding something back and eventually the black man chuckled as he went on.

'Sorry Si but I couldn't help but smile at the time as I watched you and big sister Hannah trying to make something of each other. That day you were both of that awkward age of adolescent socialising and it was difficult for you.'

'Well, from what little I remember, she was just an awkward character, very serious and withdrawn. It was as if she was trying to hide herself away', he broke off there and King made to question him further but Simon changed the subject brusquely.

'Look we haven't much time, King, but I'd like to give you an update on how things are going here and also to make a plan to meet up again in the New Year. Will you be coming to Caro and Benny's when you get back from seeing your mother?'

'For sure I will, but right now, tell me how the course has been going this term. Jeez, you're well into year two already. Before we know it, you'll be out and inflicted on the world!'

They fell to talking of other things and an hour plus passed very quickly before King Offenbach dragged himself away to start his drive back to London. Simon left him by his car, refusing the offer of a lift back to his flat. He thought he would grab an hour in the shops and get a few Christmas presents.

At the top of his list was Benny and his ceaseless demand for new sweaters. Si was confident that Marks and Spencer would provide and he set off towards their centre city store. It was not too long a walk and he wanted a bit of time to think.

Coincidence does happen, he told himself as he strode out, even if this would be stretching a point. But that day out in 1977, seven whole years ago plus some had come back to him in clear memory now. He must have been pretty gauche himself but that tall, self-possessed girl had been a fair old challenge: prickly as hell, more than a bit argumentative and apparently trying to hide herself. She had worn large, thick glasses. He could see them again as he walked. And her name had been Hannah. But it couldn't be the same, surely.

Simon spent twenty minutes browsing through the store. He bought some cards, wrapping paper and a Playboy diary which he thought might amuse Harry, also a sweater for Benny. He was doubtful about the colour but, persuading himself that it would do, he marched off to join the queue at the pay desk and was trying to calm his impatience at the delay when he glanced in front of him and saw with a jolt of recognition that he knew the tall girl who was three ahead of him and just being served. It was Hannah again, without a doubt. As she turned her head slightly to replace her purse in a voluminous handbag, he could see those enormous specs on her nose. Quite unreasonably, he felt panicked and was about to turn away and sacrifice his place in the queue when she turned on her heel with bags in hand and seemed about to stride off when she checked herself, looked straight at him and spoke.

'Haven't we met before somewhere?'

'I, uh, don't think so. It's possible of course but I don't know', Simon knew he was gibbering in front of her very direct gaze, 'anyway my name's Simon Goring and it look's like I should move'. He smiled, hoping he was recovering himself as the line of buyers moved forward and he saw that there was only one more before his turn. He got to the cashier who put everything into one bag and gave him his change but when he turned to leave, he found the girl still there, waiting for him. She didn't waste any time.

'Actually', she said, 'I'm cheating a bit. I was having coffee with friends a while ago and saw you with that great long streak of a black man. It was him I recognised and when I heard his cowboy accent, I remembered from where. A long time ago, on a day I spent with my mother in London. You were with him then. Yes?'

'Good Lord, you could be right,' Simon told her as he pulled himself together and tried to stop feeling guilty about something which she couldn't possibly know about anyway. The crowds of shoppers whirled about them as he gestured and went on, 'Too much going on around here. How about a beer?'

'A drink would be OK, so long as it doesn't have to be beer'.

They left the shop and found a pub almost next door, not a place Simon had been in before but it was reasonable, not too crowded yet, some tables and chairs as well as the bar. He chose one and went off to get her a gin and tonic and himself a pint while she was settling herself. She wasted no time as he returned with the drinks and spoke out as he was putting them down.

'I'm Hannah, by the way. Hannah Deveridge. I got here in September and I'm reading Philosophy and French. You've done a year already so you're very grown up and when we met before, we were troublesome teenagers. How time flies. Cheers!' She took a sip and sat back, waiting for his reply.

'I remember now. I was with my godfather, King Offenbach. He's the black guy you saw just now. And you were with Pente Broke Smith, you, your Mum, your brother and little sister. We all did the Jubilee together. That's right, isn't it?'

Hannah took off her glasses and fished in the pocket of her coat for a tissue. She started to polish the lens with great concentration and Simon had the sure feeling that this was a mannerism, a distraction while she was considering what next to say. He used the moment of silence to study her, especially now when she had those enormous specs in her hand and not balanced on her nose to act as a form of mask. He knew already that her figure was beguiling, but what of the face?

It was easy to recognise what was wrong with it - as she would consider anyway. The birthmark started just inside her left eye and extended in a straggle half way down that side of her nose. It was not prominent but it was noticeable especially for its colour which was an angry red where it bordered the eyeball but becoming much more subdued as it spread onto the nose. In an instant, Simon reached the judgement that none of it was too big a deal and that it must cause her far more angst than it would excite attention in those meeting her. Apart from this blemish, Hannah's face was remarkable for its beauty. The high cheekbones seemed to reach up for the forehead which was largely concealed behind her hair. The mouth was wide, quite thin lipped but with a sensuous curve. The complexion was flawless and the neck was slim and tall, forming a pedestal on which the head was mounted. The eyes were large and the very deepest colour of blue so that they appeared almost violet. Her hair was thick and the colour of late walnuts, it fell in layered waves to below her shoulders.

All of which made her an enigma, Simon thought to himself as he sat opposite her and pulled a battered packet of cigarettes from his pocket and held it up in offer. She took one and he lit it for her. Why, he mused, should such an attractive girl go to such pains to hide her compelling looks behind grotesque glasses which, in a contradiction to their presumed purpose, mostly served to highlight the one gift of nature which did not flatter her.

'I'm often told I'm awkward and a challenge,' she announced without preamble, 'you're entitled to form the same opinion.'

'Well I'm not doing that yet although I do remember thinking that you took yourself pretty seriously.'

'Yes. I suppose that's right and I still do. But we were children then and the thing about growing up is that you do learn to hide your feelings and put on the act that's expected of you. It's a pity, really. Honesty loses out to presentation'.

'Wow,' said Simon, 'this is getting heavy conversation already. I'm interested but I want to do some catching up first. Fill in a bit of background for me, would you mind? All I know is that we walked around the Embassy gardens that time while our elders were gossiping up in King's office. I can't remember anything else.'

'OK,' said Hannah, stubbing out her cigarette and leaning forward to cross her arms on the table, 'well here's the short version. I'm just into Uni. Good school, good results, pretty bright. Determined, impatient, can be difficult. I live with my widowed mother on a large and wealthy farm outside Hereford. My father died from drink. I have a younger brother, William and there's my sister Charlotte, known as Charley. I managed to lose my virginity last night. You were watching and you dropped your calling card'. She laid the Christmas card on the table in front of him.

Simon had his glass to his lips as she finished speaking and spilled most of his pint down his front.

'Jesus,' he expostulated, 'what do you do for shock tactics?'

Hannah Deveridge smiled sweetly at him as she gathered her things together and stood up.

'I can do better than that and you can do better than a grubby calendar,' she replied as she eyed the carrier bag at his feet. 'But all that can wait for another time. Happy Christmas, Simon, and thanks for the drink.'

She left him at that and made a quiet exit. Simon instinctively knew better than to follow her.

10. HANNAH DEVERIDGE — 1985

Hannah's birthday fell at the end of March, always close to the Easter weekend when spring was busy pushing winter out of the way, when there was more light to the day and spirits were lighter. She had come home to mark the changing season in the Herefordshire countryside and to recognise with quiet satisfaction that she was two thirds into her first year at Bristol University.

After lunch, she sat on with her mother Vanda at the big pine table which dominated the kitchen. Her brother William, home for holidays from his boarding school, had gone out on a mission of rabbiting with the improbably named Aaron, second son of the dairyman and an important year older. Charlotte, the youngest of them at fifteen, had left them to go to her bedroom and write up her diary. That's what she had announced as she left the table but Hannah guessed that Charley, always perceptive and wise beyond her years, had acted with the motive of leaving mother and daughter some time and space together.

Vanda had opened a bottle of wine and now she refilled their coffee mugs: they were both smoking. They sat side by side at the table, looking out through the broad bay window at the garden and the fields beyond the beech hedge which bordered it. It was a calm and peaceful scene, without diversion or distraction and Vanda was tempted to reflect that in some placid conversation but she couldn't allow herself to do that. There was a stranger in the room who stood between them: some sort of taboo which needed to be challenged or else, she sensed, the foundations of a barrier might build to become an impregnable wall. She had experience with something of just that coming between her and her own mother Trisha.

Vanda was never one to mince words and she was about to launch in when Hannah anticipated her by asking a blunt question.

'When are you going to Paris next?'

'On Tuesday week, for a week.'

Neither could help but to smile at the other. A hard and accurate serve countered by a firm return. It was so like them both: no evasion and no shilly shallying. Hannah swallowed half her glass of wine in a single gulp and fixed her gaze on her mother as she went on.

'Mum,' she said, 'don't you think it's time for you to be more honest, at least with me, about this relationship of yours? I mean in principle at least, there's nothing wrong with it. You've been a widow for over six years, so there's no reason at all for you not to have another man. It's not like it's an affair. But you're so secretive about him. As far as I know, he's never been here and you only meet him when we're all away from home. All I know about him is that he's a Frenchman and he's called Victor Sollange. And even that's a guess but I did once see a letter for the post which you forgot to whip out of sight.'

It was Vanda's turn to seek refuge in her wine. Then she refilled both glasses and lit herself another cigarette.

'Sorry about this', she said blowing a cloud of smoke, 'but I'll blame Victor. He's a horror with his fags.' After a pause, she went on. 'You're perfectly right, Hannah. I should have confided in you much more and much sooner - really much, much sooner. But you know what it is, you get into a habit and then you persuade yourself that the time's not quite right, you need a better opportunity, whatever. They're all excuses but I must say that when it started between Victor and me, I think you would honestly have been too young to take it in. I think it would have frightened you and you had quite enough to cope with without that.'

'Quite possibly, Mum. But that's a long time back now. You obviously have something now that's proved itself over time. I think that's terrific, I really do. But can't you now make more of it? I mean, where's the commitment? What's the plan?'

'There's no plan, not beyond the way we live our lives right now. We meet three or four times a year and we speak on the phone maybe every ten days or so. And you know what, I really don't want to push it further than that. He's a marvellous man, Victor: thoughtful, challenging, stimulating in every way. But also, and by his own admission, he's selfish. He's never been married, has never lived with anyone. He's had any number of women I'm sure, although I'm just as confident there's never been one as constant or as important as I am to him. But he is a lone wolf. He's always lived in the heart of Paris and wouldn't wish his home to be anywhere else. He's some sort of policeman with a very international bias and he's ruthless by instinct and professional training. So we're a pretty unlikely pair and maybe that's why it works as well as it does. I think it also works because we are on his territory. Frankly, I wouldn't want Victor to be here and trying to establish himself with either set of your grandparents. They wouldn't understand him in any sense and I certainly wouldn't want him trading arrows with your aunt Sarah and Rufus.'

Hannah nodded, raising her right hand to sweep the long hair away from her face, a gesture which her mother recognised as the means of buying a bit of time. Then she spoke again.

'But Mum, honestly, is this sort of clandestine love affair enough for you? I mean you're only just over forty. You've got half a lifetime left and I would have thought that you'd want more from it. Why not marry again or at least go public with the relationship and what it means to you - actually to the two of you by the sounds of things. I don't have to be told about the family hassles that would involve and if Rufus and Aunt Sarah have a view on all of this, I bet that's all to do with money. Well screw them, I say. You've done more than your bit for both sides of this family. You deserve your place in the sun of some happiness and fulfilment. I mean you've had the let down by Pente, then Dad and all that heartache and now this so near but so far with your Victor. Golly - give us a break or rather give it to you, I say. I mean, you could start another family - and why not?'

Hannah broke off to pick up her glass while Vanda looked at her and was unable to keep the tears from her eyes. She would never have expected such insight, feeling and support from a daughter whom she had regarded since her puberty with love and respect but larded also with a little wariness as Hannah had developed her moods and self-sufficiency to the point of remoteness. She was touched by this concern and thoughtfulness and she had to pluck a tissue from the box on the table, running it gently over her eyes whilst she smiled shyly. Only then did she feel capable of reply.

'It's lovely of you to think that, much more to come out and say it. It really means a lot to me to hear you speak like that, Hannah darling, so thank you. Thank you more than I can say. Rather than try for any big speeches, I think it's time I told you more.'

She smiled diffidently at her daughter as she picked up the bottle to pour them both some more wine. Then she took another cigarette, shrugging her shoulders at this indulgence as her smile turned to the grin of two sinners sharing their pleasures. She raised her glass in a silent toast before she started to speak again.

'I suppose it's an affliction in a way to have too many memories, too much time alone to go over them and no one to share them with. That's really not a complaint but just the way it is. The way it is for me, anyway.'

Vanda suddenly felt the tears again, pricking at her eyes but Hannah jolted her out of it, saying abruptly, 'It can't be the memories, Mum. It's the silence more like. Everyone has memories - good and bad. But not everyone can stay silent like you do. You lock the world out, keeping your thoughts to yourself, never sharing except trivial, gossipy things. It's surely that which makes you lonely.'

'Maybe you're right,' Vanda replied, feeling physically stung just as if a wasp had bitten her but also recognising the justification for her daughter's jibe and determined that she should not walk away from it.

'OK,' she went on, 'let me try. But just so you know, I'm not whingeing and I'm not feeling sorry for myself. I can cope perfectly well without wearing my heart on my sleeve.'

'Oh yeah, yeah! Just for God's sake get on with it, Mother!'

Vanda stuck her tongue out at her daughter, grinned again and took a pull at her glass before she started in.

'I'm forty-one now and I guess I'm lucky because I knew, deep down, that I was in love with the man of my lifetime when I was fourteen and a bit. I'm just sorry that I couldn't hold onto him for longer than I did'.

She broke off briefly as she saw Hannah rolling her eyes at this drama.

'Well, you asked for the history and this is it, so bloody well listen! I'm sure you can believe that this backwoods part of the world was even more remote when I was that age and I can tell you that my Rupert, Roo or Pente as everyone now calls him was just everything to me. He was my constant companion, my verbal sparring partner, my mentor, my challenge and my stimulation all rolled into one. Now, of course you can argue that I - and he also for that matter – were simply adolescents at that point, still at school and learning about life as well as maths and history. We could have grown up and grown apart, you might well say and I couldn't prove you wrong, but I know you would be. He and I were soul mates, predestined to be together and I still imagine, even dream, where we would be today if bloody God hadn't intervened and nicked him from me.

'But there is some sort of compensation. I may have lost a love but I haven't lost a friend - my friend and the one person I turn to instinctively when all the chips are down and I feel entirely desperate. Roo was only briefly my lover and I never think about what Pente may have hiding under his cassock but the two people are still one and the same man and he is my man, and always will be.'

Mother and daughter sat silent for a moment, their eyes

locked as they gazed at each other across the length of the kitchen table. Hannah said,

'Well I asked for it, Mum, and thank you for being so candid, even if it's too brief and a bit of a shock, to be honest. I always thought you two just did some growing up together. I never realised there was so much to it for you. Was it the same for him?'

'Yes, I believe it was and I honestly don't think that's wishful thinking. He did get some way towards asking me to marry him and I'm quite sure that was genuine, even if he was intent on getting his leg over at the time.' She gave a wry smile.

'But when was this,' asked Hannah, 'I mean where was he at with the priest bit?'

'That was later, but not much later. In his second year at Oxford, he upped sticks during the summer to go to India. I'm still not sure if he had by then received the Call but he certainly came back with it. It was then that he told me that he had discovered a prior claim on his life and that we couldn't be together but that he would always be there for me. I was devastated but I have to admit that he has made good that promise.'

Hannah nodded and then said, 'Tell me something about Dad, about my father'.

'Yes. That's very different of course, but it may be even more of a surprise to you and one that is welcome. Your father and I were something of an arranged marriage. I'd known him since early schooldays and I hadn't thought much of him. He was a bit weak and certainly pretty wet, often sick, never outstanding in school work or sport and not too popular with children his age or our teachers. He was a bit of a misfit really, always on the fringe and redeemed only because his family was rich and a big player in this part of the county. He and I knew each other, of course, but it was really my father, your Gramps who introduced us. My Dad saw I was pretty miserable, or at least available, after Pente defected and he was determined that I shouldn't go off to Uni even though I had a place. He's an old fashioned man and as you know, not an easy communicator. He thought that girls should stay close to home so he contrived an opportunity to get me together with Luke. I wouldn't say that I was up for grabs, it was more that I was still coming to terms with the loss of Pente and I just couldn't see what to do with myself.

'And then something really pretty astonishing: I found that overnight almost, I was revising my opinion of Luke, finding that I liked him and was impressed by the fact that he wasn't all stuck up and pretentious like his parents and especially not like his sister. He was quite good looking, no oil painting but not overweight, a reasonable height, not spotty, didn't smell and most important, he was fun. Laughing Luke, they called him, at least for a while and that did sum him up. He wasn't Einstein, but was no fool either. He had opinions and a bit of style, but of course the other major attraction was that he had money - and lots of it!' Vanda broke off then and the silence stretched between them. Both women were aware that there was ground to be covered and more history to be shared. But the chronology was all wrong. The elephant, which both recognised but of which they had never spoken, had to come first. Eventually, it was Hannah who took up the conversation.

'You know, Mum, it's your Frenchman I need to hear more about. The who and how and why. If it helps you to talk, let me say that in my heart, I believe that it's he who is Charley's father, which makes her my half-sister. True or false?'

'Quite true.'

Hannah slumped back in her kitchen chair, saying nothing, her eyes fixed on her mother. Silence again, unbroken and stretched out as Vanda returned her gaze, unblinking and unmoving but in her mind just praying that William would not choose this time to make his normal, noisy return. This was not a moment for interruption. Finally, it was Hannah who moved the tableau on, pulling herself forward to grab her glass and emptying it in a single gulp before she reached out to grab the bottle, twisting it to see the level inside and speaking as she did so in a calm and controlled voice.

'Better get another, Mum. We're going to need it, I think.'

'Probably. There's plenty more in the fridge if you like this white. You grab one and I'll keep talking. You'll want to know more.'

Vanda put out one hand and pulled the packet of cigarettes closer to her. She took one out and lit it, took a deep drag and sitting back as she stretched out her legs, she regarded her daughter as she continued to speak.

'Oh wow, Hannah', she said, 'I'm just so glad you know, gladder still that we can talk about it. But look, the history isn't complicated. My introduction to Charlotte's father was a matter of the merest chance. From the outset, from the first moment of setting eyes on each other, there was a very strong mutual attraction which was always going to turn into some sort of fulfilment, although I was pretty sure that it was going to be a brief fling, just ships passing in the night.'

'So how did you get together in the first place?' Hannah was determined to keep her concentrated.

'Well, way back earlier, right at the end of the swinging sixties, Pente's mother Constance died. I had been really close to her, both as a person in her own right but also because she was a last connection with her son whom I was still mourning. After her funeral, when I was feeling really low and dreading going back to your father, Pente persuaded me to stay on at Forty Green Cottage for a while, a few drinks and some comfort.'

Vanda looked up from stubbing out her cigarette and saw her daughter staring at her, wide eyed. She hastened on with a smile and a shake of her head.

'No, no. Not that sort of comfort! Just a hug and a good fireside chat. He told me that I couldn't go on as I was - not harried into misery by two uncaring families and a husband well on the road to perdition. I always remember how he put it: "you can't live like that for another thirty years, not even three." He told me I must have a break and that he would arrange something. It seemed to take forever but finally he rang and told me that his good friend had arranged an introduction to a working colleague, a Frenchman who lived in Paris and would look out for me if I flew over there and gave myself a holiday for a few days. I certainly did have a break. And I fell in love. That's how Victor entered my life and when I left Paris, I was carrying his child.'

She paused to sip at her wine and Hannah was poised to comment but her mother held up a finger above her glass.

'Hear me out a bit more first. Victor knew nothing about Charley's conception and birth. He and I had absolutely no contact with each other after that week of romance. Zero. And we both thought that was right. I was entirely content and of course I was relieved that your father never so much as asked about the baby, while everyone else around here assumed she was his and speculated that perhaps both he and our marriage had improved.

'I didn't set eyes on Victor, didn't speak to him for nearly nine years. And when I did both, it was at your father's funeral at the crematorium. King Offenbach came that day and he brought Victor with him. A month or so later, Victor rang me from Paris and that's when we started the relationship which we still have to this day. It's a happy surprise to me that we're still so much together all these years later.'

'So tell me again', asked Hannah, 'how did this American guy get into the picture? Did that have anything to do with when you took us three up to London? That summer trip, you remember, all about Royalty and an event for the Queen. I guess it was her Jubilee wasn't it?'

'Quite right: it was the Jubilee in 1977. Things were getting pretty bad with your father. Pente would ring from time to time and he happened to catch me on a bad day so he told me to get organised and bring you all with me to have a laugh and recharge the batteries. Pente had King Offenbach with him and at the end of the day King took us all round to the US Embassy.'

'We weren't alone either,' Hannah interrupted her, 'your Mr Offenbach had a boy with him, his godson Simon Goring. He was about my age but a bit geeky.'

Her mother looked at her in astonishment. 'How on earth did you remember him? I'm really surprised.'

'Don't worry for now. We can get back to it.'

'Well,' Vanda resumed, 'while you kids were out of the way, we three had a talk and that was the first occasion when I actually met King. Pente had spoken a lot about him over the years and the happy relaxation of the Jubilee day made me open up, plus I must say it seemed only fair to be candid. I told them both then, just as I'm telling you now, that I regret nothing. Victor is a completely wonderful man and I love him more than enough to leave him alone. Any arrangement to have us living together would be a disaster. Things work very well just as they are. We speak when we want and we meet when it suits us both. You should know that he cares very much for Charley even though he doesn't know her. When she's a bit older, we'll both tell her and she can make of things what she will.'

Hannah was uncorking a bottle as her mother finished speaking and now she filled both their glasses, shaking her head slowly as she took in all of this information. As for questions and reaction, she really didn't know where to start, so it was quite helpful that Vanda took the initiative.

'How did you remember about King's godson – Simon whatsit?'

'Goring,' replied Hannah, 'Simon Goring. I remembered because I was reminded. He's in Bristol now, at Uni but a year ahead of me and we see quite a bit of each other.'

It was a day for the unexpected, Vanda had time for the thought to flash across her mind before she recovered herself to ask questions. How had they met? When was the connection to history made? What was he like, this Simon? Had she, as a result, met King Offenbach again? Was Simon a friend or a boyfriend?

Hannah smiled indulgently at her mother and tried to make light of it in her response.

'He's just a guy, Mum, another undergrad and yes he's good company and one of the crowd I spend time with but there's nothing special, not yet anyway.'

'Not yet, is it? That sounds as if there'd a bit more to this than you want to talk about, so I won't press you - even though I'd love to know more.' She laughed out loud and she sounded so spontaneous and happy that Hannah felt herself bound to smile with her. She spoke again.

'Simon is just ... well he's just Simon! He's pretty articulate, definitely bright. He's not pushy, not moody, doesn't show off too much in spite of the provocation of his mates. He's very constant: yup, I think that's a good word for him. Constant. Plus also keen.'

'OK. And that's a problem for you?'

'No. No not exactly that. It's just that he's way ahead of me and his certainty bothers me. I don't know whether it's you Mum, your character or our family background or this funny, rather lost part of the world which is home. I don't know, but I do have an aversion to commitment. I want to remain my own person and I really cherish my independence. I never want to depend.'

Hannah shrugged as she finished and Vanda took over.

'I think I get the drift and if so, I sympathise, but of course I can't fully grasp something which you don't understand yourself yet. Don't push it, is my advice. Don't try and make yourself appreciate an instinct which is only just forming. You have to let it come to you, not the other way around.'

Hannah nodded and then replied,

'Thanks, Mum, that sounds very good to me. And since you're being so honest, let me be the same. There isn't a physical problem here. I mean it's nothing to do with sex - or not yet anyway. I haven't slept with Simon. I wouldn't mind but I've got the feeling that it would just be a distraction which would spoil things rather than add a dimension. I'm lucky here because Si is not too testosterone driven. I mean he wants it, but he can do without if there is a greater goal as he sees it. He doesn't exactly put me on a pedestal but he seems convinced that it's all going to happen for us one day provided he doesn't push too hard.'

'Golly', Vanda put in, 'that's a pretty mature vision for any man, extraordinary for a young fellow of his age.'

'I know, but at least we can and do discuss it.'

'You mean your relationship?' Vanda asked carefully, taking a sip from her glass as she did so.

'Yes, but also the specific subject of sex. You see, I've only tried that once so far. I just wanted to get the first time over with so I asked my Tutor who's quite a randy bugger but a very entertaining and obliging guy. He was happy to help – well why wouldn't he be? But the thing is that someone saw us doing it and I know that person was Simon.'

Vanda was by now draining her glass and grabbing for another smoke. She had been hoping for a frank exchange with her daughter but she now felt the whole conversation moving beyond her control. She was almost relieved by the interruption of her son William, making his normal rowdy entrance through the kitchen door.

11. TOMAS AND TETRACH — 1986

He called himself Li. This was not his name but it was easily understood and pronounced by foreigners, so suited his purpose. Li was a native of Shanghai, born and bred in the city which had witnessed so many profound changes during his fifty years of living there.

In the year of his birth, Shanghai, with its population close to three million people, had been one of the largest cities on the planet but control of every aspect of life had rested in the hands of less than two per cent of its inhabitants. The fifty-thousand odd cadre of European descent ruled every roost and after them came another similar number of Russian origins. Li's family were a long way further down the pecking order, yet by no means at the bottom. His grandfather had enjoyed reasonable beginnings for a Chinese and by dint of some good fortune and ruthless application, he had manoeuvred his way up the slippery slope of the Chinese bourgeoisie. By the time Li turned six years old in the summer of 1942, he was able to understand that he had been born lucky but also to appreciate that the luck was just running out. For almost all the years of the Second World War, Shanghai sweated under the yoke of the occupying Japanese forces and if that was particularly hard on the previously elite citizens of European and Russian background, who suffered their businesses being pirated and their home villas being turned into gambling clubs and brothels: it was tough also for the Compradors as they used to call those at the top of the Chinese tree. Amongst their number were counted Li's grandfather and his father, both of whom were obliged to steer a hazardous path through the minefield of regulations in order to hold onto their positions of influence. It was against a background of incipient fear within his family that young Li completed his primary education, one of the small crumbs of comfort being that he was already recognised as an exceptionally bright young student.

But difficult times were to be succeeded by worse. The defeat of Japan heralded the arrival of the autocratic Chiang Kai-Shek, who clung to power by ceding control of Shanghai to shadowy mobsters, of whom the most dangerous and violent were members of the Green Gang, led by the infamous Du Yuesheng. Li's family managed to hang on: they continued to live in the house in which he had been born, right in the heart of the old city and very close to the port. They lived pretty comfortably, they had money to spend and Li's education was of the highest standard available.

In 1949, however, Communism arrived to blow a searing wind through the whole of Shanghai. The People's Liberation Army, inspired and encouraged by the directives of Chairman Mao, set about reforming this city of commercial success and cultural distinction. The purges melded into a period of regression which was to endure for two decades and amongst the many victims were Li's father and grandfather. He was fourteen years old when these two revered mainstays of his life simply vanished. They were here together one day and gone the next. The most frightening aspect of this trauma was the absolute absence of explanation. Li and his mother found themselves alone in the house which they knew so well, yet which had become alien to them overnight. The hours turned into days and then weeks during all of which they received no word and were supplied with no information. It was not hard for Li to see that his mother was losing hold on reality. They were running out of supplies and money. Their neighbours were of little comfort and no help. Li continued to attend school, expecting with diminishing faith that he would return one day to find the male members of his family restored to them. No such miracle occurred but matters got worse. One day at school, Li's headmaster summoned him with the news, curtly imparted, that his mother also had left him: she killed herself by stumbling to the waterfront and throwing herself in. The headmaster despatched Li to a form of orphanage on the outskirts of the city. He was then a month short of his fifteenth birthday.

Against all the odds, things began to improve from this point. He continued at the same school – bussed in and out every day – and his results earned him commendation from both teachers and the management of the orphanage. After three more years, Li was ready for higher education and was enrolled in a State Academy in which he commenced training to become a government administrator which required him to be simultaneously indoctrinated in communist philosophy. He lapped it all up and demanded more. He loved the work but he devoured the politics, quite rapidly coming to persuade himself that his own grandfather and father had indeed been counter-revolutionaries, that they had failed to see the lights which were forever popping on in his own head.

Throughout the following years, Li grew in reputation as a most able worker and as a committed servant of the State. At the age of thirty in 1966, he returned to live in Shanghai following a five-year stint in Peking. He had become a statistician by profession and had won acclaim for his enormously complex analysis of population growth and people movement in the new China. The Authorities wanted him back in the city of his upbringing to help make Shanghai more politically correct without sacrificing its international earning power.

Now, twenty years later, he was still in Shanghai and knew he would never leave again. He lived modestly in a dwelling close to the house of his upbringing. He had never married. He neither smoked nor drank alcohol. He had few friends and no sexual preferences of any sort. It was a monkish existence except that the God of his world was the Communist state and he deplored the trend towards the profit motive, greater personal freedom and room for self-expression. Li at fifty was fit and healthy, a short, spare and self-effacing little man. He was mild of manner but with the tenacity of a zealot. He knew he would be retired in ten years and was starting to wonder how he would occupy himself thereafter. Right now, however, he was concentrating on his work which amounted to headhunting.

Li was down at the port, at the ocean liner terminal watching passengers disembarking from the P&O Cruise ship, the Oriana. The vessel did not normally venture into Chinese waters but she was on her final voyage from her base in Sydney, Australia and it had been decided that for her final hurrah, the Oriana should visit as many South East Asian destinations as she could.

Li's interest was not in the ship but in her passengers and he was working to instructions. The Politburo wanted to increase China's influence around the globe but ironically, the country was suffering from a lack of the right people. They possessed infinite resource to analyse reports and statistics but they were permanently short of solid, native born experience of life in the countries which held interest for China. Li was tasked to concentrate on Africa and therefore he needed a child of Chad or an infant of Eritrea with brains, aptitude and the potential to be converted to the values of Communist China.

Li was devoted to his work and with so few alternative interests; he was always on the lookout for possibilities amongst the crowds of visitors to Shanghai. He wasn't surprised to conclude that this was not to be his day. An unending stream of passengers filed off the Oriana, most to board tourist buses for a tour around the city. He was turning away from his vantage point and lowering his cheap binoculars when he noticed the smaller gangway from the bowels of the ship. That would be for the crew but it was unlikely that there would be interest amongst a crowd of pursers and packet rats. At that very moment, however, he spotted two men and his attention was so immediately drawn to them that he raised the binoculars again for a closer look.

Just possibly, Li thought to himself. He left his watching post and beetled along the quay to perch on a bollard with an uninterrupted view of those emerging from the crew gate. His targets didn't take long to appear and he moved immediately to join them as they stood at the side of the tramway which passed along the quay. They were standing relaxed and confident, Li noted, just taking in the sights as they discussed where to go.

Li was familiar with the English language. He was largely self-taught but he had been working in it for over thirty years since his first days of analysing American statistical papers. Reading was one thing, however and speaking quite another. Li's command of grammar was doubtful and his accent made him sound like a drunk with a lisp but after three attempts he managed to make himself understood and was quite surprised by how readily they accepted his offer of a drink to welcome them to his home city.

In the warmth of a nearby bar, Li nursed an orange juice whilst his guests tackled their Shanghai beers. Studying them across the table, Li could see that they were around thirty years old but the big guy with the brooding look and the heavy muscles was not in charge. It was his partner who spoke for both of them and was willing to open up with candid comments in broken English.

Li was happily unaware that he was already being viewed as a possible answer to a problem which was becoming ever more pressing. The Twins had been roaming the world for almost five years since their flight from Marseilles. They had tried more bar and bouncer work in Hamburg before moving on to Liege for a few months and then to Antwerp. In each location, their past combined with Tetrarch's mercurial temper had obliged them to make urgent exits but thereafter came an interlude of relative peace. They signed on as crew members on various cruise ships with Tomas progressing steadily as a Purser's assistant while Tetrarch laboured at manual work. They were reasonably paid, securely housed and always on the move so that when Tetrarch lost control and ended up in some bruising fight, it would be in Manila or Suva or Fremantle and their ship would be sailing the following day to remove them from the risk of pursuit.

But Tomas was growing sick of this itinerant life. Also, they had been riding their luck for too long for it to last. They needed to find something more permanent and an environment in which Tetrarch could settle down and grow a bit of calm under his skin. Tomas also was frustrated. Life couldn't be just about balancing bar bills and arranging shore expeditions. It would be worth listening to this funny little man, understanding what he had to offer and taking a long, hard look at China. Perhaps there was something here for them.

They spent a long time in the bar that day and even more the following morning. Conversation – all of it between Tomas and Li while Tetrarch glowered into his beer – took a long time as they battled with language and how life worked in this totally strange environment but at the end of it, Tomas was persuaded which meant that Tetrarch was as well.

The Oriana left to conclude her final voyage without two crew members who had jumped ship: nothing unusual in that.

12. SIMON AND HANNAH — 1989

June, and some decent weather at last.

Simon had found them a place just outside Padstow, the doorway to North Cornwall. 'The Moorings' was really a tarted up B&B advertised as a boutique hotel, but to be fair, Hannah thought as she helped herself to the breakfast buffet, Si had done pretty well to find anything given the time of year and the very short notice.

He had phoned her midweek, catching her at her desk in the overcrowded Foreign Office building south of the River. She had just escaped from another interminable team brief and was settling down to a long stint of dreary research. That was the way of it when you had recently joined the Service: it seemed that you were being tested as much for allegiance and patience as for brain power and initiative.

'How would you fancy a weekend in the Cornish sun,' he had invited without preamble and she had jumped at the idea. She managed to get away early enough for a late afternoon train from Paddington and Simon met her at Bodmin. From there, it had been a simple drive to Padstow but without much chance of conversation due to the blaring noise of road and engine in the cabin of the classic old Aston Martin DB2 of which Si was inordinately proud.

They stopped in the pretty fishing port to eat fish and chips whilst leaning against the harbour wall and arrived at their accommodation just before 9pm, an hour at which the proprietor was about to start letting their reservation to another customer.

The room was quite small with a particularly pokey bathroom but it was clean enough and there was a bit of a view over neighbouring fields. They had brought a back pack each, so it took only a few minutes to settle in. Simon had squeezed a bottle of fairly rough red into his and they grabbed the plastic glasses from the basin and went out for a stroll and a look round before bed.

This sort of activity was so typical of the couple, the sort of behaviour which had astonished their friends during their time at Bristol. They were together, an item, and then again they weren't: interdependent but also available. Huge mates, that was for sure but sometimes caught up with each other in a bout of white hot passion, other times content to let the space grow between them. As Simon's flatmate Harry had put it, they were like the M5 motorway in summer: you never could tell how long the fast lane progress would last! Not that any of this mattered to Simon and Hannah. Other people might struggle to understand their relationship, but it worked for them.

It had started four years previously. Almost as soon as the Bristol undergraduates had assembled after Christmas, they began to put down the roots of a relationship which would last a lifetime. A chance meeting in the street had led to a bistro lunch the first weekend of term. The conversation covered some predictably safe ground - family news, aspirations for the year of study, plans for holidays to come. Simon had just enough experience of the workings of Bristol to give her some useful pointers and he suggested that Hannah should give some thought to where she would like to live in the city come her second year. She was doubtful.

'Bit soon to start planning, isn't it? I mean that's eight months away.'

'Even so,' he replied with his mouthful of burger and chips, 'it's amazing how quickly the time goes and the best places for rent get booked up so early. More important is who you may want to share with. You can't start to think too soon about that one.'

'Are you getting ready to proposition me?'

She had paused with her glass midway to her mouth and banged it back on the table. Simon was amazed by the touchiness of this girl. Where did all the attack come from?

'No, no of course I'm not doing any such thing,' he expostulated, sitting back and spreading his hands wide. 'I'm just saying think ahead while you've got time on your side. I didn't and I was bloody lucky that it came together with Harry at the last minute. Anyway, I wouldn't want to live with girls. They're a distraction and take up too much space in the bathroom.'

He was relieved to see her smile.

'I'm sorry, Si. I've always been a bit direct. You'll just have to get used to it.'

Simon didn't make a reply but just concentrated on clearing his plate, interspersed with tipping his bottle of lager between his lips, using a few moments to make another appraisal of this girl whom he felt instinctively would remain a bit of a mystery to him however well he came to know her. He had to admit that no girl would look her best having just finished a game of tennis and dropped into Boots which was where he bumped into her as she was on her way home. Hannah was a tall girl, standing just a couple of inches less than his own six foot height and she looked spectacular even in a track suit which could do little to enhance her flawless figure. He remembered how she looked with fewer clothes on but put the memory out of his mind.

He pushed aside his empty plate, determined to get on a new track but only to hear himself ask how she was getting on with Roly Patrick, the trendy and popular academic who tutored both of them in different groups.

'Pretty good', she responded, 'but I'm making sure I only see him in company. Once was enough for the carnal bit. Still, I'm sort of glad you asked. You were watching, weren't you?'

'I was *not* watching,' Simon protested, 'I was just dropping in a Christmas present and without any clue about what was going to greet me.' Even before he had completed his riposte, Simon knew he'd been conned. With minimum effort she had caused him to give away a secret which he could have guarded for ever. 'How did you know anyway?' he finished lamely.

'Sixth sense and intuition,' Hannah replied and bestowed a

flash of that smile on him. 'I knew someone was there and then I found the card as I was leaving.'

'Honestly, Hannah, you are really something else. Not content with embarrassing me, you're now laughing at me! I can't keep up.' He sat back in his chair, all prepared to sulk.

'I'm sorry, Si, but I did warn you about being direct. Look, if it's of any comfort, I don't often feel that I'm with a friend I can trust. Never before actually so there you are, you're in a very special position and you might like to know that I've told my own mother about that little escapade and would you believe she quite approved. So … let's put the whole thing behind us. And I can tell you that Mum asked after you. She'd like to meet you again.'

So there it was. This casual, unarranged lunchtime snack came to be the starting point for an unusual relationship. It was always Hannah who led the way and Simon who had to catch up. Throughout their remaining time as students until he graduated in the summer of 1987, they were often together, usually in a group of their contemporaries, sometimes just the two of them. On a number of occasions they stayed with Simon's adopted family in London as Dulwich was cheap, comfortable and convenient if there was a concert to attend or a gallery to visit. Less frequent had been the excursions to the Herefordshire countryside for a weekend with Vanda and all of these had been successful occasions. She and Simon got along very well with banter and a teasing which became a constant.

Simon and Hannah became very good friends and occasional lovers but there was nothing binding between them, no boy/girlfriend language, no expectation asked or offered. In the long summer vacation of 1986, Hannah went off to the States for a couple of weeks at the invitation of an exchange student called Alvin and his family who lived in the Colorado backwoods. When she returned to Bristol, they got together for a pub evening and a good catch up. Hannah summarised her American venture with normal candour.

'They were nice people, Si, and showed me all the sights.

I had a terrific holiday but poor Alvin turned out to be a disappointment. I mean the sex was great for a while but honestly, he became a bit of a bore.'

Being a man with his share of male pride, Simon was not ecstatic with this frank announcement but it was so typical of Hannah that he knew he had to accept her as she was or call a final halt to their relationship. That he could not do. She was his sounding board and advisor, as well as his part time lover. She was also his closest friend by a country mile: a drug for his contented existence which he could not go without.

It was that basis of mutual regard and understanding which continued when he rang that day in the summer to suggest a weekend in Cornwall. It was second nature for both of them to polish off the bottle of wine as they strolled around the lanes close to their B&B, updating each other on latest but insignificant news, before going in to their small room with its lumpy double bed, undressing and climbing into it naked but undemanding and uncaring. They slept immediately. Tomorrow would be another day.

After breakfast, they took the Aston which growled along the lanes to Constantine Bay, where they were lucky to find a parking spot outside the stores, in which they bought sandwiches, fruit and a couple of soft drinks before walking down the lane to the beach. It was familiar ground to them both. They luxuriated in a walk along the length of the sand, watching the surfers and smiling at the antics of the children, delighting in their games whilst their parents sprawled on the beach.

They climbed over the rocks and picked their way along the path above Booby's Bay, nodding a greeting to the lifeguards who were relaxed beside their look out post. They went on to tackle the track which rose progressively steeply to circumnavigate the headland and Simon, fit and tested from his military training, was impressed with the easy manner in which Hannah kept pace with him, her long legs flowing over the ground.

They reached the highest point of their walk and by unspoken agreement flopped down onto the springy grass, Simon pulling their drinks and sandwiches from the bag he had been carrying. The sun was bright and getting on for overhead, the breeze mild even in this exposed position, the panoramic view spectacular. It didn't get better than this for Cornish coast lovers.

Simon went first, giving her a precis of his life since they had last met which had been in London around Christmas. He was now better than half way through his Royal Marine induction training and yes, it was very tough indeed, yes it was at the same time pretty satisfying and no, he had no regrets about signing up for a career to which he had committed himself before starting at university. He had had a similar conversation with his old mate Harry Bonsor only a few weeks back and Hannah's few questions now reminded him of the Harry approach. Neither of them had the slightest empathy with his career choice and Hannah in particular shuddered at the thought of a regime which permitted you no freedom of decision and precious little time to yourself.

Si knew enough to move on without reopening the debate but as ever, he reflected to himself that there could never be much future for him with this girl while he pursued what she insisted on calling his 'action man' lifestyle. But that wasn't going to spoil this weekend and anyway he wanted to ask her about his adopted mother Caroline, known to all as Caro, about whom he was having a few worries.

'What sort of worries', Hannah asked.

'Well, she's getting very vague about things, very forgetful. It's so unlike Caro who's normally a byword for efficiency, running the household, multitasking, all those good things. I haven't been home for a few months of course but just on the phone she's seemed distant and, well not always quite with it.'

'So how are things with Benny? What's he saying about all this?'

Simon chewed away for a minute or so before replying. 'It's always such a job to know with Benny and especially if you can't talk face to face with him. He's a lovely guy but he's always in another place. You know what I mean. He's so dependent on Caro running the show that he wouldn't know if she wasn't.'

Benny was a graphic designer, a gifted and creative man with his free time given over to his ability as a musician and as a leading light in a local amateur dramatic group. Hannah had come to know them both well, also to appreciate the care and concern which Simon felt for the couple - his aunt and uncle - who had taken him into their family after his parents had died in that plane crash so many years ago.

'What about the kids?' she asked.

'Well they're not that any longer. None of them is living at home now and I haven't spoken to them since I noticed this problem with their mother.'

'Look Si,' Hannah spoke to him in her normal, direct style, 'take a grip and get on the phone. It's neither fair nor helpful to keep this worry to yourself. Just get on with it and share the concern. That's the least you can do and it would anyway make for a good start.'

'I guess you're right', he replied but still sounding doubtful and before he could go on, Hannah added an offer.

'If you like, I can give a ring and shoot round there one evening. Then let you know what I find. Would that help?'

'You know it would. That would be brilliant and in return, I'll love you forever.'

'You'll be doing that anyway so don't overdo the drama. But one more thing, how old would Caro be now? Between forty-five and fifty? That sort of number?'

'Yup. Forty-nine next birthday, I reckon.'

'Well then. It could be she's just going through the change. That can have all sorts of effects and some pretty dire. I'll have a natter and see what I can find out. Happy?'

'A lot more so, thank you. And now, tell me what's going on for you. How is our next Foreign Office mandarin shaping up?'

Hannah finished her can of soft drink and stretched out on the grass, her head propped on one arm as she commenced her reply.

'I just don't know, Si, just really don't know but I can say that I've been looking forward to talking to you about the whole thing – and the latest offer.'

Simon was instantly alert, putting down the remains of his sandwich, crossing his legs as he sat bolt upright and looking as far into her eyes as those ever protective glasses would permit.

'Tell me', he ordered.

'Well, look. You don't need me to go over the dates but just to set the scene. I graduated in the summer of last year, July some time and …'

'You walked off with your First in Languages', Simon broke in to interrupt, 'almost the only student to manage it in French and Spanish.'

'OK Si, I don't need an ad campaign', but she smiled at him nonetheless.

'Maybe you don't, but it was some achievement. Anyway, sorry for breaking the flow. I'll keep quiet now, I promise!'

'Please do. So there I am. A great qualification and the world's my oyster. I could have taken some time out, maybe even a year or more but the big recruiting battalions come calling and I admit I was flattered by all the attention. So I guess I keeled over really and went for the best offer and that's the FO with the promise of fast stream entry, endless interest and lots of opportunity for advancement. Hey, I can make Brit Ambassador to Paris inside a year!'

Hannah laughed at herself as she foraged in her bag for a packet of cigarettes and her lighter. She lit up under Simon's disapproving glance but he kept his promise and his silence. She went on.

'So now it's coming up for twelve months since I started and I'm just bored to death with it all. Frustrated too as there seems to be so much interesting stuff which you're not allowed near as a new kid on the block. All I've had so far is endless training courses, three office moves, vague talk about where I may be in another few years and this from smooth talking middle rankers who aren't interested in my career but do want to get into my knickers. I know I'm pushy but really, Si, it just makes me want to scream. I just have to get out.'

Simon, so similar in ambition but so different in character, so content to accept the conventions and battle his way through them, was horrified to hear her talk this way and raised his hand, determined to have his say, but she wouldn't let him.

'Just hold on. There's more to come and then you can make your contribution. I do want your advice, Si. I will really value it because you and I approach these things so differently which makes you my devil's advocate and that's just what I need. But not quite yet as you haven't heard all the possibilities.'

He slumped back, accepting the inevitable, already worried about what she was going to tell him. 'Go on, then,' he said.

'Do you understand what I mean when I say that there are some things which you just know? There's no logic to argue, you've got no evidence and you can't prove it. But somehow none of that seems to matter. You just know and you don't need anyone to corroborate or agree.'

Simon just nodded at her. Actually, this was the most alien thought possible for him. He really didn't do gut instinct but was driven by the remorseless build up to a decision which would involve research, planning and debate. He realised with a shock that the nearest he came to simply winging it was in his commitment to this girl who was now lecturing him, and not for the first time.

'Keep going', he said.

'When you join up, one of the first things that happens is that you're allocated a mentor for your first year. It's a pretty good idea actually, a bit like having a tutor - but in my case anyway someone who will not have any extracurricular duties.' She grinned mischievously at him before continuing.

'My guardian, as he likes to refer to himself, is a lovely old guy who must be approaching retirement age. Bags of experience, originally a Soviet specialist although obviously all that's gone now and he's knocked around a fair bit in South East Asia also. Anyway, the point is that he called me in a couple of weeks ago to give me a pep talk as well as to read the riot act. Apparently, too many of the line managers I've been working for during my first year's induction have complained that I'm too outspoken, won't wait to learn, won't toe the line. You can imagine!'

Simon simply nodded and waited for her to continue.

'So when Rex waded into me - sorry, he's called Rex Trotter – as he started I thought Oh Shit, here we go. I'm going to be fired or at the least put back to do it all again and I'm not at all sure that I can bear that.

But then, all change. Rex finishes up by saying that he and colleagues have completed a review and they want me to consider a transfer to a new position with another organisation. And that's the Intelligence Service - SIS. So I have to tell him next week if I'm game to start training as a spy! What d'you think of that Si?!!

Simon put his hands around his knees and sat there, rocking himself to and fro while he looked at her. He knew there had been something coming when Hannah had started in with her little homily of 'some things which you just *know*'.

What she knew in this case was that she was going to go for this chance, there was nothing he could say which would stop her. It wasn't at all what he'd been expecting but he was pleased to find himself instinctively positive.

'Wow', he said, 'quite a development, even though I've not much idea what it will mean for you. But hey, you're very bright, you're articulate and you take no prisoners. I guess that's a good start for anyone involved in safeguarding national security. So I say congratulations, Hannah, and definitely go for it'.

'You really think so?'

'I really do. It's not so often that I react to instinct, but in this case, that's it. Plus, now you've told me, I suppose you'll have to kill me!'

'Perhaps a bit later. For right now, I've got another idea. Because it's a beautiful day in a favourite place and there's no one in sight, would you please come here!

She lay back and pillowed her head on one arm as she beckoned to him with the other. Simon needed no second bidding.

13. TOMAS AND TETRARCH — 1990

Their first year in China had been spent within a few kilometres of the quayside where their ship had berthed. Li arranged their lodging in a small house just down the street from his own. He came to spend time with them every day, chipping away gently to understand their provenance, all that had happened to them in their childhood, where, when and why they had wandered during their years of adolescence. Especially, he wanted to establish how much they knew about Africa and he was quietly pleased to discover that they were natives of the Mahgreb.

All of this took time and patience and it was a process further extended by Li's carefully composed programme of education and entertainment. He took them on many trips around his home city, showing them the sights, labouring his way through accounts of the history and making sure that he included bars and brothels from time to time, especially for the benefit of Tetrarch whose attention span for matters of culture and history was limited.

Twelve months after their arrival, it was time for the Twins to move onto the major stage of their tuition. It took the three of them a couple of days to travel by train from Shanghai to Yumen City, there to enter the State Educational Centre for Foreigners which is such an obscure establishment that no mention of it is made in official records and there is not even a sign on the door to announce its presence. Yumen is a bleak city set in a harsh landscape and punished by extremes of weather and temperature. It is a place which is little known and less understood, a location in which foreigners stand out like sore thumbs so that the Centre is for them something of a prison without walls. If it takes determination to reach Yumen, it takes much more, plus a fair slice of luck, to leave again.

As in Shanghai, Li took great trouble to acclimatize them. He made careful introductions to the permanent staff who ran the Centre and to the host of visiting professors. The tuition was interspersed with some fieldwork which included drives around the city and outlying region, learning more of Yumen and its environs which are populated by a peasantry driving itself through a tough and repetitive existence.

Living conditions within the Centre were tolerable. They were warm, fed and accommodated, their individual preferences respected as far as possible. Then there were their fellow inmates. Over time, Tomas came to reckon on a total of about thirty but it was a constantly changing number as people arrived and departed on outside training or assignment. They included men and women of different colour, age and nationality including a surprising number of Scandinavians. In spying parlance, the Centre was training 'sleepers', foreign born recruits who could in time be converted to the Party philosophy before returning to the communities of their birth to work for the benefit of their adopted motherland. Li was acting as a missionary but was training souls for the worship of a State rather than an imagined deity.

Li stayed with them for three months before he returned home to Shanghai, promising that he would be back to see them before the end of the year. It was then mid-July and Yumen was sweltering in summer heat. Tomas and Tetrarch found this preferable to the extreme cold of winter but by now, they were absorbed in their education.

For Tetrarch, the concentration was on matters physical as his instructors worked to increase his bulk and fitness, simultaneously introducing him to the wonders of weaponry with which he had no previous experience: a whole range of handguns and sniping rifles, an arsenal of explosives, a library of timing devices. He trained with throwing knives, sword sticks, fighting staves which betrayed both Chinese and Japanese origin and then there were the unarmed martial arts in which he came to excel, a bewildering menu of skills which shared the common objectives to disarm, to debilitate and to kill.

The path of progress for Tomas was less spectacular but highly varied, including economics, international politics and philosophy: there was intense language tuition so that Tomas could master standard Mandarin as well as having some understanding of the dialects. There was classic Arabic and French to be maintained plus improvement in English as the international language.

They were fully occupied as the summer months drew out and cold weather returned to take Yumen into its icy grip. With winter came Li, according to his promise, and he stayed with them until the following March, observing, advising and cajoling. Before he returned to Shanghai, he spent a day briefing them. He said that the Party saw them as an inseparable team and all the more valuable for it. It was acknowledged that their progress so far had been very satisfactory. There was more to do, of course, and they were to remain at the Centre until the end of the year when Li would come back with the brief for their first assignment. He would not say more except that it would be in Africa.

Diversions and entertainment were rare at the Centre, nevertheless the Director was conscious that life could not be all about work and there had to be opportunity to let off a little steam from time to time. Tetrarch was easily satisfied. He needed a drinking session once a week and some energetic sex on a less frequent basis. The boozing was straightforward. Often they would bring in bottles on a Monday night and there would be an impromptu party in the corner of the communal dining hall. Occasionally, they would go out in a group to one of the few bars which were within walking distance of the Centre.

There was a brothel which Tetrarch liked to visit every couple of months. It was a cheerless, depressing place, the most basic knocking shop at the back of a bar which offered for rent a motley collection of hardened women, well past their best and most of them the worse for drink or drugs. The majority were not Chinese either, many having found their way over the border from Mongolia. These were particular harridans, their naturally heavy features further debauched by their lifestyle. They were big women also, with sagging breasts and vast, spreading thighs. It was to this style of the female form that Tetrarch was particularly attracted and he would go at it like a fighting bull, spurning any form of finesse and most often causing some damage to his partner for which the Centre paid up without demur.

Tomas was not immune to some female company from time to time. Given the productivity of such a prime student, the Director was content to turn a blind eye to the succession of slinky, stylish Russian born girls who would slip into Tomas's room for a few hours, some of them for a night.

The Twins survived another broiling summer without difficulty and they were back into sub-zero temperatures before Li arrived again. He was unusually animated, very happy to receive the Director's report on their persistent diligence. After a day or so, he sat down with them. As usual, Tetrarch was motionless and silent, his mighty muscled arms folded across his chest with a bland expression on his face.

'You will be leaving here with me this time', Li said without preamble, 'you have accomplished all you can here at the Centre: both of you. We'll travel back to Shanghai, leaving here at the beginning of February. You'll be in a different house there but just around the corner from me again.'

Tomas nodded.

'Now', announced Li, 'you'll be going to the Republic of Mali and to a city there called Segou. I only know it from the map and I don't believe you've been there either but there will be plenty of time for research and preparation before you depart.'

He paused and Tomas took the opportunity to interject.

'Whatever this is, it sounds like a change of strategy. You're right that we don't know Mali but anyway, Segou is just a provincial city and not a power base. How can it be of interest to the Party?'

Tetrarch gave a grunt of approval and Li moved swiftly to continue.

'Yes, there is a change. Change is everywhere these days. The man in the street wants to have fewer rules and less allegiance to the Party.'

Tomas was amazed to hear Li speak like this. He was a stickler for etiquette and a completely committed Party man but here he was sounding casual. Li continued.

'I expect you have seen some demonstrations here in Yumen. They have been happening everywhere and the most serious occurred in Beijing last June with the occupation of Tiananmen Square. We are moving forward again now, but damage was done to our standing in the international community and it is that which brought about a shift in our strategy. Now, the priority is to provide development aid for suitable projects and places. This approach is the best way to advance our influence in poor countries which have the assets we wish to exploit. It's commercial, you see, rather than overtly political.

I expected you two to be sent to Morocco, perhaps even into Western Sahara to put some backbone into that Polisario movement. But now, it's Mali and the fledgling textile business. The Party is starting to assemble a team of experienced people in that field – agronomists, engineers, architects and building contractors – but they're going to need looking after for both politics and security. That's where you two will come in.'

Li was looking uncomfortable as he spoke, picking at his fingernails and avoiding direct eye contact. Tomas recognised the signs and decided to make no response for the present. There was therefore a lingering silence and it seemed to Li that both Twins were brooding. He continued.

'Let me give you some more detail and we will talk it all through together. It will take some time but there is no reason for us to be disturbed.'

They spent almost a week on the task and the concerns for Tomas mounted with every passing hour and with each piece of obscure information. It was plain to see how recent developments within China had come to impact on their personal prospects but what about the influences from outside the borders of the Peoples' Republic? At the Centre, inmates had access to foreign media and were encouraged to make full use of it. Tomas had been keeping track of events in Russia and her provinces: it seemed crystal clear that the Soviet Union was on a course for implosion and it was noticeable that an increasing number of students had been arriving from the Asian and Baltic republics. It seemed a fair bet that the top dogs in Beijing were now shifting their sights eastward, gauging the opportunities which must flow from this cataclysmic change in world order and content to consign Africa to a backwater for the time being.

Who was to know what would happen next? That would become clear for the Twins but not before their return to Shanghai.

14. PENTE BROKE SMITH — 1992

King Offenbach was not happy as he adjusted his step to keep level with his old friend while they walked across the garden, heading for a group of chairs which stood waiting for them under the shade of a spreading jacaranda tree.

King had spent the previous week in Nairobi and should by now be in the air on his way to the States for a routine CIA Heads of Station meeting in Washington but with a weekend intervening, he had hopped a flight down to Dar es Salaam to spend a couple of days here before crossing the Pond on Sunday night.

Pente Broke Smith collapsed his great bulk into the nearest chair and forced a smile.

'Sorry you've found me so clapped out, King, but it's very good to see you and thanks again for making the effort. I'm glad you're staying here. The room's OK, I hope? Not five star luxury but comfortable enough?'

'The room's fine, Pente, and I've had a warm welcome from your people here. So I'm well set and all ready for a bit of your news. And this is a swell spot to sit and chew a bit of fat. So shoot.'

The two men were sitting in the extensive grounds of the monastery which was the base for the Order of Saints in Tanzania. Pente nodded briefly as he gazed about him.

'You're quite right, King. It is indeed a beautiful spot this – and so quiet too. Here we are right in the middle of a humming, noisy city and yet this could be, well it could be the Garden of Eden! I have to say it's a marvellous place to be making a recovery and I'll be right as rain by the end of next week. I know my own constitution well enough by now and I've had a fair few doses of malaria in my time. You can't avoid it, not going to some of the places I've lived in!'

He gave a familiar guffaw of laughter as he shifted in his seat to rummage in his robes for a battered old silver box which King knew would contain the vile smelling short cigars to which the big priest was happily addicted. Pente saw King's glance of disapproval so chuckled some more as he continued speaking.

'Now don't start on me, King. Even a man of God is allowed one vice!'

King was disinclined to pursue a debate on the subject, knowing that he would make no progress. Instead, he posed a series of testing questions, some of which were deliberately provocative and he was rewarded when Pente expostulated.

'Oh for heaven's sake King, stop making out that I've got one foot in the grave. I know you're just trying to tempt me into ill temper and rash statements and you will quite probably succeed as you normally do! But look, really, I'm only just over fifty – which makes me about five years your junior I might remind you – and there's plenty of Pente left. God knows, I'm committed to this country and to its people. I'm not giving up until I'm carried out or no use to anyone anymore.'

Pente grumbled away into his shaggy beard but his eyes were twinkling. It was true. He would always rise to the bait of controversial argument and it was just as true that he enjoyed the needling which he had been receiving from this old friend from the days when they had been studying together at Oxford.

King was not quite finished yet. 'You're sure as hell right that I'm an even older sweat than you but the difference is that I can get myself a whole lot more molly coddling than you can. Sure, I'm still knocking around some pretty dire spots throughout Africa but I'm travelling in comfort and these days I have the help of a team of bright young sparks who are happy to do the grunt work. That's the difference, right?'

'I can't argue with that. As soon as I'm fit, I'll be back on the road to Arusha or Singida or wherever, but always in some rattling old pick-up with the heat blazing and the dust blowing. Then there's the dodgy food and water, of course, and before you know it, I collect another dose of something, most likely malaria which likes to strike where it's been before. On the plus side, though, I'm blessed with the certain knowledge that I'm doing some good. The Order of Saints is recognised for what it achieves in this country and I'm sustained by that: proud of it too.'

'As you should be. It's a brave record, Pente, and you'd be right to rejoice in it. For me, of course, it's not the same. Hell, I can look back on some high points of accomplishment but victories over the bad boys of drug and people smuggling don't make for any sort of public triumph. And then there's the internal politics. There's so much personal career ambition in the CIA these days that sometimes you feel like you're fighting the home team as much as the opposition.'

'Well my old chum,' said Pente as he rasped his old lighter against his half smoked cigar,'it was ever thus: perseverance has to be the name of our game, but to change to a happier subject, I've got a bit of a surprise for you this evening. And speak of the devil, here it comes!'

King swung round in his chair, looking back over his shoulder to follow the line of Pente's sight and then started to his feet, his hand already stretching out in welcome.

'Son of a gun!' he called, 'here's a happy appearance. What the hell are you doing here?'

The towering bulk of Hank Devine came across the lawn from the entrance to the garden, crinkled eyes in the weather beaten face and broad grin displaying his pleasure at being amongst friends. He gripped King's hand and tapped Pente's shoulder in greeting before dropping into a vacant chair and announcing in his Canadian drawl,

'Just checking up on you, King, you old renegade. Pente knew I was coming in tonight but I guess he kept that from you in case you took off at the prospect!'

The three men settled themselves and Pente signalled to a passing monk to bring another glass and a bottle of mineral water. He reached under his chair for the dimple bottle of Haig which he kept tactfully out of sight. This was indeed a happy coincidence, Pente thought to himself as he listened to his guests share some recent news interspersed with their normal, relaxed banter.

It was twenty-five years since Pente had met Hank who had heard about him from King, then tracked him to his modest lodgings in Antananarivo, capital of Madagascar where Pente was then stationed. Hank was after some introductions, especially to government people, to help him in his quest to do a little prospecting for precious metals in the south of what is the world's second largest island. Nothing much had come of this except that Pente and Hank had got to know and like each other. During the intervening years, Hank had dropped by to see Pente wherever he was living at the time and he had maintained contact also with King Offenbach so that the relationship which had started in the scruffy bar in Pointe Noire had blossomed.

It was a rare occasion for the three of them to be in one place at one time and they made the most of it. They drank and talked, went inside for a simple meal and then returned to the garden for more talk to finish off the evening. The Canadian smoked his hand rolled cigarettes to accompany his coffee and whisky while Pente puffed on his cheroots: between them, they kept the mosquitoes at bay.

These three men were of similar age and disposition and for all that they followed very different callings in life, they had the love of Africa to give them common cause. Their personal histories had started in just post-colonial times and it was experience rather than bias which made them despair of the graft and incompetence which had bedevilled the development of so many newly emergent states. But to set against this was the inspiring resilience and extraordinary cheerfulness of the peoples they encountered. Perhaps you needed also a fair helping of optimism, they agreed as they sat in the peace of that garden, but it was true that green shoots of progress could be seen appearing and the time for Africa to realise her potential must finally be approaching.

After the colonising Europeans, the USA and the Soviets had been influential, 'But now,' said Hank as he took a pull at his whisky glass and rolled another cigarette, 'now I reckon it's the Chinks making most of the running.'

King looked at him with interest. 'I'm not seeing so much of the Chinese. Not like I used to. What's your story?'

Hank Devine blew a trail of smoke and gave a great yawn before reaching for his glass as he replied.

'Aw hell, it may be just a straw in the wind but I had an interesting experience about three months back. I was up in Mali which I don't know so well and I guess that was a good part of the attraction of taking the job. It started with meeting some guy in a bar: when doesn't it? I was in Luanda which is pretty much home base for me and got talking to this dude who calls himself Abe Porteous. He hails from Enid, Oklahoma which sounds like just the place you'd want to escape from. Now lives in Tulsa which I guess is why his outfit is called Tulsa Oil. Abe would be pushing sixty, short, round and none too fit but fair company. He's one of three partners in this little outfit that's done reasonable business in cleaning up small wells, mostly in Texas, which weren't interesting to the big boys. He's getting towards retirement, fancies a change, has never been to Africa so he comes over to see some asshole buddy from his schooldays who's spent a working lifetime operating rigs offshore in Angolan waters. And this guy talks him into parting with some dollars to have a stake in a brand new venture which has bought the rights to have a look see at the country in the north east of Mali, up beyond Gao and heading for the border with Algeria. It sounded a pretty damn doubtful prospect to me but I could see that it's on the fringe of the Taoudenni basin where they've brought in a couple of wells so I guess that was the excuse for my friend Abe to blow some savings in return for grabbing himself a bit of frontier spirit. He's all set to go and have himself a look but then fate intervenes. He gets sick in Luanda, goes to a smart expat medico and hears that his diabetes has taken a turn for the worse and he's likely to be in real trouble if he high tails it into bandit country where the nearest doctor would likely be on the moon. By then, Abe has hired a couple of guys with some technical qualifications but not much savvy for operating in Africa. Abe is wondering what the hell to do next when he finds himself drinking with a Canadian rough diamond who knows a bit about oil and a lot about the bush. The guy's ecstatic.'

Hank grinned at them as he continued.

'After three martinis, I know I'm going to sign up, ride herd on Abe's rookies and head off north into parts I haven't seen for maybe ten years.

'The trip to Mali was simple enough though it took time, what with all the plane changing and goddam visas. It was three weeks before we were ready to drive out of Bamako in an old Land Rover. My ass was good and sore before we made it to Mopti, our first stop. But if you ever get the chance to go there guys, just do it. It's a good sized town and with what passes as a cathedral and every last building and turret is made of sun dried mud. I tell you it all makes a sight worth seeing.

'Anyway, we camped just north of town and next day, another helluva long drive, with the three of us cramped up front and a load full of gear behind but the road wasn't so bad and we made it to Gao. That's a dozy little spot but we could buy more fuel there and while we were getting water at a convenience store, we met a little guy who said we could sleep the night on the roof of his house, a hovel of mud hut but comfortable enough sleeping under those Sahara stars. I figured we'd have another three days to go but the going got worse. Country was more broken, way more sand and dunes, harder to see the track and the maps I had not worth a dime. It's gone midday and like a cauldron in the cab. I'm thinking it's some sort of mirage when we spot a herd of shacks on the horizon up ahead, then I figure it must be a place called Bourem in which case we're a bit West of where we should be but I'm taken up with the driving as we're in some pretty deep sand and then wham! We get on a mite of rocky incline, pick up some traction, over this rise in the ground and there's another vehicle! But it ain't going places, with its front axle down and a couple of guys grovelling around beside it. I stopped of course: gotta help each other in this sort of country.

'My guys pile out of our truck and we walk over to see what

gives. The fellows digging at the front hardly look up from work and it seems they're locals: loose fitting robes, the right headgear.

'It was an Isuzu. A short chassis station wagon and an OK vehicle but anything can catch a blowout. They've got a couple of spare wheels hanging on the back but it turns out their problem is with the jack, just a pissy little thing which won't give enough lift. I get this from a big surprise 'cos she's a woman! She's a Malian lady who looks government, dressed in a tropical suit with badges of rank. The suit's getting grubby as she's rummaging in the back of the truck, looking for any tool which might help. She seems in a powerful hurry, chattering away at me in fast French over her shoulder. It's then I notice there's another guy, sitting in the rear seat like he's expecting restaurant service. He's a Chinaman and self-important with it, tricked out in a Mao suit and looking inscrutable while he waits for his minions to deliver.

'I tap the broad on the shoulder and get her to slow down long enough to explain to me what the hell's going on here. The gal tells me she's from the Ministry of Interior, escorting the important guy from Beijing who's got a brief and a pile of money with him to give a helping hand to the Tuareg which is what took him to some pow wow in Tombouctou. Yup, fellas, Timbucktu really does exist and it's a fair way west of where we were right then so these folks had already come a few hundred miles in bad bush country. It seems the big meeting had finished awkwardly with another group trying to get in on the act and they reckoned this mob was on their tail so she was pretty damned anxious to get Mr China safe back in Bamako.'

Hank took another huge gulp of whisky and lit up the latest cigarette which he had been rolling while he spoke. Then he stretched out his legs and resumed his story.

'The first part was easy. I took my guys round to the front and did a bit of sign language. Of the two working there, one was stocky and looked to have some muscle under his robes. With four of us heaving, it wasn't much of an effort to lift up the front of the vehicle, not even with our friend still sitting inside and while we did this, the second fellow who was lighter weight but agile, he was wrestling on the spare and twirling up the nuts. Hey presto, we were ready to ride. But then I see a cloud of sand and dust coming our way rapido and next thing we have the cavalry arrive ....except it was the injuns!

'It was all a bit confused. Madam Mali was shouting abuse at these newcomers – a gutsy lady that one. There looked to be a couple of dozen of these guys to our seven and they were as mad as hell. They were riding in four pick-ups, most standing in the backs and brandishing rifles, some waving swords, and the drivers circled round our vehicles. We weren't going anywhere without sorting this out, that was for damn sure.

'There was no mistaking what they were after and that was Mr China, still sitting up in his seat but maybe a mite less inscrutable by now. For sure, this was a kidnap and ransom attempt and as for who these guys were or where they had sprung from, well I guess I've no more idea now than I did then. What was mighty clear was that they weren't going to have him without a fight. The girl jumped into the rear seat alongside their asset, meanwhile the light guard drew a weapon and stood at the back of the vehicle. The stocky guy didn't stand anywhere: he just advanced and took the fight to the nomads right from the jump. He picked out a leader, mouthing off from the back of the lead truck and Stocky just moved in and grabbed him, lifting him by the throat with one hand and grabbing the rifle off him with the other. They're mostly light and skinny these desert types but still strong and wiry so I could hardly believe what I was seeing. Stocky runs this guy's head into the truck which lays him out, then he reverses the rifle and uses the butt as flail, mowing down others standing up in the back of the vehicle. To synch in with him, his compadre now comes off point duty and opens fire at the side of truck two, strafing down the side so the guys come off it pretty damn smart and hunker down behind it for some cover. That's the moment when Stocky pulls the pin on a grenade and lobs it into truck three.

'He doesn't hesitate then, just moves straight behind truck two and goes on using the rifle he's stolen as a club to clean up on the fellers shielding there. Jesus, I can still hear the crunching as he laid into them. Then I get distracted as a couple are sneaking around the blind side heading for the back door of the Isuzu and, well you know me King, I quite enjoyed knocking their heads together!

'Suddenly, it's all over! One truck's burning, another down on its chassis, bodies all over and those that can move are piling into the last truck which was the first to arrive and taking off the way they came. I'm still gob smacked by Stocky. I've never seen a fellow fight like that: a real killing machine taking pride and pleasure in his work.'

Hank shook his head in admiration as he continued.

'I can tell you we didn't stand around for long either. My two were mustard keen to get the hell out and poor old Abe would have to wait a while to get his survey done. That and send a small army along with the next geologists.

'I knew the Isuzu would be quicker than our Land Rover back to Gao, especially with less of a load on so I piled straight in the back, shouting at my guys to follow and that way we would keep some sort of convoy. Stocky drove while Madame Mali and I sandwiched China behind. He never moved a muscle and I was able to talk over him to the woman. She wouldn't say much about herself, gave her name as Sohia. Close up, she looked mid-thirties, maybe a little older. She was smart and well-informed, no question. Also, she was boss of this little outfit and the guys up front never said a word the whole journey. Sohia told me this was her third trip to the north east, riding herd on Chinese bigwigs. She explained that Mali was getting serious investment from China for all kinds of structural projects – bridges, roads, factories, all that good stuff. She told me in passing that the she got her minders from Segou where they were looking out for Chinese technicians trying to get a textile plant going. She said the Chinese wanted more control of the north and that meant confrontation with the nomad tribes which roam this region. There's a powerful lot of space, hard country, harsh climate and a fierce load of people who'd be pretty damn testing to bring in line.

'We got into Gao around sunset. I'd been keeping an eye

137

behind me and my guys hung on OK. I reckoned on getting more out of Sohia the next day and we went on back to our friend at the convenience store. But we didn't see the Isuzu again. Either they pulled out early or maybe drove on through the night.'

Hank nursed what little remained of his whisky as he looked from one to the other of his companions.

'That's it, really guys. Nothing more to say but it was an interesting experience and I reckoned you'd both like to hear about it.'

'You're right, Hank, it's a fascinating account and a real eye opener to me,' said Pente as he shifted in his seat and reached for his cigar box. 'It's starts me thinking too. We've had a lot of Chinese money coming in here – and for all manner of projects throughout the country. Do you reckon they're after more than that?'

'No, no,' King broke in, 'no, I spend a whole lot of time on this. There are some spots where they're pushing for real political influence and that's pretty much all in the Sahel so I also have been real interested in what Hank got up to - and as always I surely do admire your talent for survival.' King smiled across at Devine before he continued, 'but for the most part, China is continuing to practice a policy that's maybe fifteen years established now. They're saying to themselves that they have skills, money and people. The last is the problem for them. They've got too many damn people and it's a population outgrowing peasantry, wanting more of a say in things and wanting more out of life than just living. All of this has translated into a sort of commercial colonialism but when the powers that be get the sniff of a chance to muscle into some territory in what you might call an old fashioned way, well, they'll sure as hell try to take it, as Hank witnessed.'

King yawned as he finished and Pente took his point. It was well after midnight now, the garden quiet and the city beyond the walls a little more subdued.

He said as he climbed to his feet, 'Time enough to sort out the world tomorrow. Let's head for bed.'.

15. NATHANIEL HABTUMU — 1993

The establishment of the British High Commission in Nairobi is larger than it first appears as there are a number of single storey buildings located throughout the spreading grounds, all of them accessed via carefully tended gravel paths which lead back to the large reception area in the imposing Commission building.

In the middle of a fine May morning, one of these outskirt offices was hosting a meeting between three people. The first was the Head of Chancery at the BHC, who gave his name as Steve Kingsmill, a bluff, long serving professional diplomat, proud of his Yorkshire origins. Sitting by him was a girl in her late twenties who introduced herself as Kingsmill's assistant although she was in truth an Intelligence officer, out from London. Her name was Hannah Deveridge.

Sitting across a low table, strewn with colourful magazines and a tray of coffee essentials, was their guest. He was Nathaniel Habtumu, aged thirty-eight, born and schooled in Addis Ababa, Ethiopia. A self-made man of means, Habtumu had founded a women's fashion label called Elegance which sold up market, ready-to-wear clothes, designed in Paris and made up in a number of developing countries – India, Bangladesh and also here in Kenya.

Habtumu had a reputation for flamboyance. He was a self-confessed party animal who loved to attract attention, very happy with all the press attention he could get. He was permanently on the move, forever available to publicise the Elegance brand. It was that which brought him to the High Commission that day. He was hopeful of an entrée into the Marks and Spencer chain, believed he would win it using clothes made up in Nairobi and Mombasa, and understood that there was financial assistance available through the UK's trade programme.

Steve and Hannah heard him out. The man was good company, spoke well and made an excellent presentation. He looked the part also. He was highly polished and immaculately turned out in his tailor made tropical suit with a shirt which spoke of Turnbull and Asser and a tie which was certainly Hermes. The whole proposition looked to be the genuine article. Hannah was quite certain that it was not.

The brief which she had brought with her from SIS concluded with a strong suspicion that there was a link between this man and the infamous bomber of the World Trade Centre in New York, just three months earlier on 26th February.

The career of Ramzi Yousef, born in Kuwait under another name, was well documented and there was no doubt in the best minds of the FBI in the States that Yousef had been both architect and perpetrator of the outrage. Over a thousand people had been injured in the explosion which he had set off by parking a rental truck in the underground car park of the North Tower, lighting a ten minute fuse which connected to a urea nitrate bomb of 600 kilograms in the vehicle and then calmly making a run for it. He escaped to Pakistan, from there trumpeting that his objective was to influence the US government to cease giving aid to the state of Israel. Yousef achieved notoriety but nothing like the result which he had planned. The intent had been to demolish both towers, killing tens of thousands but the parking placement of the truck and the fusing method had both been faulty so there were many fewer casualties, although a great deal of damage.

It was established by the FBI's meticulous search that an assistant bomb maker had been involved, an Iraqi called Abdul Rahman Yasin who was now on the run with Special Forces closing in on him. But it didn't stop there. A reliable informant in Damascus told the British that Yousef and Yasin had received technical advice, not all of which they had accepted. The source was well connected and available for contract hire at exorbitant cost given his explosives expertise. His name was Nathaniel Habtumu.

In which case, Hannah thought to herself as she listened to the man proclaiming that he was God's gift to women, why would he risk drawing attention by asking for today's meeting? It must be sheer bravado, laying down the challenge of catch-me-if-you-can which would certainly fit with this character to whom she had been listening for the last forty-five minutes. Alternatively, maybe he had no idea that the connection had been made between him and Yousef. Just possibly, of course, they might have been given bum information and this popinjay was just exactly what he claimed to be. But Hannah had developed quite a feel for this sort of situation and the sense of villainy seeped from his pores. Habtumu needed more investigation, starting with his real name: this one meant 'wealthy' in Ethiopian and she was certain he hadn't started life that way.

As the meeting wound down and Steve Kingsmill was commencing the polite formalities of what might happen next, Hannah busied herself with apparently completing her Minutes of the meeting and behaving as the dutiful junior. She was thinking to herself that this Nathaniel was, whatever else, a womaniser. From behind the screen of her overlarge spectacles, she had been observing him as he undressed her with his eyes and the odd salacious smirk. This implied that, however good the man's brain, he allowed himself to think with his balls and that was a weakness to be exploited.

Later, the three of them were walking the gravel path back to reception, from which point Habtumu would go through the secure procedure for checking out of the High Commission. There was now a good deal to think over and more research to undertake. Hannah was looking forward to it and she would make a start before a dinner date that evening.

Simon Goring was here in Nairobi and they had made a plan. He had got back into town only over the weekend, having spent the previous month somewhere remote up around Lake Turkana. 'Training', he had said darkly when ringing from his hotel on the fringe of the city and she had known better than to ask for more detail. Si was a fully-fledged Royal Marines officer, now serving with the Special Boat Service so it was to be expected that he would be tight lipped and gung ho. She would get more out of him over dinner but he was collecting her before then, direct from the BHC at tea time so they would have time to go into the Nairobi National Park and see what they might see. The Park, open to the south so that animals can come and go as they please, has a surprising wealth of wildlife and midweek it would be pretty free of humanity.

It had been six months since they had been face to face but as always, they picked straight up. There was much to talk over: family, friends, careers. That afternoon, they mixed banter and talk as Simon drove them around the Park tracks in the almost new Land Rover he had been loaned from the barracks. They were ecstatic to come across a pride of lion - mothers with young - and they lingered to watch the cubs playing until the light was fading.

They ate at an Italian restaurant in Karen. The food was good, the peace and the ambience perfect for their mood. Hannah started with news of her mother. She had been touched to find out that he had given up a rare weekend of leave to make a visit to Vanda at Foy.

'My Mum seems much happier in her skin these days', she said, twirling the stem of her wine glass as she spoke, 'I'm still pretty amazed that she's apparently content to keep on with this see-you-sometimes relationship with Victor but it's her choice, of course, and I have to say that it seems to work for both of them.'

'Yup,' replied Simon, 'But that's not new is it.' He chewed on his steak for a minute: it was a bit tough, even if tasty.

'See you sometimes', he repeated her words, 'Like mother, like daughter, then?' Then he changed the subject before she could respond.

'What about Charlotte? Your mother was more taken up with her than anything else.'

'Charley. Well yes, she is really something else and just for starters, I have trouble getting my head round her age. She was always my little sister and now, suddenly, she's twenty-three and setting out on independent life. Well, more than that really. She's been out of Uni for a year and guess where she's about to start work.'

'Go on', said Simon.

'Cheltenham, GCHQ no less. I heard just before I came out here. Of course it'll be all training and indoctrination for a year and more but even so, they snapped her up as soon as she applied. Her Double First from Edinburgh will have helped of course but mostly someone sharp will have seen what always strikes me about Charley. It's an old fashioned word, I know, but Charley's really fey. She's not exactly clairvoyant but she just gets things by instinct rather than labouring through a whole process of logic like the rest of us. And my God, don't try a crossword with her: she'll leave you for dead!'

Hannah was laughing as she finished, but she gave him no time for a reply before she changed tack.

'And tell me what's going on for you, Mr Action Man? How's it all shaping up in your cut throat career? Is it all about death and destruction or do you leave yourself time to shag a few mermaids?' She was leaning forward in her chair as she spoke, her eyes twinkling behind those huge glasses which she knew he found mesmeric, her breasts thrusting forward against the tight, white T shirt which she was wearing beneath an unbuttoned shirt in pale pink.

It wasn't a big challenge for Simon to recognise the provocation which he devoutly hoped was leading somewhere but he was glad for a few moments of interruption as the waitress appeared to check on their progress.

'There have been one or two …. well distractions', he said, 'but mostly it's all about work. A lot of it is lecture and study, some of it violent, much that's repetitive and sometimes there's something completely new and different.'

'Like what?'

'Like I did a jumping course a few months ago, as in parachuting,' he added as he could see the angle of her head frame the question, 'scary but fun. But you know, Hannah, I'm thinking that this is not a permanent way of life for me.'

She sat back, resting her knife and fork against her plate for a moment while she shot him a puzzled look.

'I'm really surprised to hear you say that, Si. I always thought you were born for this; that you'd be a Marine for life or at least until they killed you or chucked you out in your dotage. What's changed for you?'

'Nothing's changed really. I'm having a ball and learning lots, building up an experience which I can market in the future.'

She interrupted. 'That's all good surely? Where's the problem?'

'It's not so much a problem with the present. It's more about opportunity. Simply put, I want money, independence, variety. Plus – and I know this sounds a bit hackneyed – I'll be thirty next year and I reckon by then I need to have my grand plan in place, a clear vision of where I'm going. The only part I'm certain about is that I want a place to be settled in, a retreat to give me peace and comfort from time to time. I want someone to share that with and in due course I want to have some children. Mind you, that depends on whether I can wait long enough for the lady I have in mind to become available.'

There were a few moments silence between them as they munched away at dinner. Finally, as Simon was lifting his wine glass to his lips, Hannah avoided an answer by asking another question.

'What does King Offenbach think? He'd be your best mentor wouldn't he? Or haven't you confessed to him yet?'

'Yes I have. We've had long talks about it all and the options. Thing is, as he says himself, old King is by nature and background a one-trick pony. He's been in the CIA literally from childhood since it was the US Government that gave him his education. Also, he's been alone in life other than for his mother and a very short-lived marriage. So the Company is really everything to him and it would take a major upheaval for him to leave. But that said, he's not short of imagination and he's able to appreciate my dilemma even if he can't produce a winning solution.'

Hannah pushed her plate away abruptly and asked him for a cigarette which he managed to produce while refilling their glasses. He signalled their waitress over and ordered coffee, knowing that Hannah would not eat more. She smiled wryly.

'You know me too well, don't you Si? That's really why I can't understand why you would choose to see me every day instead of once in a blue moon. There's no doubt that I'm an awkward and demanding cow a lot of the time, yet if it's of any comfort, there's no one on this planet I'd rather spend time with. God knows I get enough offers from all types, from spooks to stockbrokers with plenty of wierdos in between. But I'm a bit of a loner and probably too content in my own company. Now I've got my own flat in London, I'm really happy living by myself: no more sharing for me.'

'And no romance either?' he had steeled himself to ask the question.

She shook her head. 'That hasn't come calling since I saw you last and mind you, I haven't gone looking either: but since you're sort of asking, just a little bit of lovemaking from time to time. I hope I'm as feminine as the next girl and more so than most, but when it comes to rolling in the hay, I guess I think more like a man. I can enjoy it – sometimes more than others – and then move right on along without looking back over my shoulder. That's me.'

Simon drooped his shoulders theatrically as he looked her in the eye. 'Well I guess you've always been pretty casual and calculating about matters of the flesh,' he said, 'you have been ever since I first caught you at it in Bristol!'

She threw her napkin at him but had the good grace to be laughing as she replied.

'OK and touché!', and then, 'now look Si, if you have this weekend free, then so have I! I'm due to fly home next week but we can have Saturday and Sunday together. Let's go off on safari and you can ravish me all you want. But not tonight you can't. I've got to be up early and I'm afraid I don't want to be explaining things to the girls I'm sharing this house with, so would you mind behaving properly and just driving me home now? Please?'

'But I haven't found out anything that you're doing yet, Hannah. I mean nothing about this trip and what you're doing here in Kenya. All you said was to meet this evening and of course, as per usual, I come running. So now you owe me a bit of info, perhaps even some gossip.'

'And you'll get it all, I promise. Or at least as much as I'm allowed to say without putting cyanide in your drink! No, look, I'll tell all while we're out together in the bush. But tomorrow's work and I need to be ready and eager for it.'

'I wish you'd said so earlier,' Simon sighed with a pout of resignation as he called for their bill.

'But Si,' Hannah replied as she reached down for her bag, not attempting to disguise the typical flash of irritation, 'You told me on the phone that you've got this weekend free.'

The disappointment stayed with him as they walked out to the car. It was still early and he had been looking forward to a proper conversation, undisturbed by distractions: and how typical of Hannah to make out that the change of plan was his doing. He couldn't help remaining morose as they drove off.

Hannah was staying in a High Commission house. It was located out along the Ngong Road in one of the maze of small lanes behind Woodley Park. Hannah directed but Simon's mind wandered from her conversation. It was only ten-thirty as they approached the house having twisted and turned through side streets after leaving the main road. Here, all was silent save for cicadas and the odd barking dog. They passed a couple of street vendors' stalls, here to provide for the wants of night staff at the private houses which populated this area but other than from their braziers, there was no street lighting.

Roughly parked by the kerb on their left was a matatu, the ubiquitous public transport vehicle of East Africa, licensed to carry as many people and as much baggage as could be fitted inside and on the roof. This one was typical of the breed with a bash in every panel and a message hand-painted on the back:

'God will forgive' it promised. Further on, Hannah indicated the next entrance to the left and Simon pulled into the short, straight drive over the culvert which carried the storm water drain to stop in front of the solid double gates. He sounded the horn and waited for action. Through his open window, Simon could hear the sound of running feet and then the fumbling with locks and drop bars before the gates swung open and they were greeted by a smart figure throwing a salute in his British High Commission uniform. He was standing to the left of their car and Hannah put her hand on Simon's arm as he was about to drive on. She lowered her window to speak.

'Good evening.'

'Evenin' Miss,' this with a further salute.

'Where's Distance tonight?'

'Oh he here, Miss, but now sleepin' in the quarters at the back. His evenin' off.'

'Oh OK, thanks,' said Hannah as Simon took them the short distance to the front of the house, she added, 'the normal guard is a lovely guy who calls himself Distance because all his family live somewhere beyond Kitale and he doesn't often get home. Isn't that nice?'

'Oh terrific. Now, do I drop you here or come in?'

'You do drop me, yes, and I'm not inviting you in. But you may kiss me goodnight and tell me you're looking forward to our weekend together.'

'Of course I am, yes and I'll ring you about the timing. Now, sweet dreams and work hard, but just before you go, who does this motor belong to? Pretty flash, an S Class Merc … and a chauffeur,' he added, pointing to the large figure in a peaked cap who stood by the car.

'I fancy that's Mr Peter Solberg. He's an enigmatic Swede who does water engineering or something. He's busy courting the willowy Freda who runs one of the Aid programmes. There's just three of us although the house is large enough to sleep more and right now only two as Angie is down in Mombasa for the week. You might be able to meet both of them when you pick me up, maybe even Peter with the smart car!'

Simon tolerated being teased. He gave her a brief kiss and watched her walk through the front door before he turned in the sweep which divided the house from the extensive garden. He went over the culvert and swung left, sensing this would be a shorter way back to the main road.

Inside the house, Hannah avoided the sitting room in which she imagined Freda would be ensconced with Solberg and went instead directly to her room on the first floor, directly opposite the head of the staircase. It was spacious, with a lovely view over the garden and a fine bathroom in which a brand new shower had been installed. The bed stood behind the door which she closed behind her before flinging off her clothes and walking naked into the bathroom to turn on the shower.

She felt a twinge of regret, knowing she had upset Simon. She didn't admit to any guilt and was confident she could bring him round so they would enjoy their weekend together, but … but, Hannah thought as she relaxed under the sluicing of the shower, for how much longer could she keep Simon available on an as and when basis. Is that what she herself wanted anyway? It was no answer but right now, she just wanted to get some sleep. The next two days would need a lot of concentration and she wanted to be at her best.

She wandered back into the bedroom, running the towel through her hair and deciding that it could wait for further attention until the morning. She threw the towel back behind her onto the bathroom floor: it was amazing how quickly you could get into these bad habits. She smiled to herself. Then she froze on the spot.

Across the room in an armchair placed by the door, there appeared to be a figure, seated and motionless. It must be a trick of the gentle moonlight which was the only illumination. Unconscious of her nudity, Hannah advanced towards her bed to hit the master switch and light flooded over the room. There was no trick of nature. Sitting there calmly with a welcoming grin on his handsome face was Nathaniel Habtumu. He was dressed in the same sharp suit which she remembered from earlier in the day.

Hannah was instantly petrified, literally incapable of movement and she stood there, unclothed and uncovered as she looked at him. In contrast, Habtumu seemed relaxed and he widened his charming smile as he spoke out.

'My Dear Miss Deveridge, you must please excuse this intrusion although I flatter myself in the expectation that you may come to recognise it as a welcome surprise! Anyway, it's for me to confess. The fact is that I found you most physically attractive when we met this morning. I like tall women with long legs and I am knocked sideways when they are wearing glasses! I'm happy to see you keep them on even in the shower.'

Hannah managed enough control over her wobbly limbs to move over to her bed, sitting down and using one of the pillows to cover a good deal of her nakedness. She did not remove her glasses. She knew she must keep calm and try to assert some authority.

'Mr Habtumu', she began only to be cut short be his interruption.

'Oh Nathaniel, please. Even Natty if you must!'

'Mr Habtumu. I assure you this is not at all welcome. Would you please leave this house immediately. Otherwise, I will summon the staff and alert my companions who live here.'

'Bravely said, Hannah, but difficult for you to do. I have already immobilised your staff. The young man you know as Distance will wake in the morning with a heavy head but otherwise unharmed. The other domestics are here every day but live off site and as for your companions, one lady is in Mombasa and the other, with her Swedish escort, have been detained in the restaurant of their choice which is way over the other side of town. They will be inconvenienced but nothing worse. That leaves only your date for this evening and he has left you. So you are quite alone whereas I have a team of ruffians to look after me, notably the excellent Bobu. He is my chauffeur, but is useful for many other things as well. I'll show you.'

149

He gave a barked instruction and the door opened to admit the swarthy, bulky figure of the black man she had seen as they arrived. The man stood in the entrance and, to her relief, looked studiously at his boss. Habtumu continued speaking and now there was a harder note to his voice.

'So there you are Hannah. All is arranged and in place. You might just as well resign yourself and perhaps start to enjoy the experience. What do you say?'

She concentrated on preventing the shock from shaking her limbs and quavering her voice. She spoke with as much dignity as she could muster.

'Perhaps I should be flattered by your insistence and extravagant preparations, Mr Habtumu, but rape is still rape and that is what it will be. That makes you a serious criminal and I can't see that it's worth your while. I may be white and desirable if that's what turns you on but I'm still just a low grade secretary. Not really worth going to jail for, unless they still hang rapists here in Kenya.'

Justifiably, Hannah felt proud of her defiance. Certainly it reduced the Ethiopian to silence for a full minute before he smiled and resumed his lecture with a threatening message.

'Miss Deveridge. Please give me the credit for some brain power. You are not a simple secretary. You are a serving Officer of the SIS, the British Intelligence Service and you came to Nairobi specifically to investigate me. That buffoon Kingsmill today, he was a front as the senior. It was you conducting the interview and it is you who will report back. I'm not afraid of the spooks and mandarins of Whitehall but I object to anyone poking around in my affairs. To get my own back, I am now going to poke around in you for a while and Bobu will make a handsome recording of our activities which I will send to London to emphasise my feelings. I want you to at least pretend to enter into the spirit of the affair and you can be as rough as you like. I enjoy a bit of that, but I must warn you that if you simply lie there and think of England, then I will invite Bobu to take my place and I will handle the camera. Whatever, you should be grateful you're a pretty girl and not a muscle bound thug or you'd be dead by now. Bobu would have handled that most efficiently.

'So, shall we get on with it?'

This was not really a question and Hannah felt herself quail. What was it she'd been saying to Si just a couple of hours ago? Something to the effect that sex didn't matter much to her? Well, Christ, rape bloody well does. I can't see any way out of this. What's worse, I bet he does his bit and then turns the huge black on me anyway. There was maybe just one slight and slender chance. She made herself smile at him.

'Do I have to wear my specs?'

'I'd certainly prefer it. They add considerably to your allure.'

'Then can I change these for my second best pair? Just in case there's any damage in the rough and tumble.'

As she hoped, the erotic prospect caught his imagination and he nodded.

'They're in the bathroom. OK?'

'I think so,' said Habtumu, 'but Bobu will keep an eye on you while I undress.'

Hannah felt a spasm of hope. Also in the bathroom was her travelling cosmetics bag in which she carried a small can of spray. Would it be enough for both of them? Could she get to use it on both and make a run for escape from the house? She simply had to try.

She rose from the bed, deliberately making no attempt to carry her pillow with her. She did her best to flaunt her body without being too obvious. She walked into the bathroom, up to the double basin which stood under the window. She was conscious of Bobu following her to stand in the doorway. She couldn't see him but she could smell him. She made herself move slowly and carefully as she reached for her bag.

Meanwhile, Simon Goring was cross with himself. He had found his way easily enough back to the Ngong Road and was hammering towards the city centre when he slewed his vehicle, braking hard to a halt on the dusty shoulder. Something was not right here.

Special Forces trainers concentrate on more than muscle and mayhem. They prize the ability to observe while unseen, to be endlessly patient and to analyse random information as the brain grapples it into one cohesive message. Simon was good at all of that but he had been nursing his grievance at Hannah without allowing himself to examine the clues.

First, there was that matatu which they drove past on their way in towards Hannah's house. Si's fine peripheral vision had shown him the driver slumped over the wheel, apparently asleep. But was he, and who else might have been behind him in the vehicle? It bothered him that you simply didn't see matatus standing idle in residential roads like that.

Then there was the guard on the gate: smart enough but not the regular guy and why did he stand on the wrong side of the Land Rover as they arrived? How did he know what car to expect and that there would be a passenger?

Lastly, the Mercedes in the driveway: Simon had seen that it bore the selling dealer's sticker in the rear window. It was not unusual for expats to personally import a car, but why would a Swede buy from Mr Mercedes in Hanover?

All straws in the wind but they were scratching him. He was going back to check and if that proved a fool's errand which pissed her off, he would just have to live with it.

He pulled a fast U turn and kept his foot down, following the route they had taken together. This brought him to the end of her lane and the matatu was still there having apparently not moved a wheel. He loitered past it and caught another glance at the driver, unmoved and still slumped in his seat. But had he seen a flutter of the right hand as it draped over the steering wheel? And had there been the slightest wobble of the ancient suspension at the rear?

Simon accelerated with a brief burst, then knocked the Land Rover out of gear. With his window down and the A/C turned off, he looked in his mirrors and strained his ears. The hefty diesel engine of his vehicle was hardly silent but above the throb of its tick over and the noise of his tyres on the dusty road, he caught the sound of the old van's engine come to life and he could see it move.

He felt his suspicions confirmed as he reached the entrance to the High Commission house and he freewheeled into the entrance, running over the culvert until his bonnet was almost touching the solid double gates. He kept his headlights on, moved the transmission lever forward to engage low range but left the main gearbox in neutral. He didn't want his reversing lights to ask questions about his intent. He reached into the storage box between the front seats to take a grip on the short, heavy torch that lived there. It wasn't much of a weapon but was all he had. He sounded the horn. Then he sat and waited.

Simon knew about the classic raiding tactics of African house breakers and car jackers. Get up close behind a vehicle as it waited at gates, box it in, immobilise the occupants, get what you've come for and then scarper. Even forewarned, he was impressed by the speed and judgement. The matatu swept up behind him, stopping just short of burying its nose in the Land Rover's spare wheel. In his mirror, Simon could see a burly figure swinging his legs through the passenger door before the vehicle had come to a halt and he could imagine the rear and side doors opening. There would be a further four in the back, so six including the driver plus more inside the compound. It was time to level the playing field a bit.

Simon banged in reverse gear, dropped the clutch and floored the accelerator. With an angry growl, the Land Rover took off backwards in its lowest gear with a force which threatened to pull the wheel out of his hands.

The driver of the matatu was half way out of his door when the violent impact threw him on his back in the road with one leg still jammed in his cab. He screamed and flailed about as he was carried backwards with his skull bouncing. The front passenger got clear, as did two more who escaped through the side door. The final two, trying to exit the back door, were carried clear across the narrow road and crushed into the undergrowth beyond the culvert on the other side.

Simon knew he was still outnumbered and must make the best use of surprise and the power of his vehicle. Remembering his instructor from Marines attack driver training, he grabbed for third gear and maximum thrust. The Land Rover shot forwards and was bellowing its rage as it hit the double gates which were still closed. Immediately behind them, the phony guard was battling with the padlock, intent on releasing the gates and letting in his mates. He was smashed to the ground in a bloody pulp as the Land Rover careered through and Simon swung the vehicle hard left onto the lawn. He braked violently as he released his door and rolled out onto the grass, allowing his car to keep rolling on towards a plantation of hibiscus.

Picking himself up, he took precious seconds to let his eyes adjust to the gloom of the garden. He heard shouts and screams from around the gates, was pleased to sense the chaos there. Then he took off, running for the front door and was surprised to see it standing open with a light on in the entrance hall.

The noise in the road, so sharp and sudden in the silence of the night, startled Hannah and she fumbled her wash bag, spilling the contents all over the floor. She dropped to her knees, searching desperately to see the precious little can of pepper spray, her one hope for saving herself. But Bobo was on her in an instant using both powerful arms, one between her legs and the other clasping her around her breasts, lifting her and turning to carry her back into the bedroom.

But mayhem was her friend. The second crash as the gates gave way was followed by panicked voices and an agonised scream. Bobo didn't release his hold but he swung round to stare at the window. Then he spoke.

'Sounds like a heavy mob, Boss, with gates gone. Best I take a look.'

Habtumu shouted back at him, 'Stay where you are, Bobu. Gimme two minutes to get the car, then bring the girl.'

He was pulling on his trousers as he made a dash for the door and the staircase beyond it. Bobu kept his grip on Hannah and carried her back into the bathroom. He moved to stand in front of the basins and leaned forward to open the window with one hand. Hannah screamed with pain as his other hand squeezed her breast with excruciating force before it cracked into the side of her face – a blow which made her brain whirl. Then he had the same hand entwined in her hair, caught up to the roots as he pulled her roughly towards him and used one foot to sweep her legs from under her so that she fell to the floor on her back. The huge foot descended on her stomach, driving the breath from her body as he kept his hold on her hair. Immobilised, she still writhed to escape, lashing out with arms and legs while she was held by this iron force.

It was only seconds but felt like a lifetime of struggle for Hannah as Bobu strained to hear anything of the action outside. There was some moaning, some shouting, much confusion: in the distance, the rising wail of a siren which might have meant nothing or could be that shattering the gates had triggered an alarm. Then the engine of the Mercedes revving as the car was being turned in the drive: time to go.

Bobo bent down and gave Hannah another vicious slap around the head before scooping her up, both arms around her naked, writhing body, her head lowered like a battering ram. He ran out of the bathroom, through the bedroom, making for the head of the stairs.

Simon was holding onto his torch as he fell out of his Land Rover and the impact on his grip activated the switch. The torch threw a powerful beam as he sprinted for the house. The oak double doors stood wide open and his torchlight bounced back at him from the chandelier which hung in the entrance hall. The effect spoiled his night vision but he sensed a squat figure slip from the doorway at a run and he heard frenzied feet crabbing for a grip on the gravel of the drive. He ignored these sights and sounds as he threw himself through the door.

At the top of the stairs stood an African of imposing size and build and he was holding the struggling, naked body of Hannah Deveridge. A distant memory flashed in a millisecond across Simon's mind. He had been answering Hannah's insistent questions about his career and he had told her, 'actually it's the cerebral stuff I like best but I do unarmed combat pretty well.'

Now would be a good time to prove it.

Above him, the African threw his burden away and Hannah fell on the landing floor with a sickening crash. Bobu paused to pull and open a switch blade from the back pocket of his jeans. Then he ran nimbly down the stairs to launch his attack on the man in the hall.

Simon Goring stood his ground as the black mass descended on him, a vicious grin on Bobu's face as he maximised his advantages of height, bulk and momentum. He might as well have whistled. As he came off the bottom step, Si's torch took him in the stomach, his knife arm was caught as it came scything down and was steered away to destroy his balance while a knee came up sharply to batter his groin. In his pain and confusion, Bobu lost his grip on the knife which flew from his hand to skitter over the tiles in the hall. As the big man bent in pain to catch his breath and his balls, Simon stood over him and chopped down with both hands on the exposed neck before standing back and kicking out twice at his stomach.

A red mist of anger settled over Simon. He wanted not just victory, but revenge. With a sudden burst of strength, he bent and lifted the recumbent form onto his shoulders, climbed the stairs and pivoted at the top to hurl Bobu from the landing down into the hall. There was an almighty crash as the huge body wiped out the chandelier before hitting the tiles. Bobu lay still, his limbs at awkward angles and blood seeping from the side of his mouth.

Simon turned his back on the sight, went into Hannah's room and stripped a sheet off the bed. He returned with it as she lay naked on the landing, a hand knuckled in her mouth and tears streaming down her face. He pulled her up and towards him, wrapping the sheet round her and cradling her in his arms.

'All over now', he whispered and was encouraged that her strength of spirit was surviving as she replied, 'just starting more like!'

Then he heard it too, the sound of sirens growing closer and then wheels on the drive. Hannah struggled to her feet, went into the bedroom and closed the door behind her. Simon turned and stood at the top of the stairs to see the hall suddenly populated by moving figures. He recognised the mop hair of Ian Purdey who ran Security for the High Commission but he was almost lost in a gaggle of policemen. One of them stood out, a tall, spare man in the cap and braid which singled him out as a senior officer. He looked up and it seemed to Simon that there was a glint in his eye as he called out.

'Welcome to Kenya!'

16. SIMON AND HANNAH — 1995

They smirked at each other across the genteel lace table cloth. The very idea of meeting for tea in the Regency town of Cheltenham seemed of such a different time and generation that they could only laugh at it. But the hotel which they had chosen at random was efficient in service, the tea better than adequate and it was most unlikely that they would be interrupted.

It was almost two years since the dramatic incident in Nairobi. The time for post mortem discussion was long gone and after their return home, they had spent another weekend in the West Country, talking the whole business to death.

Nathaniel Habtumu disappeared before the Police arrived. Simon kicked himself for taking his Land Rover onto the lawn and leaving the way clear for the Ethiopian's escape but Hannah told him he was being absurd. He had no idea what was going on in the house and had focussed on finding her: thank God he had! If he hadn't followed his gut feel and come back, to say nothing of all his tough guy action when he got there, well she would certainly have been raped and quite likely murdered. She couldn't go on forever proclaiming her gratitude but she would surely never forget it.

There was a police investigation but no further action. The giant Bobu survived being chucked over the bannisters and was well enough to be roughly hauled off to jail. The injured gang members were detained and it was reckoned that two or three more got away. The British High Commissioner personally thanked Si and sent a commendation to his Commanding Officer. Every effort was made to keep the incident quiet and there was only subdued reporting in the press.

Hannah returned to London for extensive debriefing at SIS Headquarters. The view, to which she subscribed, was that

Habtumu was a dangerous man, unpredictable because he was prepared to risk his cover for the sake of self-gratification. At least they and the Americans had a clear ID and would be keeping watch for him.

But there was no comfort for the lasting damage which had been dealt to Hannah herself. Her confidence had taken a severe knock and as the months passed, she came to the painful realisation that she must seek an alternative career. She talked about this to Simon. He mixed compassion with a little steel in trying to persuade her that her talent as an SIS investigator was not to be wasted. Give it some time, he argued, a determination to concentrate on other things and she would recover to put Nairobi entirely behind her.

Hannah instinctively knew better. She was damaged goods and there would always be the haunting fear that panic would return to assault her just when she needed to be at the top of her game. She spent several weekends at Foy, taking strength from her mother and the two never failed to reach the same conclusion. It was time to make a move. Today in Cheltenham, she was ready and able to tell Simon what that move was to be.

'Strangely, Si, the answer has been close at hand all along and I've been a bit of a mug in not thinking to ask Charley sooner. Actually, I never did ask her. It was she who brought up the subject while we were both at Mum's a while ago. Charley's well established here at GCHQ and she told me they want to strengthen up some areas with people of the right experience. She encouraged me to at least go along for an interview. The panel seemed impressed but thought I was a bit young. Anyway, they let me go on to the normal endless round of assessments and tests, after which, would you believe, they made me an offer. So during the next three months, I'm going to be moving down here and starting work. I'll be able to have Cheltenham tea quite regularly!'

She laughed as she stirred her cup and the manner in which she held herself was enough to tell Simon that she was seeking his approval.

He nodded at her. 'It sounds right to me. It's a chance that must have been waiting for you and I'm a great believer in how fate works things out. I'm proud of how you've stuck at it since Nairobi. You could have resigned immediately and gone for something totally different. Now this turns up so you can stay with the work we know you're good at but from a different angle. Bloody good for you, I say.'

Hannah leaned over the table and blew him a kiss. 'You're my favourite man, just such a tonic for me!'

He smiled at her, pleased with her reaction, then asking 'tell me again, though, what exactly does Charlotte do here? I mean as much as you can tell me.'

'I'm not sure of the correct title but she's one of the team they call the Listeners. There're a lot of them because they have to go 24/7 and in a whole load of languages. But basically, they're there to monitor the sophisticated comms equipment and listen out for what the villains of this world are saying and planning. GCHQ is top standard. Best in Europe, they say, and perhaps better than anything the Yanks have.'

'Where does Charley live?'

'She's got a nice place, very Charley in that it's a bit different. She rents an apartment over the garage block in quite a big old pad, almost a stately home somewhere between here and Gloucester. I've been there of course, not that often as she shares it, but they're managing to fit me in while I find a place of my own.'

'And is she very dedicated to her job?'

'Oh yes for sure. I think she especially loves it because she's so bloody good at it. She has a touch of our great grandmother in her, has Charley. She has a sense. She has the vision.'

'And you two get on? As well as ever, I mean?'

Hannnah nodded vigorously, 'Yup, we certainly do, better than ever as we've got older. We're a close knit lot in our family, I'm happy to say although the relationship with our brother Will is more superficial. That's not so much a man/woman thing: it's more to do with his farming obsession. The property is his whole life and he does a marvellous job with it, but it's a bit limiting for the rest of us, Mum included.'

'Limiting?'

'Well, boring to be honest. He's pretty one track really. Cry rape to Will and he'll ask which field!'

They smiled at each other, both luxuriating in the instinctive understanding which comes with a long friendship. They talked some more about her new job, Simon prodding for more detail of which there was little she could reveal except about the endless process of interview. Then he changed tack.

'How long can you stay with Charley after you start?' he asked.

'Not long, but there's a bit of flexibility. I kick off next month, the beginning of August which suits both SIS and GCHQ pretty well. Then first on the training timetable is a residential course for a week and after that Charley goes off to France and Italy for two weeks leave so I'm planning to find somewhere of my own from September. I think it'll work out.'

'So you'll be there with whoever she shares with? You mentioned someone.'

'That's Liz. Lizzie Maynard. But no, I'll be there on my own. Charley and Liz will be on holiday together. They're an item you see.'

'Ah', said Simon, temporarily lost for words.

Hannah continued, 'Yes. It's a lesbian relationship'. She lifted her teacup and grinned mischievously over its brim at him. 'There now. Have I shocked you Mr Upright and Proper?'

Simon couldn't get cross with her but he was surprised, unsettled even and that made him reply more forcefully than he intended.

'Absolutely not! I'm sure they make a great couple.'

This started Hannah laughing so hard she had to put down her cup.

'You're a gem, Si, really. What an alpha male response! But since you ask, yes they are a great couple. Liz is a rather powerful lawyer – property I think – and she and Charley have been together for nearly three years now so I know it works well. More surprising but just as good, the two of them get on well with Mum and even Will seems quite comfortable with it. Much more amazing is Charley's father Victor. I'd have put money on the lessie bit being anathema to an extremely hetero Frenchman like him but no, he embraces Lizzie in every way and he's their first port of call on their summer holiday. But look, Si, that's enough about me for the moment. Tell me what's going on for you? What's the next posting or training or whatever?'

'I'm leaving the Marines, Hannah, that's what's new and next for me. I've resigned my Commission and I've got myself a new job. So there you are: you're not the only one.'

As Simon sat back with a slightly smug expression on his face, Hannah was clunking down her cup in surprise. Her wide eyed look of astonishment told him to get on with the explanation.

'It's a bit like for you in one respect. Funny how these things come together when you're not expecting it. In my case, I've got King Offenbach to thank for steering me into some lateral thinking. I suppose he could see me getting unsettled and he came up with an idea which has worked out.'

He paused in reflection and Hannah snapped at him. 'Don't stop now, for God's sake. Tell me more.'

'OK. Well, it goes back to King's time at Uni, at Oxford in the sixties when he was over from the States. He became a good friend of Pente and they were close mates with three other undergrads. They were so much a group that they were known as The Oxford Five. One of the others was a guy called Conrad Aveling, a true blue Brit from an old fashioned family who went into the Army via Sandhurst. He did very well, a bit of an action man, saw interesting times in the Far East and married while he was out there. They came back here and Conrad went on to do tours in Germany and Northern Ireland. He was starting to wonder what next when he had a visit. Connie's wife had a guardian when she was orphaned, a Frenchman called Roger Mantel who lives in Singapore with his son. Together, they set up a successful outfit which provides security to private clients, mostly companies. You know the sort of arrangement?'

Hannah nodded as he continued. 'Well it seems they were doing so well with the enterprise that they wanted to expand into Africa. Their problem was in managing the volume of work, plus of course the distance and time zone. So they approached Conrad to get a subsidiary going, based here in the UK. He did that about twenty years ago and it's been growing ever since. Plus I hope the company will go on growing as I'm the latest recruit!'

'What's it called?' she asked as an instinctive first question.

'Bastion,' he replied, 'Bastion Security and the company's based at Farnham, but there's a fair bit of travel involved. It's not a big set up, about thirty employees, two dozen major contracts and a great shoal of smaller assignments that come and go. Plenty of variety anyway and I must say that I do like my new boss. He's quite quiet, looks a bit pressured which he must be but he knows his stuff and in every way we speak the same language. I've met his wife also, a super lady who is Cambodian born. Name of Antoinette but known as Tepee and in due course I expect I'll be able to tell you how that came about. They have three children, twin boys and a girl. Oh, and just to finish the introduction, I'll be able to start sometime before the end of this year.'

Simon shuffled his feet and started toying with a sandwich. He looked at her expectantly, anxious for her reaction but Hannah took her time in responding and even then there was more question than judgement.

'It's a big move, Si, isn't it? It does sound right for you although I don't know enough about military life to be certain that you should be turning your back on it. But then I don't need to: you are sure in your mind, that's obvious, and I'd always back you to know what you really want. You're that sort of man.'

There was a pause before she continued. 'The only question I've really got, Si, concerns what you haven't told me. Because there's something else, isn't there? Something more on your mind? I know I'm right. I can always tell with you.'

He groaned theatrically. 'You're a bloody nuisance with your sharp brain and your perception, Hannah. There is something else which I had wanted to keep to myself for the moment but I can see I'm not going to get away with that. Look, it's all about my grand plan and a lot of that's about you. I think you and I are really good together and that we can develop a great lifestyle to last us into our dotage. If there was ever a complementary couple, that's us. But I'm not making any grand statement today and I'm not getting onto one knee next to the tea table. I'll bide my time until I believe the moment's right.'

He sounded so serious that Hannah could not resist teasing him some more.

'I can hardly wait, Si, and I'll be fascinated to see what moment you choose as the right one. But tell me one thing. What's this got to do with a career change for you?

'Teasing me is one thing,' he said with mock severity, 'but it's not like you to be slow in spotting the obvious.'

'And that is?'

'There is no way that you could or would live a military life. You're just not made for it.'

'But I could manage Farnham?'

'I don't know that. Not yet. I simply don't know if I'll be on the right road to win you over forever, but I do know that at least I won't be on the wrong one'.

They smiled at each other and called for more scones. This conversation had called for suitable celebration.

.

17. TOMAS AND TETRARCH — 1996

There can be few more beautiful places in the world than the Loire Valley, especially if a warm sun is shining on an early evening in June. The Twins paused in their work of clearing bramble and ivy from around the immature trunk of a small oak tree and permitted themselves a look back at the house which was now their home.

Tomas and Tetrarch had come a long way from Segou in the Republic of Mali. They had returned to Europe in 1993, arriving in Paris on a direct flight from Bamako to be greeted by freezing February weather.

Tetrarch was happy to be out of Mali and stimulated by the prospect of putting down roots somewhere in the French countryside. Tomas was preoccupied with worries about the Chinese and whether a long arm of retribution might be reached out to attack them. The Twins had, after all, spent over five years in China and in all that time, they had been fed, watered and trained by the State, a total investment which they had squandered by walking away from the project in Mali simply because they were bored.

Following that incident with the Tuareg tribesmen, Tetrarch had driven through the night to get Mr China safely back to Bamako and all the little sod had done was to read them a Politburo lecture before he stalked off without a word of thanks. As they were driving back to Segou, Tetrarch had vented his frustration.

'You know, Tomy, I'm getting well pissed off with this. We might be here like this until tomorrow or for another year and for however long, we'll be waiting for some fuck-whit to make up their mind for us. It's up to you but for myself, I've had enough of taking orders. I want us to decide our own future. And something more, I want to have a place of our own. I want my own garden and I want to find someplace near where our mother's family came from in France.'

This was a long speech for Tetrarch and Tomas took due note. Maybe he was right and it was time for them to make a move. It took some thought and planning, also patience while waiting in vain for a reply from Li. Finally, even Tomas was worn down by the inactivity and they bade their farewell to Bamako.

They had to stop looking over their shoulders and concentrate on the future. They were now thirty-five. They had ideas but no funding therefore money, serious money, was the absolute priority and they had the sort of luck here which comes from knocking on every possible door.

When they fled from Marseilles fifteen years previously, they left the train at Dijon and struggled to end up in Hamburg. There, the best cash income came from casual work in the bars and clubs and brothels which were productive sources for documents pilfered from drunken seamen. Over time, they got their hands on two passports which, suitably doctored at no small price, allowed them to get employment on the cruise ships which had been their next stage of life.

It was therefore as Lotz and Achleitner that they arrived in Hamburg from Paris, struggling to remember their way around the city and enough of the language to get by. They found work and somewhere to live. They were making good subsistence money but nothing like what they would need for a new start, so Tomas spent time making the rounds, looking for hints, clues and contacts, trying to find the lawless enterprises which would pay very well for the skills they could supply.

But it was Tetrarch who made their mark when doing a bouncer's job, spotted while he made easy work of a couple of large Latvian seamen who were causing a ruckus one evening. Casual contact and a couple of beers led to Tomas being summoned and a serious conversation in the back room of a nearby bar in which there were no unwelcome ears to hear.

Tomas sensed immediately that this might be leading them into the big time. The introductory talk was all about a major robbery, location and substance unstated but with the promise of a harvest of earnings, payable in cash. Tetrarch pricked up his ears but Tomas was wary. For this sort of money, why them? Their informant explained that his associates were searching for particular ability, also people who were newly arrived in the city, had no records and could be judged reliable. If they were interested, they must return for a detailed briefing. From this, the Twins knew that they would be marked down for extermination if they talked to anyone else on the subject.

Ten days later, they met the leader of the heist. His interest was in Tetrarch because he needed a man of strength, experience and silence. In conversation, however, he warmed to Tomas who evidenced the brainpower which was ideal for the purpose.

There followed weeks devoted to planning and practice during which time the Twins picked up some retainer money while continuing to work at their temporary jobs around the Port. Finally, they left Hamburg by night with Tetrarch at the wheel of a high roofed panel van which had been stolen to order. His passengers included Tomas and four other gang members: the load bed was full of specialist equipment, chosen to meet exacting requirements. They had no difficulty in the journey and the leader, with two more accomplices, met them at the safe house in Frankfurt.

This was the background to an art theft which briefly dominated international news. In late July of that year, three famous paintings were stolen from the Schirn museum in Frankfurt, including two by Turner which were on loan from the Tate in London. It was the start of a story which would run and run until these precious works were recovered by paying a ransom for their return, but the involvement of the Twins was merely short, sharp and profitable.

It was Tomas who played the first key role, paying to enter the Schirn as a visitor at midday, wandering around the exhibits throughout the extensive building until an hour before closing time, then changing clothes in a washroom to become a cleaner and finally hiding in a corner of the cafeteria when the building was secured for the evening.

Five hours later, in the quiet of the night, Tomas opened a fire escape door on the lower ground floor to admit the first three collaborators who were to shut down the alarm system. There was a risk that the fire door might activate a distress call but the great building slumbered on as the full team went about its task, emerging just after midnight to find Tetrarch waiting with the van in a side alley. They loaded carefully and moved off at a sedate pace. It was at the end of this narrow service roadway that Tetrarch earned his corn. The alley was one way only and the leader had not thought to check on its junction with their exit road. It was here that they were halted - not by a barrier, not by a Police road block, simply by a hole in the road. A deep, wide trench was running along the main road and straight across their alley. The leader in his seat by the window with Tomas in the middle goggled at the sight and thought furiously. Could they turn? Could they reverse? But Tetrarch didn't hesitate. He knew he had been sitting there for hours with his window open. He had seen no lights, heard no voices. There had been no sound of machinery and no sirens either. Therefore these roadworks must be a project lasting days and with German efficiency, there would be some sort of bridging for use during daylight hours. Tetrarch got out of the van, leaving his door open and the engine running. He sauntered over to have a closer look and on the side of the road he found what he was expecting: a pair of long, thick, steel tracking plates to be placed over the trench when required. They were very heavy but Tetrarch managed to carry the two together in a crabbing walk to the trench. He didn't worry about the noise as he dropped them in position and he continued to appear the lonely night worker as he made an unhurried return to the van and climbed in. They took off over the ramps and made it to the safe house without incident.

In the garage there was a nondescript small Peugeot which

had been stolen from a French tourist the previous week. The leader pushed the Twins towards it, handing over a fat manila envelope and watching them drive away. A fair bargain, the leader thought. He had been impressed by their performance but was glad to have them gone. Tetrarch might have been noticed by a passer-by and possibly Tomas in the Schirn but he and his other accomplices had been masked and in the background throughout the operation.

The Twins had no difficulty with their onward journey. They crossed the borders into Switzerland and thence into France, motoring quietly across the country into Poitiers where they exchanged the car for an older but larger estate version. Tomas took care of the manila envelope: a fair bargain indeed.

They based themselves in the Loire Valley town of Loches which they knew to have been the birthplace of the maternal grandmother whom they had never known but whose ghost seemed to be beckoning them home. About a month later, whilst meandering in the district, they stumbled across the Chateau du Mesnil and bought the place for cash.

At first sight, this didn't seem a sound decision. It was more of a large farmhouse than a chateau and it was nearly derelict. There were several holes in the roof and water stood in pools on the floor. The outbuildings were half collapsed, there was no electricity and there was an infestation of rats. But it was also home. Both of them were delighted and set up camp in the most habitable part of the old building. They were surrounded by ten hectares of scrubby, long abandoned land which came with the place but they had fine views over the remote countryside which placed them about halfway between St Senoch and St Flovier. They visited both for buying provisions and they settled to make improvements to the Chateau.

The weather was cold and it was getting close to Christmas when a smart looking Citroen drove into the yard and sounded its horn. The chauffeur stayed at the wheel while his passenger climbed out and looked around him.

It was Li.

In the dying light of the short winter day, Tomas had been inside trying to apply plaster to the walls of one of the reception rooms while Tetrarch was at work on the roof of the former cow byre. Visitors to Mesnil were rare, so hearing the car, both converged on it from opposing directions and stopped short in astonishment.

Li said, 'It's good to see you both again and it has not been easy to find you. Is there somewhere we can talk?'

Tomas shook his hand, smiling, and replied, 'We are short of comfort here and only camping. Where have you come from?'

They didn't linger. The Twins started up their old car and followed Li's driver to Loches. Li took rooms for them in his comfortable hotel and they settled down to talk. They soon gathered that Li had received the letters which Tomas had written to him and that he understood their reasons for leaving Segou. He had found them as much by luck as judgement. The first part was intelligent guesswork, recalling that in Yumen, Tetrarch had spoken of the countryside of their ancestors. The luck came when he engaged the hire car as the driver enjoyed mysteries, was born and bred to the area and knew that someone had acquired the old chateau. It had been worth a look.

Li talked of home. 'Things have been changing fast in China,' he told them, 'the facility at Yumen is still operating but the students are all from Russia and central Asia, some from India but no more from Europe and Scandinavia. Today, the focus is on commercial interests, not political ideology.'

Li chose his next words carefully. 'I am permitted by my Director to tell you all that I know. That is because my Director remembers you well. He was favourably impressed by your behaviour when you looked after him in Mali.'

Tomas stared at him, recalling all the botched arrangements, the fight with the wild Tuareg and the abrupt dismissal after Tetrarch had got them back to Bamako. It sounded as if Mr China had moved much further up the ladder of the People's Republic.

Li continued, 'I am here because of Chechnya,' he said, 'do

you know where that is?'

'Yes, I suppose. But only approximately.'

'This small piece of land is not important to us in China, but it is important to Russia and that's why it matters to Beijing. Let me explain.

'The break-up of the Soviet Union in 1991 was welcome to us because we were intimidated by the size and power of our neighbour, always concerned about the true objectives of the Kremlin. When the USSR was finished, we knew that there would be times of turmoil while the new Republics were becoming established. Therefore there was the chance for us to make allies and develop influence, especially in Kazakhstan. We knew it would take time for the new Russia to reorganise and for the power struggles in Moscow to be resolved. While China was modernising and developing new policies for the future, it was helpful that the Russians had their own domestic problems.

'To give ourselves a little further advantage, we have been giving support to some dissident groups which are in conflict with the Russian government. If Ministers are distracted by local matters, there will be less time to consider their strategy for the future and this buys more time for China, time in which we are growing in our commercial strength and influence.'

Li raised an eyebrow and Tomas nodded: all understood so far.

'The PRC's greatest effort is in Chechnya which has declared its independence from Russia and is now at war with its former motherland. There should not be a contest here. Chechnya is a very small enclave of territory and Russia has enormous military power. However, the Chechens are a fierce people and fine guerrilla fighters; also they are passionate about their country which is mountainous and remote terrain. The Russians have already lost many soldiers and a vast amount of equipment in the battle for Grozny, the Chechen capital and they have been unable to win.

Beijing has already given assistance with money and weapons but all this must be very carefully handled. We cannot afford for our support to become known or it would destroy our relationship with Russia. You understand?'

Another nod: it wasn't hard to get the point.

'OK. Now here is the project which we wish you to undertake. The Chechen separatists have a new battle plan. They believe it will drive the Kremlin into granting them their independence. The Chechens need a master bomb-maker and they know who they want. They have asked us to recruit him and pay him. Beijing is willing but cautious. The Bomber is talented but he is an unreliable character so my Director wants you to be our intermediary, to take charge and to watch over this man while he does his work.

'I have a great deal more detail here,' Li paused to tap his head,' including your fee but first, you must tell me if you are prepared to accept.'

Tomas allowed a time of silence between them before posing a question.

'And what if we do not agree to take the job?'

'You are the only people whom my Director will consider. If you refuse, I am to walk away and we abandon the Chechens. Officially, the matter would be over but since you have become my friends over a long period, I must add that I think your own lives would be at risk.'

'So we play nursemaid to a powder keg and be well rewarded or refuse and have to keep looking over our shoulder. Is that it?'

Li simply nodded. Tomas barely had to glance at Tetrarch before confirming their acceptance.

'Very good,' said Li, 'I am pleased and relieved. The man will come to you shortly. His name is Nathaniel Habtumu, another African like yourselves.'

'No', said Tomas immediately. 'you must tell us where to find him. This place is our home, Li, and we will not risk exposure – especially not if this Habtumu is as unreliable as you say.'

There was a long pause before Li, unaccustomed not to be taking the initiative, was able to nod his head in agreement.

'Very well. I will leave you with a contact number in Paris.'

Tomas was sorry to see Li depart and pressed him to stay one more day. The two of them spent it in Loches, leaving Tetrarch at the chateau to continue his work on the roof. As they settled to talk in the hotel lounge and later at a brasserie in the town centre, Li became increasingly animated in his account of all that had happened to him and the changes in the long established political environment, especially in Shanghai. He was delighted with the progress in his country, seeing China grow ever stronger on the world stage, becoming not just the world's most populous nation but also the most significant in economic growth. Tomas wanted to understand more of the philosophy of the Politburo and Li told him all he could, but emphasised that his guess might be informed, but it was still a guess. Li went off the following morning and watching his smart car and driver bear him away, Tomas was conscious that they would be unlikely to meet again.

During most of the following day, Tomas coached Tetrarch through a detailed brief. They wanted this assignment, Tomas reasoned. It would discharge their debt to the Chinese, it would secure their financial security. It would provide time and maybe contacts for developing a long term strategy for their future. But it was essential that in their dealing with this Ethiopian, Tetrarch must be seen to be operating alone. Tomas wanted nothing to do with him – certainly not to meet him. Habtumu was a short term means to an end: it could be seen from the reports in society magazines that he was a blustering, flamboyant character with a blabber mouth. Tetrarch could handle him and give nothing away but Tomas must stay in the background, providing discreet advice as needed.

The invasion of Russian territory by Chechen separatists under the leadership of Shamil Basayev is well documented. On June 14th 1995, a column of fighting men carried in trucks disguised as a Russian Military convoy crossed the border from Chechnya and travelled unchallenged for over a hundred kilometres into the Russian city of Budyonnovsk. Here, the Chechens stormed the City Hall and raised their flag. Under pressure from defending Russian troops, Basayev's force regrouped in the main hospital in which they held over 1500 hostages.

Over the next four days the world held its breath as demands were followed by negotiations which then descended into bloodshed. A resolution to the crisis was reached on 18th June through an agreement to negotiate a form of independence for Chechnya in exchange for the Russian hostages but by then, more than one hundred and fifty people had lost their lives and many more had been injured in the fighting. Russian military action to free the hostages had failed on three occasions and the political ability to manage such an incident had been found wanting. It didn't help that the morale of the separatists was flying high with their leader, Basayev, receiving a hero's welcome in his village of Dargo when he crossed back into Chechnya. David had slain his Goliath.

Behind the bald accounts, it's difficult to assess the performance of individuals as events moved quickly and because neither side held to a consistent strategy. Three of the invading Chechens claimed that the hospital was to be prepared for demolition with the hostages still inside. They were instructed to protect the Bomber while he set his charges but were moved before he could finish the job. From the Russian perspective, witnesses from the elite Special Forces reported that their unsuccessful efforts to overrun the rebels had been blunted by frequent changes of direction from their political commanders.

The collateral damage to the city was immense, with over fifty municipal buildings destroyed or badly damaged. Survivors insisted that many of these were located nowhere near the fighting and that some had 'exploded spontaneously'. It's possible that Basayev redeployed Habtumu from the hospital to create drama and to cause confusion to the rear of the Russian fighting troops. Whatever the facts, it's certain that Habtumu was feted alongside Basayev when the triumphant Chechens entered Drago and this speaks volumes for the extent and skill of his work.

Tetrarch had returned quietly to Loches from Chechnya

themselves uncomfortable. But Father Basil, who's now been in post for about ten years, would have none of that and set about changing us.

By then it was drink time and Simon was becoming less surprised as Pente produced a bottle of whisky and dispensed it before searching for his cigar box on his overcrowded desk and lighting up as he cradled his glass in one meaty hand. Simon warmed to him anew.

Later, they went down to the Refectory for dinner. This, and the kitchen, was housed in one of the separate buildings, all being accessed from the courtyard and on the short walk there, Pente pointed out the accommodation block in which newcomers were first lodged during their training.

'Adequate but pretty basic even though it's a lot better than in my day. But you don't want the novices to be too cherished. Much better that a man tries us, finds it's not for him and leaves before it's too late.'

'You mean, before he takes his vows?'

'Yes, that's right, although here we talk about "commitments." It seems to suit the modern age better.'

The supper was fine and wholesome if not very imaginative. They sat at long tables which reminded Simon of his boarding school. There was plenty of conversation and Simon had the chance to meet Father Basil and to enjoy some of his quiet humour. But nobody lingered there for long and after another drink in his rooms, it was time for Pente to attend chapel, the cue for Simon to be shown to his single visitor's room at the other end of the long passage on the top floor. He was happy to make an early night of it and to sleep soundly.

After breakfast the following morning, they set out together to walk the extensive grounds and tracks. Both men were clad in boots and heavy topcoats as rain was threatening: there was a biting wind but Simon found the whole place refreshing, especially with its majestic outlook.

Their opening conversation sought common ground through shared reminiscences. They knew each other slightly but opportunities to meet had been few and far between.

'Well after all,' remarked Pente, 'we're of different generations and while you've been travelling, I have spent most of my life in Africa so there was never going to be much of a chance.'

'The thing is,' said Simon feeling that he must grasp the nettle, 'I asked to come and see you because I need your advice and perhaps your help also. It's about Hannah, you see, but also about her mother. Plus it's really important that they don't know I've come to you.'

'Well you're in the right place, that's for sure. Women aren't allowed here!' He gave his great bellow of laughter: humour was never long absent from Pente's language. 'But sorry for the interruption. Tell me what's on your mind.'

'I will, and I'll hold nothing back, but I won't spin it out either. First off, Pente, you know where I'm working now?'

'I do, yes. You won't need telling that I get most of my information from Vanda and she is, of course, close to her daughter. So what Hannah tells her Mum mostly gets passed on to me, suitably expurgated of course, and I'm sure there will be things she keeps to herself. But she does trust me with confidences and she knows full well that they're safe with me. Sorry for too long a reply. But I do know. You work for my old chum, Connie Aveling, and you're one of his top dogs at Bastion Security. That's right, isn't it?'

'It is, yes. I've been with him for two years now and I think it's a success for both of us. He's a first rate operator and an excellent guy, although I'm developing a bit of a worry about his state of mind but that's a different subject and perhaps for later. The point right now is that in the New Year, I'm going to be transferring to the staff of Fergus Carradine. You know who I mean, I believe?'

'I do, yes.'

'Well, that means I'll be based with him in Asia and I won't be back here in the UK for a couple of years. That's if the whole project works out and, incidentally, I don't even know exactly where I'll be going yet.'

'You're in good company there, Simon. I don't know either.'

Simon was astonished, stopping dead in his tracks. 'Really?'

'No. That's really the truth of it, Simon. Look, let me just fill you in on a bit of background. I came out of Africa in May this year. I relinquished my post in Tanzania on health grounds, not so much because I hadn't recovered from my last bout of malaria because I had by then - and recovered well. No, it was more because it was obvious that if I had stayed on, it would have recurred and gone on doing so, but probably getting worse each time. The Abbot here took a view that I wouldn't be damaging only myself, but the Order of the Saints also and of course, he was quite right. So I was content to follow his instruction and come back here. I'm still settling in, mind you, only been here a month or so but I feel it's been a good move and there's one further advantage. We may be cut off here but it's a damn sight closer to London and old friends than I was in Tanzania.'

'London, you say. Is that significant?'

The priest looked sharply at him as they walked stride for stride, the sharp wind bringing tears to the eyes.

'Let's take a break while I fill you in on some background. I could do with a smoke anyway.' Pente veered of the path and went to prop himself on a large bough which weather had brought off a giant oak nearby. He went through the performance of getting his cigar lit and puffed contentedly before resuming.

'When I was at University thirty years ago, I fell in with a crowd of particularly good friends who have remained so after all this time. One of them is your Godfather, King Offenbach although he was only there in our final year. Another is your boss, Conrad Aveling whom we always called Connie. The third is a beautiful, gutsy lady called Alexa Labarre who married, was widowed and now lives in Hong Kong. The last is David Heaven who has spent his working lifetime travelling in and out of Africa. He started and runs a conglomerate called the Mansion House.

'Our group was always hanging out together so we became talked about as 'the Oxford Five'. We've kept in touch since those days too, helped each other out from time to time, had the odd reunion when there's been a special occasion and schedules have clicked together. Of us all, I suppose it's me and King who have retained the closest contact. OK so far?'

'Of course, and I certainly know the Mansion House. In fact I've done business with some of their people but I've never met David Heaven and didn't know of his close connection with Conrad.'

'Well, Connie has always guarded his confidences and more recently, well I guess that's the whole point.'

Simon made to interrupt with a question but Pente waved him away and by unspoken agreement, they resumed their walking as the priest continued.

'David Heaven is putting together a very grand plan. His passion for Africa and his despair at the shattered state of so many countries on that continent has driven him to conceive the notion of taking over one of them - and then starting again. I know it beggars belief, but it's true.'

'I suppose that if any organisation could take a tilt at such a thing, then the Man......'

'No.' Pente rounded on him. 'No, this isn't the Mansion House. This is a personal mission. I've already broken a confidence, Simon, and I can say little more. Indeed I don't know much more, not yet, and I won't until David is ready to talk about things in greater detail. But the point is that I've said what I've said for two reasons. The first is that the Heavenly ambition has brought about a severe rift between him and Connie Aveling who thinks he's mad, bad and wrong. I think you need to know that before you commit yourself elsewhere because in moving, you will certainly be held to be breaching Conrad's trust and there will be no going back from that. And my second reason is that I reckon you've come to see me for a personal reason. Instinct tells me you deserved to know this much.'

They must have walked fifty yards in silence before Simon replied. 'Thank you, Pente. I very much appreciate your frank honesty and your faith in me. You'll be surprised to hear it, but actually Conrad does know where I'm going and I do have his blessing – his encouragement even. Plus he has said a lot about looking forward to my return to the fold. You see, he's talked about my taking over from him when he reckons it's time to hang up his boots and he's mentioned the benefits of further experience which I can gain from working with Carradine: nothing wrong with any of that though I have the feeling there's more, as yet unspoken. I've never met Heaven, of course, but my gut is telling me that I'm some sort of olive branch which Connie's offering to repair bridges with his old mate.'

Pente sighed. 'You just could be right, Si, and by God I hope so. It's a tragedy to see such a long established relationship fractured and here you have two punchy and honestly quite selfish characters that have not, of course, become more malleable with age. But put the two of them on one side for a moment. What's your most testing problem and how can I help?'

'In one word, Pente, it's Hannah.'

'Ah! Yes I thought we would get to her! What's the problem?'

'The main part is down to me if I can find a way forward. But I think I'd better start from scratch even if you already know most of it – from her mother I mean. Anyway I can summarise it pretty quickly and you just stop me with questions as and when.'

Pente was amused with the notion of receiving a brief on a love affair in the manner of some military report, but he held his peace and waited for Simon to go on. They had walked to the top of a rise in the ground which commanded a long view down the valley, dropping away from them, before the younger man stopped abruptly and swung round to speak quite fiercely.

'Hannah can be the most frustrating girl in the world because you just don't know what she's thinking, have no clue about the road she wants to travel. Sometimes, I don't believe she knows herself'. He paused to puff out his cheeks with the effort of controlling his emotions before going on.

'We've been together now for … well about ten years

really, since our days at Uni, at Bristol. But it's only ever been off and on. I don't mean bust up's and start up's, it's not been like that. We've each had a career, of course, with demands of time and place but there's nothing unusual about that. You see, my problem is that I want to move our lives closer together - intertwined in fact - but somehow she keeps getting away from me. The relationship is terrific when we're together, and I mean on every level, but there's always something that holds Hannah back. She won't commit, but she doesn't want me gone from her life either. I mean I've even changed jobs mostly with her in mind. I came out of the Marines because I knew the military wife life would never be for her but I didn't get any real signs of encouragement. It sounds pathetic, Pente, I know, but I'm at my wits end. Talk about cherchez la femme.'

Pente said, 'I'm going to get cold just standing here. Come on and we'll do my valley circuit before lunch. And just keep talking Si. I think you'd better tell me the last bit before I offer any comment.'

There was a nod of agreement from Simon and they resumed walking as he continued. 'So now I've accepted the latest assignment. I'm to go out to Singapore at the end of February. This is all to do with Heaven's grand plan, of course, and professionally speaking, it's an extraordinary opportunity. But that said, I have as yet no idea of precisely what, where or when. All I do know is that, whatever the outcome, I'm going to be out of touch for about two years: incommunicado in some godforsaken spot at the other end of the world, for Christ's sake. Sorry', he finished with an apology for the blasphemy.

Pente took no notice but posed a question. 'What happened between you after that business in Kenya? That was what? Three or four years back now? Vanda told me about it, or as much as she knew anyhow. You did well then.'

'I thought it was a turning point – *the* point actually. Of course I wouldn't have wished for something like that to happen but while she was getting herself back together, we were able to talk about things, especially the future. She was over the top grateful to me, really. What I did was not too special, not with the training we get and anyway I lost it at the end, did some guy much more damage than was necessary. Not too professional, I'm afraid.'

Pente just nodded. 'OK, just finish it off. What's particularly bugging you now?'

'It's Hannah's job, Pente, that's my worry now. There are demands on her now that she's working at GCHQ and there is loyalty to consider as well. If I was to tell her even as little as I know about where I'm off to and why, well she'd be duty bound to investigate a bit further. That's the sort of thing which her outfit is there to keep an eye open for and actually, I guess the same would apply if she was still with SIS. So I can't say anything, but if I simply vanish without a word, how can I expect her to be still around if and when I get home?'

Pente paused long enough to relight his cigar in the lee of the hill. The butt of it was looking a bit damp from the rain and after a couple of attempts he chucked it away in disappointment. He put an arm on Simon's shoulder and turned him so that they were standing face to face.

'Now, Simon Goring, you just listen to me. You've let yourself *and* your Hannah down by being so incredibly wet for far too long. What d'you think you're doing with all this poncing around waiting for the girl to come to you? What ever happened to good, old fashioned courtship? You're meant to propose, for Heaven's sake, not slouch about in a fit of the vapours until she disposes!'

Simon bridled instantly, but Pente wouldn't let him interrupt.

'Just hear me out. You can't go back. You can't undo the past and you certainly can't back out of your imminent commitment. Not professionally and not personally either. But what you can do is to let me give you a helping hand. Just go off to Fergus in Singapore and leave the communications to me. I will contrive to speak to Vanda and together we'll cook up how we inform her daughter. If you've got what she wants, she'll be waiting for you. And if you haven't, well you may be miserable but you'll have lost nothing, will you? The one thing you must do is to tell her all you can before you go and if I were you, I would make it a marriage proposal that's got to wait for a while but nowhere near as long as you've already been waiting for her.

'One other thing which I reckon will bring you more comfort than it brings me, Simon. There's an irony here which would be delicious if it were not so painful. Endless years ago, I threw over the certainty of being with Vanda for life in favour of a different call which was to serve my God. I don't regret that but I do still mourn for what might have been. Hannah might have been my daughter but I believe she would still have inherited so much of her character from her Mum - a remarkable lady of huge strength of personality who has continued to give me more friendship than I deserved. I think both of us would believe that Hannah couldn't do much better than you - warts and all - so while you're away, we'll be doing our best for you.'

Simon stood there, wordless as he nodded his agreement and gratitude. Pente grunted his acknowledgement and they moved away together, up the hill and back towards the Monastery.

'Let's go in for a decent lunch and we can have a bit more time together afterwards before you leave. There may even be time enough for you to help with the ironing!'

The woolly beard shook as his boisterous laugh rang out across the bleak hillside.

19. TOMAS AND TETRARCH — 1997

The Twins left the Chateau du Mesnil in the middle of August when much of France was on its annual holiday.

Tetrarch had little enthusiasm for this expedition and the further they travelled from the Loire, the more he missed the chateau and his occasional forays away with Nat Habtumu. But Tomas had decided so there was no more to be said. The great hulking figure might brood a bit but he wouldn't argue.

They left their car at home and took a long distance bus, reaching Bordeaux where they spent a week while Tomas did more research at a library and a specialist bookshop in the city. Tetrarch perked up while he occupied himself in a few bars of doubtful reputation before Tomas announced that it was time to move on.

They flew now, taking a plane to Istanbul where there was a shorter layover of just forty-eight hours as Tomas checked more background history, then on again with another flight into Ankara where they switched back to bus transport and spent days bumping slowly east before swinging south towards Diyarbakir and eventually crossing over the border into northern Syria. They made an uncomfortable overnight journey to Aleppo, squeezing into an overloaded minibus and Tetrarch complained that there must be an easier route. Tomas told him the journey was important and there was more research to do there.

Aleppo took another two weeks by the end of which Tetrarch would have been dangerously out of his mind with boredom had Tomas not found an introduction to a little known clique of fighting men whose favoured weapon was a variation on the South American bolas. Tetrarch was getting pretty competent by the time they left again, this time in a half decent old Mercedes with an owner driver called Yaman, whom Tomas hired to drive them east in slow and gradual stages clear across the entire country until they left Syria and moved on into Iraq.

They left Yaman at the border and went back to bus transport, travelling a little south of east to Arbil, north of Kirkuk and after that by roads little better than tracks through remote country to cross another border and eventually find themselves in Saqqez, northern Iran. Tehran came next, but only after long days, endless roads and blinding heat. When finally they did arrive, the sprawling capital city was a pain to Tetrarch with no drink and no women. He spent dreary days by the small pool of the scruffy hotel in which they lodged, wishing that the Shah had not fallen twenty years previously as this place had apparently been the right sort of hot spot in his day.

On two separate days, the Twins hired a car to take them the hundred kilometres north east from Tehran to Alamut and the centuries old castle perched on its mountain top. Tomas had spent time studying all that had been written about this ruined citadel and the importance of its history. Tetrarch loafed about and refused to climb closer than was necessary to look at what was left of it through a pair of powerful binoculars.

At last, Tomas was satisfied and with an urgency which pleased Tetrarch, they took a plane east to the city of Mashhad which they found to be spread out and dreary. They stayed just long enough to get their papers in order so that they could cross over into Afghanistan. The border formalities took most of a day and they had to slum it in a travellers' shack before they were able to climb into a pretty comfortable Toyota minibus from which they alighted some hours later in Herat, in the west of this challenging country.

From this point, the Twins became conscious of hostility and latent danger all around them. They agreed it was strange now that they were nearing forty years old that they should be sharply reminded of nervous travelling when they had been teenagers. Tetrarch took the lead, confident in his ability to fend off all comers as might be necessary, but Tomas was much less comfortable and didn't want to dally.

The journey was painful. They took big buses and minibuses, once even a donkey cart, but day-by-day they progressed through the arid, harsh countryside with the no less hard inhabitants. They made sure they carried water, ate what they could and slept wherever reasonably safe. They passed through both Mazari Sharif and Baghlan, keeping well to the north of Kabul. The country became steadily more wild and the roads more precipitous as they penetrated the Hindu Kush. The last few hundred kilometres seemed to take an eternity as they forded the rivers and toiled up and down the steep and stony mountain passes. It was while they were following on foot a train of nimble, sturdy mules that they passed from Afghanistan into Pakistan. The going was no easier and the peaks looked even higher but Tomas was encouraged to know that they were at last reaching their destination.

A day later, the Twins walked into the large town of Chitral and gazed up at the pinnacle of Tirich Mir, towering 7700 metres into the clear, cold sky. They felt a sense of welcome coupled with the fulfilment of arrival but Tetrarch was still left wondering why they had come. They found a basic boarding house which suited them with its relaxed atmosphere and acceptable catering. They spent two months there, starting with days of wandering the town and the surrounding countryside which seemed calm and contented, sparse of population and complacent in the grandeur of the scenery.

The inhabitants they met were wary of strangers. It took calm to penetrate the reserve, to master some means of communication and to learn the etiquette of local habit. Tomas had to mix persistence with patience before it became possible to converse with the old men whom they had come to meet.

On their last night before a leisurely departure which would take them south in gradual stages to Islamabad and eventually to a flight which would carry them home to France, Tomas spoke to Tetrarch. In a little speech which was calculated to inform a man of immense brawn but stunted brain, Tomas spoke carefully and slowly.

'We have come a long way and thank you, as always, for being with me. Your strength and protection is all I need and now I can tell you why I wanted to make this journey. You remember the first part?'

Tetrarch just nodded.

'Over eight hundred years ago, a man came from Iraq, where he was born, to Alamut in Persia or Iran as it is now called. The old castle at Alamut is near Tehran and we went there twice.'

'God, I remember that well enough: a pain in the arse, that journey, to and from.'

Tomas smiled at him. 'Quite. Well, it was important to see because this man went there to start his training to become a member of a powerful group. He learned well and he was promoted to go and rule a large area of Syria - all the country we travelled through with Yaman. Yes?'

Another nod.

'Many years later, this man managed to defeat the conquering army of an invader. He convinced the leader that he had divine power, so the invaders went away.'

'What d'you mean by divine? Did this man have weapons? What did he use?'

'It was more what he said, Tetrarch. He did have weapons and he had his own fighting men, but even more than that, he had the power of authority and the invader believed him.'

Tetrarch kept on nodding and Tomas waited patiently. Finally, Tetrarch spoke again with another question.

'What has this do with us, Tomy? Why do we make this long journey for a man who died so long ago?'

'Because of his name, Tetrarch, that's why. I'll explain a bit more.'

There was more nodding and knuckling of the brow under the thatch of black hair as Tetrarch leant forward in his chair and linked his hands together over his knees as he prepared to concentrate.

'The birth name of this man was Rashid. His full title was Rashid ad-Din Sinan and he went by other names as well, but we needn't bother about all that. I started to read about him before you went to Chechnya. I used to go to the Library in Loches and I studied on the Internet. But even before that, Tetrarch, it was you who put the idea in my mind that I needed to do all this research.'

'Me?' The big man didn't try to conceal his astonishment.

'Yes, you. Really! When we were back in Mali, you told me that it was time for us to live our own lives: and you were quite right. I started looking back and I saw a steady pattern in all we've done so far. OK, so we've survived, getting richer and stronger and with a better place to live, all that. But other people have always decided our future for us and we've gone along with them. In childhood it's different of course, but you and I, we stopped being children when we were very young. We became independent, yet still tied to the instructions of others. You remember Dhaou in Tunis? Then Marseilles, then all those years on the ships. Yes?'

Tomas knew that Tetrarch had to get the prods and make the responses to keep his attention. Now there was another slow nod but this time accompanied by a deep sigh. That was good. He was tuned in.

'All the time in China was good for us both - Shanghai and Yumen where we learned much. Even so, we were completely under the control of Li and he himself was a puppet of the State. And we still went back to him for the Chechen job. So all the while, sort of doing what we were told.'

'OK Tomy, I got it. But that still doesn't tell me why we've got to bother with some poor old sod who's been dead for centuries.'

'Because that old sod went through the same as we have. And then he decided that wasn't good enough for him. He decided to take control for himself, stop being under instruction. So that's what he did. He founded a sect – that's like a group or organisation – of followers who would do anything he told them. They came to be feared and respected. They were called the Assassins.'

'Hah. So you mean they went around killing people?'

'Yes, they did a lot of that. Those were dangerous days and hard lives. But don't get the idea that this was just a gang of thugs. They were much more than that. They chose that name, Assassins, to frighten people and to build their reputation. The Sect members and their leader, this man Rashid, their whole purpose was to control and dictate. Rashid made himself and his organisation available for hire. He didn't want to own things. He didn't want to be a King or a Prince or an Emperor. He had his own home and refuge. That's the castle at Alamut.'

Tetrarch made to interrupt so Tomas signalled for him to speak.

'So this outfit was a sort of enforcer, like we have today?'

'A bit of that but a lot bigger and better. They didn't just enforce, they did all the planning, all the arrangements. Rashid would have a contract for a job and he would have complete control, so enforcing was only part of it.'

The lightbulb went on. 'And you think, Tomy, that we two could be doing the same sort of thing today?'

'Very good, my brother, that's just what I think.'

There was a long silence then while Tetrarch shuffled his feet and flexed his arms, the biceps bulging as he did so. Finally, he asked his next question which surprised and impressed Tomas.

'So, If this guy and his people were so big in Syria and Iran all that time ago, what are we doing up here in the middle of nowhere after ploughing through half of Afghanistan?'

'I told you that Rashid had several names. There was one which is very important. Friends and enemies called him the Old Man of the Mountain. That was his title as the founder and leader of the Assassins. He used to come up here, into the high country of the Hindu Kush, to renew his spirit. When things were tough and he was weary, I believe he would make his way east through all that hard country, just like we've done. I think he avoided fights with the Afghan tribes so he could get up to the top of the world and give himself some peace.

'That's why I wanted to come all the way here myself, Tetrarch, and I couldn't have made it without you. And now we've been here and I've talked to some important people, I know where you and I are going and confident we can make it.'

'OK. Well you know me, Tomy. If you're happy then I guess I am too. But don't go wearing out your batteries too quickly. I like it here too, but I'm not in any hurry to come back.'

20. VANDA DEVERIDGE — 1998

The Easter weekend fell in mid-April and the weather was kind. On the Saturday morning, it was warm enough to sit out on the terrace, enjoying a bottle of champagne before lunch. Vanda was determined to make the most of having both her daughters with her: it didn't happen often. On cue, she heard the back door bang noisily, the sound of dogs' paws scuttering on the worn flooring of the utility and then heavy padding as the large young man in his stockinged feet and farmer's working overalls came striding through the kitchen and out to join them, the normal beaming smile splitting his weatherworn features and the untidy mop of straw coloured hair flopping on his shoulders. Even better, Vanda thought to herself, now I have all my children together and that's rarer still.

'What's this, a coven of drinkers?' her son William demanded as he advanced on them, bending to kiss each in turn and waving off the bottle which his mother offered as he yanked at the ring pull of a can of lager.

'You smell of cow, dear brother', his sister Charley told him as she put a hand under her nose.

'How strange, and with this a farm too! Whatever next!' He boomed a great laugh and dragged up another chair, slumping into it with his can raised in a general salutation. 'Happy Easter all!'

Vanda looked at him fondly. As always, it amazed her to see his extraordinary likeness to his father, Luke. Not in build, of course as William at thirty was a far bigger man than his father had ever been but in the colouring, the features, especially the eyes and the firm, jutting chin, but the likeness stopped right there. Will was now an established and successful young farmer, already one of the pillars of this rural community. There was never an idle minute for Will, never a moment when he wasn't working, worrying, plotting some new scheme for expansion or general betterment of Home Farm.

This was a big business now and turning some handsome profits, so much so that Will had the full support of his uncle Rufus Slessor, side-lining the harpish Sarah. She continued her vendetta of sniping at Vanda but seldom descending from the grandeur of her Chelsea house to do so. These days, Sarah came down to Foy only on day visits to see her parents and they found these occasions as much of a burdensome duty as she did.

Tom and Majorie Deveridge had moved into their eighties but were behaving as if they were ten years younger. Tom had rediscovered his zest for life as his grandson was happy to pick his brains over plans for the future, harvesting the experience of bygone years as he developed his own strategy for the farmland which they both loved. Then there was the new baby. Will had married his Mhorag, the girl from the Welsh Valley north of Aberfan who had been a fellow student at Agricultural College and just three months previously, she had given birth to their first child, a son called Edward. Everyone in the family was delighted but none more than Majorie and Tom, for whom the baby signalled so much hope for a future which they had thought was lost.

It was news of Edward, of course, that his aunts demanded as they sat on the sun filled terrace watching his father swigging the lager. Hannah had popped over to meet the baby just after he was born in the small hospital in Ross-on-Wye but Charley had yet to be introduced.

'He's doing fine', Will announced with proprietorial pride, 'and we're expecting you all to come over to us for tea. Great grandparents are coming too, so Mhorag and I reckoned on doing a bit of head wetting. Are you on for that?'

'Terrific,' said Charley, 'just try to keep us away. And what's all the other news, Will? How's it all going here down on the vaarrrm?' She drew out the word with a suitably rural twang.

She and Will liked a bit of leg pulling and he responded in kind.

'All going pretty good, Charley thanks a lot, but of course it's classified news. Can't tell you or you'll go leaking it to the damn Cubans or someone!'

He slapped at a ham like knee as he laughed at her with Vanda and Hannah joining in. Charley grinned as she lifted her glass. It was always good to have some merriment and she was well aware that Will couldn't take his sisters' profession seriously. National security and farming at Foy really didn't mix as subjects. In keeping with the thought, he got stuck straight in to telling them all of the latest projects and progress at Home Farm, scarcely drawing breath for the next ten minutes. Then he glanced at his watch and said he must be getting back.

'I'll leave you girls to your lettuce leaves or whatever you're having. I've got one other thing to do on my way home to lunch and that's going to be a treat. I want to see how Hector's settling in.' And looking at the question marks on their faces, he added, 'Hector's my new bull: I bought him at market last week and I reckon he's going to be a winner. There are certainly plenty of ladies waiting for him and I've just got to hope he doesn't turn out to be a raving poof!'

Vanda was, as always, both surprised and content that there could be this sort of open badinage in the family about Charley's sexuality. What a changing world, she thought to herself as she walked into the kitchen and waved at her son's vanishing figure before turning to get out the quiche and toss a salad for lunch. There was some decent cheese too and they would have a bottle of Provencal to wash it down – perhaps two. There were things she wanted to talk over with her girls and at the top of her list was this house and what to do next. Will and Mhorag had taken a small cottage in the village: it was owned by the family but normally used as a holiday let. Now Edward had arrived, it was getting pretty cramped and she thought it was time for her to be making a move from the big house and allowing it to welcome the next generation. In the event, they hardly got onto that subject. When the three of them were sitting in front of loaded plates and full wine glasses, she bored straight in and asked Hannah the question which had been so much on her mind.

'Well. Have you heard anything from Simon yet?'

Hannah hadn't even picked up her knife and fork by then and she didn't move to do so now. She lifted her glass and took a sip at the very pale rosé before she turned to face her mother.

'Nothing like a direct question, Mum, but actually, yes I have, although it was only last week. It was a good long letter, a dozen pages or so, but he has been gone a couple of months now and that was the first I've heard from him.'

Charley put in, 'A letter? That's a bit old hat isn't it? Might be very romantic but it's stone age stuff.'

Hannah was grateful for the interruption. 'I know what you mean, Charley, and you're right. I had been expecting a phone call, E Mail, Text, whatever – even a bunch of flowers but to be fair, I had no idea just how cut off from civilisation he is until I got to read this letter. It was sent from Singapore, incidentally, posted by the first man out for some leave or whatever. Anyway, the point is that what they're up to there is not just hush-hush, it's also bloody remote. Apparently they're somewhere in the Highlands of PNG – that's New Guinea, north from Australia – and they're completely cut off while they prepare a camp and do a whole load of planning and training. It's obvious he can't tell me much more because he doesn't know himself. But I've got to tell you both that not being able to maintain any sort of normal contact is making me miss him more. I'm not sure if this was meant to be his novel idea of courting technique, but it does seem to be working.'

'Well, Darling, I'm happy for that at least,' said Vanda and really meant it for all that it sounded a bit trite and sloppy.

Charley came in to say, 'what I don't understand, Hannie, is that I thought Simon's outfit was Africa specific, so what's he doing on the other side of the world?'

Her sister shrugged her shoulders. 'Search me, honestly. I just don't know and if I asked, he wouldn't say. I'm just having to hang on to see.'

'And for how long?'

'Sometime next year. That's the only promise.'

'And what if some desirable, wealthy James Bond turns up in the meantime?'

'In that unlikely event, Charley, he can have me for a Big Mac and chips - unless of course I manage to get to him first!'

The two girls broke up with laughter and Vanda was happy to join in. She moved to change the subject.

'I've never asked before and I'm not looking for any details, but how much of each other do you see at work?'

Hannah replied. 'It depends, Mum, and it's surprising how much it varies. Sometimes not for days or weeks on end, then something will come up which involves us both and we might spend full working days together. That may sound strange but GCHQ is a vast organisation and there are so many of us scurrying about. The fundamental reason, though, is that Charley and I do such different work. She gathers information from a huge variety of sources whereas it's down to me and my lot to try and decipher what all the data means and how we should react to it. And there's one other big difference. Other than for emergencies, my working hours are fixed and I'm a sort of Monday to Friday civil servant.'

'But for me', Charley took over, 'no two weeks are the same because I'll be working one of three shifts and even within those you can move around depending on need and your language specialisation.'

'Golly', said their mother quite wishing she had never asked, 'it sounds pretty exhausting', and then she continued, surprised at her own daring because Charley's lesbian relationship was still something which she was making slow progress in understanding and accepting, 'how does Lizzie cope with these changeable hours? How difficult is it to plan your lives together? I mean I imagine that as a lawyer, she must work daytime even if it's not nine to five?'

'Yes, you're right Mum. It's not easy sometimes and it does lead to stresses and strains. But what relationship doesn't have those? Whoever you are, if what you've got is what you want, well - you've just got to find a way through all the shit, haven't you?'

Vanda steeled herself with another gulp of wine before she asked her next question.

'But you and Lizzie. Is it for life?'

Charley stopped eating and plucked a grape from the bowl in the middle of the table. She seemed to be considering the question while her mother and sister gazed expectantly at her. Finally, she formed her reply.

'First of all, thank you for asking. It means a lot to me because just asking that means you're taking me and Lizzie seriously. So, thank you.

'Look, I guess the answer is that she and I are growing closer and that's because we're managing to jump the hurdles together. The work bit is easy enough but the social taboos are tough, getting past the point at which friends and colleagues *permit* us to be together and getting to where they really accept us as a couple. We're going through the process of getting a legal partnership and when the law changes, we might get married but I'm not sure about that step. Neither of us wants children by any means or machinations and for myself, I'm still not comfortable with parenthood for single sex couples.'

'What does your father think?'

'Wow, Mum,' Charley expostulated but grinning at her, 'I'm really getting the third degree here. I'll be glad when it's your turn again,' she said smiling across the table at her older sister. Charley continued.

'It was an eye opener talking to Victor.' She always spoke of her father by his given name, never by some familiar diminutive. 'For a guy who's so one hundred percent hetero, I was really surprised by his reaction to my telling him that I'm gay. I mean there was no reaction. Not really. He just murmured something about going with whatever suited me and saying that now you can be whatever you want. Then he went straight on to talk about my career and what he's doing with his time. I must say that I was very moved. The one person from whom I'd expected outrage and horror and what did I get? Acceptance and support without any questions! I'm sorry, I don't mean to say that I've had anything less from you two – or Will and Mhorag come to that, it's just that I really didn't expect it from Victor. But there you are: life and people surprise you, don't they?'

There was an interlude of silence between them. Charley resumed eating, Hannah reached for her water glass and Vanda rose to make coffee. She was on her feet as she said to them.

'I hope he's going to relax a bit more. He's trying, I know, but he still spends too long at work.'

'But Mum, Victor's retired now, surely?' said Hannah.

'Yes he is and that helps. But he's still not making the life changes which he should. And that's before you take account of what time he's spending on this new passion of his. Tell her, Charley. You've seen him more recently than I have.'

Victor's specialist area of knowledge had been the drugs trade from South East Asia into mainland Europe and in retirement, he had set himself to write an investigator's manual in which he would set out all that he knew and how he had come about the knowledge over so many years.

'I must say', Charley was saying, 'he was looking well when I saw him a few weeks ago. Definitely a better colour, more relaxed in his manner, very stimulated by his work on this handbook or however you might describe it and absolutely fascinated by his research into all these bad guys of the East over generations past. He looked rejuvenated to me but he's not going to slow down, is he Mum? He's his own man with his own commitments and I can't see that will change while there's breath in the grand old body.'

'No,' said Vanda in reply, 'No you're right Charley and I accept that. I couldn't change him and I wouldn't want to try. But I don't want to lose him either. As you know, I love him and our brief times together. I just comfort myself that he'll last longer now that he's left the daily working grind and if he can cut back even a little on the lifestyle. When I was last with him, he had at least changed to fags with filters and he wasn't smoking in bed.'

Hannah cheered the tone of conversation by remarking, 'Well he wouldn't do that anyway, Mum, not while you're with him. He'll have better things to do than smoke!'

They all laughed as Vanda brought coffee cups to the table, but Hannah waved hers away.

'Have another glass of wine then. Or would you like some tea? You haven't eaten much, Hannah, is it my cooking?'

'Certainly not that, Mum, no. I'm just a bit off it all, probably because I'm pregnant.'

Charley goggled and her mother dropped a mug on the floor. Hannah wiped tears from her eyes and tried to smile at them. There was a prolonged silence, finally disturbed by Vanda as she wandered to the sink for a cloth and returned to start clearing up after the breakage. Finally, it was Charley who spoke.

'You're sure, are you?' and then hurrying on without waiting for a response, 'well yes of course you're sure. And about the father?'

Vanda gave a gasp of surprise at the question but Hannah didn't seem offended.

'Absolutely certain. There's been no one else and anyway, I know the day of conception. It was during the last weekend we had together. That was in February, cold and blowing in the West Country with little else to do but stay in bed.' She attempted another smile before going on, 'It was the last time I saw Si before he went off abroad and this letter is the first I've heard from him since then.'

'So he doesn't know?' Vanda kicked herself for asking such a stupid question but her daughter was gentle in reply.

'No Mum, he doesn't. He wouldn't have a clue. And he isn't going to find out.'

'But surely …' Charley started before her sister cut her off sharply.

'No, Charley. No to both of you. Simon doesn't know that I'm going to have his baby and we are *not* going to tell him. Not me and neither of you. Mind you, you'd struggle to make contact with him in the back of beyond and although I could probably get a message to him through Bastion, I'm not going to try and I want you both to promise me that you won't either. He's away, but he'll be back.'.

21. CIA LANGLEY — 1998

The huge complex of buildings sprawled in the sunshine of the autumn afternoon, the majesty of the fall colours not yet fully developed. Pedestrians and vehicles moved purposefully about their business and there was bustle throughout the offices and echoing corridors. The hub of the machine which exists to guarantee the security of the United States was beating with the activity which never ceases and numerous coloured signs gave warning that the status of alert was high.

In a conference room located on one of the upper floors, another meeting was getting underway. The attendees filed in to find their Chairman punctilious as always and in his place at the head of the broad, long table, his back to the window which gave a fine view over the spreading grounds. He was Stanton Aird the Third, old school Washington and money, a patrician figure with his carefully pampered, greying hair, beautifully tailored clothes and immaculate manner. He was long experienced in conducting such a gathering. He was also a realist, an imminent retiree from government service and within a year he would be on his way to the Hamptons, the golf courses and the charity dinners which would sustain him for the remainder of his days. But this afternoon, he would manage another trawl through the efforts of the worker bees, the grunts who represented departments at the CIA, each an area of specialist expertise. Aird was there to garner and sift the results of their efforts before presenting his own report to the President's National Security Advisor. He didn't expect much new today.

It was nearly three months since the bombing of two US Embassies in Africa. On 7th August, terrorist attacks in Nairobi and Dar es Salaam had killed nearly 250 people, injured over 4000 and caused extensive damage to buildings which stood, in effect, on US soil. America was horrified and outraged. President Bill Clinton had ordered a hard hitting retaliation, identifying targets in Sudan and Afghanistan. Less publicly, the President had railed at the CIA and the Intelligence community for their failure to anticipate such events and the lack of data to ensure that excesses by mop haired jihadists were discovered and strangled at birth. These passionate instructions from the Chief Executive had energised Langley into a maelstrom of investigation and analysis, underpinned with determination to leave no stone unturned, no contact untapped, no pressure less than fully applied. Weeks of constant work later and they were still at it and the Chairman would ensure that if there was a further nugget to be scooped from this group of relative juniors, he would find it. It would be good for his career to finish on an upward note, better still for the prospects of his only son, Stanton Aird the Fourth who was currently making unspectacular progress through the ranks of the State Department.

Instinctively, the Chairman rose to his feet to pull out a chair for the remarkably pretty girl who was there to represent Ballistics. She smiled at him with a touch of flirtation but as he opened the meeting and invited her to speak first, he had to admit that she was competent and self-assured in her role. Nonetheless, Ballistics had little new to report. She could now confirm that three victims in Kenya and one in Tanzania had all been killed by a close contact weapon of unusual make and calibre …. But. She allowed the unspoken conclusion of 'so what' to hang in the air.

Next to speak was Analysis, a heavy set, middle aged man who expanded in dreary detail on the likely provenance of all the attackers in both cities. He offered nothing which was not already known.

The Chairman moved on to Communications, a tall beanpole of a fellow whose prominent Adam's apple wobbled as he spoke. Comms reported that they had not intercepted any fresh transmissions during the past week which he could state positively to have relevance to the attackers in Africa. He was, however, awaiting further comment from 'our friends at GCHQ, Cheltenham, England'. The Chairman thought he had covered his ass sufficiently and invited the latest thoughts from Special Ops.

This muscled young man gave every impression that he would be happier killing people efficiently than addressing a conference but it became evident that he was constrained by knowing nothing more of whom to kill.

The Chairman turned to Language, a dumpy little woman of middling years and uncertain origin. He had come across her before but could not remember if she was born in Turkey or Teheran. Language gave them fifteen minutes of recap, delivered in her mellifluous tones with just a touch of American idiom and finally came out with some new news. Did they all, she asked, remember the triumphalist message over a satellite phone to a landline in Lahore, Pakistan which the Brits had intercepted just after midday local on the day after the attack? Yes, of course, they all remembered. Well, announced Language, she and her colleagues were now convinced beyond reasonable doubt that the speaker's native tongue was Pushtu. She had picked that up from the very few words decipherable amongst the whoops and cheers, also from the accent in which the caller had finished by speaking in guttural English '..... and Praise to the Fountain Head.'

There were twelve of them round the table and the Chairman could see that there was appetite for debate over this announcement but he cut it off smoothly. There would be time for sparring after they had heard all contributions, so he called next on Ordnance. He didn't expect a revelation from this quarter and wasn't disappointed. The slightly built, sandy haired man with the trace of a Scots accent told them his Department had nothing further to add. They had pored over all the fragments of bomb material which had been recovered from the sites, they knew precisely what it all was, how it had been put together, primed, carried and detonated. They knew also with absolute certainty the identity of the bombs' designer and he was the Ethiopian, Nathaniel Habtumu. It had been skilful, sophisticated work but he had left a clear calling card in the materials used and the manner of construction. It seemed that he wanted to be recognised.

The Chairman continued to invite contributions in his calm, unhurried style. They heard from Transport about the vehicles used, from Pathology, from Dentistry and from DNA, all three of whom confirmed information about the identity of the attackers who had died at the two scenes. Finally, they heard from Statistics who did add something new, namely the very latest headcount, an unfortunate expression, of all who had died or been injured.

Stanford Aird noted that there was one attendee who had yet to speak. Consulting his notes, he identified that it was Records, placed at the far end of the conference table. Records was a young man to be marked down as an academic by the look of his shaggy hair and scruffy clothing. He responded to the Chairman's invitation with diffidence.

'I should explain, Sir, that I am from Records but my subject is actually history'.

'Very well, Mr History,' said the Chairman, 'kindly tell us what you have to report.'

'OK, Sir, it's this. I have no qualification in language or matters cultural so when I question this transmission which includes the reference to the "Fountain Head", I'm not challenging the expertise of my colleagues.'

Just as well, thought the Chairman, or we'll be here all day with the ensuing turf war. But already a pudgy hand had gone up and he thought he'd better let Analysis come back with whatever was clearly riling him.

'Thank you, Mr Chairman. Look, I just want to emphasise that we've raked over those few words every which way during the last coupla months. We've used our most sophisticated gear and we've run them fast, slow, forwards backwards, every damn thing we could think of. But the words were spoken quickly, indistinctly and there was a helluva lot of background noise - gunfire, shouting, something being dragged - all that stuff. Now, no question the guy says "Praise" and for my money, I'm damn sure he says "Fountain". I'm not so certain about the "Head", but it does make sense. Fountains, as we know, play an essential role in the Islamic faith. Mosques provide the means for ritual washing, so our man here is simply rejoicing at what they've achieved and paying thanks and tribute to his God, to Allah, for their success. He's laying a sort of claim to the bombing sites as instant shrines, suitable to become Mosques with all the necessary accoutrements.'

More hands were being raised around the table but the Chairman spoke firmly to maintain his control of the meeting.

'That's interesting. But it's not new, is it? We've been through all this before and I don't see that we have cause to ponder the imponderable any further. You may well be correct in your deduction,' he paused and nodded in the direction of Analysis,' but whatever the motive for that terrorist comment in the heat of the moment, we are still no closer to identifying the speaker or the person to whom he was speaking in Lahore. I have, therefore, nothing further to report onwards and upwards. Is that not so?'

He looked round the attendees and could see from their expressions that there was to be no questioning his conclusion. Except from one. At the end of the table, History had his hand up, perhaps he had never dropped it, and the Chairman was conscious that the scruffy young man had been cut off by Analysis. He signalled History to proceed.

'Sir, this is just speculation but I suggest it's possible that the attacker didn't say "Praise to the Fountain Head", but rather, "Praise to the Mountain Men". That could be significant and I can explain why.'

Encouraged by a nod from the Chairman and the heightened interest in the room, History warmed to his theme and spoke fluently.

'The Mountain Men were a secret sect of fighters who originated nearly a thousand years ago and flourished for about a century. They were hard as nails, highly disciplined, very skilled in their performance and ruthless in action. They were known also as the Assassins. Their main area of action was in what is now northern Syria but there is record of them operating much further East and many were recruited from the high country of the Hindu Kush, which lies in both Afghanistan and Pakistan. Essentially, the Mountain Men were guns for hire, or you could say mercenaries.'

Sensibly, History paused at this point to allow his words to sink in. No question was posed and he could see the Chairman sitting forward in his seat and concentrating. History continued.

'The Mountain Men were more than just muscle. At the insistence of their founding leader, they operated to a contract which gave them the responsibility and the power not just to execute an action, but to plan and control it as well. So they accepted the brief, agreed the terms, made the strategy and evolved the tactics. The whole shebang, therefore, from start to finish.

'Now the Mountain Men themselves are long gone of course, but we're wondering if, maybe, the ideas and the title with it have been resurrected. Our thoughts have been sharpened by something else. Global atrocities in the past have been horrific and bloody, but also haphazard. The World Trade Center bombing is a good example. Bad as it was, it could have been a whole lot worse and would have been if the bombers hadn't made mistakes.

'But Nairobi and Dar are different. Here they got it right. Here were two attacks which went, as far as we can judge, exactly according to plan. What's more, they were precisely coordinated: two bombings, two cities, same day, same time. We're wondering if they got their act so well together by employing someone to do it for them. Maybe a master planner who's got none of their passion or ideology, doesn't care about the end, is simply there to be the professional who guarantees the means. A guy or a group called the Mountain Men.'

History concluded and sat back in his chair. He had successfully lit the fuse on his own sort of bomb, the Chairman thought to himself as he presided over an enlivened conversation which would now take up a further two or three hours. At least when he finally did get clear, Stanton Aird would have something new and significant to report back to Washington.

22. IMOGEN — 1998

The baby was born at 3 o'clock in the morning of Thursday 19th November. The birth was normal, quite straightforward and reasonably swift. Mother and child were enfolded in the care of seasoned professionals at the small cottage hospital in the Herefordshire countryside. Joy at this happy and healthy arrival was unconfined even if it was incomplete.

Three days later, Vanda drove her daughter and granddaughter home to Foy and Hannah started to busy herself with the miracles and mysteries of motherhood. After the birth of a child, life is never quite the same again - not for either parent but especially not for the mother. How often had she heard this sort of wise and knowing expression from a relative or a friend? Well, thought Hannah to herself as she watched the baby gurgling happily at her breast, she had her own twist on this experience. There must be innumerable absent fathers, but not so many who would have walked across the world to be there. Si would have done that but he had never known of the developing existence, let alone the entry of his daughter onto the stage of life.

Hannah was sorry but she didn't feel guilty. She trusted her instinct and knew she was right. But that hadn't made the secret any easier to keep and during the months of her pregnancy, there had been any number of occasions when she had been so tempted to let him know, but the difficulty in communication had always helped her to keep to her resolve. The greatest test had come at the end of October. The clocks had just changed bringing darker, longer evenings. She had stopped work and moved to live with her mother at Foy. She felt huge and uncomfortable, wishing the baby would hurry up and get on with it. Time had slowed to a crawl and she couldn't even have a drink to help it pass. She heard the phone ring and the gasp from Vanda as she answered. She heard her say:

'Good heavens! Simon! Where are you?' and then, 'yes, she's here. Hang on while I pass you over.' So saying, she chucked the remote at Hannah and made an exit from the snug room where they were sitting by the fire.

'Well, here's a surprise!'

'I know,' Simon said, 'I can't tell you how frustrating it's been the last few months, being unable to ring you - or anyone else for that matter.'

'So how come now?' Hannah checked herself as she spoke, realising that she was sounding petulant already. The baby kicked violently and she shifted herself to try and find a more comfortable position.

'I'm in Singapore', he was telling her, 'flew in from Port Moresby yesterday. In a helluva rush to replace a bit of kit we broke and I've got to go back at midday. It's in the early hours for me here and I've been desperate to reach you. I tried your flat number and your mobile but I didn't risk the office. I finally guessed you must be at Foy – but why midweek?'

'It's just for the night,' Hannah lied fluently, 'Mum's not been very well so I nipped over. But don't worry about all that, Si. Tell me what's going on and tell me when you're coming home. I miss you.'

He gave a great sigh and she heard him take a gulp at something: no doubt a decent drink, the lucky bugger. Then he was going on.

'Well, that's good to hear anyway. And my God I'm missing you too but I hope my letters have been getting to you?'

'They have,' she replied thinking of the all the pages sitting upstairs beside her bed,' and they are a real comfort, I promise, except that you can't cuddle a letter.'

'Tell me about it! It's no better when you're writing them, that's for damn sure! But give me some news, Darling one, and I'll tell you mine.'

They talked for an hour and more. Hannah was all the while conscious of what she was inventing, improvising, and even more of what she avoiding. It made her feel better to hear Simon glossing over his details of the camp they had built and their activities, devoting more time to talk of the terrain, the weather, the people and the discomforts. She understood that he could not, would not dwell on their mission. That made two of them. It also had the effect of bringing her closer to him than she had ever felt before. He would be worth the wait..

23. TOMAS AND TETRARCH — 1999

The Mountain Men spent most of the year at home in the Loire, plotting and planning. Following their success in Africa, they had a brief now, a new and larger contract. The understanding which had developed in conversation with the quiet old men in Chitral had blossomed over time. The language barrier had diminished with the introduction of the unnamed, unseen Interpreter. By now, Tomas had confidence in him and the use of English worked satisfactorily for them both.

Each week, Tomas and Tetrarch left the Mesnil and drove to Bordeaux or Toulouse, sometimes to Orleans, once to Tours. They would use a one time, throwaway mobile or a public phone in a crowded, city centre site and Tomas would make the call for never more than four minutes while Tetrarch stood to one side in unwavering concentration on their surroundings.

Travelling back from one of these excursions in May, with an endless evening light and little traffic, Tomas reflected that the Interpreter reduced communication to an exchange of facts and operational intentions. There was no need to be diverted into philosophy or passion. Tomas knew the old men were not like that. For them, the objectives could not be discussed without discourse into the myriad reasons for their discontent which led to how their God was inspiring their efforts. None of that mattered to the Mountain Men. They were the professionals. They were unmoved by any expression of piety, any noble endeavour in the name of God or Mammon. Let the politicians and prophets spew out their call to arms, let them preach their claims of injustice and let them rant their blood-curdling hymns for revenge. In the end, they depended on the Men of Action, those who could see clearly without the contamination which arrived with high flown ideals. Tomas understood that to succeed, you needed to be devoid of involvement, pure of principles. It was exactly that clarity which had guided the Mountain Men of old and it was no less correct a thousand years later.

The long summer broiled its way past. They had their commission from the Elders of Chitral but the timing for its execution was tight and it was already clear that there would have to be some delay. They didn't lack for money or weaponry. There was no difficulty with people either. They were not expensive and were perfectly prepared to die for their belief. The problem was location. To prepare for this operation, it was essential to find a site which guaranteed space and peace. It must provide access for heavy equipment, living accommodation and buildings in which training facilities could be constructed. It had to be sufficiently remote to be secret. Their existence must be unknown and unsuspected until they were ready to move.

As Tomas researched and planned, Tetrarch would slip away from time to time to spend an evening carousing with Nat Habtumu. He was never late in returning but made plain that he enjoyed these outings – usually in Poitiers, sometimes Paris and once for a couple of days in London. When they were not up to mischief, Nat was happy to talk about his life and his exploits. Tetrarch would listen in his normal heavy silence but he took it all in and reported it back to Tomas. Nat was inordinately proud of his ability with explosives: he delighted in recalling his activities in Chechnya and Nairobi. He bragged about other episodes, especially the World Trade Center bombing six years previously.

Tetrarch was primed by his twin to ask Habtumu why he didn't worry about his security as he must be on the wanted list of a dozen Agencies around the world. The reply was typical of the man.

'I swear the Elegance fashion label gives me cover, that's why. Not even my cousin in Addis who runs the outfit knows everything I get up to and all those fuckin' smartass security guys reckon I'm just one fine lookin' sassy pouf makin' my fortune dressing ladies round the world. They don't see a prime bomber in stylish Natty Habtumu!'

Musing on this, Tomas thought Habtumu was living in a fool's paradise but he could go his own way provided he didn't drag Tetrarch with him. It was a worry but Tomas would find comfort by slipping off to the other side of Loches to dally with the slim and sultry woman and her extraordinarily exotic body which had grown lonely since she abandoned her husband.

In September, the Twins drove through the Pyrenees into Spain to look at two sites between Santiago de Compostela and Lugo in the north west and then a third just over the border into Portugal, near Braga. All three had features to recommend them but none was quite right. On the long drive back to Loches, Tomas started to think about North Africa and asked Tetrarch for his feelings. They talked about it as they took the fast route through Bilbao and crossed the border with France to travel home via Biarritz. They found themselves in agreement. Morocco, Tunisia, Algeria, even Western Sahara, any of these might well offer the sort of sanctuary they were seeking but they would be bolt holes which could easily become cul de sacs. Beyond that, they had been children and teenagers in these countries, fleeing for their lives and surviving on their wits. They were long past all that now. They were the Mountain Men and they didn't wish to revisit their early days.

By this time, the countryside around le Mesnil was wearing autumn colours and the days were growing shorter. So too were tempers and conversations with the Interpreter grew more testing as he struggled to be diplomatic whilst putting across the message from the old men of Chitral that they were becoming frustrated. Tomas had promised results and a commitment for the new century. Why now such a delay?

Action was needed, so before the end of the year, the Mountain Men flew back to Pakistan, to Chitral for a conference with the Elders. They arrived in Chitral on the 22nd December after a plane changing itinerary and an endless drive by hire car north west from Rawalpindi. They took a day's break in the rest house and met the Elders on the 24th which was a Friday.

There are occasions on which God and Allah move in a mysterious way. As they talked over green tea and sweet cakes, news came to them of the hijack of an Indian Airlines Airbus which had been in flight from Kathmandu to Delhi when it was taken over by masked gunmen. There followed an extraordinary saga lasting a week during which the plane flew with its captors and captives from India to Pakistan to Dubai and finally to Kandahar in Afghanistan, then under the control of Taliban authorities, who arranged for the 190 hostages to be released and the militants dispersed.

Tomas could not have wished for a better backdrop to his talks with the Elders. Here was a perfect example of how not to stage an incident in support of some grand cause. As was evident from each day of this developing farce, the hijackers were completely disorganised. Their demands were vague, they were unable to coerce the pilot to fly to their intended destination because the plane was not carrying enough fuel. As the drama unfolded, they kept changing destination, changing requirement and changing conditions. They permitted one hostage passenger to die of stab wounds inflicted more in panic than by design. They were helped only by a correspondingly chaotic response from the authorities in India. The whole enterprise was a disaster, said Tomas delivering a harsh verdict, and it failed because the hijackers had not been prepared: they did not have a plan. They had been gung ho, shooting from the hip and hoping for the best. Their reward was a shambles and they had been lucky to escape with an ignominious ejection from Afghanistan. Such an outcome would not happen with the Mountain Men in charge, but sound planning was essential and that took time and great care.

The Elders of Chitral were suitably mollified and impressed. As the week went by, they became progressively more relaxed and amenable. They had questions to ask and suggestions to make but it was clear that their faith in the Mountain Men was restored. They were content to wait a little longer and see their patience justified by the excellence of result.

Part Two

HUBRIS

presumption towards the gods

1. NEW YEAR'S DAY — 2000

It was not until the second day of the new century that news of a coup d'etat on the West Coast of Africa spread around the world. Even then, most people were more interested to hear that the dire predictions about the date change on computer systems had proved to be without foundation.

Then the news bulletins and the commentators made it clear that this was not a normal coup, not the sort of bloodletting and overturning of one faction by another which was a familiar occurrence on the continent of Africa.

This was different and it was not a coup at all: it was an invasion.

The perpetrators had spent years in planning and a fortune in investment to provide for the required equipment and personnel. They were led by an Englishman of retirement age, a successful entrepreneur who had spent a working lifetime travelling throughout Africa. His name was David Heaven and he came in from the ocean with three ships and 3000 people in the small hours of the new century. His aim was to take control of an established sovereign state and to replace it with a new country, a new order and a new society. The nation was renamed as Millennium and the coastal capital at which they landed took the title of Century City.

Kingston Offenbach and Pente Broke Smith didn't need to hear an announcement. They were party to the ambitious undertaking conceived by their old friend David Heaven and on New Year's morning, they were flying with him and others over mainland Africa, approaching an airport which they hoped would be flying a new flag to greet them. In the spacious comfort of the 747 which was configured to carry both passengers and cargo, Pente and King tried to relax although they were both buoyed up with nervous anticipation. There was no turning back now. They were committed.

Hank Devine heard a report in the evening, local time, of the 1st of January. It had been a bitterly cold day in Peace River, Alberta and he had spent it inside, arranging the small workshop which was integral to the house he had bought only two blocks from the prairie hospital in which he had been born. He had kept the log burning furnace hard at work all day and had been comfortable as he constructed shelves and cupboards. He made himself a meal and was sitting down to it in front of the TV when the national news ran a piece on the coup in West Africa. Hank listened to it all, fork poised halfway to his mouth, before he laid it back on the plate and rose to pour himself a stiff Scotch. He raised it to a distant horizon and drank deeply. Putting down the glass, he banged his great ham hands on the table and gave a spontaneous guffaw.

'Jeez,' he said to himself, 'I just knew King was up to something he wouldn't talk about and goddam if I'm not right. He'll be mixed up in this for certain sure and it wouldn't surprise me if he had Pente with him. Aw, shit, I wish they had me too!'

Natty Habtumu spent the New Year weekend in London. There was an Elegance fashion show in Kensington on the Friday at which he officiated in his flamboyant style but found time to notice the large black African, draped in a superbly tailored suit, who sat in the front row with a ravishingly beautiful women on either side. At the drinks reception which concluded the occasion, Nat made sure that he was introduced to this impressive giant who turned out to be the son and heir of the President of a West African State. He had a charming style and a wandering eye. Nat recognised a fellow mischief maker and they went on to spend a riotous night together in the company of these spectacular girls and a few other hangers on.

At the Chateau du Mesnil, they got a full report on the television evening news. It was Sunday 2nd January and the coverage was extensive because a large number of French and

Belgian expatriates lived in the country - many of whom had been there all their lives. There was a piece from a stringer on the largest circulation newspaper in the Ivory Coast. The guy had been homeward bound to Abidjan from an assignment in Burundi, changing planes when he got caught up in the firefight at the airport, a priority target for the invading force. He made a brave job of reporting on the violence in the airport, specifying how the attackers had shepherded bystanders away from the action. It was all voice-overs, of course, but editors in Paris had inserted photographs and some footage of the airport buildings which added to the quality of the account. Switching off the TV at the end of it, Tomas was impressed. The military operation seemed to have been well executed. It would make for another good example to put before the Elders.

Simon Goring didn't need to wait for any form of news. He'd been making it himself.

At three o'clock in the afternoon of Sunday, 2nd January, Simon was stretched out on the bunk in his very small cabin on the vessel which had carried him into this country. He had been sent to get some rest by his boss, the Strike Force Commander Fergus Carradine, after thirty-six hours of continuous action but now he found that he couldn't sleep. He wasn't really surprised. So much had happened, there were so many images taken from the recent hours which kept popping back into his mind. As soon as he closed his eyes, he was back in the airport control tower, the euphoria of success overtaken by adrenaline as the first of the opposition arrived in their trucks. Then the confused fighting, the firing, the running across the tarmac of the runway, expecting a spray of shots to cut him down in pain and blood at any second: sprawling on the ground beneath that colossus aeroplane, his chin grazed by the rough surface: standing on the shoulders of his back-up to jump for the belly cargo hatch and dangling there while he fought to pull himself in, anticipating again the blast of fire which would take him out for ever.

It was all as he had been told when he first enlisted in the Marines. You can practise forever but nothing can quite prepare you for action in earnest. And now it was all over and he had not a scratch to show for it, all he really wanted was not sleep but the distraction of conversation, to talk it over with someone else. He just had to speak to Hannah.

Simon swung his legs off the bunk and jumped to his feet. He was still in boots and battledress, grubby and bloody in places. He was un-showered and unshaven: he must have smelt like a Barbary ape as he picked up his helmet and his weapon, heading for the Bridge and the Communications Room, located just behind it. Sparks was a heavily bearded Welshman whom Simon had come to know well during their long sea voyage from Asia to Africa. In response to the question, he had a quick and welcome answer.

'You needn't bother with my hi-tech kit, boyo, just pick up your mobile and make your call. Easy as that. We may be pirates in a strange land but nobody's told the telecoms guys anywhere. It's business as normal so far.'

Simon took his phone and found himself a quiet spot on the afterdeck. It was Sunday: the New Year and New Century weekend. He punched in the landline number for Foy and knew with certainty that she would be there.

Vanda answered on the third ring. 'Just hold on', was all she said and then the familiar, slightly husky voice was with him and he could picture Hannah pushing back her huge glasses onto the top of her head - a gesture when speaking on the phone about which he had always teased her.

'Well', she said, 'and where are you this time?'

'Wherever you like to imagine', he replied, 'but it's very good to have arrived and to be getting established. Not so good as to be speaking to you again.'

'You're certainly making the news here now. Lots of Press and TV coverage, with commentary ranging from gung-ho to outraged. I guess we're all a bit out of practice for Francis Drake stuff these days.'

He gave more of a grunt then a laugh, giving Hannah a clue and she went on.

'You sound pretty knackered, Si. Tell me about it.'

So he did, pouring out more detail than he should although he named no names, no places. The security risk didn't seem to matter, whereas the relief and relaxation he derived from talking to her was immeasurable. He answered her questions as best he could, painted a picture with all the imagination he could muster.

It took half an hour before Hannah gently interrupted him.

'You should stop now, Simon. Stop and rest. You're going to need all your strength in the coming days and I hope there won't be too many more of those before you can come back.'

'Me too,' he replied, 'I'll let you know'.

Ringing off, Simon returned to his cabin and his bunk. He would sleep now and then he would go and talk to Fergus. It was about six weeks short of two years since he had taken the appointment and started on this journey. It was time to go home.

2. APRIL — 2000

Spring came reluctantly to the Loire Valley. At le Mesnil, Tetrarch was busy in his garden while Tomas was forever occupied with scheming, research and regular contact with the Interpreter. Pressure from the Elders in Chitral was growing again. They had an army of recruits ready to go. They wanted action and were chafing at delay.

For Tomas, the same problem remained. The elements of strategy were dropping into place – the targets, the timing, the numbers and equipment required. But they could not move without training, repeated practice to make sure that the grand and complex plan unfolded to perfection. The Mountain Men would not risk a botched operation. Preparation was vital and for that, Tomas had to find a secure base.

Help and a solution came eventually, but it was from an unexpected source. Towards the middle of the month, the Twins were sitting over supper one evening when Tetrarch started one of his rare monologues.

'Nat phoned yesterday,' he announced between mouthfuls, 'says he's back in Paris and wants me to make a trip. Stay over a few days and talk about this new friend of his in London who wants a bit of help. Is it OK with you, Tomy?'

'I think so, yes. We can make a call to the Interpreter tomorrow but you mustn't be late back as I'll need you for the next one. Who's the friend?'

Tetrarch shrugged his massive shoulders. 'Nat hasn't said much. It's some black guy he met in a club. Name of Jago. I don't know the rest but Nat says he's a big wheel. Son of some African President - or was. His papa got taken out during that coup at the New Year and this Jago is busy trying to get himself back in charge. Nat says he's a good operator but needs some muscle. Might be a chance for us.'

Tomas was interested and became more so when Tetrarch returned from his binge in Paris with the full story. It was all so typical of Nat with his supreme self-confidence and lack of discretion. Following his New Year celebrations – momentous in every way – he had finally woken in his hotel room to find himself still accompanied by his striking companion from the night club. From her he discovered the name of their host, he being a regular and generous client of this girl. Nat took it upon himself to pay a visit to show appreciation and in the hope of further action. It was midday on Tuesday 4th January when he marched into the Embassy building in Holland Park and asked to see Prince Jago Bourdier-Tamalou. Nat was gratified to be shown straight into a luxurious office in which his benefactor was seated behind a desk the size of an aircraft carrier. Only then did the wheels turn in his head and he sharpened up his act in an instant. This young guy, who couldn't be more than thirty, had been set to inherit a kingdom but someone had just stolen it from him.

With his accustomed good luck, Habtumu had timed it just right. Jago had moved during the long weekend from debauched insensibility through shock, then horror, then impassioned anger to the point where Nat found him immaculate in charcoal suit and Hermes tie, toying with a silver propelling pencil as he considered his options. Only of one thing was Jago implacably certain. He was going to get his country back: it belonged to him.

Their first conversation was brief but for Nat, it was immediately promising. He gushed with sympathy for Jago's predicament, promising an attentive ear and all the help he could offer. The paunchy young African beamed his thanks and took a phone number as he stood to escort Nathaniel out of the building, towering over him.

Jago was good for this commitment and they spent a lot of time together over the next three months. Nat came to understand that 'Prince' was simply a nickname, the 'Bourdier' had been invented by Jago's grandfather to enhance his own status after he had grabbed power in a military coup thirty-five years previously and 'Tamalou' was the name of the tiny bush village which provided the origins of the family.

Whatever the humble background, this family had done well for itself, bestriding an African nation as it tried to shake off its colonial provenance. The first President of the newly independent country had been no more than an appointee of the colonising power. Jago's grandfather had disposed of him and his clique with bloody efficiency and had been no less ruthless in securing his own power base. His son, Jago's father, had built on these foundations and had stamped sharply on internal dissension in recent years. Jago explained that restive factions had been encouraged by the widely publicised discovery of a new oil field off the country's Atlantic coast.

'We call it the Tamalou Trench', he told Nat, 'and it's just huge. The Yanks found it and proved it, the French want to drill it and the Brits want to buy in. Why wouldn't every bugger want a slice? It's high quality crude, there's more than can be measured so far and it's ours. Or it was, until those fuckers, whoever they really are, invaded on New Year's Day. I was only here in London to celebrate the Century before going back to help my Dad and now I've lost him as well as the country. But I'm not giving up. That country, that oil, all that money – that's my birthright and I'm sure as hell going to get it back.'

Jago and Nat didn't just talk as they got to know each other. Nature had given them much in common. They were both genial souls to meet and provided entertaining company. Both loved to party, to drink, to dabble in some mild stimulants and both had a powerful sex drive.

As the weeks passed, Jago gave him more background. He detailed the power of his position, the status which came with being President in waiting and he fulminated against the carpetbaggers who had arrived out of nowhere to steal his future. He never failed to finish one of these frequent diatribes with a vow to win it all back.

To massage his new friend's ego and to ensure benefit for himself, Nat was quick to tell Jago of his own exploits and especially to emphasise that whilst women's fashion was a successful commercial cover, his real talents lay in his ability as a bomber.

'I'm the best you'll ever find, Jago, and I'm yours for free: at least until we get you home and in your palace!'

There was no great rush. Jago was encouraged that the Embassy here in London remained unmolested and the same went for Paris, Brussels and Berlin. It was clear that the establishment by force of arms of this new country in Africa which the invaders had christened Millennium remained unfinished business for the major powers of Europe.

This was still the status when Nat Habtumu came over to spend time with Tetrarch in Paris and after hearing all the details, Tomas was intrigued by the possibilities. It was a bit far south in Africa but at least in the right time zone for Europe and it did seem likely that all the action was confined to the Capital and the coast. Tomas imagined that for the present, there would be vast swathes of bush country which would be more remote than ever and where better to hide that amongst uncertainty? They could offer Jago help for this domestic dispute and he need never know that they had an additional agenda. Tomas gave Tetrarch a brief for Habtumu to present and an instruction for him to get back to London and Jago with urgency.

Nat took an overnight bag to Charles de Gaulle Airport the following day and checked it onto his Air France flight to Heathrow. He received his boarding pass with a polite farewell from the lady at the counter.

'Alors, bonjour Monsieur Habtumu, et bon voyage'.

Nat didn't notice the bronzed, fit looking young man who was standing immediately behind him in the check-in queue. Equally, Simon Goring didn't recognise Habtumu as they had never met face to face, but the name was seared on his memory and the quick flash of an Ethiopian passport attracted his interest. He made sure he was close enough in the queues and on the plane to study the face, the features, the build and height. He used his phone to grab a quick photo.

Simon had endured a weary trip out of Africa. He had wanted to leave much sooner but Fergus Carradine had been very persuasive in asking for a little more help and he had been backed up by King Offenbach. Added to that was the difficulty with travel as even three months on from the invasion, only charter flights were landing in Century City with none of them returning directly to Europe. Eventually, he hitched a ride on a scruffy old cargo plane as far as Lagos and two days later, he took a scheduled commercial flight to Paris. Arriving there, he bought a ticket to London and was waiting his turn when he heard the name which jolted him from his travel torpor.

At Heathrow, Simon loitered behind Habtumu as they waited for their luggage. Then they went their separate ways, Simon too keyed up at the prospect of seeing Hannah for any further thoughts.

Nat took the Underground into Central London and went straight to the Embassy building in Holland Park. He now had an offer to put to Jago and they would need to do some talking. But first, some entertainment was called for and he had no difficulty in persuading the African into a night out on the tiles.

About a hundred miles away, Simon was arriving by coach in Cheltenham and taking a taxi to the address she had given him. It turned out to be a comfortable, pretty large apartment in one the town's renowned Regency buildings. She was waiting outside on the pavement as his cab drew to the kerb. A late midday sun was shining but it was chilly in the wind and she was wearing long boots and a coat with the collar turned up, her hair billowing around the usual large glasses perched on the top of her head. She looked reassuringly familiar and irresistibly attractive but their greeting was subdued as they felt instinctively shy with each other. She took him up in the lift, through the hallway and into her light and airy kitchen where she had a pot of coffee waiting. They embraced again, this time more warmly and with a hint of rising passion but

Hannah broke it off to smile and tell him that he smelt of tiredness and travel. They started to talk at once and then stopped in unison. Simon rested his back against the floor to ceiling freezer, letting his gaze wander over the tailor made units which lined the walls and the centrally placed work surface with its gleaming hob and eating counter on which stood a vase of spring flowers.

'It's been a long, long time,' he said simply.

'I know: two years and a bit. We have an awful lot of talking to do, so let's make a start. Why don't you go and have a bath and change. Then we can go out on the town and take things from there.'

He nodded and picked up his bag.

Ten minutes later, he was lying in the bath and wondering what was to happen next. It was bloody marvellous to be back home in the UK, very much better to be with Hannah again but they had been a hell of a long time apart and he told himself to take it slowly. He was much impressed with this pad – a fine big sitting room, two double bedrooms both ensuite and another room but with the door firmly closed. She must be doing pretty well at GCHQ. The only downside was that he was, right now, definitely in the spare room.

Simon's jumbled thoughts as he rubbed shampoo into his hair were interrupted by a strange sort of noise which he simply couldn't identify. Something had come into the bedroom and was making its way towards him. He sat up abruptly and splashed water over his ears, trying to make it out. It sounded like the squeak of wheels: was his suitcase being moved? Surely she couldn't be appearing with the Hoover?

There was a soft clunk of wheel on wood as the bathroom door was pushed open and he was alert, completely confused, reaching for a towel and about to emerge when he stopped, transfixed as the front wheels of a little pushcart appeared. He took in the random jumble of small, coloured bricks which it carried and then his eyes widened as the figure behind it advanced cautiously into view. A child stood there, supporting itself on the handle of the cart, regarding him with wide open eyes of curiosity.

They studied each other for what seemed an age before Hannah stepped into the doorway, relaxed and smiling with a transparent pride.

'Simon Goring', she announced, 'allow me to introduce you to your daughter. Her name is Imogen.'.

3. JULY — 2000

From the first of the month, Habtumu rented an apartment in a tower block overlooking Lord's Cricket Ground in St John's Wood. It was expensive but he overrode objections from Loches by saying that it was convenient for Holland Park and important for keeping up appearances with Jago. He said nothing about its convenience for visiting women.

Back at le Mesnil, they were occupied with other matters. Since the beginning of the year, the Interpreter had been supplying names and contact details for those loyal to the cause who had come, for varied reasons, to be living in Europe. There were nearly fifty of them, scattered through Germany, France and the Low Countries and all had been told that they could expect contact from the Mountain Men with instructions which they must obey to the letter. They included both men and women, single and married, in jobs ranging from railway worker to paediatrician. According to the Interpreter, all these people were of the highest quality but that would be simply the opinion of the old men of Chitral and Tomas would not take their judgement on trust. So during the months of June and July, the Twins were almost constantly on the road, days spent on travel, meetings and interviews. It took time, particularly because Tetrarch conducted all the conversations by himself, moving ponderously through an agenda of questions prepared in advance. Tomas remained in the background to listen and observe.

Tomas was also absorbing the quantity and quality of media coverage on the new African country of Millennium. Coups d'etat don't grip the public imagination for long, especially not if they have taken place in a little known African State which most people would struggle to place on the map. But the affair in Millennium wasn't the normal blood feud with one brand of chaos succeeding another. This was a land grab, an act of modern colonialism which would horrify most people except that, by all accounts, it seemed to be welcomed by the locals down there. There was no shortage of eye witness reports, even coverage on television by intrepid foreign correspondents in Century City canvassing opinion and meeting new citizens who had arrived from around the globe.

The guarded optimism in the Press did not please all of the big hitting politicians. Some of the European Premiers were indifferent or hinted at admiration for the new regime, whilst making it clear that they had weightier matters to concern them. The Belgians, however, were very doubtful and their Prime Minister, Guy Verhofstadt, spoke darkly about 'turning back the clock of civilisation,' while Jacques Chirac, the French President, fulminated against what he called a 'tyranny'. The whole affair had nothing to do with Great Britain except that UK citizens had been the chief perpetrators but that did not discourage Prime Minister Tony Blair from speaking out forcefully against 'outrageous piracy'. And from Washington, President George Bush chose to echo Edward Heath with talk of 'dark acts of capitalism'.

This seemed like hypocrisy to Tomas. The politicians made no mention of the oil, the off shore find in the Tamalou Trench which had been confirmed before the invasion. It had never been formally announced but the well informed knew perfectly well that he who controlled Millennium now controlled also a massive income to be harvested from one of the world's most valuable commodities. This was the tactfully unspoken reason why there were now murmurings about the need to pose a challenge to the invaders, to make it clear that they must abandon their takeover or face the prospect of a European force of arms to evict them and reinstate the former regime, leading to discussion of how the oil bonanza might be best managed. It wasn't subtle, but it might well be effective.

The diplomatic machinations rumbled on. It was confirmed that the former President had died in the invasion and that his son had succeeded him in exile. Jago was now holding the reins but keeping to the shadows and speaking softly to Downing Street. The Prime Minister was very much interested in progress and snarled an instruction to his minions:

'I want to know when a mouse farts in Century City.'

'Of course, it's all pretty absurd', Hannah was saying to Simon as they climbed the Cornish coastal path. It was the last weekend of the month and they had stolen a couple of days before the full rush of summer holidays to enjoy the sea views which were their particular favourites. The sun was out but there was a fair breeze in their faces and Simon was burdened by Imogen on his back, snoozing in her papoose. Hannah continued talking, puffing from the exertion of the walk and from her sense of outrage.

'We're expected – ordered even – to dig the dirt and find something which is supposed to threaten national security but basically, it's all about self-interest and money.'

'Well,' said Simon in reply, 'I guess that's politics for you. It's just exactly what King was afraid would happen. I remember him saying to me before I left Century that given the choice, they'd have been better off never finding the bloody oil in the first place.'

'I know, Si and I'm sorry to drone on but the whole deal does just piss me off. Most of the European Union countries don't seem too concerned one way or the other: they've got their own bigger fish to fry. But the French and the Belgians are up in arms about international piracy and breaches of human rights – all that sort of thing. The Yanks are the same, spouting that it's an outrage and an affront to new century behaviour. The surprise for me is that our own PM is so outspoken. It's not as if this was ever a British colony but of course it's UK citizens who have done the invading and he's all for international action to restore the status quo. It's typical politico speak: a whole lot of righteous language while the whole bloody lot of them are really manoeuvring for a crack at that oil.

'Actually, while I'm feeling all fired up, there's another thing which is upsetting me.'

He raised an eyebrow in query and Hannah continued. 'You remember that photo you took? The one of that guy in front of you in CdG airport? Well, as I've told you before, it definitely is that creep Habtumu: I'd recognise the bastard anywhere, even in a crap photo and with some clothes on. But can I get anyone at work to take him as a serious risk? Can I hell! They're all full of what's going on at the moment and tell me I'm overreacting to bad memories and something which happened seven years ago. He's all burned out and history, they say. But I haven't given up. Charley has been working on it for me, just on the quiet of course. She managed to find a tape of that meeting in Nairobi and using that as a template, she says she's getting voice recognition now. He's in London, seems to be living there pretty much permanently and spends time talking to a number in France. Charley's listening but says it's hard as they're using some sophisticated scrambler down there. I'm going to get more, though, I'm sure of it and I'll keep you up to speed.' But anyway, let's talk about something else. How's the business going for you?'

'Christ, what do I say? I still feel the ghost of Conrad Aveling at my shoulder! Before I even left Millennium, Pente and King told me a whole lot more of the circumstances which led up to the stroke that killed him. It was such a tragedy for Connie himself, his family and the rest of us as well. He was a talented man in his field, a gentleman and a born leader. He's so hard to replace but Sebastien is brilliant with his support from Singapore.

'The work's absorbing certainly and full of promise: lots to do, more contracts piling up, no shortage of pretty good people – most ex forces of course – lining up to work for Bastion. So look, it's exciting but it's also frightening. I just feel a huge responsibility and the fact Seb mostly leaves me to get on with it, well that's very flattering but it makes me feel – well lonely I suppose.'

Hannah nodded. 'I can understand that. But hang on in there and just keep going. It's pretty early days yet, only three months or so, and already you're well regarded.'

'Says who?'

'Apparently by just about everyone there. It's funny how communications work these days, but Bastion people speak to Connie's widow, Tepee and she chats to Pente down in Millennium who tells my mother and she tells me!'

He smiled at her. 'That's very damn reassuring! It may not be a commendation from some high flown business guru, but it's a comfort, just the same! Thank you: and how about we sit down for a bit? There are other things to discuss.'

Hannah lifted Imogen from her father's back and all three of them flopped down on the springy grass. Hannah pulled a grubby stuffed rabbit from her back pack, followed by a drinking beaker and a biscuit so the child would be amused for a few minutes as she lay in her mother's lap. She went on talking to him as she busied herself.

'Si, what about Imogen? I know we've talked about her so much since you got home and I must say I still laugh when I see you sitting in that bath and goggling. I don't know which of you was the more surprised!' Hannah started giggling again at the memory before she went on. 'But seriously, I still don't know if I did the right thing in keeping the knowledge of her from you during all those months. I've asked you often enough, but you've never really told me. There's always been something to stop you before you got started talking about it.'

Simon produced a pack of cigarettes, taking one for himself when she refused. 'I shouldn't be smoking,' he confessed, 'but I'm nervous. I'm always nervous about things that really matter to me personally: subjects of the heart, you could say, opinions which once voiced, you can't modify or take back.'

He broke off to lean forward and stroke the baby's cheek with his forefinger. Imogen smiled at him and grabbed for the finger, chuckling as he moved it down to tickle her under the arm and through the light little parka jacket she was wearing against the summer wind. Her father went on speaking.

'Part of me, Hannah, is still living with a protest. I can't imagine how you could have lived with such a secret for so long and really, I don't think you should have tried, let alone succeeded. I hate the expression but I was truly gobsmacked when I found out - especially the way I did. So I started out with a fair bit of resentment and I know you were conscious of it.

But there's another side to this coin. One way or another you could have got a message to me at any time between Imogen's conception and her birth. Plus also, you could have counted on me resigning my position and getting the first boat, train, plane out. I would have done just exactly that, without a second thought. But I'd have been wrong to do so, I can see that and therefore a lot of me ends up being grateful to you for taking a courageous decision and for having the resolve to stick to it. That can't have been at all easy for you.'

Hannah said, 'No, that's right. It was very hard at times and never worse than when you rang from Singapore, only a few days as it turned out, before she was born. But throughout, I kept telling myself that it would have been the same for generations past, when couples were separated for absolutely ages during the war years and didn't even know if the other half was still alive.'

He nodded slowly before going on. 'Well, I know that alright. I know also how independent you like to be, how self-contained you are and I've been fretting over the last few weeks that at heart, you want to stay solo and keep our daughter for yourself.'

Simon looked agonised as he took a deep drag on his cigarette and they looked at each other. Finally, she smiled at him and said,

'Simon Goring, you are a serious wimp. Why don't you just ask? And do it properly: fag out and on your knees!'

And so he did and she accepted his proposal, saying in reply, 'Well of course, but what's kept you? I've been waiting for this since you got back in April!' Even then they couldn't do anything traditional. There could be no kissing or hugging or holding until they were back from their walk and he held Imogen while she rang Foy and told her mother. Simon's sense for the conventional was mollified as he heard Vanda laughing with sheer joy. It was a very happy day which culminated in champagne and a particularly good dinner at the smart hotel he had extravagantly chosen.

Later, when the babysitter had gone and they were lying in bed, drifting towards a contented sleep, he dared to ask.

'All that time I was away, was there anyone else?'

Hannah had been lying on her side, curled up with her back to him but now she turned, lifted herself to lie on top of him and gazed into his eyes as she spoke.

'You, Si, are an absolutely typical alpha man. But you know me: you don't ask a straight question without getting a straight answer. And that is No, there's been no one else while you've been gone. No action whatsoever and one good reason is that producing and nurturing a baby is a very damn consuming business - so don't go thinking that only you are irresistible!

Hannah paused for a moment, watching the smile start to wrinkle the corners of his mouth. Then she asked,

'And what about you, Mr Lothario? What about all the girls in grass skirts where you've been? Tell me!'

'I confess to a slight indiscretion in the fleshpots of Manila but as for where I spent most of my time, I was untouched, I can promise you. The women there are not the most alluring, in fact I reckon they're equipped by nature to be pretty much rape resistant.'

This had them both laughing so much that they had to get up and pour themselves another drink which led to other things before they finally slept. It had been a good day.

4. OCTOBER — 2000

Tomas sat in a folding canvas chair, a bottle of lager in one hand and a cigarette in the other, watching Tetrarch as he prepared their evening meal. The sun was dipping towards the western horizon, the heat dissipated only by the breeze which was forever blowing over this vast and lonely land.

They were camped at the Palace and had been there for two months. In addition to the Twins, there were twenty in the party but they were billeted in some of the construction huts half a mile away. Tomas needed some isolation and their quarters lay in a slight depression with a couple of acacia trees for shade and a bore pipe from which they could draw water. Now, with awnings spread between old containers, latrines dug and a generator to hand, they were comfortable and self-sufficient.

The Palace had been easy enough to find. Jago had given a fair description of the extravaganza which his father had been constructing at the time of his overthrow. It was sited near his birthplace in the north east of the country which was now Millennium, outside the bush town called Tamalourene which gave most of its name to the President's family. The settlement was about five hundred kilometres from the Capital, a full day's drive over dreadful roads so the airstrip at the complex was a vital component.

The Palace was perfect for their purpose – utterly remote, all the space they could use and easy to exit in the event of crisis. Tomas was content and especially pleased that they could occupy the Palace for as long as they wished in return for being available to help Jago as and if he called for it.

The bargain had been struck in late July by Nat Habtumu, coached by Tetrarch on the instructions of Tomas. Jago had dropped anchor in Holland Park despite its uncertain future and while he talked to Nat, he was simultaneously waiting for an approach from the British Government. Smooth contact came eventually from Greville Thornton, a career diplomat temporarily assigned to the staff of the Prime Minister's right hand man, Jonathon Powell.

Thornton's position never varied.'I'm just here to keep myself informed, Prince,' he would say whenever he dropped into the Embassy or came on the phone, 'you see, the Government is concerned for the welfare of the British expats who were living there at the time of the coup and HMG is playing a leading role – with the French and the Belgians – in formulating an EU policy as to what should happen next. There's a variety of options, including the possibility of sending a European Force down there to restore the status quo and while the talking's going on, it's very helpful to get all the news and views we can. Absolutely in confidence, of course: I report only to No 10.'

Meanwhile in France at this time, Tomas was processing the commentary which flowed from Habtumu like water from a tap and from the best of it, developing ambitious plans. These were passed to the Interpreter, along with requests for more money and people. The funds and the help started to appear. It was time for the Twins to move.

They left Loches in mid-August and travelled by rail to Marseilles. They paused in familiar surroundings for a day or so before making the sea crossing to Algiers. They carried modest hand luggage and used the German passports which they had acquired years previously. Arriving in North Africa, they made their way south overland, travelling slowly and in discomfort but attracting no attention. They journeyed by way of Niger and Chad into the Central African Republic. A week later, they were knocking at the gates of Millennium on its northern border.

Eight months after the invasion, the new rulers of Millennium were concentrating on priorities. From the start, the number of immigrants from around the globe had exceeded expectation and most of these aspiring citizens arrived by sea or air into

Century City. It was not surprising that travellers from the north found little in the way of formalities to delay them and they crossed the border without being conscious of it. At the first small bush town, they commandeered an ancient Nissan taxi van. The owner drove his new clients the short distance to their destination and soon afterwards, left again to take one of them to the capital, a journey which might take two days each way allowing for breakdowns. Tetrarch took with him a considerable stash of US dollars and a shopping list which included a four wheel drive pickup.

He was gone for nearly a week while Tomas subsisted on limited rations and explored on foot. The site was simply enormous: by following a straggling wire fence to the point at which it turned at right angles, Tomas estimated that it was a fifteen kilometre square.

A succession of buildings, courtyards, sports fields and gardens sprawled out on all sides from the centre piece construction which was a vast mansion on three floors with a full sized basement. A straight kilometre avenue had been bulldozed through the bush to join the dirt road which wound through the village of Tamalourene. At the junction, a form of guardhouse was built and occupied. Squashed inside were three families whose men folk were supposed to ensure security for this enormous construction site. No, they reported, the President's architect and project manager hadn't been near them for months, none of them had been paid and the gangs of workers had drifted away. There had been no deliveries of materials but plant and machinery was still around somewhere and, the spokesman added, his cousin and family were living in the control tower on the airstrip: he waved a vague hand into the middle distance.

When Tetrarch reappeared, they worked together through the Palace and its grounds, noting the quality of materials, making calculations of the cost of this extraordinary folly which could now be only a memorial to the President who had commissioned it. That said, it was ideal for their purpose and

240

Tomas was relieved that not a single soul came calling. They had found magnificent isolation.

They mapped the estate and made an inventory of the equipment, the condition of the part-completed buildings and the extent of stores and materials. Of particular interest was the airstrip. An all-weather tarmac runway had been properly constructed at huge cost so that the great man could visit from the capital to check on progress and so they could fly in transports with most of what was required for build and maintenance. It was impressive, if sinister in its loneliness.

There were journeys to be made also. Two weeks after they established themselves, the first of the recruits started to arrive, flying into Century City as immigrants. All but one was accepted by the authorities, the exception being an Iraqi born engineer who made the mistake of travelling on an out of date passport. It was normally Tetrarch who made the long drive to collect these people but occasionally they went together. There was no phone or internet connection at the Palace and Tomas needed to report progress to the Interpreter.

At the beginning of October, Tetrarch called Nat Habtumu in London. Tomas wanted him for a solo mission which had two objectives, one which he knew all about and the other of which he knew nothing.

On Thursday, 12th October, the United States guided-missile destroyer, the USS Cole, was attacked by suicide bombers as she was refuelling in the harbour at Aden, Republic of Yemen. At around 11:00 local time, a small boat made an innocuous approach towards the destroyer and went unchallenged. The two occupants guided their craft to rub gently against the port side of the warship as 300kg of explosive was ignited by the terrorists who perished in the attack. The blast blew a sixty foot gash in the side of the Cole and entered a storage space beneath the ships galley, killing seventeen crew members who were queuing up for lunch. A further forty were injured, the total damage was considerable and the blow to American prestige was immense. It was the most serious and successful attack on a US Warship for fifteen years.

It very nearly didn't happen at all. Habtumu had arrived in Yemen a week earlier and as Tomas had expected, he found a shambles of organisation and the rudiments of a bomb which would hardly have scratched the paint from the USS Cole. It hadn't taken him long, however, and by the time the destroyer steamed majestically into Aden harbour, they were ready with the right shape and size of bomb, a means of delivery and the same two suicide volunteers.

Reckless of the consequences to himself, Nat stood as close as he could to the dockyard and waited for whatever he might be able to see or hear. He was not disappointed and he became increasingly triumphant as news leaked out of the naval base. Thirty-six hours later, he went on to fulfil his second mission. Having exhausted the opportunities that existed in Aden for suitable celebration, he booked himself on the first flight out and took out his phone as he waited. There was no one at Loches, of course, and no communication possible with the Palace but London was easy. He phoned Jago: it was just for a chat, he told himself and he would give no details but still manage to convey something of his brilliance. Tomas had been depending on exactly this indiscretion.

5. DECEMBER — 2000

Work at the Palace continued with remorseless energy and no distraction. They were on schedule and the quality of work was satisfactory. To save time, Tetrarch did well to find Patrice, a local man with a small truck who was happy to ask no questions as he drove to the capital to ferry home whatever was required.

During the week before Christmas, Xerxes and Petraeus flew in to land their Boeing 737 without difficulty. The pilots were respectively natives of Albania and Greece and they knew each other from working together in Oman. The plane had been acquired from a scarcely functioning transport outfit in Togo and they had followed a circuitous route to arrive. Xerxes said the machine was tatty but serviceable and he seemed confident it could be kept flying, provided there was fuel. Tetrarch took him to inspect the underground reservoir which had been one of their earlier discoveries and Xerxes was suitably impressed: all that was needed was the hard labour of pumping it into the machine.

On the ground, they were now well organised. They had power from a generator, backed up by a standby. They had a kitchen, refrigeration, a dining hall, four dormitories and a number of shower rooms. There was no air conditioning but as bush camps go, the accommodation was quite habitable.

They made the most of all the space, both inside the shell of the Palace and on the ground surrounding it which was littered with storage sheds fashioned from sea containers. A form of assault course mushroomed over nearly a hectare and a gymnasium was set up in the basement. Scale models were patiently constructed in classrooms on the ground floor of the Palace.

243

The team was now complete, numbering twenty-one men and five women. Tomas was pleased with the way they had settled together, also relieved to have Tetrarch on hand to settle any disputes. Contact between them and the villagers grew naturally and brought benefits. Patrice, the truck driver was followed by cleaners and kitchen helpers. There were a few who had been helping on the construction work so the numbers snowballed to about thirty. This was fine: the relationships were harmonious and the work output was quite effective in an African style but of course, it involved more communication and gossip. Tomas was not surprised when officialdom came calling, particularly not as they were approaching the New Year celebrations – a time for generous gifts. But it was a surprise to see a European step out of the smart beige Land Cruiser with a light bar on the roof.

Their visitor turned out to be Police Inspector Marc Pierron whose base was in the distant Regional Barracks at Oykambo in the centre of the country. He had a large patch to cover, including Tamalourene which had been important until the Palace construction stopped with the coup nearly a year ago. So what was going on here now?

Tomas and Tetrarch made the Inspector welcome, inviting him into their rooms for refreshment and conversation. It turned out that Inspector Pierron had been born in Charleroi, Belgium, coming out with his parents as he finished school. He had spent a working lifetime in the police force here and would have been due to take his retirement shortly, but now he simply didn't know. The new order seemed to be well established in Century City and no doubt its influence would spread out into the provinces in due course but for the moment, all he had to do was to submit his normal monthly report. He made for pleasant company, knocking back his beers and undemanding in conversation. He was quite short and running to fat but still well turned out in a uniform which sparkled with badges of office and a peaked cap which he laid on the table beside his chair, accompanied by his Ray Ban dark glasses. He wore a side arm and handcuffs in his belt.

Tomas saw that there was calm intelligence behind Pierron's apparently casual questions. After an hour or so, Tetrarch announced that he was ready and must leave for Century in his pick up: a routine trip to collect materials and provisions. The Inspector rose to say farewell and to wish him a good trip. He would look forward to making another visit in a few months. Tetrarch grunted and then he was gone as they heard his vehicle rev up and move off.

Inspector Pierron remained with Tomas for lunch and several glasses of wine. He did not press to be shown round and Tomas did not offer. Instead, they talked of world matters and the chances for this new regime here in Millennium. The Inspector sipped at a glass of Armagnac with his coffee, accepted politely his host's New Year gift which he knew from its shape to be a carefully wrapped brick of bank notes and then made his own departure. The Toyota moved away slowly. The return journey would take up the remainder of the Inspector's day but he would have much to think over. There were undoubtedly matters here to report and his sharp nose smelt mischief in the air, his main focus being on Tomas who was a strange one to find out here in the bush and in charge.

Meanwhile in Europe, short days and an imminent holiday season made for inaction. Jago was determined to keep calm and wait developments but he was becoming anxious and Nat Habtumu's swashbuckling confidence didn't help.

'You can be fuckin' sure man,' he announced with his normal swagger, 'I've got the connections but better than that, by Christ, I can make things explode! Even if we have to turn Century into another Mogadishu, we'll sure as hell get you back where you belong.'

In Gloucestershire at GCHQ, it was now routine and straightforward to keep tabs on Habtumu. It was almost too easy for Charley Deveridge. She had never before monitored the phone of someone quite so indiscreet as he would speak to anyone at any hour. He talked freely about the USS Cole and his role in the attack on her. He spoke just as readily about his 'connections'- his friends and people of influence in Millennium and all about what was planned to turn the place into another rogue State, a second Somalia or perhaps a North Korea.

If the technicalities were easy for Charley, the situation was horribly frustrating for Hannah and her colleagues who were tasked with analysis and recommendation to authorities in London. It was plain that Habtumu was a dangerous terrorist. They knew exactly where he was, with whom he consorted but what he was going to do next was anybody's guess. So why not pick him up or even simply make him disappear? Well no, the answer kept coming back from Whitehall. He's performing a function in looking out for Jago and that's important for us. So, we just keep riding herd on him for now and see where he leads us. He's focussed on Millennium and so are we, so leave well alone for now and don't tell Washington that we know who blew up their ship. It won't bring anyone back or mend the hole.

In Africa, Tomas would have been delighted to know of Nat's performance. He was spreading exactly the misinformation which Tomas had planned. And two hours out from the Palace, Inspector Pierron drove slowly over the long and lonely road. It was in terrible condition, more of a dirt track, but at least he knew it and had been motoring in Africa all his life. He was continuing to muse over Tomas and all he had just seen and heard, just starting to turn his thoughts towards the minder, the big, muscled guy who seemed almost mute.

At that very moment, he saw Tetrarch, stripped to the waist and leaning into an extension bar which was locked onto one of the rear wheels of his pick-up, itself lifted clear of the rough ground. Just a punctured tyre, Pierron thought, but it had happened at an awkward place – just short of the point at which his route branched left towards Oykambo and the more used track continued towards Century. It was narrow here, the track skirting higher ground with a drop off to the right, not too steep but a long descent through rock and scrub.

The Inspector stopped and climbed out. Tetrarch dropped

his bar and fished a handkerchief from the pocket of his shorts, wiping the sweat from his face as he came up with a hand outstretched in welcome. Pierron took it instinctively and felt himself being turned and pulled into a bear hug of unbelievable strength. Then the grimy rag came across his face and he recognised the stench of chloroform mixed with sweat before he began to pass out. It seemed an instant only before he recovered and was relieved to find himself back in the driving seat of his vehicle. But then the panic started to set in.

His feet were bound together, thrust beneath the pedals and tied to them. He tried to move his arms but found that he was secured to the steering wheel by his own handcuffs. The wheel was locked and he could see that the ignition key had been removed. He looked up to see that his Land Cruiser had been moved, angled to the right and pointing down the valley. Glancing down, he noted the gears in neutral and the hand brake released.

There was no sign of Tetrarch and he began to fiddle his feet about, hoping to lift and place them on the footbrake. He felt movement and looked in the rear view mirror to see the naked, broad back of Tetrarch as he began to push backwards. Pierron had time to swear and to shout once before his rolling coffin went over the edge and picked up speed as it bounced through the scrub and rocks. It slid sideways and rolled three times with increasing speed before straightening and sliding ever faster until it hit a collection of much larger rocks at the bottom of the hill. There was no fire but the vehicle seemed to groan with pain as the dust settled about it.

Tetrarch walked down the slope, picking his way through the rocks which he used as stepping stones as he approached the Toyota. The driver's window was open as he had prepared it. All the others were smashed by the impacts. He wound the rag round his hand and reached in to search for a pulse in the neck of the rag doll figure, slumped over the transmission tunnel. There was no life to be found. Tetrarch reached down with difficulty – the door would have been impossible to open – and pulled at the release knot he had placed around the feet and pedals. He retrieved the cord and found in his pocket the keys to undo the handcuffs. The Inspector's hands fell away from the steering wheel. Then Tetrarch replaced the ignition key.

Before the long climb back up the hill, he stood still and looked around. The scene appeared as he had intended. Sleep or drink or plain inattention had caused the driver to lose control: an accident, one that might take days or weeks to discover..'

6. JANUARY — 2001

The New Year started slowly.

The political inactivity in Europe persisted and British Prime Minister Tony Blair was frustrated with French President Jacques Chirac who was discovering reasons to make haste slowly. At a routine meeting of European Foreign Ministers, the topic of Millennium didn't even make it onto the agenda.

In London, the smooth talking Greville Thornton was summoned to be told that he had better become inventive in finding a way to 'rev things up a bit – and soon'. Across the skyline from the splendours of Whitehall state offices, Jago was brooding in the Holland Park Embassy which remained open and trying to operate with a normality which was becoming a farce.

Nat Habtumu was in London, waiting for word from the Twins. He had returned to St John's Wood, a different apartment but in the same tower block with its views over the cricket ground. The location appealed to him as a good base from which to cruise the night spots and brag about his exploits in Aden to anyone who would listen. Charley Deveridge had no trouble in tracking his movements, listening to his phone calls and discussing it all with her sister. Hannah kept pressuring her management at GCHQ to recognise the guy as a serious threat and to take action against him. But the mandarins and the politicians they served were determined to be either dense or devious, insisting that Habtumu be left to blow in the wind until they were ready.

Towards the end of the month, he managed an excess of behaviour which both broke the log jam and sealed his own fate. On the evening of Friday, 25th January, he left his apartment soon after 9pm and took a cab to an address in Notting Hill. His destination was a gambling club of poor quality and outrageous prices but well regarded by its dodgy clientele for the variety of contacts to be found there. Nat spotted his target as soon as he walked up to the bar and ordered a double whisky and water. She was sitting on a bar stool, her short skirt well above her shapely knees, a long tall glass of something and an illegal cigarette in one hand, breasts straining against a tight white T shirt and the whole of one arm which was spread out along the bar top covered in tattoos. Unusually, however, what really caught his eye was the hair – an amazing mane of flame coloured tresses which cascaded down past her shoulders. Just the very ticket for me, he thought to himself and immediately engaged the girl with his own brand of suggestive conversation.

Her name was Maeve and it didn't matter that he could hardly understand her wild Dublin accent but he gathered that she was a biker's girl, just abandoned by her man who was going mad and violent. She had not much money and no place to go. She quite fancied a bit of chocolate. The rest didn't take long and they were back in St John's Wood by eleven with Nat pouring them both a large vodka while she wandered around the apartment, cooing with delight.

The sex which followed almost immediately was way better than he had expected. He didn't need to decipher the detail through the accent to understand her commentary with its instructions for her pleasure and demands to know his preferences. She never stopped smoking throughout their first, protracted bout and as she sat back in his biggest arm chair and watched him thundering into her, she raised his game by drawing the glowing tip of her cigarette across his stomach just above where his manhood was hard at work before chucking half a glass on vodka with ice cubes onto the exact same spot. Habtumu howled with shock and excitement, further energised by the delight of finding that the hair down there was as bright and prolific as the mass which whirled around her head.

They were taking a break, Natty strutting around with a wavering erection, pouring vodka and fetching more ice from the fridge. Maeve grabbed the canvass bag which she had carried away from the club and sat, naked and cross legged on his carpet as she rummaged through it, coming up quite casually with her heroin kit contained in a grubby plastic bag. Turning with glasses in hand, Nat saw her pull out a plunger with an already bare needle and he gave an involuntary shriek as he freaked. He didn't care about narcotics one way or the other, but needles for him were like spiders or rats to others: their effect on him was one of sheer, unreasoning terror.

He shouted at her and she shouted back. He saw her reach for the tie for her arm, suddenly realised why the tattoos spread from shoulder to wrist and he swung the glass in his hand to bash away the needle from his sight. It skittered off out of view under the sofa and she was suddenly on her feet, hitting out at him and swearing that he was a great, black, clumsy fucker. Maeve dived for the floor, pushing the sofa back on its castors but then he was on her, pulling her by her hair, grabbing at some of her clothes as he hauled her towards his front door. She was crying, screaming and swearing as he fought to hold her with one hand while he opened the door with the other.

He pulled her through, still shouting enough to wake the dead, still struggling as he tried to push the call button for the lift. She lifted one knee with an instinctive aim born of much practice and in the agony of its impact, he lashed out at her, letting go his grasp of her hair as he did so. Maeve gave a cry of pain, her bare feet scrabbled for grip on the tiles of the hallway and she fell away in a tangle of limbs to crash down the stair well which was adjacent to the lift. It was not a long fall to the next half landing, but she lay there, very still in a crumpled heap.

Nat started down the stairs towards the girl, then stopped and ran back, remembering his front door which would close on its own to leave him stark naked with a corpse to indict him. He struggled to control his panic, forcing himself to think.

First, he stood in the doorway and listened. The stairwell with its grisly burden yawned at him. The building was silent which was not unusual. He seldom saw his neighbours and the place was frequently deserted at weekends. He went inside the apartment to fetch a chair to prop open the front door. He dressed himself, swigging vodka from the bottle as he did so. He returned to the hallway and descended the flight of stairs. He grasped the tattooed arm and heaved the pathetic bundle of body over his shoulder, turning to look as he did so. There was no blood. He carried Maeve into his sitting room and laid her full length on the sofa. The hair colour continued to dazzle him but her neck flopped ominously to one side. He collected her clothes and bag, dropping them in a pile by her side. Then he went to the bedroom and pulled off a double sheet which he spread over the lonely body with its small collection of belongings. Maeve was neither mourned nor remembered: she was just an unwanted complication which had interrupted his lifestyle.

Nat sat in his kitchen while he considered. Here in London he could turn only to Jago for help and probably he would find refuge in Holland Park, at least for a while. But he wasn't sure that the Embassy's status could now offer him security and anyway, Jago would connive at many things, but not murder. Then there was Paris where he had many friends and useful contacts but he rejected that also. The city and its police were too close in every sense to the British authorities and a hideaway could soon turn into a trap without an exit. No, he told himself, he had to get much further away. He had to get himself south into Africa, to this new country of Millennium, to find his mate Tetrarch. He needed help.

Decided, he put down the bottle with a clunk and returned to the bedroom, giving a passing glance to the shrouded figure on the settee. He packed a case with his best clothes and shoes. He filled his pockets with essentials – his wallet and a second notecase filled with sterling and euro notes, his two passports, French and Ethiopian. He made sure he had his Elegance Gold card: you never knew when it might be useful.

He was ready as the time approached 2.00am. He stood the case by the door and returned to the kitchen, sitting on a stool and leaning on the counter in the centre of the small room as he smoked and drank more vodka. He dozed before noticing that it was 4.30 and time to go. He turned out all the lights and quietly closed the front door behind him. He was very confident that the apartment, with its sole occupant lonely in death, would remain undisturbed until Monday morning. He felt it was a good omen to find a black cab before he had reached the end of the road. He climbed in with his case and gave directions. He would take the first Eurostar train of the day to Paris and there make a decision about the next leg of his journey.

Nat failed to recognise that he was not alone. There was a companion travelling in his pocket in the form of his mobile phone. A hundred miles away in Cheltenham, GCHQ was keeping a permanent monitor on his number and although Charley Deveridge was not on duty that weekend, her colleague on the night shift made easy note that their target was on the move and he rang Charley early on the Saturday morning. Charley abandoned her breakfast and her lover, making haste into the office where she sat all day and most of the next, tracking Natty Habtumu through Paris to Avignon, from there into Spain to Barcelona and on to Lisbon. The phone went silent as he boarded a direct flight for Century City.

7. FEBRUARY — 2001

King Offenbach sat on the balcony of his fine, third floor apartment in Century City with its spreading view over the ever restless ocean and he picked at a problem the way a dog gnaws at a bone.

There was sustained international pressure for a United Nations mandate to take action against Millennium, calling for a military campaign to reinstate the old regime under the former President's son Jago, now living in London and biding his time. It was the British and the French who were sounding the loudest cries with voluble support from Belgium and crucially, from the United States. The rationale for public consumption was that the invasion had been simply not proper by 21st century rules of international diplomacy. It was different, which was bad enough, and successful which was worse. But behind the rhetoric lay the significance of the oil. King could wish that geologists had never discovered the blasted Tamalou Trench.

He sighed to himself as he poured another rye and water. It was no good thinking that way: you couldn't uninvent things and you couldn't hide what was known. Best to concentrate on what you could do to manage things and that was his strong suit. Which led him back to the niggle of worry which he had been scratching all that day. King was a time-served CIA professional, a clandestine all his life. It was the accumulated experience which alerted him and set his antennae of concern zinging.

For some time, he had been fretting that they didn't know enough about the country which they had taken over. For sure, the invasion itself had been well managed, the transformation of life and conditions in the Capital had exceeded expectations and they had made some progress in pushing out into the provinces. But even so, it was now over twelve months since they had arrived and there were still large swathes of this great landmass which they did not know, had not yet visited, certainly could not claim as converted territory. The process had been hindered by the early retirement of their leader, David Heaven, and whilst his successor as President, Hugh Dundas, was a towering success as an administrator and financier, he was not a son of Africa and couldn't feel the touch of history on his shoulder.

Just two days back, King had dropped by the office of the National Police Chief, an excellent man who had arrived in the first wave of immigrants and had a great track record of running a paramilitary force in another African state. Consumed by many projects, he had skated over the inconvenience of a rural Police Chief who had gone missing. It was over a month before a search had discovered him dead in his vehicle, smashed up in a mashed up car at the bottom of a boulder strewn ravine. Probably an accident but the sparse facts bugged Offenbach. It seemed unlikely that a man like Marc Pierron would meet such an end: not impossible, of course, but certainly unexpected and assessing it was made all the harder by the fact that not one of them here in Century had any notion of what the country was like in the region where he died. They should go and have a look, was King's thinking. First, however, he would get a night's sleep and then share his reflections with his old friend Pente Broke Smith.

King walked round to see him the following morning. Pente was installed in one of the small houses, built for clergy, which lay in the grounds of the Cathedral. King found the priest in his kitchen, the bulky body standing with arms spread on the table as he read the day's edition of their newspaper, The New Century. A kettle was boiling busily and Pente interrupted himself to supply a noisy welcome.

'Coffee ready for spooks and sinners,' he said beaming, 'and I do believe it's straight black for a black!'

King took no offense at this accustomed banter. 'I guess it's your normal brand of pretend coffee? Direct from the jar?'

They continued their jibes as Pente filled a couple of mugs which they took out onto the patio at the back, getting comfortable in the big chairs around a wrought iron table, Pente immediately searching for one of his smelly cheroots. Without preamble, King got to his point.

'Pente, it's like this. I'm worried we're going too slow in pushing out to the borders of the country. We've been here now for over twelve months and we still don't know the whole of what's out there. We're not halfway to the east yet, maybe a bit more north but that leaves a helluva lot of territory which is just a blank…' he broke off as Pente put down his mug and interrupted, blowing a cloud of smoke as he did so.

'King, we've done this conversation before but I'll tell you again. You've seen a lot more of Africa than I have but all short stay stuff. You haven't lived in one country, in one place for months and years. But I have. I've had the thick end of forty years of it. There's a lot of continuity in Africa and things just move very slowly, especially way out in the bush where folks live a quiet and repetitive life. Out in the boondocks, they will mostly not even be conscious that we've arrived and what's more, they won't give a damn either. I reckon myself that the original plan was right and we should stick to it. Get the Capital sorted out – pretty much done now – then move on out in stages which is just what we're doing now. And the further out into the bush we get, the smaller the population there will be and the faster we can go. Mark my words, we'll be well into the last and smallest village of Millennium within another six months.'

King Offenbach was leaning forward and clasping his hands between his knees as he gave his measured reply but there was a fierce glint in his eye.

'Pente, I hear you. I know the policy and I appreciate the progress. I don't have a problem with your estimate for the next few months either but what if events don't wait for us? What if there's something happening somewhere out there at this very moment? We could be surprised just because we haven't taken a good goddamned look for ourselves.'

Pente registered the strength of anxiety.

'There's something else bugging you, isn't there? Something new?'

'Yup, there surely is and my old nose is telling me we should be taking real urgent notice. You remember when that guy was reported missing a coupla months back? The Police Inspector?'

Pente furrowed his brow. 'Two months ago is asking a lot of my tired old memory,' he remarked with a deep chuckle, 'but yes, I do recall that. I thought it was unusual because the guy held a bit of rank and was Belgian born, also with a great deal of experience.'

King nodded. 'That's my conclusion too, Pente. We'll make a spook of you yet. Of course, we never knew he was there and I guess we'll never know why he sat in his outpost for so long after we arrived but as you say, life moves slowly in these parts. No one contacted him and maybe he reckoned he was only hearing rumours. What's bugging me, though, is that they found him last week.'

Pente's shaggy eyebrows raised a notch in enquiry and his eyes bored into King's face but he said nothing, waiting for his friend to continue.

'Yeah. Well it seems that one of his officers searching the bush tracks found his car and what was left of him. It seems like an accident, vehicle came off the road and over a long, steep drop. Car got all broken up and so was Pierron. Of course there wasn't much left of him, what with animals and insects but they got him back here, did a post mortem, found no sign of anything to argue with the accident verdict. No gunshot wound or sign of attack: everything consistent with an auto wreck.'

'So where's your problem?'

In answer, King tapped the side of his nose. 'Just intuition, I guess, but it just seems unlikely to me that a guy with that background and experience of living in the deep bush country would crash out that way. Course it's my gut feel, that's all and

I know our Chief of Police isn't about to take it further: can't blame him either. He's a helluva good man and he's got a whole raft of things to do which must seem more important.'

'So?' Pente knew his man well enough. He knew there was an action plan coming.

'So. Well I guess I'm gonna take a ride out into that country myself. Just to have a look around and while I'm about it, I'll do a bit of a sweep down south too. I'd sure as hell feel happier doing something rather than sitting around wondering if there's a crisis waiting round the corner for us.'

There was a pause between them before Pente spoke again, but he was reassuring.'I can understand your thinking King and it seems to me you have a point plus I've got a healthy regard for your intuition. Will you take anyone with you?'

'I reckon not, no. With my colour, it'll be easier just drifting by myself but I won't pretend to be a local. I've seen Fergus Carradine and I'm borrowing one of his military jeeps - well Land Rover to you.' He gave one of his languid smiles and continued, 'the thing that's not so good is there's no mobile phone coverage beyond a hundred odd k's out of Century so I won't have communication if I need it. That's mostly why I dropped by now. To let you know and to say that I'll leave tomorrow morning and I'll be gone for a week maximum. If I'm not back by then latest, please send out the cavalry.'

'Of course', said Pente , giving King a sharp look but knowing that he'd get no more out of him. 'But first, I'm getting out my map and you can mark me out your route plus when you expect to be where. When we've agreed on that, don't you dare deviate.'

That's a promise, Pente, and thanks.'

While this conversation was taking place, communication was the name of the game also for Nathaniel Habtumu. Having got himself unscathed to Century City, he was ensconced in comfort at the prime hotel in town, the old Majestic which had been vastly improved under new management. But he was getting bored and wanted to make contact with Tetrarch but couldn't find him or call him. He was unconcerned about what he had left behind in London. Certainly not the girl – he was struggling to remember even her name – but he was comfortable that there would be no hue and cry for him down here. There would be bigger fish to fry for all the big hitters than retribution for some squalid little hooker and her murder.

Habtumu was right about this but wrong to underestimate the interest which he was attracting. He kept his phone charged and turned on which was all that Charley and Co, so far away in Cheltenham, needed to tell them where he was. They would have willingly listened to his conversations and scanned his messages had there been any of either but as the days went by, Nat stayed silent. That changed on Sunday 25th February when he was finishing a late breakfast in a café down the street from his hotel. Whilst pondering what mischief he could find before the weekend finished, he tried Tetrarch's French mobile for the umpteenth time and was astonished when it was answered by a guttural voice which he didn't recognise. This was Patrice the truck driver and sitting beside him on the fringes of sleep, Tetrarch heard the talk and grabbed the phone. They had been in Century the previous day, picking up supplies including some heavy weights with which Tetrarch had come down from the Palace to lend a hand. It had been a long day and a heavy evening. As they were clearing the traffic and settling for the long haul back, Tetrarch was relaxing but the phone call and the voice brought him to startled wakefulness. He couldn't speak to Tomas so he did what seemed best to him. He told Patrice to turn around and within an hour, they were back on the road but this time with an excited Natty Habtumu jammed in the truck cab between them.

They were two hours out of the city and getting onto rougher surface with huge potholes when they met a travel stained Land Rover travelling carefully in the opposite direction. It was driven by a black man who appeared to be unaccompanied. The occupants of both vehicles gave each other a casual wave of greeting as they passed and King Offenbach gave the matter no further thought as he continued into Century, happy to be nearly home.

In a dark and cold United Kingdom as that Sunday drew towards its close, GCHQ at Cheltenham was staffed as normal. So too was the seat of national Government at No 10, Downing Street as the Prime Minister was spending the weekend with official entertaining at his country house.

Charley Deveridge was at her desk, surrounded by her screens and phones and modems, backed up by the unseen paraphernalia of communications which were the cutting edge tools of her trade. Her sister Hannah sat beside her, each as frustrated as the other by their problem, ironic in the circumstances, of passing a simple message to London. Everyone in the battalions of UK security professionals knew the name of Nathaniel Habtumu. It was understood and accepted that he had 'form', although there were differing views as to his significance and the urgency with which he should be intercepted. But now, thanks to Charley, they knew pretty much exactly where he was. They knew also, from just one very brief transmission that he was in contact with a man - probably of North African background judging by the accent - who answered to the name of Tetrarch. Yet now, and for the past four hours, they simply could not get this message through to the powers that be.

Charley pushed a redial button and was connected again to the No 10 switchboard. She found herself speaking again to the same, fruity voiced woman who had taken her message on two separate occasions earlier in the day and had failed to confirm, despite her promise, that the PM had been informed. Now this woman was sounding irritated, not accustomed to being taken to task.

She said, 'As I've told you before, the Prime Minister is returning to London and must now be en route. I will ensure he gets your message in due course. And please, you don't need to repeat it yet again!'

Hannah leant forward, pushing Charley out of her way to reply.

'Look, madam, whoever you are. I'm Charley's sister Hannah Deveridge and I'm a senior analyst here at GCHQ. Mr Blair has instructed me personally that he wants to hear if a mouse farts in Century City. Now, you let him know that it's not a mouse, but there is a fucking great elephant down there - and it's about to shit!!'

There was a squawk of disapproval as they broke the connection.

Satisfied with the reaction, Hannah grinned at her sister.

'Can't do more, so I'm out of here now. Si's had Imogen for most of the day and he's got to get back to Farnham, probably leaving me with a week's worth of clearing up. Wish me luck!'

8. MARCH — 2001

It was a cold month in Paris and a fine, blowing drizzle which felt more like sleet greeted Charley as she alighted from the airport shuttle bus at Porte Maillot. It was still early as she went into the queue for taxis and at the head of the line, she climbed into a Citroen with a garrulous driver who gossiped all the way to Montmatre.

Victor Sollange had moved house the moment he retired from the Deuxieme, the French Secret Service, buying a two bedroom cottage with a bit of a garden and a fine view down the hill in his favourite part of the city which had been home to him since he had left Corsica as a child. He was a solitary man, hoarding his privacy as if it was a cache of fine art, a strange characteristic for a person born on an island where family is everything.

Charley and he kept frequent contact. She came to visit him every six months or so as he would never again leave Paris. She habitually addressed him as Victor, never Papa or the like, and most of their conversation revolved around work. Victor had no difficulty with her love life and he never failed to ask after her partner, Lizzie, but his enquiries were superficial as were his comments on his garden and the opera, the two interests which nourished his relaxation away from professional life.

Charley dropped her overnight bag in the spare room and they went out immediately for coffee and croissant. A walk in a local park followed before a bistro lunch and an afternoon in front of the fire at the cottage. During all this time, they exchanged working news. Charley reported on how things were going for her at GCHQ, how much she saw of Hannah and how well they combined together. Victor, in his turn, took her through the detail of his grand retirement project, a lengthy exposé of the twenty-first century Silk Road which transported people and poppies between the high hill country of Asia and the lush pastures of the cities of Western Europe. They spoke French, in which Charley was only a little less than fluent and Victor was solemnly helpful in correcting her grasp of idioms. His English was growing rusty and was masked by a heavy accent but he touched her by switching briefly into the language to make a comment about Vanda.

'I have been lucky to know many women in a long life, Charlee, but your mother has been, and is still, the only love of my life.'

Shortly after this commitment to which no reply was expected or offered, Victor banked up the fire and Charley went to her room before they left for dinner at the latest of Victor's favourite brasseries. It was only then that Charley made her request.

'I need your help with something special, Victor. Especially, I need to tap into that phenomenal memory of yours.'

'Eh bien', he replied reaching for his glass, 'what are the clues?'

Charley took a final mouthful of her turbot with sauce mousseline, pushed away her plate and launched in.

'There are so many things I can't talk about over the phone', she began, 'but when we were together last, which I think was late last summer - early autumn? Around then any way, and I know I told you about our trace on Nathaniel Habtumu, the Ethiopian?'

Victor just nodded and she continued. 'A bit after that came the attack in Aden on the USS Cole and I picked him up in Yemen so we can be pretty sure Habtumu was involved in that.'

'Yes,' he replied, 'that makes sense. A wild card, pretty crazy operator that one, but for sure a prime bombardier. I got a reliable report on him being linked with the Chechnya mob going back a few years and I'm sure he played a part in the US Embassies atrocity in Africa. But King Offenbach gave you information on those incidents, surely?'

'Yes he did, Victor, and I'd love to talk it through with him right now but not only is King retired, like you, but also he's down in Millennium and none of his old comrades in the CIA are game to share confidences with him.'

'Of course: I understand that. It's a pity, though. He's a clear thinker with imagination, useful qualities. But I have to say I'm inspired by what those guys are doing in Africa. It was a very ballsy move and they seem to be building on it. But sorry, I'm interrupting.'

'No that's fine', Charley said shaking her head, 'and as it happens, Millennium is very relevant to all this, especially because that's where Habtumu is now. Over the winter which he spent in London, I've been tracking him via his mobile and believe me, Victor, it's not been hard! He's the most indiscreet blabbermouth you could wish for and it's frustrated the hell out of Hannah and me that our people haven't been prepared to move in and pick him up: too late for that now. About a month ago, he scarpered in a rush, took the train over here, went down through Spain and caught a plane to Century City out of Lisbon. He mooched around there for a week or so, often ringing a French mobile but never getting a reply until two days ago and since then an absolute blank. I'm guessing he's gone somewhere well out of town, out of Century I mean because there's no service once you're out in the bush country. Whatever, that doesn't matter so much. What does matter is the name. You see, Victor, he spoke to somebody he knew and I'm trying to get a lead on who that might be. It's a Christian name, maybe a nickname but it's unusual and I'm thinking it's just possible you may have heard it before.'

Victor broke in now. 'Hang on Charlee, I'm a retired spy and policeman, not a bloody word magician! I can't just pluck a name out of nowhere – even though I'm quite prepared to try and I'll do so, but not quite yet! You're holding out on me, aren't you? There's something else you're after, you fille mechante!'

Charley sat back laughing. 'OK Victor, you win! Yes, there is something else but I wanted to mention it after this name business. I didn't want to confuse the two subjects.'

'Hah! You can leave me to worry about that. I may be an old

dog but I'm still learning new tricks. Now then, what's this other matter?'

'Well it also involves Nathaniel Habtumu, but perhaps indirectly, and it's also about a name. What can you tell me about the Mountain Men?'

Victor whistled through his teeth and abruptly called the bill, saying to Charley 'this is something better discussed at home.' They left the restaurant and took ten minutes walking back to his house. Charley put on coffee while Victor stoked up the fire, fetched a bottle of Armagnac and placed an ashtray and a packet of Gauloises beside his chair. As they settled, he said:

'It's not Men, it's Man singular and he's a figure from ancient Asian history,' he announced to his daughter. Then he went on to tell her much the same story as the Twins shared when they arrived in Chitral after their epic journey. Victor had the knowledge to go into greater detail and it took him half an hour to complete the history of the Mountain Man. Charley was spellbound but not prepared for his finale.

'Right up to today', Victor told her, 'the high country of the Hindu Kush has remained a stronghold of inspiration for fighting men with their passionate principles. Even more important for me is the town of Chitral, in the extreme north west of Pakistan. It's a peaceful looking place, not very large and in a beautiful, mountainous setting. But behind a façade of tranquillity it houses a hotbed of plotting, a centre for intrigue. More than that, it's the point of origin for smuggling - drugs, people, armaments, all moving from East to West along a modern version of the Silk Road.'

As he broke off to put more wood on the fire and to light himself another cigarette, Charley asked him if he knew the place at first hand.

'No,' replied Victor, 'not me. My priceless informant, a Kashmiri, he told me about it and he had a great talent for making pictures out of words. But he lingered there too long and they caught him. They tore off his balls and hung him on a tree with nails through his ears and another through his penis.

It took him a week to die in the scorching sun of their summer months. Chitral is an evil place.'

'Jesus', was all the response Charley could muster before Victor continued, 'the latest I've heard, but only since I retired, is that the name of the Mountain Man has been revived, trading I guess on the long history, but I've got no more detail.'

'And you haven't heard of it in the plural – not the Mountain Men?'

'No. But that means nothing. There could be something new but I'm out of the loop these days and growing more out of date. It's bound to be.'

'OK. This is fascinating and valuable stuff, Victor. I'll tell you now that our man Habtumu, he once mentioned on his phone while he was still in London that he was himself one of the Mountain Men, those were his very words. But the guy is a braggart and a bullshitter. I can't believe he would ever have been invited into the sort of secret society you've been describing.'

'You'd be right. He'd be lucky to survive a day,' said Victor, 'but again, he doesn't sound like a type who would be able to invent such a thing. He must have got the name from somewhere or someone.'

'I agree.'

'So you're wondering about the man he's just hooked up with in Millennium. You're wondering if the name you've heard him speak could be one of today's Mountain Men?'

Charley smiled at him as she tilted her glass of Armagnac in salute. 'It's no wonder I'm so bright', she remarked, 'not with a father like you!'

He returned her smile as he asked, 'So give me this name now.'

'Tetrarch.'

'Tetrarch. You positive? Couldn't be any mistake?'

'No, Victor, we're sure. It wasn't a good line but you know the sort of kit we have these days. There was more than enough to work with and it helps that you're dealing with some strong letters here. It was Tetrarch, no doubt.'

'Not a French name?'

'No, although it translates: but in English, it dates from Roman times, meaning "a subordinate ruler"'.

There was a very long silence between them during which Charley finished her drink and yawned. Victor scowled with concentration and smoked some more. Finally, he spoke to say,

'You must be tired, Charley. You get to bed and leave me to ponder on this one. What time must you leave?'

'I'm booked on a mid-morning flight. I need to get back for an evening shift tomorrow – or rather, today.'

He nodded, already deep in thought and when she appeared the following morning, he was still in his chair before the long dead fire, a mug of fresh coffee and an overflowing ashtray at hand.

'I've called for a cab in thirty minutes, but I can say that I'd had a bit of luck for you. That name struck a chord so I spent the night chasing it down and getting a few people out of bed. Finally, I got round to an old chum of mine who used to be on the Murder Squad in Marseilles years ago. I spoke to him an hour ago. It's a tough city, Marseilles, plenty of violence but not so many spontaneous killings. They tend to be more pre-planned so harder to bottom out and perhaps that's why Louis remembered this one. It was at a bar in le Vieux Port, as much a brothel really and this was back in '80 or '81, sometime around then. A great big thug of a guy known as Poillu, who was meant to run the joint and was up to every known fiddle, he was topped in his office down in the cellar and there was never a doubt about who did for him. It seems that twins who originated from North Africa had been working there for a while, one as a bouncer, the other a bookkeeper. There's a fallout and Poillu ends up as a bloody mess on the floor. The twins skip town that same night and are never heard of again. According to Louis, the bookkeeper was called Tomas and the brother was Tetrarch. There's no way of knowing if there's a connection here, Charley, but it's an unusual name. I hope that helps.'

9. APRIL — 2001

Tomas was content with the progress at the Palace.

Come the right time, there would be three teams, one for the USA and two for Europe. In addition, there were the two pilots, Xerxes and Petraeus whose job was to keep their old aircraft in reasonable shape while it was used for training and a few short hops. Tetrarch roamed the site, keeping watch and reporting back to Tomas who remained isolated, refining plans and procedures, paying special attention to support and backup arrangements. The routine was interrupted only by the regular drive to the fringes of Century City to make a brief call to the Interpreter: thus were the Elders of Chitral kept informed.

They kept the teams training as one. That way, each individual had to become familiar with all the tasks and all the locations, and of equal value, it meant that each man and woman had the chance of constructive input to all the attack plans. Of course, all these volunteer terrorists accepted that their own lives were forfeit and they were encouraged that there were to be no exceptions: Tomas and Tetrarch themselves would be paying the same price for eternal glory.

Tomas was worried by the arrival of Nat Habtumu, grinning from ear to ear from his squashed seat in the centre of Patrice's truck but it was a bonus to have his services. The Ethiopian was a genius of design and build with his explosive devices, the range of disguises, the means of transportation and activation. The work kept him busy, too occupied to be boozing and too tired to go chasing after the women. Midway through the month, Tomas started to count in days: only forty-five until the first team would move out.

In London, a significant meeting took place on Tuesday, 17th

April, just after the Easter weekend. It was held at the Foreign Office in Whitehall and was chaired by Sir Geoffrey Smithers, a retired Ambassador in his late sixties. Smithers had been recommended by the Chief of Staff at Downing Street and personally appointed by the Prime Minister. He was a good choice for the job, with much professional experience in the Arab world. He had a sharp brain and was an excellent administrator. It helped that he had a high opinion of himself and was unable to resist this opportunity for some autumn glory.

Prime Minister Blair had been enraged to be told that the combined multitude of his Government servants had been so occupied in bickering amongst themselves that they had let slip Nathaniel Habtumu. This slimy character with a loose mouth and missing morals had been allowed to flounce off to Millennium despite the fact that they knew he was screwing around in St John's Wood. To make it worse, he had only left because he panicked after murdering some wretched tart.

They told him that Habtumu had information but the PM knew quite enough already about the progress of those fucking pirates in the renamed country which they had stolen. There were articles in the international press, even television documentaries, devoted to covering the 'miracle of Millennium'. So much pap for him because the greater interest was the Tamalou Trench, that ocean of oil just waiting to be exploited and if there was a way, through diplomatic guile, for the UK to get a share, then he was going to find it. He expected a decision by late June on getting a European force into action to restore the previous regime and allow for a deal to be struck on the oil. His gut feel told him that the window of opportunity would close about then and in the meantime, he wanted a concerted effort to tie up loose ends.

Hence the appointment of Smithers and that's what brought them all together that day. Present were both Charley and Hannah Deveridge, also their big boss who ran GCHQ. Greville Thornton was there, two from the Security Service, a couple from Trade and Industry, an Assistant Commissioner of the Metropolitan Police and a scattering of technical support specialists. They had been talking all day and Sir Geoffrey thought it was time to sum up so they could break by 6pm.

'We know that the Ethiopian, Habtumu, is in Millennium but we don't know where. We have no assets in the country. We do know the American, Offenbach, who was a participant in the coup but he is now persona non grata with the CIA and we don't wish to excite the attention of our friends there because Habtumu has been implicated in the bombing of the USS Cole.

'We know that whilst in London, Habtumu became a close associate of President elect Jago. We know from tapping Habtumu's phone that he boasted of having the influence to bomb Millennium into the state of another Somalia. Both his character and his phrasing make clear that he would not be the prime mover in such an action, more of a valued subordinate.

'GCHQ has established that Habtumu, after his arrival in Century City, spoke to a man named Tetrarch. We know nothing of this person but there is speculation that he may be one of twins with distant criminal records in France but unconnected to terrorism. It's nevertheless conceivable that these two are Habtumu's senior partners and that he fled to them in Africa after he committed murder here in London.

'In short, Ladies and Gentlemen, we don't know who we're looking for, we don't know where they are and we don't know who to ask. This is a bleak outlook which I must report to the Prime Minister but let us now concentrate on trying to find more background on these mysterious twins. It's a shot in the dark but the best we can do.

'We'll return here in two weeks' time for our next review.'

As Smithers closed his meeting, King Offenbach was sitting by the sea in Century, a deeply troubled man. Since returning from his tour of Millennium's borders six weeks previously, he had been trying to investigate the possibility that they had some uninvited visitors within the country. He was certain in his own mind but had to admit that his conviction was based more on instinct than firm evidence. His concern started as he drove into the village of Tamalourene and stopped at a wayside stall to buy fruit and a bottle of water. There was a bit of bustle to the settlement which surprised him. He knew he was close to the former President's grand project but expected to find it abandoned. He had planned on having a look around, but from casual conversation with the large woman minding the stall, it was clear that villagers were working there and getting well paid in cash.

He drove past the grand entrance to the place and noted all the wheel tracks in the dust. The dead straight approach road was so long that even with his binoculars he could make out nothing of detail. The outline of the mansion was clearly visible but it would have been so whether occupied or a simple shell. He dared not linger. He had to assume that if interlopers had taken over the place, they would be hostile. King was too old and wise to be suckered into a fight which he couldn't win so he drove on to reach Century a day later, having seen but not appreciated Tetrarch and Habtumu being driven by Patrice in the opposite direction.

Thinking to share his worries with Pente Broke Smith, he walked into an entirely fresh crisis. That morning in April, he couldn't find Pente at home so he wandered into the Cathedral. He found him on his knees in front of the altar in the Lady Chapel. The great bulk of the priest seemed to dominate his surroundings and he was quite unconscious of King's appearance. He was obviously in deep conversation with the Almighty so King left him in peace while he wandered around the Cathedral, wondering again how they managed to build a roof of such height a couple of hundred years ago.

His reverie was disturbed as Pente erupted into the aisle and caught sight of him.

'That's one prayer answered anyway. I was just coming to find you, King, and I'm very happy indeed to see you. I need some counsel, old friend, and I need it now. Have you time to talk?'

'I sure have. That's why I'm here but it sounds like my problem should fall in line behind yours.'

271

'Come with me and I'll make some coffee while you read what's just come in on E mail. There's a storm about to break'

Pente led the way and once in his small sitting room, he gestured King to an armchair and left him with the three page message. King had never met Father Basil, the Abbot who ran the Order of the Saints in Hexham, northern England but Pente had told him much about the man who was both leader and mentor. He could write a good letter too and his message drove any other consideration from King's mind.

Father Basil described how he had been in his office when surprised by the sight of three vehicles coming up the drive through the parkland. Two of them were marked police cars. The Abbot left what he was doing and descended to meet them. The Police Inspector introduced himself curtly and said that he had come to collect some personal possessions belonging to the priest, Rupert Broke Smith, now living in Africa and not expected to return. He produced a warrant authorising his action but declined to state what he was seeking.

The Abbot felt obliged to cooperate and accompanied the Inspector with four of his men to the top floor of the Monastery. He explained that Pente's chattels had been placed in a storeroom. The Inspector proceeded to remove everything which the Abbot identified. In addition to all the boxes and suitcases, the officers removed Pente's computer. The party then descended again in the lift - it took a few trips - and shortly afterwards the cavalcade of loaded vehicles departed, leaving Father Basil none the wiser but full of foreboding.

It took only thirty-six hours for the news to receive national coverage on television, radio and in the Press. The investigating authorities had found hundreds of indecent images on the priest's computer. All were of pre-pubescent boys and the reports spoke darkly of other electronically filed material. An arrest warrant had been issued but since Broke Smith was one of the ringleaders of the country grab in Africa on New Year's Day 2000, he was unlikely to be detained immediately.

Father Basil was hugely distressed. He knew that this sort

of report, whatever the truth of it, would do great damage to the Order. But he was also a Christian and he had been a good friend to Pente over many years so he concluded his message with as much encouragement as he could offer, saying he was confident that an explanation would be found. He was also shrewd, King thought to himself as he put down the final page and turned to face Pente as he lumbered in with a coffee tray. This would for sure be a sting operation and it had the hand of dirty tricks department written all over it. King had no doubt that the wretched photos and films really were on Pente's computer, no doubt either that it had been some geek in the bowels of Whitehall who had contrived to put them there. And the purpose? Well, that was easy and obvious. Demonising a key character would ramp up the pressure on the makers of Millennium, just at the time when the Prime Minister was hoping to persuade European leaders to join the plan for an international force to turn the clock back. All this, however, would be very painful indeed for Pente Broke Smith and King would now have to work hard to bring him any sort of comfort.

Meanwhile in London, Greville Thornton was feeling pretty pleased with himself. It may not have been original, but the notion of rubbishing reputation was always productive and never more so than when you could drag grubby sexual practice into it. It would be interesting to hear what people had to say at the next Smithers meeting but for now, he was especially pleased at how they had latched onto the story in France and Belgium. Nothing like a bit of muck raking and if you can't find it, well just invent it! He chuckled to himself and went off to the pub.

It was unfortunate but not surprising that the news was out and shouting on a day when Patrice was making his collections in Century City. One of his standing duties while in town was to pick up a couple of copies of the national newspaper and since he had to overnight in the capital, he managed the following day's edition as well and this carried reactions in European countries and in the States. He gave the whole batch to Tetrarch as soon as he arrived back at the Palace and Tetrarch, who was not a great reader, passed them straight on to Tomas.

The effect which this news produced was fierce. Reason said that these were charges against the priest but that, as yet, there was no proof and no conviction. But Tomas was instantly convinced of his guilt, wanting to believe. There might be many such cases all round the world but this one felt personal. Here was another bent priest, cocooned in comfort in another city, another version of the depraved man who had damaged Tetrarch for life. That one had got away with it but this one wouldn't. Tomas felt a seething against this Broke Smith and made a silent vow. As soon as the first team had left, there would be a few clear days during which they would go – just the Twins together as they had always been – and they would mete out a terrible vengeance.

10. MAY — 2001

The storm in the international media over the Pente Broke Smith allegations blew into a hurricane. A quiet satisfaction was enjoyed at No 10 when the subject of Millennium worked its way back onto the agenda of European Foreign Ministers who were due to meet in Brussels at the beginning of June.

Isolated in his cathedral home in Century City, the pressure which Pente was feeling mounted inexorably, testing all his faith and values. He made one or two calls to Vanda back in Herefordshire and their conversations brought him comfort. He leaned heavily on King Offenbach who kept him going during these dark days and talked him out of a series of knee jerk reactions.

At the Palace, things were going smoothly as they entered the final stages. The first team would leave at the beginning of June as they had further to go. Tomas had complex plans to slip them into the USA through various entry points from Mexico to Alaska, each individually but with a single destination deep in the desert of Arizona. If one or even two should be detained, the remainder would be able to manage. That was the basis of their training and the same applied for the second and third teams who would leave for Europe a month later.

Tomas was particularly pleased with the performance of the two pilots, Xerxes and Petraeus. They were the only two hired guns in the party, recruited for their skills and having no commitment to the project beyond their professionalism and the good money they were earning. But their dedication had been the equal of the fervour and passion which drove the remainder of the group and they both showed great initiative. Operations around the railway and city centre targets had been straightforward to plot and rehearse but the complex activities involved with a plane hijack were much more demanding and Tomas had learned the lessons from the botched attempt in Pakistan and Afghanistan.

The pilots had taken charge of all this and the training regime which they devised was rigorous. They created a mock-up of a typical airport check-in to demonstrate standard procedures and next to this they set up a classroom in which they could teach the teams the rudiments of navigation and communication. In addition, they made full use of the aircraft they had flown in. It was old now, out of date and much smaller than the planes which were the teams' targets but it was still useful for training in deployment and how a small group could control a large number of passengers and crew. Xerxes and Petraeus had done an excellent job and would be missed but it was nearly time for them to move out and Tomas talked to them about their route and the disposal of the old 737.

The Smithers Committee convened again in the middle of the month: all of the established participants were present under the Chairmanship of Sir Geoffrey. There was a suggestion from the senior SIS man that they could easily introduce Special Forces personnel into the influx of immigrants making their way into Millennium and thus give the Government assets on the ground if needed. The Chairman gravely noted the value of this possibility but made no commitment.

Then Hannah had to admit that they were no further in either identifying the Twins, nor in reviving the trail to Nathaniel Habtumu. She didn't add that her sister Charley had spoken again to Victor in Paris who had not been able to help further with either line of enquiry.

After this, the senior officer from the Met Police came in with more encouraging information. Through Interpol connections, the French authorities had located the renovated Chateau near Loches in the Loire which looked to be the home base of Tomas and Tetrarch. The place had been found through a mixture of paid informers, speculation and a bit of guesswork. Sir Geoffrey perked up at this news and demanded maximum efforts to take matters further.

A week later at the Palace, on Sunday 20th May, they reached the point of first departures. The old Boeing stood at the end of the runway, lined up for take-off, the engines spinning comfortably as the pilots ran through their final checks. Petraeus was in the command seat with Xerxes beside him.

Nat Habtumu was standing with the Twins up in the unused control tower. He put his hands to his ears as the engines spooled up into a scream and the plane started to move, gathering speed with swift and smooth acceleration. It was almost level with their watching post and close to take off when there was a puff of smoke mixed with dust and they could see the plane slump forward as the nose wheel collapsed. A second later and a much louder explosion announced the failure of the port side landing gear so the Boeing tilted crazily. With a tearing, graunching, tortured howl the aircraft veered off the tarmac runway into the boulder strewn bush land at a barely diminished speed. The engine noise was dying away as the pilots shut down but they had no chance to regain control before the plane was tripped by huge rocks into a more extreme angle and the full to capacity fuel tanks exploded with thunderous roar.

The entire episode had been a masterclass, demonstrating the pinnacle skills of Habtumu with the design, the setting and the activation of his explosives. An expert technician at his peak, he had reason to feel pride in his achievement.

So now he turned towards the Twins, a seraphic smile on his face and his arms spread wide in triumph as he sought to embrace them both and to receive their congratulations. Before he could take a forward step, Tomas shot him cleanly and neatly between the eyes.

Tetrarch hadn't questioned the decision and he understood the reasons for it but he had baulked at doing the deed. Since Natty Habtumu had appeared, he had become as much of a friend as Tetrarch had ever had and his absence would hurt. But Tomas was right: Nat simply had to go. He was a constant source of concern for what he knew and his loose mouth. That had been contained by their isolation here but the potential for disaster would have increased away from the Palace. Tetrarch would miss his company, however, his fun and sense of mischief and so would others, none more than the Madam and her girls in Poitiers.

Tetrarch proceeded to bury the body with care, enlarging by pick and shovel one of the excavations which had been started years before for a reception building next to the Control Tower. While he worked, the wreck of the Boeing burned its way towards extinction and when he had completed his task, he returned with Tomas to find the Attack Teams still busy with their training.

On Wednesday, 30th May, King finally put together the conversation which he had been seeking to arrange. He took Pente with him and they went to the Treasury building office from which Hugh Dundas preferred to operate. Already there, they found Fergus Carradine who had been the Strike Force Commander for the invasion on New Year's Day, 2000. The four men helped themselves to coffee from the urn which was ever present on Hugh's side table and then they sat down to talk.

Each man contributed to the conversation in his accustomed style. Pente rambled a little as he continued preoccupied with his own travails. King slumped in his chair, drawling in his laconic style but with no word wasted as he recounted his journey around the country's borders and his concern at the environment around Tamalourene. Fergus Carradine was clipped in his speech and searching in his questions. Hugh Dundas was unmoving and unmoved, quietly jotting the odd note on the pad before him. At the end of an hour, Hugh moved to sum up.

'Let me see if I have this right,' he started. 'We have, as yet, no definite evidence. We are simply suspicious and we're speculating. Nevertheless, we have reason to do so. This country is a substantial landmass, of which we do not yet have full detail, let alone experience. It's perfectly possible that interlopers have arrived in our midst without our knowledge. We're relying on King and his drive past the Palace when he could see very little but felt much. It's a significant location but more important for me is the effect it had on King. I respect his gut feeling.

'And so, gentlemen, it seems clear to me that we must take action and if our further investigations reveal nothing sinister, we will be all the better for knowing it. In truth, we should have moved sooner and I blame myself for the delay. So, where do we go from here?'

King was the first to speak, pulling up his chair to the conference table. 'I'd say more information is the top priority. We need to know what's going down there, especially how many. We need another recce.'

'I agree,' put in Fergus Carradine, 'as yet we don't know what we're up against but assuming the worst, I've got to get a team together - and with the necessary equipment. That's possible but it will take time. It's eighteen months since we invaded and after that, we disbanded the Strike Force. Many of them are still here but it's still going to mean a hell of a lot of preparation.'

The others nodded in understanding and Pente went on to make his contribution, pulling at his shaggy beard as he spoke.

'Normally, I'd recommend the bush telegraph. It's remarkable how news travels through rural Africa. Even in the most remote spots, word gets passed from mouth to mouth so I've not much doubt that we could eventually get more information about the Palace that way but the drawback is that it would take days or probably weeks and we simply don't have the luxury of that much time.'

Hugh Dundas opened his mouth but Pente raised a giant hand to cut him off as he went on. 'Excuse me for a minute more, Hugh,' he said, 'as I've got another thought. It's true that we don't know quite who we're looking for, nor how many may be there. None of that. But we do know that the British Security people are busy looking for one man, a terrorist suspect, and they believe that he's here in our midst, probably right here in Century. I reckon it's a good guess that this individual is mixed up with the gang at the Palace.'

With this announcement, the Priest stood and moved away from the table to light up one of his cheroots. King smiled peacefully to himself but the other two looked startled and it was Hugh who posed the question.

'Where does all this come from, Pente?'

He got a reply through a cloud of smoke. 'Through a fair bit of personal indiscretion, Hugh, that's how! Look, King knows most of this. A very dear friend of mine - she and I maintain a bit of contact, especially recently as she's been concerned for me with the computer business at Hexham – well, Vanda has let slip that the British Government, using GCHQ in Cheltenham, is trying to locate the guy. Vanda has two daughters, both working in that organisation. She gave me no name and no doubt she and her girls would be shot if word got out that she had mentioned it to me of all people but, well you know how it is, sometimes these things just sort of happen.'

Pente stubbed out his cigar in an ashtray on the window sill and resumed his seat at the table. There was silence for a while before Hugh Dundas started to speak again.

'So,' he said cautiously, 'does this revelation amount to a further problem for us? Or is it perhaps an opportunity?'

King came in immediately, 'I'd say the second, Hugh, that's for sure. And why? Because it gives us reason to take a gamble and up our communication with the UK. Could be that a shared cause would improve relations and get Mr Blair and his people off our backs.'

'What d'you think, Fergus?'

'Yes, my instinct is to agree but I'll leave all the contact and machinations with King. I'm going to have my hands full getting a military show on the road. The only thing to add is another one for you, King. What are your buddies across the water going to say?'

'Fair question, Fergus and truth be told, I don't have a damn clue but I'll get on with finding out.'

'OK,' Dundas was back in charge now and wrapping up,

'let's agree actions for now. Pente, you keep going with your lady friend and we'll risk any damage that could arise from intercepted contacts. King, you handle all the spooks wherever and see what more intelligence you can gather. Fergus, you'll get a fighting force together and you make the best estimate you can of how many and what they need. For myself, I've got my hands full with steering Millennium and the economy in particular but I've one other suggestion. I see a bit of Arnie Schwartz, the South African guy who flew us in here. Arnie's a top class pilot and lives for flying. Suppose I take him into confidence and ask how he would go about a look at the Palace from the air?'

The others nodded their agreement and they finished the conversation with the arrangement to meet again daily, same time and same place.

Part Three

NEMESIS

Agent of downfall

FRIDAY, 1st JUNE 2001

King Offenbach chose to make the call on the landline from his sea front apartment. The time for subterfuge was past so he rang the international number for the main switchboard at GCHQ, Cheltenham, England to give his name and to ask to speak to Miss Hannah Deveridge in Department A84. The request was received without query and he sat waiting for the connection, reflecting on the strangeness of modern life and communications. Here they were, regarded as being close to a rogue state, unable to take a direct flight to London, much less to pass its borders and yet there was no problem with a phone call, an E Mail message or access to information on UK Government organisations via the Internet. His thoughts were interrupted as she came on the line with a cheery greeting.

'I must say that you're one of the last people I expected to hear on my office line, King, but it's all the more of a pleasure for that! What's to say?'

'Well Hi Hannah,' he chuckled in reply, 'It's good to hear your voice and sorry to surprise you but I figured we need to talk.'

'Go right ahead but just so's you know, I'm recording you.'

'Sure. I was counting on that. I'll make this direct, Hannah. The way we understand things down here, I reckon you guys are looking for a certain man, an Ethiopian, and a fella you've run across personally in your past. You believe he's right here somewhere in Century City. Now for our part, we figure he's hooked up with a mob of pretty doubtful characters who've sneaked under the radar into our territory and are holed up in the bush a helluva long way out from here. We know where but we don't know why.'

King paused deliberately and let the silence of space hang

between them before he finished off. 'I'm calling to suggest we help each other by pooling information but I'll understand if you have to confer some and then call me back.'

Another silence.

Then she said: 'This may come to be a career changing moment for me, King, but this is so important to us that I'm taking an initiative. Please go right ahead and tell me what you've got. And to be clear, we are talking about Nathaniel Habtumu? Correct?'

'You've got it. He's the guy OK. But can you say anything about why you've got such an interest in Habtumu?'

'Yes, I can King. It's a directive from on high, can't get higher, and the main reason is that Habtumu is well in with the possible successor to the regime you displaced down there and the incentive is that huge great resource you've got sitting offshore. You understand?'

'Oh sure, Hannah, I get the message.' King drawled his reply: he had known all along that the Tamalou Trench would haunt them in Millennium despite its vast value.

'There's more, King.'

'I'm listening.'

'First off, we know for certain that Habtumu was involved in the USS Cole. Probably, it was him who made the device as he has a lot of talent for that. So far, we've kept that information from your former colleagues and you won't need me to tell you why'.

'Check.'

'Next, Habtumu has bragged about their ability to turn the country into a second Somalia but we think that would take organisation beyond his ability and anyway, what would be the purpose.'

'Yeah, I hear that. But you said "their", Hannah. Who's "they"?'

'That's the point. Habtumu skipped out of London to avoid arrest on a murder charge. He killed a woman and did a fast runner. He made his way to Century and we've heard him there so we know it for sure. Why there? We believe he fled to join up with his senior partners and we know practically nothing about them. They may be plotters and planners or they may be action men. The most we have to work on is that there are two of them, they're siblings and probably twins, about forty years old and their names are Tomas and Tetrarch. They may also refer to themselves as the Mountain Men.'

She heard King Offenbach exhale wearily down the phone line.

'This is pretty damn hard, Hannah. If you guys with all your resource and equipment can't find more of a trace, there's small chance I'm going to do any better.'

'I know. It's all very sketchy, very flaky and we don't know how much time we have either. But at least we're in touch now and you might be encouraged to hear that your old mate Victor Sollange is on the case too. I've a feeling that you two old warhorses will come up with something more.'

King laughed. 'It's good to hear about old Victor and please tell Charley to give him my best. I'll get to work, Hannah, and let's you and me speak again in a couple of days.'

'Agreed.'

They broke the connection. Hannah went straight off to warn her boss and her colleagues. King went onto his balcony to watch the sea as he thought.

SUNDAY, 3rd JUNE

Tomas had them all assemble in the dusty turning circle at the top of the long entrance drive. They stood in front of the Palace. The imposing building formed a backdrop which would look well in photographs.

The first sun of a new day was stealing over the landscape as the departing group, accompanied by all their colleagues, came down from the dormitory buildings, humping their bags. They looked like a group of itinerant tourists, about to move on to the next destination and to add to that impression, the two women were toting a little more luggage than the seven men. Approaching the spot where Tomas and Tetrarch were standing, they could all hear the sound of the truck, with Patrice at the wheel, as it came around the building from the garage sheds at the rear and braked to a halt at the spot which Tetrarch was indicating.

There was little conversation, no speeches and no further instructions. All the talking had been done and it was time for action. Those remaining were destined for a different glory on another continent. They had the best part of another month to spend at the Palace and there was envy in their restiveness as they watched their comrades in arms load the bags onto the truck. Only one of the bystanders was active and he was the former pharmacist from Palestine who was a keen photographer. He circulated amongst the group, snapping as he found his opportunities, recording the raised, clenched fists, the grasping handshakes and the clinging embraces. Watching from a distance, Tomas was confident that here was stinging publicity in the making but the pharmacist wouldn't see it for himself. None of them would. There were no farewells to be said, only goodbyes. All of them were embarking on the trip of a lifetime and Tomas marvelled at the determined enthusiasm of twenty-six healthy humans now in the prime of their existence and all going to a certain and violent death.

They came together for a last time as Tetrarch gesticulated and they formed a small crowd in front of the grand entrance to the Palace. The photographer handed his Nikon to Tetrarch and took his place, the lens fluttered and the image was captured. Immediately, the nine took their uncomfortable places in the load bed of the truck and Patrice moved away down the long drive. The A Team had departed.

Tomas could do no more. They were heading for the United States but infinite care had been taken with planning how they would get to their appointed targets and the journey would be protracted and dreary. Patrice's bone-jarring truck would take them to the northern border of Millennium after which they would swing a little East, trekking for some thirty kilometres before they would pick up transport to take them further North and then a long way West. In about ten days' time, they should be arriving in Dakar, Senegal from which port they would take a ship for the Caribbean islands, from several of which they could slip with relative ease into the USA and then disperse as the plan required. None of this was too hard, especially not for the sort of people they had now become but it did mean painstaking travel over a long period, very different from the fast flight alternative which the other seventeen members of the Europe Teams would be experiencing when their turn came to leave the Palace.

MONDAY, 4th JUNE

The Smithers Committee assembled in Whitehall at ten o'clock sharp and half an hour later, Sir Geoffrey was growing petulant.

He had read his briefing papers carefully on the train into London, noting that Hannah Deveridge, at her own initiative, had shared sensitive information over a telephone call with the black man who had defected from a lifetime with the CIA by participating in the Millennium coup. This seemed highly improper to him and noting that not just her immediate boss, but also the Director of GCHQ had elected to attend the meeting, Smithers had prepared a general censure of her performance. He heard her out before delivering a monologue critique of the damage she was likely to have caused.

But after he finished and an awkward silence ensued, it became clear that the Director himself had endorsed her actions and was present to give her his full support.

'It's unusual, of course, Sir Geoffrey but so are all the circumstances. I'm conscious also that the Prime Minister himself is very explicit in his instructions. They are that we are to find this character Habtumu by whatever means and as fast as possible. He is very upset indeed that the man eluded our grasp whilst he was in London.'

The Director paused briefly to manage an accusing glance at the representative of the Security Service before he continued.

'Mr Offenbach is now searching for Habtumu throughout Century City but he is hampered by having never set eyes on the man. We have sent him photographs but they don't provide personal experience and of course we have no identification whatsoever for the two men whom we now suspect of representing a far larger threat – that's to say the mysterious twins going by the names of Tomas and Tetrarch.'

Further down the long conference table, the Officer from the Metropolitan Police raised a hand and the Chairman nodded towards him.

'I wanted to contribute the additional information which we've just received from our friends in France', he announced, 'they haven't got a surname and personally, I doubt we'll ever get one. In fact, my guess is that Tomas and Tetrarch are just aliases or nicknames but it may be helpful that we do now have a photo, although of one man only. It shows him doing some martial arts training and was taken by another member of the club he used to frequent in this place, Loches. He looks a pretty tough customer.'

The Commissioner proceeded to hand around copies of a black and white photo which showed Tetrarch, stripped to the waist and wielding fighting sticks. The body did indeed look fit and fearsome but the facial features were obscured as he was grimacing with effort. The large woman representing Trade and Industry flicked her copy aside and interjected with a sensible question.

'Returning to Nathaniel Habtumu, we should not overlook the fact that he used to be high profile in the fashion business. Why don't we consult people from that background? There must be many who could give us more details of how he looks, sounds and behaves. More photos even?'

The Chairman himself responded, re-grasping the reins of the meeting.

'It's a fair point and we may well have to come back to it. For now, however, I don't believe we should risk giving this manhunt the wings of general publicity, especially not as Habtumu is the only link we have to these twin brothers who have become our prime target. We don't want the populist media, now encouraged by the priest scandal, to devote too much attention to Millennium.'

Then came the turn of the GCHQ Director who had been biding his time.

'Chairman, I have a further proposal. Like it or not, we have no choice but to work with Offenbach in this matter. That could be interpreted as giving succour to the current regime there of which HMG officially disapproves, therefore the Prime Minister should be made aware of what we are intending to do and why. If we can get over that hurdle, I think we should be getting assets down there on the ground and providing support. It may be that we should share this with the Americans but I leave that judgement to others.'

The senior man attending from the Security Service opened his mouth to come in with a comment but Smithers was alert and held up a hand, indicating that the Director should finish speaking first. He continued, hunching forward with his elbows on the table so he could look around the assembled gathering.

'It happens that a member of my staff who is with us today, Hannah Deveridge, has had dealings with Nathaniel Habtumu and has suffered at the man's hands. This was some time ago - Nairobi in 1993 - but it was not an incident to be forgotten and she retains a clear memory of how he looks and acts. She knows Kingston Offenbach, as you have heard, and I've every confidence that she would acquit herself well in Century City and be of considerable assistance to the American. But in a candid conversation prior to this meeting, Hannah has come up with another suggestion which I believe provides a better solution.

'Hannah has a particular friend - actually he is her fiancé - who also has close experience of Habtumu, having been present in Nairobi and having seen the man much more recently.'

He went on to describe how Simon Goring had stood in the airport queue at Charles de Gaulle Airport and taken photos of the Ethiopian.

The Director continued, 'Goring was a regular Royal Marine but he resigned his Commission and went to work for one of the major international security outfits. That was in the mid-nineties but later he was seconded to what became the invading Strike Force which established Millennium. It seems that

Goring was influential in the planning and led the team which successfully assaulted the airport. So he's seen action and he knows the place. He came back to the UK a bit over a year ago and now runs the Bastion business which covers contracts in Africa. Hannah believes he will go back in there for us and I back her judgement that he would be the best man for this job.'

This idea produced a flurry of conversation which Smithers worked hard to channel into a reasonable action plan. It was eventually agreed that Simon Goring's record should be checked out and he should be accompanied by SAS personnel working undercover to watch his back and no less to watch him.

The plan would now have to be approved by No 10 but it did represent real progress and Sir Geoffrey broke up the meeting feeling justified in looking forward to his late lunch.

THURSDAY, 7th JUNE

Patrice had taken almost three full days to return to the Palace. After dropping the A Team at the unmarked northern border and seeing them march off through waving grassland, he turned his truck and bumped his way back onto the better worn route towards Century City for another load of supplies. On his return trip, he stopped at a familiar watering hole in the little town of Singahala, a place where he could get a meal and a few beers. During his stayover he saw the hotel proprietor using a mobile phone. He was told that a new mast and relay station were now operational which meant that communications had moved 200 kilometres closer to the Palace.

This news was good enough for Tomas to change their plans. It was important to report to the Interpreter in Chitral that the A Team had departed as planned and he could now do this in a single day, leaving Tetrarch to keep a watchful eye on the camp. Tomas drove out of the Palace before dawn and a couple of hours later, the establishment settled to another day of routine.

An unwelcome visitor arrived shortly before midday. Arnie Schwartz was enjoying himself and had been since he took off from the airport at Century that morning. Arnie was a true birdman, never happier than when he was in the air which was his natural habitat. He was barely seventeen when he went solo and at twenty-five he was a seasoned professional in South Africa's air force, qualified for combat in fast jets. But the routine and discipline of Service frustrated him so he resigned to take a job with a major international airline. This profession provided him with enough money and free time to indulge his passion for stunt flying and in sharp contrast, to give flying lessons. As a tutor, he surprised himself with his own success, being extraordinarily patient and understanding, perhaps because he was himself so completely confident from the moment he became airborne.

Arnie Schwartz met Hugh Dundas in Hong Kong in 1989 when he was spending four months of accumulated leave flying for an Executive Jet company. They got on well together and Arnie formed a high regard for this behemoth of the business world who managed to keep his humour and his manners intact despite his soaring success. They kept in touch and Arnie hadn't hesitated to take up the offer to fly the big Boeing which Hugh had bought to bring them all down from Europe on invasion day. He was Hugh's man now, content with his life in Century City and delighting in the variety of work which came his way.

He had borrowed a Cessna for this outing. There was a wide choice of aircraft at the flying club which was attached to the main airport and most of the machines were standing idle having been abandoned by their previous owners after the invasion. But this Cessna was an exception, being the property of a Belgian born rancher who ran beef cattle on the lush ground of the Central Highlands. He had been living here for years and was happy to welcome the new order. Arnie was friendly with the owner, sharing tips as to how to get the best from his machine which was never flown with passengers but did have an auxiliary fuel tank.

The sun was high in the cloudless blue sky of Africa as Arnie consulted his map and confirmed that he was a bare fifty kilometres from Tamalourene. He gained some height and described a very wide circle to starboard as he picked out the main features of the Palace as it had been introduced to him a week ago in Hugh's office by another long term resident, an extremely competent African who had been in charge of the cartography office for the previous President. It had been a busy time since then, what with choosing his machine, getting the owner's permission to borrow it for a day and making sure that it was prepared to his exacting standards. But he had forgotten none of the African's brief and now he could see clearly enough the two outstanding features, the towering skeleton of the Palace and a distance away from it, the black scar of tarmac which was the private runway.

Arnie made up his mind and turned in sharply, then side slipping to lose height fast as he made his approach. Straightening up in an instinctive move, he simultaneously shut down his throttle so that his passage at about a thousand feet was almost silent. He could see no movement on the ground as he passed over the main building, all the workshops and outhouses, the control tower and finally the runway. The whole place seemed to be deserted which, according to the brief from Hugh Dundas, was entirely possible but he needed to verify and the best way of doing so would be to land and have a walk round. It would be hot on the ground and a fair march but it was the only way of getting the job done so he put on power and pulled up the nose as he swung into turn and lined up to put her down. It looked as if he would need to taxi for several hundred yards before he got level with the Tower.

Ever watchful, Arnie caught a glimpse of trouble while his machine was still a few feet off the ground. There was a flash of movement on the roof of the Tower and he put on power while holding down the nose so that he was increasing speed but not height. He passed the wreck which he had seen on his first pass, recognising the outline of a burned out 737. His excellent peripheral vision flashed a warning to him and his actions became instant and automatic. He slammed the throttle fully open, hauled for height and banked away sharply, his port wing uncomfortably close to the ground and disaster but he was happy to be taking the risk as it was a better option than the small arms fire which was pouring in at him from points on both the roof of the Control Tower and from somewhere behind the wreck.

A few seconds later, Arnie was clear and cruising again, heading straight back to Century with a report for Hugh Dundas. He couldn't say who and he couldn't say how many but for certain sure, there were residents at the Palace who were determined and unfriendly.

SATURDAY, 9th JUNE

They caught up with him in Uganda. Simon Goring had started one of his whistle stop tours in Zambia a week ago and after a couple of days in Lusaka he moved on to Nairobi. Since he had been running Bastion Security from its UK base, he found that these little and often visits worked best for keeping a finger on the pulse and the frequency of appearance held undoubted appeal for the clients.

Entebbe was to be his final port of call on this trip and when he checked into his hotel, he took a call from the PA to the British High Commissioner asking him to come by for a drink. It sounded like an instruction and having arrived at the attractive colonial residence at 6.30 that evening, he found himself almost immediately on the telephone, speaking to Sir Geoffrey Smithers in the study of his country house outside Marlborough. The conversation was as brief as it was surprising to Simon. Smithers explained how he and his Committee were working at the express instruction of Downing Street, how matters had progressed and the nature of the assistance which they were now asking of him. Sir Geoffrey managed to convey that his cooperation would be highly valued in some manner to his benefit, whereas his refusal might have less warming consequences. Simon was inclined to accept this on the spot but thought better of it and promised instead to return for another conversation before Sunday lunch the following day.

He hung up and arranged permission to make a second call which was to Hannah. This went on longer while they took advantage of a secure line for her to tell him more of the background, the machinations and the time it had taken to gain the PM's agreement that Government should now be taking help from one of the hands which had 'practiced piracy'. They had a laugh at this, uncaring of the certainty that their conversation would be recorded and then Hannah continued with the latest speculation about the identities of Tomas and Tetrarch.

They left themselves time to share some intimacy, news of how the wedding plans were developing for late September, her latest ideas for a honeymoon destination and counsel that he should avoid the tarts of Entebbe and hurry home to her bed instead. Then Hannah continued with a theme which started a current of electricity running through him.

'The couple of days we stole before you left on this trip: remember?'

'Well, of course: why wouldn't I?' he replied forcefully as his memory reeled through some of the highlights of their time together. They had been spending too much time on the phone and too little in one place as Simon grappled with the demands of his business and Hannah responded to the unceasing imperatives from GCHQ and Whitehall. There were pressure cooker days as he lodged in Farnham during the working week and she struggled home to her Cheltenham apartment, risking being late for the devoted child carer, Winnie, and then too exhausted to enjoy the pleasure of looking after Imogen. One evening, Hannah's patience snapped and she called her mother on a whim of desperation. She was insistent with Si and late the following afternoon, he joined her from Surrey and they drove together to Foy, leaving Imogen with Vanda who was ecstatic at the prospect of her granddaughter to stay. Then they put their mobiles on silent and started a meander through the matchless countryside of the Cotswolds.

They made their base in the village of Bledington, staying in the pub with rooms on the Green and they spent two days blessed by June sunshine, blissfully content as they wandered by car and on foot through calm and compelling surroundings. Over dinner on their second night, they started in on their worries and challenges before Hannah interrupted herself to wag her knife at him.

'Enough already, Simon. Just whilst we can, let's talk about ourselves and where we go from here. Specifically, I have a suggestion. I think I should go about selling the flat and we should start looking for somewhere to live around this part of the world. It sounds corny and provincial, Si, but I want a home for after we're married: I don't want a smart pad, I want a garden and wellies and a dog. Also, I want a couple of siblings for Imogen and right now, I want some more wine.'

'Does that come first,'he smiled as he lifted the bottle between them,'or do we have to go upstairs right away?'

'Don't you dare mock me,' she said, lifting her glass to her lips and as she drank, Simon surprised her completely by saying simply,

'I agree.'

'With which part?'

'All of it actually but mostly for now about a house. Funny, but I've been having much the same thoughts myself. Anywhere round here is easily commutable to Cheltenham for you. It's a fair way for me but possible and anyway there'll be days I can work from home. Then there'll be the overseas stuff. Will you be OK with that?'

'I can manage well enough on my own when I have to, Si. I think I've proved that already.'

He lifted his glass in acknowledgement of a fair point and paused before changing subject.

'Why did you call her Imogen?'

Hannah gazed into his eyes as she replied.

'I like the name. But also, it has three syllables.'

'And that's important?'

'Yes, very. Because her surname has only two: Imogen Goring. They run together, you see. There's a cadence and it sounds right. She was always going to be Goring, no matter what – or at least for now!'

It was drizzling the following morning and they slept on, happily unencumbered by Imogen and recuperating from too much dinner and drink followed by some gentle and fulfilling lovemaking. Approaching nine o'clock, the rain stopped and the sun appeared, encouraging Simon to think about breakfast and another day. He was stretching with both arms vertically above his head when Hannah turned over on her back and reached up to lock her fingers with his. He made to lower their arms but she resisted him.

'Don't do that, Si. We're tumbling.'

'Tumbling?'

'Yes. We're birds, you see: very particular birds and my favourite breed. We're eagles.'

'OK,' said Simon, humouring her as he kept his arm outstretched, 'and are we of any particular variety?'

'Yes, certainly. We're of the family of the Bald Eagle.'

'So the symbol of the USA?'

'Correct. We're beautiful, dominant, majestic. We cover vast distances but when we come home, it's to a strong, huge stick nest which we've made for ourselves way up high in a tree somewhere which gives us a terrific view on the world and great security.'

'Go on,' he said, intrigued by this imagery.

'Before that stage, of course, we have to get together and to do that, we must have a spectacular courtship. We lock hands and fingers – well talons – and we fly linked together. We soar and swoop, we turn cartwheels and plummet at huge speed. We tumble towards the earth and pull out of our dive together just before we hit the ground. We are masters of flight and of our own survival.'

'It sounds impressive. Is there any other special characteristic of our performance?'

'There is, yes. We mate for life.'

Simon moved over to kiss her and their hands fell away.

And now he sat staring into space as he gripped the telephone in Entebbe and listened to the soft breathing of Hannah, picturing her in the kitchen of the apartment in Cheltenham.

'I remember well enough and I'm coming home soon. Then we can build ourselves a new nest.'

'It can't be soon enough. Take care of yourself. And remember also that there are two girls here who love you.'

She blew a kiss and there was a buzz on the line as she broke the connection.

At the Palace in Millennium at same hour, Tomas was deliberating on what to do for the best. It turned out that when the little plane had flown over the Palace, Tetrarch had been in his home-made gym, working out with a variety of weapons as he did every day for an hour or so. He had heard nothing and even if he had, he would have been much too late to avert the course of history. It was the Ukrainian called Aziv who overreacted at the prospect of a landing on their runway and then when it seemed the pilot intended a low level flypast, Aziv blazed off a stream from his machine pistol. There wasn't much chance of hitting the aircraft but what he had done was to announce their presence and attitude. They should have allowed the guy to land and taken their time in questioning him and his passengers before, in all probability, despatching them. As it was, Tomas had returned to the certain knowledge that their position had been compromised. There was nothing to be done about that now but the consuming question now was how to react. It needed thought. No benefit would result from speedy action.

TUESDAY, 12th JUNE

Simon Goring arrived in Century during the early evening. He was tired and apprehensive but able to appreciate the swift advance of changes in Millennium since his departure over twelve months ago. The city seemed to be buzzing with new building and repair work. There were more shops selling more goods and apparently at all hours. The taxi which he took from the airport was relatively modern and immaculately clean. His hotel, always his favourite for its position on the waterfront, was spruced up and offering a much improved level of service. He settled in for a comfortable night having made a plan to meet Pente and King Offenbach for breakfast.

Simon was touched by the warmth of their welcome and as they finished eating in the hotel restaurant, he was happy to speak of the bargain he had made on the telephone from Entebbe.

'I told them that I would accept their commission to do all I can to help in finding Habtumu and his confederates. I said that I would charge a fee but that it was not to be paid in cash. I told them that I wanted to see a full announcement in all the media that an investigation had proved the child abuse accusations against you, Pente, to be entirely without foundation and that you were offered a full apology in absentia.'

The Priest dropped his coffee spoon with a clatter of china and looked dumbfounded.

'Well', said Simon, 'the whole bloody performance is absurd. There's no evidence to take it to a courtroom where it would be dismissed out of hand. This was trumped up for political gain and it's a complete disgrace. I'm pleased to say that my ultimatum was accepted.'

Offenbach beamed in relief and admiration at the initiative. Pente buried his face in his hands and came up with just a single question.

'But Simon, how could you know for sure that I'm not guilty?'

'I'm surprised you of all people asking that. It's a matter of faith. You may not be able to prove it but you know.'

'Good God', Pente told him, 'and I do mean that. Thank you most sincerely and what a marvellous way to start the day.'

Shortly afterwards, they walked together to see Hugh Dundas and found him in his office, together with Fergus Carradine and Arnie Schwartz. The six of them settled in for a conversation and to make two plans for action. The first was concerned with the search for Nathaniel Habtumu and the second revolved around Arnie's recent experience over the Palace and how Carradine's people should deal with the place.

As they schemed and debated amongst themselves, five hundred kilometres away across the country, Tomas was talking to Tetrarch.

'I have decided. The best we can do now is to move the schedule forward by a week. We will never know what the pilot of that plane saw. We don't know if it was a chance arrival or if there was a plan to reconnoitre. We don't know how many were on the aircraft, where it came from, what it was doing but the best guess says it was sent by the government in Century City. Because it came at all means that they suspect we're here but don't know who we are, how many we are or what we're here for. Aziv has told them they have something to worry about but nothing more and, praise be, they don't know that our first arrows have already flown. We must now expect them to follow up and how long that takes will depend on who they have in charge. We must expect the worst but I think they will come by road and that it will take them some days to get organised. So I'm going to pull forward our departure date. We'll leave here this Sunday and spend seven days lying up in the bush. If anyone protests, they can blame Aziv. We'll hold a meeting in the morning and tell them.'

Tetrarch nodded. The thinking wasn't for him but he'd be content to follow the order and to back it up if any of the group felt argumentative.

SATURDAY, 16th JUNE

They were ready to leave the Palace. The exit wasn't going to be as smooth as Tomas had planned but they could manage. It had been an exhausting few days during which they had drawn heavily on Tetrarch's strength and Tomas was played out by the constant attention to detail, with the object of leaving nothing behind to speak of their identity or purpose. They would move out at midday tomorrow and Tomas went to get some rest still undecided about the fate of Patrice who had been a good and loyal servant but in doing so had seen too much.

In Century City, meanwhile, there were mixed feelings. After a scratch pasta meal, they had gone to King's apartment and were now sitting on his balcony in the cool of the evening, drinking coffee with Armagnac and talking things through. There were four of them with Hugh, Pente and Simon. Arnie Schwartz was not present and Fergus Carradine had left the previous day, taking two of their military Land Rovers, loaded with a total of nine including the two SAS soldiers who had arrived in Millennium to support Simon Goring. Fergus had plotted a route which would avoid the normal road to Tamalourene but would short circuit the trek which King had followed. It was a sound plan, but it involved using tracks and in one section a bash through virgin bush so Fergus had allowed plenty of time to get themselves into position for a dawn attack on the complex. Allowing for delays on the journey, he reckoned they would make the assault on Monday morning. King and his guests raised a glass to their survival and success.

They turned then to an analysis of their own efforts over the last few days. In credit, they could reflect that they had scoured every likely location throughout Century City which might be giving safe haven to Habtumu and the Twins. The debit side of the ledger was much less comforting. Not finding someone was not the same as proving there was no one to find. They were gnawed by doubt and could only hope that Carradine's men would find their targets at the Palace.

SUNDAY, 17th JUNE — 02:00

The best laid plans may be undone by chance, by carelessness or by equipment failure. Sometimes, pure fate may intervene.

Tomas woke from a dead sleep at this lonely hour of the night. The pain was extraordinary and coming in long waves, between which there were intermissions which promised a return to normality. Tomas stuck it for an hour, then crawled out of bed and staggered to find Tetrarch who was snoring like an ox in the next door room. These were their private quarters, well away from the dormitory blocks which housed the attack teams.

Tetrarch was instantly alert as Tomas stumbled in with arms and hands twisting and flailing in a desperate effort to contain the raging pain before collapsing over the bed, fighting for breath. Tetrarch contained his own sense of panic and leant over the gasping figure.

'What is it, Tomy?' he whispered and bent lower to catch the reply which whistled softly through tortured teeth.

'Don't know. It's from my stomach clean through to my back. Can manage, but it's bad. Need help. Get me in the pickup and' ….. , but the message was cut short by a further shudder and a barely muted shout of pain.

Sweeping the agonised figure into his arms, Tetrarch ran for the door and their vehicle standing outside. He manoeuvred Tomy to lie on the rear seat and returned to his room to collect a sheet, a pillow, a blanket and a litre bottle of water. He checked there were jerry cans of fuel in the load bay and was getting behind the wheel when he heard another gasp which made him lean over to catch the message.

'Tell someone.'

Tetrarch nodded and drove over to the nearest dormitory

block which was reserved for some of the men in the party. A figure appeared out of the night and a dulled torch beam glimmered briefly.

'What's going on?'

Tetrarch stuck his head out of the driver's window.

'Tomas is sick. Will be OK but we need help. It'll take a day. You guys just work as normal and we'll be back tonight.'

Tetrarch was happy to have found himself speaking to Aziv. That one owed them something and he wouldn't let them down a second time. He gestured a farewell at the torch and then gunned the pickup away down the long drive. He had already decided that speed was more important than comfort.

Thus started a truly dreadful day, ten hours and more of torture for them both with Tomas falling in and out of consciousness as the pain bit ever deeper while for Tetrarch, the concentration of maintaining speed over poor to wretched surfaces mingled with fear at losing Tomy's control and guidance. He knew the roads pretty well and gained some time by taking a scarcely visible track through the bush which by-passed the section on which he had disposed of that Police Inspector. Then came Singahala, the only place where he made a stop as it had a fuel station. Tetrarch bullied the owner into filling the tank and he ransacked the shelves of the scruffy little shop for any worthwhile drugs, coming up with a dusty old packet of codeine and a fresh bottle of water.

Tomas was groaning on the back seat as they pulled out and went on, one hand claw like as it grasped a grab handle, the other locked behind the knees which were drawn up into a foetal position. The steady gasps were punctuated by an occasional shriek of pain as the vehicle hit a rougher section but Tetrarch continued as fast as he could.

The final two hours and a hundred kilometres were quicker as the surface improved with a central strip of long laid tarmac but Tetrarch was forced to make occasional swerves to avoid potholes, other vehicles and ox carts. Passage over the ground may have been quicker but it was no more comfortable for the patient curled on the back seat.

It was past midday when they blasted through Century City's suburban traffic and Tetrarch needed almost a further hour to negotiate his way to the main medical facility of the Hospital of all Hope which was centrally located. He drew up outside the spreading white building and ignored the shouted protest of a uniformed guard as he dashed for the front door and the reception desk.

MONDAY, 18th JUNE

Fergus Carradine was late. The assault team was forced behind schedule as they battled through a brutal stretch of virgin bush country. The short cut which he had planned turned out adding to their time elapsed since leaving Century and he now regretted having left the decipherable track which wandered around a low escarpment, describing the shape of a huge bottle. They had cut across its neck, aiming to save at least a hundred kilometres, and it started well. But when they were about a third through they hit shale ground which trapped rain water and turned the conditions into very heavy going, made worse by the sharp elephant grass which grew head high. The weight of their vehicles hadn't helped, the two specially equipped Land Rovers being burdened with armaments, communications equipment, fuel, water and food: all necessary but heavy components of a load which had to include six men. It hadn't taken long for Fergus to offload ten guys including himself to slog on foot through the bush while the two drivers ground their vehicles forward in low range and low gear. Almost immediately afterwards came the first of three punctures which made for yet further delay.

The result was that they were dog tired and twenty kilometres from their target at 0330 on Monday morning, so unable to hit the Palace and its surrounding compound until after dawn which was too late for his battle plan. Fergus was forced to delay his attack and he took his force into the slight cover of a stand of acacia trees, deploying his camouflage nets and setting a guard of two while the remainder of them prepared a rough camp and some food. Then they slept.

Meanwhile at the Palace, two of their opposition were on guard, hoping to see Tomas and Tetrarch reappear but there was no sign of them that morning or during the daylight hours which followed. As the dusk of Monday crept over them, they settled into another evening of routine and two of them, one man and one of the girls, took the first watch. The weather was calm and so was the general mood. They were all looking forward to leaving, to taking the first steps towards carrying out their missions. All were confident that the Twins - the Mountain Men - would return before dawn although anxiety gnawed at Aziv: only he had seen them leave and Tomas had looked pretty bad in the glimpse of the torchlight.

Tomas was looking a lot worse to the emergency team who arrived with a gurney at the back door of the pickup. Tetrarch was lucky in the Hospital reception, almost falling over an experienced nurse who had arrived with the First Fleet from Hong Kong and she took one quick look and called for a crash wagon. The wasted, bloodless face was screwed into a rictus of pain and the body was clenched into such a tight ball that she suspected death had already occurred until she caught a tremor of a pulse and raised the alarm. In seconds, Tetrarch was left on his own as the two male nurses dashed for the Emergency Room with Tomas curled on the stretcher between them. The engine of the pickup was still running and Tetrarch moved mechanically to find a parking space.

Thus began a long night for Tetrarch, with an even longer day to follow. He sat silently without complaint in the waiting area off reception as the shifts changed and the human traffic passed by. He walked around the extensive car park, helped himself to the occasional cup of coffee, accepted a sandwich from time to time, smoked a great deal and managed to bum another packet from a sympathetic cleaner. But he remained withdrawn and in a state of shock. He was frightened and the last time he had felt this sort of fear was when he had been abandoned in the cathedral at Rabat, his mother dragged from him.

It was late afternoon, twenty-four hours after he had driven in, when they came to tell him that Tomy had survived an operation but remained in intensive care under heavy sedation.

Tetrarch should go to get some rest and return in the morning. The messenger was the same nurse who had rescued Tomas and she was persuasive. He could make no contribution here and he looked done in. Tetrarch thanked her and took directions to the nearest budget hotel which was just around the corner. He was installed there and fast asleep within half an hour.

In Century City that Monday evening and through into the small hours, Simon Goring worked alone to seek any sign of their quarry. The face, the stance and some of the mannerisms of Nathaniel Habtumu were all ingrained in his memory and knowing the man's reputation as a party animal, Simon did an extensive round of the hotels and bars and clubs. He was deliberately indiscreet, asking questions and laying claim to a friendship with this flamboyant character: somebody must have seen him. By two o'clock in the morning, he'd had enough and zero to show for his efforts. He was not to know that Habtumu was already long dead and lying in an unmarked grave on the other side of the country. He didn't know either that Habtumu's far more dangerous friends were now almost within touching distance, one asleep and the other in an induced coma.

TUESDAY, 19th JUNE

Carradine and his force of eleven were now rested, vigilant and keyed up for action. At precisely 0345, their two vehicles in line astern and each with a crudely muffled exhaust pulled off the village road and onto the dead straight kilometre of track which stretched away in the still of the African night towards the Palace. They paused while Fergus alighted from the leading Land Rover to run a final check with the occupants of the second vehicle. Satisfied, he was returning to his seat when his sharp ears picked up the growl of another engine, still some way off but apparently approaching.

With hand gestures, he directed his two drivers to move off into the scrub, one on either side of the track and to kill their engines. The Land Rovers bulked in the gloom but they might not be noticed if this new arrival on the scene was a local, familiar with the surroundings and keen to get home. To add distraction, Carradine beckoned to Trooper Joe Hawkins, one of the SAS soldiers from the UK, and together they unhooked a sand ladder from the side of the second vehicle and stretched it across the track. They lay prone on the ground, camouflage painted faces well below a headlight beam, and waited.

Patrice's old truck came up from out of the village and turned on to the drive. He was alone. A creature of habit, he had been worried by the lack of instructions during the previous day. He had grown content to trundle his old truck up the drive each morning to receive his orders for the day, always from the big man, from Tetrarch. This had become his life until yesterday when he had been told that the two leaders had gone away and it was not known when they would return. It would not be long but he must stay at home until he was summoned again. This hadn't been enough for Patrice and he had been restless and unhappy. With the instinct of a hunted animal, he had sensed the presence, then heard the very dim noise of a car moving quietly through the village. They must be back, Patrice thought to himself, and he slipped out of his shack, climbed into his cab and rattled off. The noise of his passage was familiar to his fellow villagers and not a dog stirred in response.

When he saw the modest obstacle looming in front of him, Patrice was more confused than concerned and he slowed, peering through the fly specked windscreen and letting his lights pick up more detail of whatever lay across the track. He had no time to do more before both his cab doors were yanked open. Hawkins grabbed him by the throat and hauled him out into the dust of the track while Fergus reached over from the passenger side and knocked the truck out of gear. It came gently to rest with its front wheels kissing the sand ladder, lights spearing into the night and the old engine wheezing away.

Carradine flashed his pencil beam torch to take one look at Patrice and made up his mind. Hawkins was using one knee to keep his man on the ground and he had one meaty hand at the scrawny neck. Fergus spoke softly but with urgency.

'We don't have an argument with this one so he can go. Take three with you in the truck. I bet they'll know it at the Palace so it should give you a bit of cover with your vehicle up its arse behind. I'll hang back a hundred yards with the others and see which way they jump. Go.'

They moved off, Hawkins driving the truck with three of his team behind him in the open load bay, one to each side and the third looking over the tailgate to their Land Rover which followed a bumper's width behind with its driver and a sixth fighter. The old truck made as much noise as ever and its headlights pierced the night but the shadow behind it dribbled along quietly in complete darkness, guided by the single working tail light and the gestures of the man sitting at the rear.

Fergus Carradine stood in the track and watched them go. He looked at Patrice, now standing dishevelled and confused beside him. Carradine jerked his weapon in the direction of the village behind them and spoke in English.

'You go. Tell the others there is a new law here now. You must stay away from this place.'

Patrice nodded and turned to shamble away. Fergus had no idea if he understood but Patrice was already clear in his mind. Unless the Twins came back very soon, then all would change again but the villagers were accustomed to taking whatever comes and making the best of it. He quickened his steps and didn't look back as he heard the second Land Rover move up the track.

Sitting beside his driver, Fergus had some time to reflect as they motored in silence. This had to be the dodgiest episode of his experience and his stomach churned as he imagined what might lie ahead. Around him, he had some good men, most of whom he knew well and all with some background of conflict in Africa. They had fought their way into this country eighteen months ago and had taken control of an entire city so half an incomplete palace with its surrounding compound should be straightforward, especially with the supreme training of the two SAS guys to help. But to set against that, he had no idea how many they were up against, no idea of their capability. He had no plans of the building complex, no clue about defence obstacles which may have been erected. There had been no photographs to study in advance and he was depending on the instinct of King Offenbach and the sightings of Arnie Schwartz on his fly-by that this track ran dead straight to the grand entrance. Fergus hated to be short of intelligence and now he felt naked.

There was a single guard on watch at that dead hour of the night. Her name was Katya and she was one of the three remaining girls, a large woman who came from rural Romania where they breed them strong and silent. She was not easily alarmed, she had excellent eyesight and she was extremely fast on her feet.

Katya heard the engine, made out the outline of the familiar truck, was wondering what the hell Patrice was doing and then

314

saw the second vehicle which was so close to the tailboard that it appeared to be on tow. She sprang up from the old chair by the ever open double doors to the complex, whirled around and sprinted for the inner courtyard which gave access to the dormitory blocks beyond. The automatic weapon dangled from her right hand and she slipped off the safety as she ran.

Fast as she was, she wasn't fast enough. From his position in the back of the truck, the sharpshooter Kenny Crowe, who had been a key ally for Fergus during the invasion, caught a glimpse of her body movement. He swung up his rifle and loosed off a steam of shots which caught her in the legs and back. Katya went down, dying if not yet dead and firing her weapon into the night sky. In doing so, she gave a vital warning and in their beds and bunks, her colleagues were jolted into instant reaction. All of them slept clothed after a fashion with their armaments immediately to hand. In an instant, full battle was joined.

Carradine's vehicle swept up, its lights now blazing and disgorged its load as it came to a halt. His full force dispersed at the run, some following Hawkins as he dashed for the inner courtyard, others moving to circle around both sides of the huge building. Fergus delayed to keep Kenny Crowe by Patrice's truck, watching for any who might try a break to the front.

As he shouted his instruction, Fergus had time to be grateful to Katya. She had proved that whoever these people were, they were for real and fighting back. He stooped and ran for the courtyard, hearing gunfire from all directions and conscious of the chaos developing.

The action raged for nearly two hours, diminishing in noise as the time passed. The stun grenades which had come in with the SAS men were valuable, particularly in one of the three dormitory blocks which they stormed. Equally effective was a device which Fergus had never seen before: little mini torches mounted on a spiral coil of wire with a rubber base, coated with a powerful adhesive. They would stick to most surfaces and when left to wobble on their wire, they acted as decoy and could easily be mistaken in the pitch darkness for a moving man with a helmet light. Some of them caused the terrorists to blaze away, thus revealing their own presence and position.

Carradine was worried about casualties and still guessing at the total enemy number. The estimating became harder as they pushed into the complex and could appreciate the size of it. The Palace was five storeys high with unfinished staircases in place but few interior walls. There were gaping chasms designed for lift shafts, apertures awaiting windows, piles of building material scattered at random. It would have been testing to walk around in full daylight and was a lethal arena for a running gunfight in pitch darkness.

Fergus jumped for the stairs, wanting to investigate the upper floors and to gain some height. A big, burly fellow named Anders Moran appeared at his side to provide back up. Moran was a former policeman from South Africa, shrewd, competent and experienced. They got as far as the third floor before giving up. Dust in their torch beams was heavy on all the surfaces which were unmarked by footprints so it was clear that the enemy force had never patrolled here which was surprising because the view would be panoramic for a look out so they must have felt unthreatened by casual visitors.

Fergus was running back down the final stairs of undressed concrete when his eye caught a dull glint from the hallway below. He missed his footing and lurched sideways as he launched himself into a jump down the last three steps. Immediately behind him, Moran made a clear target, his moving bulk standing out against a starlit sky which could be seen through the great window spaces on the staircase and a fusillade of fire from a corner of the hall caught him squarely and cut him almost in half.

Fergus heard, guessed but didn't look back to confirm. He dropped to his knees as he landed, rolled himself into a ball and came to lie face down, squinting into the corner from which the attack had come, his hand gun extended in front of him and gripped in both hands. Almost immediately, the gunman appeared, flitting over the intervening space to see if he had scored once or twice. Fergus was a very fine shot and, despite the poor light, scored with two shots to the head. The body sprawled and he could see that this had been a girl.

He didn't look back. Pressing himself against the cover of the walls, Carradine went through to the inner courtyard and on to catch up with the rest of his men. The diminishing sound of gunfire told its own story and suddenly it was clear to him. These people were a terrorist force, brave, technically competent and perfectly ready to die. This place was a training complex, marvellously remote in itself and all the better for being lost in Millennium which was itself outcast from most of the world. He didn't know about their targets or timing but it was clear to him that they had been preparing for attack, with not much thought given to defence.

He had been bloody lucky: his small team ought to have been decimated, completely cut to pieces given this labyrinth of a place with all its space complemented by its hidey holes. But they hadn't expected interference, had given no thought to a pre-emptive strike against them, setting a guard against a casual visitor but not allowing for an attack force. In addition to which, he had also been bloody lucky with that truck: without that, they could never have got so close without sounding the alarm.

WEDNESDAY, 20th JUNE

Across the globe, the day started in waiting.

Far to the East and shortly after dawn prayers, the Old Men of Chitral gathered in the cool of the morning to sit in their cane chairs under their favourite group of trees and to hear from the Interpreter that he had no further news to report. But that was not a surprise. When Tomas had called almost two weeks previously, it had been to confirm the departure of the A Team, on plan and on time, and to add that the others would leave Tamalourene sooner than expected but would still travel to Europe and their targets according to schedule. Tomas had not enlarged on this and the Interpreter had assumed it was a measure to provide additional security. The Old Men heard him out and sat back, content. Long life and accustomed practice had taught them all the value of watchful patience.

In London that morning, another meeting of the Smithers Committee heard that the Police in France had found nothing new at the chateau outside Loches. The place remained quiet and undisturbed but they would continue to keep a watch. They heard briefly from Charley Deveridge but she had little to add. Nathaniel Habtumu seemed to have vanished into the ether along with his transmissions. Her sister Hannah came in then as the senior representative of GCHQ on this occasion and she was able to report that Simon Goring was in Century and had provided a detailed account of his search throughout the city for the elusive Ethiopian. He had found no trace of the Twins either. Sir Geoffrey Smithers was listless in his Chairmanship: he had been hoping for more and better and knew that his report onwards and upwards would not be well received.

Later that afternoon in Century City, Hugh Dundas organised

a meeting with King Offenbach and Pente who came with Simon Goring. Fergus Carradine arrived travel-stained and weary but he soon had their collective attention.

Fergus started with a quick account of their journey out and the difficulties which had delayed them. He went straight on with the attack and ensuing fire fight, his own exploration of the Palace and the loss of Anders Moran which made Pente catch his breath and start scrabbling for a cigar.

'That was bad,' said Carradine, 'he was a very good man. But mercifully, he was our only casualty bar a couple of flesh wounds. We found a total of seventeen, fourteen men and three women all of whom were heavily armed, determined and dangerous. We destroyed them all, every last one eventually, but it was a long process. Our greatest difficulty lay in the location. That place is a massive sprawl of buildings that stretch out behind and on both sides of the Palace which is huge in itself but probably only a third finished. As a construction project, it has years to go and all around there are workshops and store sheds, old shipping containers, a mess hall and purpose-built dormitory blocks. Further out you find the airstrip with a proper tarmac runway, a half done control tower and another group of support sheds and shacks.'

Fergus broke off to empty his coffee cup and the others waited in silence for him to go on.

'They weren't really prepared for us. King and Simon, I think you two will understand this best. They were canny fighters, those guys, and brave too. They were familiar with their weapons and they had a fair range of them. All good kit, modern and well maintained with any amount of ammunition. There was never any panic, no suggestion of turn and run. They used all the cover well and we had to be patient and move slowly to flush them out. It became easier with daylight but it took time - especially when you remember that we didn't know how many were waiting for us.

'But here's the thing which really struck me. They weren't properly together: they were seventeen individuals, not one group.

Oh, they would and did support each other but that seemed to happen by accident rather than design. Overall, they were an attack force, not concerned with defending themselves or their ground: highly trained all right and expert with their weaponry, but each with a mission and unprepared to fight as a group.'

There was silence in the room as Fergus continued to muse but none of his audience was prepared to interrupt. He held the floor and would complete his account in his own time and style. Finally, he resumed.

'It would have been 0730 or even a bit later before I felt confident that the battle was over and we could start the clearing up. By then, we had pressed right through the palace complex and were up on the airstrip where we killed the final two, except that was a best guess, of course. I didn't know how many should have been there and I wasn't going to take risks that weren't necessary so we moved very carefully and thoroughly, starting where we were, in the control tower, and working our way back down to the palace complex. But first, one thing to add: one of my guys did check out the wreck of that aircraft, the 737 which Arnie spotted on his fly by?'

The others nodded their understanding.

'Well, it's clear that at least two died in the crash as what's left of them is in the cockpit seats. Beyond that, it's anybody's guess what happened, whether the plane was taking off or landing and nothing to say whether it was an accident or intended: it's just a grisly scene.

'Anyway, we went on checking the outbuildings one by one, removing the bodies as we found them and alert for anyone left behind and for booby traps. We had a few scares but we ended up back in the Palace and I climbed back up those stairs, as much to see the views as anything but I'm glad I did because that's how we found the last of them.'

Pente couldn't resist bursting out with 'D'you mean more terrorists? Alive?'

Fergus held up a hand as he said, 'Just hear me out. Questions later, OK!' He smiled at Pente as he continued, 'I was on the second floor and went to the window gaps, looking west towards the airstrip. When I peered down, I could see the roof of another building, just a shed but with a couple of containers tacked onto it. It was partly concealed behind a clump of scrub growth and I knew we hadn't fought through there so I took Joe Hawkins with me to check it out. And I have to tell you that there were two people living there, they're not there now. What's more, I don't believe they were present when we came calling.

'What we found was, in effect, a two bed apartment complete with a bathroom and a kitchenette. It's sparsely furnished but adequate for long stay: there's a bit of a seating area which has bookcases, a filing cabinet, a desk, a video player with screen – power from one of the gen sets, of course. It was all neat and tidy when we went in but Joe took a lot of trouble checking it out for traps. I had a quick browse, found a list of names and then a set of what you'd call personnel files: there were seventeen of them. There was a sort of training schedule as well and I was looking at it when Joe gave me a holler to join him in one of the bedrooms. The first of these was very bare, hardly any furniture except a cupboard and the single bed which was all messed up with a pillow trailing onto the floor. But the second was different and that was where I found Joe, looking at photographs. They were all stuck on one wall, it seemed in random arrangement. There were a couple of martial arts posters, perhaps pulled from magazines of which there was a great stack on the floor in one corner. The photos were all of one guy and they must cover quite a period of time as you can see the age change in his face. But the subject is always the same – a big, heavily muscled man who looks to be of Arab or maybe North African origin but pretty light skinned. He's always posing for the camera, always in fighting stance and generally holding a wide variety of weapons, everything from guns to staves and sticks. I've got all of them with me also so you can have a look for yourselves in a minute. But one was the exception and it's this.'

Carradine took from his shirt pocket a dog eared black and white photo which was grainy in finish but perfectly clear to read. He passed it around the group so all could study it and emit their gasps. Face on to the camera, the big man was stripped to the waist and had his arm around the shoulders of a lesser, jolly looking figure who was recognisable as Nathaniel Habtumu. A handwritten inscription had been scrawled at the bottom and it read 'Two of the Mountain Men.'

Fergus said, 'I've never seen either of them and they definitely weren't amongst those killed in the firefight.'

He spoke as the photograph was circulated from hand to hand and it was Simon Goring, the only one of them to have seen the Ethiopian in person, who passed it back to Fergus. There was silence while each man present grappled with the implications of this discovery. Then Hugh Dundas took charge of the summary.

'This gives us proof positive, doesn't it,' he said, and confirming his own judgement he continued, 'First, these Twins do exist and it was presumably the second of them who took the photo. Secondly, they have adopted this nom de guerre, whatever it may mean. Thirdly, they have pretty much literally embraced the Habtumu character.'

King Offenbach, his analytical brain working hard, took over.

'Right, Hugh, but there's more: Fergus and his team have broken up a terrorist cell. They've taken out most of it, but a third of them had already gone, so the questions are where and when and why? I reckon we have to assume that the Twins and Habtumu are now together but where are they now and why did they leave the Palace in what seems to be a helluva hurry?'

'Could they have been frightened off?' questioned Pente, 'could they have had some tip off?'

'My best guess would be no,' put in Si Goring, 'Everything says to me that the Twins, Tomas and Tetrarch, are the management. They've been directing this outfit but they're not part of it.

'So where would they go now,' asked Hugh Dundas, 'and why leave when they did?'

'As to where,' Simon replied to him, 'my bet is that they're now amongst us here in Century and I can't help but remember the warnings that GCHQ picked up through Charley, all Habtumu's threats to make another Somalia out of this country.'

'So', said Hugh, holding onto his patience while his frustration mounted, 'what the hell do we do now?'

'Just hold on, Hugh, and let's assemble the facts and features.' King Offenbach made the proposal and proceeded in the calm manner which was his hallmark.

'First off, you have to make some reasonable assumptions in a case like this. You can't guarantee but you can call the odds and take decisions accordingly. Now Fergus, with his guys, has done a great job but he has also established that a third of those training have left already, therefore presumably now on a mission but he got there before the others were ready to jump off. That's good – score one for us.

'I agree with Simon that the Twins aren't part of the team. They manage it but they don't own it. They're professionals but not caught up in any of the ideology. On the other hand, I don't buy this Somalia theory, not some terrorist strike to waste our country. Why would you train thirty-odd to do that and then reduce your force by a third?

'OK, now go back to the Twins. We don't know much about Tomas and Tetrarch but from what Fergus found, they seem organised and disciplined. They cleared out in a hurry leaving some mess in their quarters which doesn't sound typical and leaving no clear authority to act for them. It's just a guess but my bet is that Fergus would have had a really rough time, might well not have managed it at all, if the Twins had been around to manage their side of the battle.'

Fergus was nodding his head in profound agreement as King continued.

'Something caused them to leave, if not in a panic then certainly in a rush and it can't have been part of the plan. My gut tells me it was temporary only, that they would be heading back as soon as they had dealt with some emergency and what might that have been?'

He answered his own question, going on before there could

be an interruption. 'It seems to me that it most likely was connected to all our searching here. All our efforts to trace Habtumu and that topped off by your enquiries, Si. My bet is they've come looking for you and us, a pre-emptive strike and I figure we need to meet that head on.'

He sat back then and let them mull it over. A full minute passed in silence before Hugh spoke out again with a question.

'Fergus,' he asked, 'how did you leave things there?'

'We buried the bodies: just a mass grave, I'm afraid, using a digger we found on site and we had to leave Anders with them. Then I pulled out, taking three of mine with me. We left late and drove through the rest of the night. Joe Hawkins and his mate from the UK are still there. Those guys are very good at lying up out of sight and they'll make for quite a surprise if any of the opposition returns. The second Land Rover and the rest are in bivouac about 50k's down the road and they'll go back for Joe and Bernie in forty-eight hours.'

'Good,' said Hugh, 'that's good. Now for us, I say we follow King's hunch and go straight back on the hunt. We're looking for three men now, not one plus two possibles. I'll speak to the Police Commissioner and we'll get his men on the case. I can't see that we need to play this quietly any longer.

'So, King, I'll ask you to coordinate this search please. We don't want to leave a stone unturned throughout Century City. Simon, you can float as you judge best but to start, please spend some time on the phone to Hannah. We can now share everything we have with London and can consider ourselves to be working on the same side. And you, Fergus, please get some rest with the grateful thanks of us all, then I suggest you work in with King and give us some more tactical advice. Let's meet here again in twenty-four hours to review progress.'

They all responded to Hugh's clear direction and were getting up to leave when Pente Broke Smith spoke.

'I'll be on call to help any way I can,' he said, 'and as soon as possible, I'll go up to Tamalourene and speak for all the departed. There are no distinctions in death.'

FRIDAY, 22nd JUNE

Hugh Dundas called their daily meeting forward to lunchtime and they shared sandwiches and coffee in his conference room. They were all getting desperate. Thursday had been a never-ending day with nothing to show for it as they passed midnight and that was all the more frustrating as it had started with encouragement.

In the mid-morning, Simon had been checking the more up-market hotels when King called him to divert urgently to meet a uniformed policeman who had found something interesting in one of the City's southern suburbs. Simon had difficulty with the address but finally found a scruffy looking motel, really just an extended bungalow with garden parking. The entrance hall served as a minute reception and office. The policeman was draining a can of coke and the tired owner was looking truculent when Simon showed up but it seemed they had struck gold.

Copies of the photos which Fergus had brought with him had been circulated amongst the Police force and the motel owner had made an instant and positive identification.

'No question,' he said to Simon and wondering why he had to repeat himself, 'that's the guy who was staying here,' and he tapped the photos of Tetrarch in the gym and posing with Nat Habtumu.

'What about the other one?'

'Nope. I never saw him.'

'But the first man, the one who stayed, he's coming back?'

'Nope again. He was here three nights, left a deposit and paid the balance in cash when he checked out this morning, 'bout four hours ago. Didn't tip, didn't pay extra for messing up the room.'

'Messing up?'

'That was last night. He brought a tart in and they were hammering away. Broke some bits of furniture, bed legs and that.'

Simon was hard pushed not to smile. 'Why didn't you get him to pay?'

'Huh', said the owner with a mirthless grin, 'he was a big fella: not a man to argue with. 'Sides, I'll get some extra: commission from Phoebe.'

'She's the hooker?'

'That's right. I make the introductions and generally, I use her.'

Here was a bonus, thought Simon to himself and half an hour later, he was talking to the large and slatternly Phoebe who also identified Tetrarch without hesitation and went on to give a graphic account of their activities, finishing off with a simple summary.

'He was a damn hard fuck, that one, but he paid well.'

Simon shared all this with King over the phone.

'Tetrarch must have been killing time while his brother and Habtumu are up to something. That's the only thing that makes sense, Si. Could be they're done now, they've linked up and hightailed it out in which case they'll surely be heading back for the Palace where they'll catch a surprise. But just possibly, Tetrarch was told to move camp after three nights. In that case, he'll be checking into some other joint, probably in the same area. I'll send some more help and you go on searching all the other dives in that area. But Simon, be very careful.'

But by the end of that day and into Thursday night, the trail had gone cold again with no more sightings and no other word. By the early hours of Friday, they were despondent and by the lunchtime meeting, they were despairing that their birds had flown.

They settled into conversation and encouraged by Hugh Dundas, it was a reenergised Fergus who was driving them through a methodical review of all the places they had searched for their targets.

'What about public places,' he asked. 'Not all the restaurants and cinemas and clubs, I know we've been combing through those, but what about Churches, libraries, art galleries, community centres, sports halls?'

'What about the Cathedral?' Pente interjected, 'and there's the Monastery just out of town. What about the hospitals? Maybe one of them is sick or injured.'

'Yup,' replied King Offenbach, 'we've had our people around just about all those you've both mentioned, except perhaps that monastery. I've not heard tell of that so I'll organise for us to take a look. We need to go everywhere there's a collection of people. We've got to search by word of mouth. But as for the hospitals, Fergus, we've been right through All Hope, the other two and the emergency clinics. We've found plenty of guys sick and suffering from all sorts including gunshot and knife wounds, but none called Tomas or Tetrarch. Not a sniff of Habtumu either.' He broke off and reached for the coffee pot, just as Hugh's landline rang. It was Hannah calling from Cheltenham GCHQ and hoping to speak to her fiancé. Hugh waved Simon through to the adjoining office so he could have some privacy.

'Hi Si,' she could never resist this greeting, 'it's your secret spy lover calling.'

'And James Bond to you too, sexy. What have you got to cheer me up?'

'Well a lot, but none of it will stretch a few thousand miles so you'll have to make do with my voice: tell me everything.'

Simon did just that but it didn't take him long as they had spoken in the early hours of that morning, just as he was about to snatch a few hours' sleep and there had been little enough development since.

Hannah heard him out and sighed in sympathy. Then she said, 'This will sound pretty barmy, Si, but I've been speaking to my mother this morning and you know her and her intuitions. She just said for me to tell you not to forget the morgue.'

'Oh terrific idea', he expostulated, 'what sort of info are we going to get out of a stiff!'

'You can mock, my love, but she may have a point. What if one or more of them is dead - for whatever reason? You know what two of them look like now, so maybe worth doing?'

'Yeah. I get the point and thank her for me. Say at least she's not suggesting I try the Cremo. That would be harder.'

They laughed together and exchanged a few more words before hanging up. Simon went back to join the others. They finished their scratch snack in Hugh's office and then Simon got in his car and drove to the City Morgue. It was not far to go and he found a surprisingly old building, situated just off the central park. Minutes later, he was inside and speaking to a tall, uniformed African in the reception area. The man was suitably impressed by Simon's note of introduction from the President's Office, signed by Hugh himself and he was happy to talk, revealing a sunny, cheerful disposition which Simon thought must be essential for working in such a place.

'Oh yes,' the guy told him, 'this heah's one of the oldest buildin's in town, datin' back to colonial days. They had a whole lot of customers back then but fewer now 'cos people turn up to claim their own pretty damn quickly.' He gave a cheerful grin and put on a pair of spectacles to study the photos which Simon handed to him.

'No, I reckon not 'cept just possibly the pretty one,' he said tapping an enormous forefinger on the smiling face of Nat Habtumu. 'Had one come in yesterday but he was well messed up in a car crash. You care to have a look?'

Simon nodded and steeled himself as they walked together down an aisle of oversized filing cabinets before his guide pulled one out with a soft sigh as the seal around the drawer parted. The body bag inside was unzipped and Simon could see immediately that the man had been too short and too wide to be Habtumu but he made himself look at what was left of the face before he shook his head.

'Too bad', said the black man reaching to pull back the zip, 'this fella gone clean through the windscreen of his pick-up and we don't know nothing 'bout him or the vehicle so I just thought.'

They returned to the reception desk and Simon was saying his thanks before leaving when the attendant said 'Course you should check the other one too.'

'What other what?'

'The morgue at All Hope: the Hospital you know. They's got their own place there on account of the folk who don't make it through treatment' and his teeth flashed in another beaming smile.

Simon drove himself back to the huge white complex which was All Hope and found a slot in the car park. He was climbing the steps to Reception when he noticed that one of the posters which they had distributed around the city was displayed on the main glass door. It featured the photo of Tetrarch and Habtumu above script which invited anyone who recognised them to come forward. A nurse who looked Chinese in origin was studying it closely and Simon quickened his step towards her.

She was happy to talk after he had introduced himself and showed her the President's letter which introduced his authority. She was called Enyang Yang, nicknamed Sammi which made it easier for everyone. She looked to be in her early thirties and was a native of Hong Kong. She had arrived with the invasion fleet on New Year's Day 2000, nursing on the big cruise ship which had brought them here. She was enjoying her new life in Millennium and had been away from work for the last few days while she moved apartment. She was happy to help and yes, she could definitely identify the big man in the photograph. He had arrived in a rush last Sunday afternoon, jumping from his pick up outside the main door and shouting for attention. Sammi had been on her way out and summoned help for his sick passenger.

'Did you see the man he had with him?' Simon asked, wishing that they had a photo of Tomas but thinking that it might have been Habtumu.

Sammi the nurse gave him a quizzical look as she considered this calmly. Then she replied, 'I think I better take you to talk to the Professor: it was Muntz who operated.'

Without waiting for his reply, she set off, a slight, determined figure walking briskly down the long, wide corridors of the hospital so that Simon had to lengthen his stride and there was no opportunity for further conversation. Sammi paused eventually by a set of double doors and pushed her way through into a quieter area, a narrower corridor carpeted in deep blue, a name on each office door to each side. She knocked on one to her right and went straight in. It was a neat and tidy outer office, speaking of calm and organisation but made austere by the lack of natural light.

There was a smart looking woman sitting behind her desk who exchanged a smile of welcome and then Sammi was knocking at the inner door before slipping through and closing it behind her. Simon stood irresolute and nodded at the lady at the desk who gestured for him to take a seat but before he could move, Sammi reappeared in the doorway and beckoned him forward.

He entered the main office which was much bigger, dominated by a huge desk, an examination couch, cupboards, small tables and two comfortable looking armchairs. A large picture window looked out over the hospital grounds.

The man who rose from his chair and came round his desk had a lean, aesthetic look about him. He was of medium height and with his neat features he carried the promise of being efficient and perhaps a little intimidating. He shook Simon's hand as he introduced himself.

'I'm Professor Erwin Muntz and I understand from Sammi that you are here to enquire about our mystery patient. Also that you act with official authority?'

Simon nodded and passed him the letter signed by Hugh Dundas. Muntz glanced at it as Simon said, 'the matter is extremely serious and urgent, Professor. I would appreciate all the information you have on this man.'

'Of course'. The accent was Germanic, the voice calm but full of authority. 'Please have a seat while we talk, Mr Goring. It will not take long.'

When they were installed in the armchairs with Sammi still standing against one wall, Muntz surprised Simon by asking him a question.'

'What do you know about endometriosis, Mr Goring?'

Simon raised his arms helplessly as he snapped back, 'Precisely nothing.'

'No quite, that is understandable,' said Muntz, unabashed at the tone of impatience. 'It is not uncommon as a complaint and is painful but it can normally be corrected with the right care and drugs of course: but if it is not treated promptly and the condition becomes advanced, it can be serious, even life-threatening, as was the case with this patient. The only remedy to which we can then resort is a surgical procedure.'

'And what is that?' asked Simon, bursting with frustration.

'It is called a hysterectomy, Mr Goring.'

Muntz sat back, anticipating the reaction with detached interest. Simon opened his mouth and shut it again. He goggled at the Professor, searching for words to express his astonishment and then he sprang to his feet, whirling around so that his glare could take in Sammi who was standing mute before he burst out with a reaction.

'This is not correct, Professor Muntz. Something is wrong here. It was a man who was brought here for treatment, not a woman.'

Muntz allowed himself a thin smile as he gestured towards the chair, saying, 'Please sit down again and try to relax while we talk'. Simon found himself doing as he was told and the Professor continued.

'Mr Goring, before coming to live in Millennium last year, I was a Fellow at the University Teaching hospital in Leipzig where I lectured in Gynaecology so I have considerable experience in the female anatomy. I can assure you that my patient was a woman - aged about forty years I would estimate, functioning quite normally and capable of bearing a child although not now, of course. The endometriosis would have developed over quite some time and would not, in her case, have been affected by sexual activity as she seems to have had little of that. I expect she tried to ignore the worsening symptoms – perhaps she was unable to seek medical advice – and thus her problem was built into a crisis. In the final event, she is fortunate to have survived.'

Simon heard him out, his mind reeling at the repercussions from this bombshell revelation. He said in reply:

'I'm sorry for my reaction but this news has come as a serious shock. Even so, we have been looking all over Century these last few days for a terrorist who we believe poses a grave danger to us all and such people can be women as well as men. So may I please interview her urgently? Is she well enough now for that?'

'Yes probably, but no you can't Mr Goring and that's for the very good reason that the patient whom we knew only as Ms Tetrarch discharged herself about five hours ago. She acted against my most earnest advice, but she went anyway.'

'Oh Jesus,' Si was in turmoil as he stood and paced to and fro across the room. First they found him, then it wasn't him but her, and now they'd lost her again.

Muntz, still seated calmly behind his desk, spoke up to say 'Please stay still, Mr Goring. You're making us dizzy. Why don't you take a breath and tell me more about the background to all this. Maybe we can still do something to help you.'

Simon stood stock still, his balled fists crammed into the pockets of his old bush trousers as he fought to compose himself.

'There's Anna, Mr Muntz, Anna Stride who was the Ward Sister on duty when the patient was collected'. This came from Sammi, speaking in a tremulous voice from her position against the side wall. Muntz turned his gaze towards her as he replied.

'A good suggestion, Sammi, but I have already talked to Anna because I was so concerned for Ms Tetrarch's welfare when she left our care. That was just before Anna went off duty but perhaps we can contact her. Meanwhile, would you please fetch the senior nurse who was there: the dark girl - from Chile, I think.'

'That's Rosata. I'll see if I can find her'. Sammi slipped out, lithe and bustling and while she was gone, Simon resumed his seat, gathering his composure as he explained the background to the Professor who had his own questions to pose, a great number of which Simon couldn't answer with any accuracy. They were still talking and Si's respect for Muntz was growing when there was a soft knock on the door and Sammi reappeared, accompanied by the heavily built, dark complexioned Rosata, whose doubtful English made clear that she was alarmed by this summons.

Muntz was careful and gentle with her as he extracted all the information she had to give. Rosata had been at the right hand of her superior, Anna Stride, listening to the Zimbabwean born Sister as she had repeatedly warned the woman about the dangers of taking herself out of hospital and then hearing Anna shift gears when it became obvious that this steely personality was determined to leave. After that watershed, it had been a question of doing all they could to help. Rosata described how she assisted her down to Reception and been on hand while the large man who claimed to be her brother carried her over to the old truck standing by the entrance, a verminous looking old guy at the wheel. The big man had placed her with infinite care in the front to lie over two seats while he jumped up behind into the load bed and the vehicle ground away. All that had been at midday and it was now five in the afternoon.

When Rosata left, accompanied again by Sammi, Simon spent a few more minutes with Professor Muntz, gaining some further information about what Ms Tetrarch would need to look after herself and how long it might take for her to recover strength. He thanked Muntz who escorted him back through the labyrinth of corridors and left him at the front door with a final message.

'Contact me if you need further advice, Mr Goring. Here is my card with all my numbers'. He turned on his heel and vanished back into All Hope.

Within the hour, Simon was back in Hugh's conference room and the gang of five had reassembled. Si gave them all a rundown on his afternoon's discovery and they were rocked by the gender revelation. Fergus Carradine put it all together for them.

'The smelly old guy in the rust bucket,' he said, 'that just has to be the fellow we met on the drive. My guess is he waited until it all went quiet after we left. He found his truck and sneaked out. I'm not sure why my guys didn't spot him but he's an old hand and it's his country: doesn't matter now anyway and he rattles down here to Century, finds where Tetrarch is hiding up and that'll be a place they've used before. Tells him the camp has been wiped out so Tetrarch assumes the attackers will be coming after him now. So he goes to hospital, tells his sister and she says move. God knows where they are now but the team is destroyed and the boss is incapacitated so could be they'll call it a day and hope to vanish.'

'Maybe you're right, Fergus,' said King in response, 'but I'd sure as hell be happier if we knew that for certain: happier still if we could catch up with that gal. She's gotta be dangerously clever and very well connected to have organised this whole show which, face it, we only stumbled over by chance and their bad luck. It worries the hell outa me,' he finished, shaking his head.

Hugh Dundas took charge.

'We'll do it this way,' he announced tersely, 'we keep looking – and as hard as before except that it should now be easier. That old truck is a bigger target and you, Fergus, know what it looks like. Find the truck and we pick up the trail. Plus our quarry is wounded and I don't want to give her time to recover.'

They were impressed by his analysis and authority. They dispersed immediately and went back on the hunt to prove without much delay that Hugh was correct. At about eight in the evening, another uniformed Police Patrol man located what he suspected to be Patrice's vehicle, cold, stationary and abandoned behind a crowd of long distance heavies in a truck stop south of the city on the main highway. Fergus went down to identify it and that was easier than expected because Patrice was still in his cab, his scrawny neck broken and a look of indignation on his face. It was impossible to establish in what alternative vehicle Tetrarch and Ms had escaped: and they would have had plenty to choose from.

Throughout that night and all the following day, they went back to a search of all the hotels, motels, boarding houses, clubs and caravan parks, reasoning that secure accommodation was the prime requirement for the Twins. The searchers had with them the old photo of Tetrarch, enlarged by excising the image of Nathaniel Habtumu whom Hugh was now guessing to have been taken out of the picture in more ways than one. But all depended on finding the big man.

They would have done better to stay at the truckstop. It had been a favoured haunt of Patrice, with women available at a very cheap price in the long, low building behind the restaurant. The Madam there was obliging for the right fee. She had none of the skills of Professor Muntz but she had a lifetime's experience of womens' workings and was prepared to provide a small room with an adjoining bathroom, both of doubtful cleanliness but she could guarantee privacy, with the occasional moan which escaped from Tomas being shrouded by the animal noises which pervaded the rest of the bungalow. Towards evening on the Saturday, Tomas sent her brother out on an errand and was cheered by the news he brought back.

SUNDAY, 24th JUNE

Pente Broke Smith left with Arnie Schwartz at dawn. Arnie had borrowed another small aeroplane and squeezed the priest into the passenger seat alongside him. Pente was no stranger to travel in light aircraft and didn't need to be told to keep himself clear of the controls as Arnie lifted off into a cloudless sky and set his course for Tamalourene.

The excursion had been agreed the previous evening. Hugh Dundas was not enthusiastic but he was tired and dispirited by their lack of result and he relented in the face of Pente's passion. They were all exhausted and Hugh ordered a break for both them and the ranks of police officers who had been deployed. They would meet again on Sunday evening.

Pente had another reason for leaving Century so early. When he had arrived with the invasion eighteen months previously, he had been horrified by the condition of the Cathedral and its grounds which had been allowed to slide into decline over passing years. By force of personality, he managed to draft in a team of volunteer workers who had spent months clearing undergrowth and accumulated rubbish, digging over flowerbeds for replanting and resetting in concrete the old headstones which had become unsettled and were lurching at random angles. In front of the enormous double doors which gave entry to the Cathedral, they were tackling the ornate fountain which had not operated for years. The water supply, originally straight from the harbour, had been replaced by a feed from the desalination plant and a framework for the three enormous cherubs who blew water from their celestial pipes had been fabricated and erected so that the display would start to shower again as soon as they were mounted to it, three metres high. Pente's workers were labouring over the weekend and they reckoned to have the first cherub in place that Sunday evening. The twenty-fourth of June was an important day in Pente's Church calendar because it celebrated the birth of John the Baptist. It was a good day for the fountain to live again and he was determined to be there to see it happen.

Simon found himself unable to sleep properly, so he turned out to drive Pente to the airport where Arnie had arrived even earlier to do his pre-flight checks. They didn't talk much as the priest was busy going over his preparations and kept obstructing Simon at the wheel as he turned to make sure that his vessel of sacraments was safely in the back seat. They had a moment together as Simon parked by the hangar and he was touched when Pente held out a hand in farewell and spoke simply.

'I really don't know how we would have managed this far without you, Si. Thank you and God bless you. Our respective ladies would be extremely proud of you.' He smiled briefly and then clambered out and walked away. A moment later, Simon could hear his boisterous voice wishing Arnie a grand good morning.

He put the car in gear again and drove slowly away, relishing the start of a new day and enjoying the quiet roads as he drove back into town. He parked at the hotel and went up to his room, planning more sleep before more searching and then King's place for lunch. But he kept stirring restlessly and sleep eluded him as his thoughts insisted on returning to Hannah. He got out of bed to turn off the air conditioning and opened the doors onto the small balcony. The gentle noises of Sunday morning rose from the street and the air felt fresh on his naked body. He picked up the phone: it was earlier still in England but he couldn't and wouldn't wait any longer.

She answered at the third ring and said sleepily 'What do you want?'

'You'.

'Well bad luck,' he heard her adjusting pillows, probably sitting more upright. He heard slithering sheets and the brief clink of glass on table. The intimacy of the scene in his imagination aroused him.

'You're out of sight, my Simon,' she continued, 'and I'm out of bounds, off limits, unavailable and …'

'But not off games?' he interrupted.

'Certainly not just now, no: but I am otherwise engaged. I have with me Raoul, the Polo player from the Argentine. He arrived last night with his string of ponies and a hefty mallet. He has great skill and energy. I think he's about to play another chukka.'

Simon was squirming. 'You better let me speak to him now. I'll send him away to attend to his divots.'

'I would but he won't understand. He speaks only Spanish and right now his tongue is occupied. He has a fine moustache which is tickling the inside of my thighs. It's rather nice.'

Hannah sighed with pleasure and went on to say, 'If you took the trouble to call, you must be alone and bored?'

'Well not exactly. I just wanted to prove I can multi-task even though I'm a bit distracted.'

'By thoughts and worries?'

'Not only. Right now, I'm playing chess: with slim Aphrodite, minus her nightie. She's surrounded my king with her bouncy castles and impressive turrets. Now she's attacking my white knight.'

Pause. Then, 'I just want you with me, Hannah. I'm lonely and alone. Horny, but now just a bit satiated.'

'Has Aphodite done her stuff then?'

'After a fashion.'

'Well. I guess I'm flattered to have such an effect. Not bad from thousands of miles away.'

Simon pulled himself up and reached for a sinful cigarette. He lit up and took a long drag before he started speaking again. He could hear her soft breathing.

'Look,' he said finally, 'there's some new news and it will rock you'.

He took her through the events of Friday and the revelation

from Professor Muntz, at which Hannah butted in with a gasp of astonishment and made him go through the conversation again.

'Christ. A woman. This is pretty game changing isn't it. But surely you've heard of endometriosis Si? Wasn't that a big clue? Not that you're pronouncing it properly anyway.'

'Whatever,' he said shortly, 'and no, I hadn't. Why should I? I've no idea of how you girls work. I'm OK as far as reception but pretty hazy of what goes on in the engine room.'

'Bloody hell, Mr Goring, you're an ill-educated chauvinist. But I'll forgive you for now if you tell me what's been going on since then. It's Sunday morning now.'

So he described their searching during all the hours of Friday night and Saturday, all the fruitless enquiries, knocking on doors and endless quartering of the city.

'But nothing so far. Just zero, like those two have vanished into thin air. And it's all the worse because we should have found them by now without too much problem given that she just can't move too far or too quickly.'

'You're right.' Simon could almost hear her collecting her thoughts before she went on. 'You know, Si, instinct tells me you should concentrate on places where there will be other women around. It'll be a sort of herd protection thing.'

'You could well be right and anyway, God knows, we need to try something different – just anything. But we don't have too much time, that's for sure. The power and resilience of this woman is already amazing.'

'I'm not arguing: but first, you just have to get some rest. You sound completely exhausted and going on that way won't be productive - and it could be dangerous, lover. Look, you sleep a bit and I'm going to round up Charley, our mother and Victor to give them all this news and to brainstorm some ideas. Let's speak later and I'll leave you with Aphrodite for a while.'

He chuckled, 'Ok then. But I'll miss you.'

'You'll see me soon, that's a promise.'

They hung up and Simon slumped back in his bed, a

marvellously relaxing lassitude overtaking him. He pulled a sheet over his naked body and was instantly asleep.

As he slumbered, Arnie was making his descent onto the runway at the Palace, the tiny aeroplane dwarfed by the immensity of tarmac. Pente had enjoyed the flight from Century City. The views were spectacular, the weather calm and clear but even if that had been different, there was a special kind of relaxation which came from being piloted by a birdman such as Arnie, a terrestrial being who was more at home in the air.

They touched down and rolled to a final halt by the half built Control Tower. Arnie shut down the engine and turned to Pente.

'Why don't you go ahead and I'll walk on down to join you as soon as I've checked over the machine and got her ready to leave again. You don't mind being on your own?'

'Hah,' said the big priest in reply as he started to struggle with his exit manoeuvre, 'I've been that for long enough in all parts of Africa!'

Arnie watched him pad off down the track towards the intended palace and its village of surrounding buildings. It looked close at hand but must be the best part of a kilometre distant. He turned back to his machine and started to busy himself with the familiar procedures.

As Pente strode along, he was conscious that the day was already very hot, the sun brazen and scorching above him as it pushed towards its zenith. He was astounded by the size of this place. Outbuildings went with construction sites of course, but the number and disparity here really seemed extreme and they were mostly interlaced with the sort of general detritus which spoke to him of Africa. It was terrific to acquire a machine for whatever purpose, better still that it should be of complex sophistication and a joy to behold but if it ceased to work, well you just leave it where it stopped and get on with something else.

Pente made slow progress as he poked his nose into the sheds and containers and motionless trucks which were festooned about the place. As he approached the centre of the compound, he could readily identify the encampment of those who had lived here recently – the mess hall, the dormitory buildings, the shower blocks and the working offices. He lingered in the largest two, formed by sea containers and roughly roofed with hardboard sheets providing huge spaces, one of which was arranged to resemble an airport check-in area while the other was a close replica of the interior of an aircraft with seats and galley, even laying down the uneven spacing of a row which gave access to an emergency exit door.

He was still working his way through all the exhibits when Arnie joined him and Pente was glad of the company as they approached together the skeleton of the grand palace building which stood gaunt and lonely as the sun blazed down on it. They entered through the rear courtyard which had seen such action during the hours of the assault. They climbed together up the rough, unfinished staircase and looked out over the long approach drive. They could make out the small village which now danced in the heat haze. As they descended, they passed the spot at which Anders Moran had died before leaving the building to walk the short distance to the mound under which lay the bodies of the fallen. Pente had no need to refer to the notes which Fergus had given him: here lay his destination for the day.

He put down his sandlewood box which contained the Sacraments and went about his preparations. Arnie moved away from him and stood quietly to attention as the priest called for universal respect and forgiveness as he said prayers over the mass grave. Pente was calm and unhurried as he concluded with the General Thanksgiving which he recited from memory. Then he lowered himself to the ground and knelt forward, his large hands burrowed into the loose soil of the burial mound, eyes tight shut, forehead lined in concentration and beard flowing as he called down a silent blessing. He remained motionless for just a few minutes which seemed like an eternity. The pilot finally broke the silence when he said simply,

'You don't know who they were. Not even how many are lying here.'

'They are known unto God', Pente replied as he pushed back onto his haunches and opened his eyes. Then he continued in quite a different tone of voice, 'Come on Arnie, we've got to look at the devil's haunt', and he raised a ham hand to point at the other camp which Fergus had found.

The two containers were set at right angles to provide a courtyard of beaten earth, covered by corrugated roofing panels. Door apertures had been cut into the containers and these were covered by neatly fitted mesh fly screens. They entered the first, standing just inside to take in the truckle bed with an upturned carton beside it, the run of timber planks resting on concrete blocks to provide some shelving. Stuck around the walls were the posters and photographs which Fergus had described. This was the lair of Tetrarch.

Across the courtyard, the second room had more furnishing and home comforts. A water cooler stood in one corner with a chest of drawers beside it, and against another wall, a chair in front of a simple desk. Pente advanced but Arnie checked him with a comment.

'Don't take long: we should be getting our wheels up shortly. I reckon the weather's turning against us.'

Pente pulled open the drawers of the desk. The contents were ordered and everyday – pencils and pens, a stapler, masking tape and a box of drawing pins. At the back of the last drawer he found a battered cardboard box and inside it, a crucifix. It was plain without frills, a thin veneer of silver plate covering the lump of steel which formed the cross. Pente took it out and weighed it in his hand. It was heavy, made more so by the bulky chain which he looped over his head as he pulled away the tissue paper which lay beneath it to reveal a photograph. He held this to the light. The photo was old and dog-eared at the corners, the colour faded and further obscured by layers of kitchen film which had been applied to preserve it. It was not pretty, but it was precious. It showed in close up a young woman of maybe twenty-five or thirty. She was good looking but careworn, smiling uncertainly at the camera as if she didn't have enough reasons to be happy. Pente flipped it over to see what might have been spidery writing on the back but he couldn't make out the detail and, conscious of Arnie at his side, he put it carefully in the pocket of his robe and they turned to go.

They walked directly back to the airfield, refusing to be side-tracked into further investigations, but it took time before they came up to the little Cessna standing forlornly on the tarmac. Arnie busied himself with flight preparations while Pente wandered across to gaze at the burned-out wreck of the Boeing. Men had died in this fireball, so he bowed his head and said a prayer for their souls. The sun was still blazing fiercely but he could feel the stirrings of a breeze as it fluttered at his beard. With his experience of Africa, Pente recognised the sign. They were in for a storm and it would be coming soon on the wings of the wind.

When the small plane touched down in Century, Pente was glad to ease his frame from the confines of the cabin. He had enjoyed the flight, even with its very rough interludes as Arnie hopped around the edges of the storm, his calm and certain movements at the controls in such contrast to the bucking bronco antics of his machine. They landed at about four-thirty on that Sunday afternoon and an hour later, Arnie was dropping Pente outside the Cathedral, just in time for him to prepare himself for the evening service which he would conduct at 6pm in the Lady Chapel.

As Pente was absorbed in his thoughts and actions, Simon Goring was being woken in his hotel bedroom by the shrill tones of the telephone beside his bed and as he picked it up and announced his name, the responding voice with its clipped southern African accent made him instantly alert.

'Mr Goring, my name's Sarah Stride. I'm a Ward Sister at the hospital – at All Hope – and I understand you want to talk to me about the patient who discharged herself last week. I'm sorry I haven't called before but a group of us have been out in the bush for a few days. I only got home a couple of hours ago and found that Professor Muntz had left a message. He's authorised me to tell you what I know about Tomasina.'

Si pulled himself up on his pillows as he replied. 'Thanks for calling, Sarah and do call me Simon. Please go ahead: I'm all ears and I'll interrupt if I need to'.

Ten minutes later, he hung up abruptly and jack knifed his body out of bed, pulling on the first clothes that came to hand while replaying in his mind the priceless information which the nurse had given him. She didn't know the woman, of course, had never met her before and hadn't formed some instant bond with her. It was nothing like that, simply that Sarah was an excellent medical professional, recognised that it had been a lifesaving operation and that the patient needed expert nursing to help her pull through the surgery and trauma. So Sarah spent time with Tomasina as she struggled her way out of anaesthesia and pushed down the medication which was required to keep her comatose as her body fought to heal itself. Whilst in this state, she babbled in delirium but later, the semi-conscious talk became more focussed. She was very specific about her brother and how he must be protected from further damage.

Sarah Stride had no difficulty in identifying her brother as the morose, hulking man who spent so long sitting by her bedside and getting in the way but she puzzled over why such a prime physical specimen should need protection, even though she picked up that he might be just a little simple of mind. But then her patient moved on and started in on a barely coherent rant against the dark side of the Church and her determination to confront its evils. At this point, Tomasina was speaking mostly in French but Sarah recognised the often repeated word 'Cathedrale'.

Three days after the operation, as Sarah was leaving for her out of city break, Tomasina's fever dropped, she lay more quietly and ceased to thrash about in her bed. The procedure had been successful but as she moved towards recovery, her communication petered out. She lay there, entirely cooperative with the nursing staff as they carried out their checks and measurements, accepting the medication and even muttering a word of thanks to Muntz but it was clear that she was giving nothing further away – she was back in control of her tongue.

It was not until the nurse was reaching the conclusion of her account that the penny dropped for Simon Goring and he kicked himself for being slow as he struggled into his clothes. It seemed crystal clear to him now as he grabbed his car keys and headed for the lift. This woman had been the power at the Palace. It was she who plotted and planned, she who proposed and disposed. Tomasina was the brain and her twin brother Tetrarch the brawn. She must know all about Carradine's raid on the compound: the old man with the truck which had collected her from hospital would have told her that and she had killed him for his pains. She was still here in Century, hiding somewhere while she licked her wounds and planned another action. Perhaps the target had always been in her sights or maybe it was her last roll of the dice. It didn't matter now which or why but Simon thought he could see the big picture without any of the detail. The mighty Tetrarch was a powerhouse but he needed her brain to direct him. There was something in his background which was driving her now and Simon was struck by the force of the woman's fevered mutterings to Sarah Stride about the state of the Church and particularly about the Cathedral. Who lived there, he asked himself, and who had been set up on high profile suspicion of child abuse?

Emerging from the lift into the underground car park of the hotel, Si ran for his car as he plucked a phone from his pocket. He would need help with this. The Twins would be waiting for Pente at the Cathedral. Probably, Tomasina would have discovered that he was expected for this evening's service to celebrate the birth of John the Baptist. The Twins would be there to meet him which put Pente at terminal risk. But unwittingly, he was playing the role of tethered goat to attract the tigers and that gave Simon the chance to finish this business.

He drove up to street level before calling Fergus Carradine. Si was lucky: Fergus was loafing at home and it took just a few seconds conversation to get him moving. He would come straight to the Cathedral, bringing back-up with him. At this point, Simon changed his mind. He pulled into the kerb, got out and left his car. It was no more than a ten minute walk and he was unarmed. Better to take a little longer but to arrive in quiet and caution, blending in with whatever crowd of Sunday evening promenaders happened to be about. As he walked, he tried Pente's numbers and was not surprised that they went immediately to his answering service. He called Hannah who came on the line as if she had been waiting for him. He told her about Sarah Stride, what he had made of that and where he was now. She gasped and blurted out,

'Christ, Si, be careful, won't you!', and then, 'I'll have a word with Mum and between us, we'll keep trying to get through to Pente. He's impossible when he wants to be incommunicado but if anyone can manage it, she can.'

They broke off as he was approaching Cathedral square and he was pleased to see that the place was a hive of activity. It was now a quarter to six and he reckoned this volunteer army must be packing up soon: perhaps some would be going into the Cathedral for Pente's Service.

Simon stopped by one of the stone bollards which separated the busy main road from the cobbled approach towards the tall doors of the building which stood open in welcome to the passing world. He put a foot up and retied a lace on his boot, giving himself the chance of a quick appraisal. His heart thumped in his chest as he made out a distant figure, a man moving slowly towards him with arms behind his back and head bowed. It was Tetrarch, Simon was instantly sure and he felt himself quail. The man looked formidable, a dangerous combination of bulky power propelled by sinuous energy. Si didn't doubt his own ability but he instinctively knew that he would not be able to live for long with this adversary.

The Twins had arrived by taxi at 5.30 and Tetrarch walked with his sister to the main doors, leaving her to enter the Cathedral by herself. He went on a circuit of the imposing building, pushing his way through the small trees and overgrown shrubs which had been allowed to throng the land on either side and at the back of the Cathedral, right up to the boundary wall beyond which the ground to the west fell away sharply down an escarpment towards the distant docks area and the ocean beyond it. Tetrarch felt comforted in this extensive wilderness area and calmer than he had been for some days. The sight of Tomy walking, painfully but firmly, had been balm to his soul as it meant leadership and control coming back into his life. Whatever she said would go for him. At the same time, he was offended by the neglect of the grounds he was walking through and memories of his garden at Rabat came flooding back to him. That had been much smaller of course, but he had kept it in such perfect order. He wondered how things were now at the Chateau outside Loches and when they might return there. He would like to be in France again, tending to his planting and encouraging his flowers. His interest sharpened as he returned to the front of the building, noting the work that these people were doing amongst the formal beds, knowing that he could do it all just as well and probably better. They would have to take care with that fountain, he thought, and he advanced slowly to see what they were doing.

Simon was watching the big man meandering towards him when he felt a touch on his arm and heard Fergus speak softly to him.

'That's Tetrarch, I imagine. I have eight men with me, all armed, but we need to be careful with all these workers and watchers.'

'We do, yes. We certainly don't want a pitched battle, but also Fergus, we want him alive and well. Mentally, he's the weak link and if we can get him talking, however long that takes, I think he'll tell us all the background, where they come from, what they've been doing here.'

Fergus nodded. 'OK, so we need to start with an orderly arrest. I'll get my guys into a horseshoe and we'll approach him slowly. No weapons unless he produces a firearm. You stay back to observe and take action if need be.'

'Got it.' Simon stood his ground and watched Fergus arrange his cordon of uniformed policemen, himself in the middle of it. They advanced in slow formation on the rising ground to the left of the cobbled walkway, passing around and through the volunteers who continued to work on the flowerbeds. Simon had a clear view of it all and it seemed to him that Tetrarch had simply not noticed. He continued to walk very slowly towards his intending captors until he came to a halt by a large, circular rose bed which he studied carefully while the officers grouped around and beyond it. They would soon have him completely surrounded and it would all be over: almost an anti-climax in its simplicity.

But they had misjudged this man. Tetrarch's apparent nonchalance had drawn them into his orbit and now he was to teach them a bloody lesson. In a blur of movement, he moved to grab the policeman closest to him, swung him into the air with careless ease and threw the man bodily at his neighbour in the circle. There was a crash of limbs as they went down together over a gravestone but Tetrarch had already turned in the opposing direction, diving forward with outstretched hands and kicking up and over with balletic grace to catch his next man in the chest and under his chin. The speed of his movements had caught them all unawares but now another three of the force rushed together across the rose bed to confront Tetrarch as he sprang back on his feet. Watching from his saddle stone, Simon could not but admire the extraordinary combination of skill, strength and speed. The policemen might have been children trying to stand against the onslaught of this man who fought with both his fists and his feet in a kaleidoscope of action.

There was a moment when two of his assailants had managed to grab an arm each and one of those who had fallen over the gravestone was back on his feet and charging in to help. Simon could clearly see Tetrarch's biceps bunch with the effort of sweeping the men holding onto his arms into each other and he heard the horrible smack as their heads came together but miraculously, the guy accomplished this whilst standing on one leg as the other extended to catch Officer Gravestone a mighty kick between his legs and he gave an agonised yowl as he collapsed, writhing.

Tetrarch was enjoying himself and Simon could see that he must be relishing the audience. All the volunteer workers had downed tools and were watching this astonishing spectacle. The sole exception was the driver of a back hoe digger which was trundling on its tracks over the rough terrain towards the skeleton of the rebuilt fountain, the first of the renovated angels swinging gently from its telescopic arm which had been extended to full height. The driver needed to concentrate, and both his vision and hearing were limited by his machine so it was not surprising that he hadn't taken in the fight scene which was absorbing his colleagues.

Events moved even faster: Fergus motioned with both hands at the remaining policemen and in unison they started to advance across the rose bed, looking to box in this fighting machine and weigh him down by sheer force of numbers. But Tetrarch leapt clear of the human shambles he had just created and took some long steps backwards, giving himself space. He moved in fluid, graceful bounds seeming to glide above the uneven ground and as he went, Simon saw him pluck at something which was hanging around his waist. He feared a weapon and was shouting a warning to Fergus when Tetrarch spun round in a full circle and let fly with his set of bolas, three steel balls the size of billiards, each on its own cord and the three tied together. He threw underhand with power but it was the speed and accuracy which were extraordinary. The bolas whipped across the intervening space with a whistle which Simon could pick up above the other noise and they wrapped themselves around Carradine's legs just below the knee. Fergus dropped on his side like a felled steer and his men paused in uncertainty. Then one drew a hand gun: despite orders, he was not going to fight further with this superman but would stop him for good. His colleagues were rushing forward and Tetrarch was preparing himself to meet them, Fergus was lying on his side and trying to free his legs, the gunman was taking careful aim and the digger driver - still blissfully unaware - was grinding his way behind Tetrarch towards the fountain. Tetrarch must have seen the threat of the levelled gun because he turned and sprinted for the protection of the digger at the same time as Fergus bellowed 'NO' and swung his bound legs against the policeman as he took his shot.

The bullet could have gone anywhere but it happened to hit the digger driver in the upper part of his right arm. It wasn't a serious wound but it was a shock and it was painful. In a reasonable reaction, the man slapped his left hand over his right arm and drew his knees up in an instinctive move. Without either hand or foot on the controls, the emergency braking system on the digger activated and it stopped with a tilting jerk which caused the angel hanging from the arm to sway dangerously and the fixing which held it there was inadequate for the unplanned circumstances.

Simon saw it all. The angel fell and it fell on Tetrarch who had just reached the security of the machine. He grabbed at the rocking digger for a handhold as he looked back towards the group with Fergus still lying in the middle. He did not look up and probably never saw the ton of angel which knocked him to the ground and reduced his head to a bloody pulp.

There are moments when time stands still and this was one of those for Simon. He took in that Fergus was barking commands while he unravelled himself from Tetrarch's flying balls, he could see the policemen gathering around the fallen figure and he could hear the digger driver bleating. But for himself, just for an instant or so, he was struck dumb and motionless. This outcome was simply not in the script, not however they might have imagined it. He had started with a confidence that Tetrarch would be overwhelmed by sufficient force but then he'd seen his capabilities and was beginning to think that the guy would walk away from them in his own time. It seemed demeaning to all of them that he should fall victim to a form of traffic accident.

Then the shock left him. Simon didn't move a foot but his

brain was burning. Tetrarch hadn't been running, not even hurrying. He'd been leading them on, fighting an action to keep them all focussed on him, trying to wear him down. They would have followed him right through the gardens, over the wall and down towards the docks. Tetrarch would have given just enough ground to keep them with him as if they had been tethered bloodhounds.

And why? It was bloody obvious! Simon went from standstill into a wild sprint for the Cathedral doors. Tetrarch had not come here alone, so where was his sister? She must now be in the Cathedral, secure in trust that Tetrarch would be drawing off the pursuit while she went looking for Pente Broke Smith. As he ran for it, Simon heard the great bells far above his head commence their toll to mark the hour of six o'clock. The service was about to start. Pente would be concentrated on its perfect conduct, unaware of any threat. Simon increased his stride and flashed into the building, pulling up short as the gloom enveloped him.

The Lady Chapel in Century Cathedral is unusual because it has a small vestry with an exterior door so that it can be entered from the outside of the building. No one had been able to tell Pente why it had been designed this way but he was grateful for the convenience of being able to walk from his house directly into the Chapel. He was in the vestry when his phone beeped at him. On a whim, he picked it up and saw in a flash of recognition that he had a message from Vanda in Herefordshire. It was always a treat to hear from her and his large fingers managed to push the right buttons to read what she had to say. He was not to know that this was her last throw of the dice. For most of the day she had been trying to ring him, to put him on his guard with the news she had received from King Offenbach and from both her daughters. All three of them had been trying to warn him and in final desperation, Vanda sent him a text. She would have been surprised that he troubled to read it, only minutes before he left the vestry to begin the service.

Pente chuckled out loud as he read the message: just four characters, followed by her x for love as always. It read simply

'1113' – nothing more but it meant something to him. He knew that it referred him to the first chapter of the first book of the Bible and the thirteenth verse. He knew without looking that the script read 'the serpent beguiled me' and his memory lanced back all those years to their happy adolescent days on the hillsides above the village of Foy. He gathered his robes about him and walked through into the Chapel. All was prepared for him and for the simple service of Said Eucharist. One of his curates, a pleasant young man born in Argentina, and two altar boys were already in position, the Sacraments had been made ready and the candles were burning.

The Chapel could seat about fifty people on linked, plain wooden chairs arranged in rows. About half were taken with a few groups and individuals scattered throughout and at a glance, Pente recognised some familiar faces. He started with an embracing smile and some warm words of welcome. Then he spread his arms wide to lead the congregation in the Lord's Prayer and he felt the heavy crucifix which he had found at the Palace bump against his chest.

As he spoke the familiar words, he was conscious of a figure entering the Chapel from the Cathedral and advancing down the aisle towards him. The pace was slow, the gait a little awkward as if restricted by pain. He could see nothing of the face beneath the cowl above the full length robe which brushed the stone floor with each step but the body beneath it was slight: a woman.

Here was Eve, beguiled by the serpent and intent on retribution. Pente's jumbled thoughts didn't interrupt his enunciation and didn't distract the congregation as she walked right up to the altar rail and stood looking up at him. He was mesmerised by the unflinching stare, the judgemental look in the piercing eyes and he broke off at the point of reciting … 'deliver us from evil'. He bent forward a little, sensing that she would speak and that her words would be faint. Behind her, the congregation was mute and confused.

'You have stolen our mother's cross. It is you and others like you who condemned my brother to be damaged for life. It is you who are evil and I will deliver us from you.'

As the woman spoke, she reached into a pocket of her robe. Pente knew she would produce a gun and he knew he was about to die. He said not a word but simply closed his eyes and clasped his hands together in prayer.

'STOP!'The shout of desperation was shocking as it burst from Simon Goring, skidding to a halt in the entrance to the Chapel. There was a pandemonium of reaction as those kneeling or sitting on their chairs ducked and turned and gaped. The curate and the small boys dropped behind the altar.

Simon shouted again,'Tetrarch is dead!'

The woman seemed unmoved: she held her gun close to Pente's chest as she looped the crucifix from off his shaggy head. Then she turned in a whirl of movement and loosed off two shots, the crack of her pistol horrifying in the calm of the surroundings. Simon dived for the stone flagged floor and there was further uproar as Fergus Carradine arrived behind Simon with two of his men, both with weapons drawn. Pente struck out at the woman in front of him, his hands still gripping each other and since she had turned with her firing, he caught her in the small of her slender back and she fell away from him, collapsing on her right side.

Tomasina was down, but not yet out and the gun in her hand spoke again before it flew from her grasp as she hit the floor but not before her final shot found its mark. One of the policemen screamed in his pain as he clapped both hands to his stomach and his tunic changed colour with his blood.

Pente let the woman lie there as he strode up the aisle to join Carradine who was trying to help the stricken policeman whilst bellowing for help. The priest was expecting to find Simon back on his feet but instead, he almost tripped on the still recumbent form, lying stretched on the flags with his face down and his arms spread out in the manner of a worshipping postulant. When they turned him on his back, they could see that Simon Goring was quite dead. One shot had caught him exactly between his eyes.

Pente fell to his knees with a moan of anguish. When he looked round, the woman had gone, dragging herself away and leaving only smears of blood which must have escaped from the wounds of her operation. The signs continued through his vestry and onto the cobble stones outside. Then they disappeared. The woman had vanished like a wraith in the night.

EPILOGUE — MAY 2015

In the still, early hours of the Washington night, the Harvard Professor was summing up.

'So there you have it', he said as he raised his hands in a gesture of completion, 'that's my story. I've told you all I know about the Assassins of Persia in the thirteenth century and the Mountain Men. There's more detail, of course, and I could take you through the centuries and show you when and where the same group cropped up again and again. Successors of course, with different leaders of differing nationalities but consistently operating to the same principle: you propose and we will dispose. If we approve of your objective, if the conditions and reward are right, we will act to realise your dream. But we will do so only in our own time and by our own means of which we will tell you nothing. We will retain absolute control. We will use our name: we are the Mountain Men.

'Come the twentieth century, the Sect became quiescent during the two World Wars which changed the globe but as we move into this new century, the Mountain Men are back.'

The National Security Advisor, Susan Rice, broke in smoothly to take over from him. An elegant, carefully groomed lady, she exuded control and confidence as she addressed her audience.

'You all have the advantage over me even though much of my career has concentrated on Africa. You were all in post, even if at a less senior level, nearly fifteen years back when these events took place. Some of you may have attended briefings managed by my predecessor of that era – another of the same colour, gender and name as myself. Condoleeza Rice and her team did a fine job in the aftermath of the attacks on America and all of your organisations contributed to the bank of information which we have accumulated.

'Let me summarise the aspects which are most relevant to us now.

'First, no trace has ever been found of that woman but we know that she was born in November 1960 and named Tomasina by her French Algerian mother Monique al Jabri, nee Dorcas. We know a certain amount about her early life and a great deal about the six months or so prior to her twin brother's violent death and her own disappearance.

'Second, we can still speak to some of the key players - Carradine, Broke Smith, Offenbach: they're all still alive and living in Millennium. That country is now firmly established on the world stage. It's a member of the Commonwealth and a significant trading partner for the USA and EU countries. Millennium is seen as the model for progress in Africa and its capital, Century City, is the hub for political development across the continent. Ironically, the founders there got a boost from the drama created by Tomasina because the UK and US authorities suddenly had the need to work with the people down there. Immediately after the crisis, the interim President Dundas proposed that the Tamalou Trench oilfield should be controlled by an international corporation owned by the US, the Brits and the French. He wanted just a dollar a barrel left in Century but his condition was that the company should be named Millennium Oil. It's a colossus today and the Dundas masterstroke was that we could hardly accept the name without also accepting the country.'

Rice paused to look around her audience before continuing.

'Ok, now third, we have full access to the forensic studies, the ballistic analyses and the intelligence reports which were compiled in the weeks following Sunday 24th June 2001.

'Forensics proved conclusively that the blood in the vestry came from the woman so she must have been hampered and in pain as she made her escape. We may presume she was suffering worse from the loss of her brother. To survive, she must have had help and a safe haven, enough to shelter her for a few days, even a few hours. Maybe she didn't make it: maybe she killed herself or died in some back alley. But her body was never found and with all that we do know about her resource and resilience, I for one wouldn't care to bet against her survival.

'The ballistics experts could never agree. Some said the bullet which killed Simon Goring was a chance, just a lucky strike which hit a fatal spot, but others point to earlier evidence that she was a crack shot and it's certain that she hit the policeman whilst she was falling to the ground and presumably in pain.

'Then there's Intel: specialists from the US and the UK swarmed over all the ground and the buildings at the Palace compound and they processed every last thing they could find. They dug up the bodies and established an ID for most of them, including the Ethiopian Habtumu. Another clue was in the mock-ups of the two airport facilities which they built for their training. One was certainly Paris and the other an American airport, probably in Washington.

'There was a lot of material on the two teams heading for Europe before Carradine's force destroyed them. There was proof of their targets and timing. The plan was to hit Charles de Gaulle Airport in Paris and the City of London at the same hour on the same day and the detail shows that they would likely have created absolute mayhem. It's not surprising that this information – all neatly filed in old fashioned ring binders – was just sitting there waiting to be found. The master operator, Tomas, would not have left it intact except in an emergency and it was her own medical collapse which provided exactly that. In contrast, no information of any sort was found on Team A, the group which left about a month earlier.

'Whatever the missing facts, the balance of probability condemns the A Team as responsible for 9/11. The preparation at Tamalourene was impressive and professional: the timing of their departure at the beginning of June is significant. Above all, they were so well organised and that in itself speaks volumes. But we don't know and we'll never know beyond doubt. We've seen all the evidence we'll find and the date is now long gone in time if not in memory.'

Ms Rice took another break as she allowed her words to linger before she resumed.

'All of you invited here have experience and positions of great responsibility. You spend time looking back over the years as you struggle to anticipate the risks and the chaos of the future. You ponder over the rise of Islam, you wonder if the threats to civilization which you have to counter have their origins in Iraq regime change, in the war of retribution in Afghanistan, in the turmoil of the Arab Spring.

'There may be something more and the purpose of this convention has been to share it with you. I'll leave the Professor to present his conclusion.'

She sat back and nodded at the man from Harvard who tweaked at his tie and started to speak.

'The picture which I've been sharing with you proves to me that there's a force out there and it was Collette who strengthened my conviction.

'As she approached her deathbed, she felt able to let down her guard and to reveal the secrets of a professional lifetime. The most valuable of these concerned her client Tetrarch, the lethal giant of a man with his ferocious physique and his mind of a gentle child. She told me how, little by little, she came to develop a relationship with him. How he started to have conversations with her in the genteel parlour of her bordello in Poitiers, cloistered in its suburb behind net curtains. He spoke in simple terms about his pleasure in nature, the fulfilment he found in planning and developing his garden, the enjoyment of an undemanding friendship with the Ethiopian, the relief of understanding with help from Collette that his sister wasn't weird because she preferred sex with a woman.

'Most critically, he talked without question or regret of how he was in total thrall to his sibling, the girl and then the woman called 'Tomas' or sometimes 'Tomy'. Of how this sister controlled his life, how she had rescued him, provided for him, guided him and of her plans for him to help her as she changed the world around them.'

The Professor paused to change tack.

'We can only guess at the effect which the death of Tetrarch inflicted on her. Not only did she lose her powerful guarantee of personal protection, she lost also much of her own raison d'etre, blaming herself for his fate. But against that, of course, she had already achieved much success according to her own lights and perhaps as a form of memorial to Tetrarch, she determined to proceed with the conception and management of acts which mean horror to us but spell accomplishment to her.

'My conclusion is that the execution of extreme terrorism is now let under contract to a twenty-first century edition of the Mountain Men and my belief is that the woman of Tamalourene is responsible. Tomas not only survived but she has grown and prospered. I don't know what she looks like or where to find her but I am convinced that we will have no peace or reconciliation while she remains alive.

'And finally, here's a thought which may be more than a flight of fancy. These days, we're all too familiar with the word "ISIS" which we take as an acronym to mean Islamic State, to be associated with the various terrorist groups operating under that umbrella title.

'But we should remember that Isis is also a name from Greek mythology, dating back to the days of ancient Egypt. Isis was a deity, worshipped throughout the Roman Empire as an inspiration to the downtrodden and the marginalised. Isis was a goddess. Isis was a woman.'

Even as he was speaking, at the other end of the day and across the world, the Elders of Chitral were gathered under the same trees, refreshing themselves with the traditional drink and some of them puffing at their pipe. There was the same number of them but the group now included new faces and others had departed in faith. The conversation was, as always, calm and ordered and polite with due deference given to the most senior amongst them. They were content. Their resolve had remained unchanged and determined down the years and they could bask in the knowledge of the help which was available to them to fulfil their dreams.

In Washington, as the Professor delivered his final comments, one member of his audience is both present and several thousand miles away. The delegation from the United Kingdom includes a senior executive from GCHQ and her name is Charlotte Deveridge. Charley is now forty-five but looks older. She wears little make up and her hair, flecked with grey, is scraped back from her forehead and tied in a bun. Her pleasant features are furrowed with the efforts of too much concentration over too many hours. Her figure has become a little fuller. She is a consummate professional but she has suffered through constant devotion to her work.

Charley still lives with her partner Lizzie in their converted coach house outside Cheltenham. She no longer goes to Paris, not since she lost her father Victor two years ago when he expired in the act of lighting another Gauloise. But the women drive every month on a Sunday over the hills into Herefordshire where they spend the day in the village of Foy with Charley's mother Vanda and with Hannah. Sometimes, when the farm permits, her brother William will be there with his brood. He now lives in the big house and Vanda is comfortably installed in the former stable block.

Hannah bought Forty Green Cottage ten years ago and lives there permanently. She resigned from GCHQ in October 2001, having suffered a breakdown after the crisis in Century City and the death of Simon Goring. She was obsessed by remorse, blaming herself for volunteering him in her place and then failing to give him warning. His murder was not just her responsibility but it was also, and much worse, her loss. Others had mourned him, had admired his efforts, had sighed over the act of chance which snuffed out his life. But his death was an accident of war from which the world must recover by moving on. For Hannah, the burden and the pain were constants which left her with no closure, no peace, just the agonies of regret and sadness.

But she did have a consolation and she was just about coping with day-to-day life, putting one foot after the other, working routinely, smiling vacantly, when the pivotal blow struck her. On Monday 1st October, she lost the baby in a flood of blood and pain. She had been home alone at the flat in Cheltenham, dressing and trying to work up a spark of enthusiasm for the day ahead, for the weeks and months which would follow, when she felt the agonising start of a process which she knew would destroy her completely. The instinct for survival gave her strength to phone Charley and then there was the kaleidoscope of gore and groan, the crash as her door was kicked open, little Imogen screaming in terror, the bilious yellow of the paramedic's jacket, the flash of blue light as they carried her into the ambulance, the blaring siren, the intruding hands, the voices murmuring reassurance and the brief moment of calm in a virgin white hospital bed before the demons started to assault her. The medics told her that she was a perfectly healthy young woman, that these things did happen, that there was no reason why she should not conceive again.

Hannah knew better. Her mind, her psyche, her whole being was balanced precariously on the edge of abyss. She knew with positive certainty that the baby had been conceived on that summer morning in the Cotswolds when eagles dipped and flew. They had mated for life and now the very last of Simon had been flushed from her womb and into the hospital incinerator. Unless she could start again, the rest of her was set to follow.

It took her over a year to recover but with that time and immense effort, she picked herself up and now runs a successful charity for refugee victims of war. She operates from Bristol and spends three days a week there. She will soon be fifty but looks ten years younger. She is vivacious and flirtatious, good looking and always immaculate. She has a busy social life and has enjoyed a number of inconsequential affairs over time. She has never married nor had more children.

Vanda is seventy-one. She wears her years well and is content with her village life. Like Charley, she misses Victor but is happy that he went out like the flame of a candle, leaving memories of a life lived to the full. Vanda and Hannah are very close, getting together most weekends and speaking more frequently. They share a robust sense of humour and joke that they are the two widows of Foy, one created by the murderous action of a woman they will never know and the other through the intervention of the Almighty.

Once a year, Pente Broke Smith flies up from Millennium and stays for a few days, lodging with William in the big house. He shows Hannah the latest photographs of the Cathedral gardens and the white marble memorial stone which stands guard over Simon's ashes. Not all of the ashes are there and Pente struggles up the hill behind Foy, the walk he used to skip as a teenager. Vanda is at his side, and he says a little prayer at the spot overlooking the valley where they left a part of Simon.

Hannah walks with them and sometimes, so does Imogen who is now a lively teenager, approaching seventeen. Hannah is always accompanied by her dog, a second generation red setter. Like his predecessor, she calls him Goring and when people remark that it's a strange name for a dog, she gives her winsome smile, saying that she likes the sound of his name when she calls to him and that he is her constant companion.